Estelle Ryan

The

Morisot Connection

The Morisot Connection

A Genevieve Lenard Novel

By Estelle Ryan

First published 2015

Copyright © 2015 by Estelle Ryan

Acknowledgements

For a short while, I considered my writing to be a solidary pursuit. I was wrong. I have so many amazing people in my life supporting me, checking up on me and cheering me on that I honestly cannot say that I'm alone in my writing career.

This time I'm changing things around and first thanking my wonderful readers. Each email, each Facebook message, each comment has such incredible value to me. I'm deeply honoured by your support and the love I experience whenever you respond to one of my 'Woohoo!' posts.

My vocabulary is simply not sufficient to express my heartfelt thanks to Charlene, Linette, Moeks, Anna, Jane, Ania B, Maggie, Krystyna, Kamila, Jola, Ania S. Your constant presence in my life is something I treasure. R.J., you make my books shine and for that you have my lifelong thanks. Anne Victory for your professionalism. Hubert, your daily assistance, support and ideas have added pleasure and growth to my writing process.

Dedication

To Julie

Chapter ONE

"Thank goodness, Doctor Lenard. You're here." Timothée Renaud looked behind me as I stepped out of the elevator into the elegant reception area of Rousseau & Rousseau. "Where's Colin?"

"Not here." For the last six months, the assistant to Phillip Rousseau—the owner of this high-end insurance company—had been reluctant to be in my presence without Colin Frey acting as a buffer. I did not understand why the young man needed my romantic partner to be present in order to communicate with me.

"Oh." Tim took a step away from me, flexing his hands. "Um, will he be coming soon?"

I stopped and studied Tim. Today he was wearing suit trousers, a tailored dress shirt and a knotted silk scarf instead of a tie. It had been interesting to observe how he'd changed in the year and a half he'd been working as Phillip's assistant.

Until eight months ago, I had been working with my team from the offices of Rousseau & Rousseau. An art crime we'd been investigating at the time had brought violent men to the office. We'd escaped the gun battle mostly uninjured, but parts of the richly decorated space had been irreparably damaged.

That event had been a catalyst for many changes. I'd taken a short break from investigating cases, we had moved our team headquarters from Rousseau & Rousseau to a secure floor in the adjacent building and Timothée had become leery of being alone with me. People usually became severely uncomfortable when I studied their body language and micro-expressions. But that was the only way I was able to understand the true meaning of their communication. Neurotypical people very seldom verbalised their true intentions. Most often their words and their thoughts did not correlate.

"Um, Doctor Lenard?" Tim swallowed, his voice tight.

I blinked a few times, trying to hold back my opinion on what I'd observed. I couldn't. "I'm autistic. Not dangerous. The expression that just flashed on your face implies that you are scared of me. What have I done to instil fear in you, Tim?"

"Um. Nothing?" He shifted on his feet, his muscle tension increasing.

"Then why are your feet pointing away from me?" I shook my finger at his feet, then at his torso. "Even your upper body is ready to flee from me."

He closed his eyes tightly for a few seconds. Typical blocking behaviour. My understanding of the neurotypical brain and behaviour was academic. In order to relate better to my unwelcoming family and a prejudiced society, I had rigorously studied nonverbal communication as well as psychology to have a better grasp of how the average human reasoned. Intellectually, I understood. Yet I couldn't truly comprehend why Tim thought closing his eyes would prevent me from pushing this topic to its conclusion. I waited until he opened his eyes.

When he did, his expression was contrite. "I'm so sorry, Doctor Lenard... er... Genevieve. I'm just worried that I might say or do something that would hur... offend you."

"Hurt? Offend? When have I ever appeared offended?"

His eyes shifted up and left, recalling a memory. "Never?"

"Are you asking me?"

He straightened his shoulders. "I don't know how to behave around you. You never look offended. But you also never look happy, pleased, angry or even tired. I can't read you."

"I know." It was a problem I had been made aware of numerous times during my childhood. My emotions seldom made their appearance on my face. As a young child, I had tried to emulate facial expressions, but had confused my parents even more. They, and their high-society friends, had been more comfortable with my neutral expression. I'd never felt the need since to placate people with artificial expressions.

"That's it? You're not going to offer me any tips on how to understand you better?"

"Do you really need to understand me?"

He thought about this. "You know? I would really like to."

"Then I shall make a point of telling you whenever you hurt or offend me."

"And maybe you could also tell me if I do something that makes you happy."

"I'll consider that." Muffled sounds of a heated argument reached us. I looked towards the conference room. "Is Manny in there?"

"Oh. We're finished bonding. Great." His smile indicated an amusing inner dialogue. It didn't interest me. I wanted to know what was vexing Colonel Manfred Millard. Tim walked down the tastefully designed hallway to the conference room. "They've been going at it like this for the last twenty minutes."

Tim slowed down before we reached the conference room doors. He flexed his hands again. I stopped with an inner sigh. "What is causing your distress now?"

"Um." He straightened his shoulders. "If I say something to offend you, could you please tell me and not anyone else?"

"Why would I..." I studied all his nonverbal cues and added the context of our conversation. "I can't believe that you would want to keep anything from Phillip."

"No, no. Not Phillip. This job and his mentoring are the two best things ever to happen to me."

I thought back over the eighteen months Tim had been working at Rousseau & Rousseau. If Tim wasn't keeping anything from Phillip, only one other person was the logical choice. "Vinnie? Why?"

"He's a very big man."

"True." Vinnie was not only tall, but also very muscular. Colin's best friend, one of my closest friends, Vinnie had used his size to build a reputation as a ruthless criminal. It had helped him and Colin numerous times when Colin had had to retrieve a particularly sensitive object that had been stolen. Vinnie was also our housemate, the self-appointed guardian of our team and at times over-protective. And he enjoyed intimidating Tim. "Why don't you want Vinnie to know if you've offended me?"

Tim's lips trembled briefly. "He threatened everyone with bodily harm if we did anything to upset you."

I wasn't surprised by this. "I'll speak to Vinnie."

"No!" Tim's eyes flashed open in horror. "Please don't. You know what? Just forget everything I said. Listen to Colonel Millard shouting. You need to go in there." He opened the conference door and waved me inside. "I'll bring a fresh cup of coffee for you."

Deciding that I'd analyse Tim's reaction to Vinnie at a later time, I stepped inside the spacious conference room. Lining the taupe walls were paintings by Ian Francis, David Choe and Yoskay Yamamoto—artists who were making their mark in the contemporary art scene. The heavy cherry wood conference table in the centre of the room could easily seat sixteen people. Today there were only two men sitting at the far end of the table, glaring at each other.

I recognised the gentleman sitting across from Manny. Twice before I had met him when I'd had lunch with the first lady of France. He looked like a cover model for a business magazine with his tailored suit, styled hair, manicured nails and trimmed beard. As the director of public relations for the president of France, public image was his top priority.

Our team was under direct supervision of the president and frequently we investigated cases he assigned to us. After one particular case, the president's wife and I had become friendly. Ours was a professional friendship, but I did enjoy her company. I did not enjoy the company of Lucien Privott, the man now turning his glare towards me.

His reaction when he saw me was the main reason for the intense distrust I had towards him. The moment he recognised me, his expression changed with practiced intent. His thinned lips became soft, his *risorius* muscles turning his downturned mouth into a fake welcoming smile. He moved his flaring elbows closer to his sides and turned his arms to reveal the insides of his forearms. Strategic nonverbal communication to convey the message of being harmless and friendly. Lucien Privott was anything but.

"Doctor Lenard!" Lucien got up, his fake smile widening. "I'm so happy to see you."

I stared at him for a second. Then I looked down at Manny. He hadn't moved. As usual, he was slumping in his chair. To the average observer, the only law-enforcement member of our team might appear unfazed. Not only was I one of the best nonverbal communication experts in the world, I also knew Manny. He was most definitely not unfazed. His fists were pushed deep into his trouser pockets and the supratrochlear artery on his forehead was prominent.

Lucien walked around the table, his hand outstretched. I took a step back at the same time as Manny got up, putting himself between me and Lucien. "Sit down, Privott. You're not fooling Doctor Face-reader."

"I'm not trying to fool anyone."

"Yes, you are." I waited until he was seated before I sat down next to Manny. "All your nonverbal cues are practiced and not very convincing. You pulled at your shirt collar and leaned back when you said you weren't trying to fool anyone. Those are indicators of stress and, taken in context, deception."

Manny's lips twitched, but he managed to prevent his smile from surfacing. "Maybe now you'll tell me the real reason for this little visit of yours."

"I've been telling you nothing but the truth."

"Doc?" Manny turned to me.

"He's not lying." I'd spent most of my adult life observing people and looking for the true message behind their words. I looked at Lucien. "But I posit that you carefully chose what to tell Manny. Ah. I'm right."

"Half a truth is as good as a lie, Privott." Manny raised one eyebrow, his look of disdain unhidden.

"Half a truth is half a truth. Not that truth can be measured." I closed my eyes, distracted by Manny's silly statement. When I opened my eyes, Lucien looked decidedly less confident and aggressive than when I'd walked in. "I don't know how long you've been here and frankly, I don't care. But I do value my own time and I refuse to waste any of it if you are not going to disclose the genuine purpose for your visit."

"What she said." Manny nodded towards me, not taking his eyes off Lucien. "Start from the beginning so Doc can hear everything. And I mean everything, Privott. Don't leave out the interesting parts this time."

Lucien pressed his lips together so tightly they disappeared from view. Then he took a deep breath, adjusted his tie and looked at me. "Benoît Faure was murdered seven nights ago in a hotel. The maid found him the next morning when she went to clean the room. Nobody had heard anything during the night and there weren't any signs of a struggle. He'd been overpowered, manually strangled and then shot in the heart.

We are pretty sure the murderer used a suppressor—a top-of-the-range suppressor that will make a gunshot sound like a loud click. A gun going off at night would have drawn attention, even in that kind of hotel."

"What kind of hotel?" This was only one of the many questions I had.

"The kind where you can rent a room by the hour."

"Why would anyone want to do that?" I frowned at Lucien's extreme discomfort and turned my attention to Manny. "Why is this hotel an embarrassing topic?"

Manny snorted. "Because Mister Hipster here is a prude. Oh, never mind, Doc. People, mostly men, hire rooms by the hour because they also hire company by the hour. And when I say company, I mean prostitutes."

"Oh. There is nothing embarrassing about that." I looked at Lucien, who was pulling at his shirt collar. "Men have always paid to have their sexual needs tended to. There has to be a bigger issue than prostitution. Is this a case of human trafficking? No. Hmm. Then you'd better explain who this Benoît Faure was."

"Benoît Faure. Yes." Lucien's relief about the change of topic was almost comical. "He was a sixty-two-year-old import-export businessman. Despite Strasbourg not being a major port or import-export hub, he always insisted on running his business from his home town."

"He was born here."

"Yes. And his family has a history going back hundreds of years in the city."

"Your micro-expressions imply that the history is not a benign one."

"To say the least. Legend says that his family line goes back to the marauding Vikings. As far back as we have police records, the Faure family name has been connected with illegal acts. Extortion, fraud, violence in all its forms— anything you can think of, someone in that family has been accused of it."

"Benoît Faure?" I wasn't interested in inaccurate legends.

"Well, he made quite a name for himself in the late seventies as one of the most ruthless crime bosses in France. But he was arrested only once. For putting the man who punched his sister into hospital for three months." Lucien shrugged. "Not really an organised crime boss' worst delinquency, but that was a wake-up call for him."

"Did he serve time?" Manny asked.

"Nope. The case never even made it to court. Even at the tender age of twenty-two, Benoît Faure was a very smart man. He hired the best lawyer in the country and got off scot-free. Then he cleaned up his act. Since that day not a single crime could be directly traced back to him. The police's organised crime unit started calling him Mister Teflon."

"Because nothing sticks." Manny nodded.

If it hadn't been for Vinnie's insistence on using Teflon pans to make crêpes, I might not have understood the reference. "You still haven't explained why the president wants us to investigate the murder of a criminal."

"President Godard is concerned that this might incite a turf war. He's also concerned that Benoît Faure's family might retaliate."

I stared at Lucien. Until he shifted in his seat and touched his collar again. Women usually played with their necklace or rested their hands on their throats. Men often adjusted the knot of their tie or pulled at their collar whenever they needed comfort. Covering the suprasternal notch, the hollow just above the sternum, was a pacifying gesture, indicating insecurity or emotional discomfort. Lucien Privott was clearly not comfortable under my scrutiny. I didn't care. "That is the rehearsed answer. What is the full answer?"

"Oh, shoot. Mrs Godard warned us you would see right through that answer." He threw up his hands. "The president only recently discovered that he is connected to a few unsavoury characters."

"Unsavoury?" I hated euphemisms. "It would save us a vast amount of time if you would suspend all politically correct expressions and call everything and everyone as they are."

The look of consternation was one of the few honest expressions I'd seen from Lucien. He leaned towards me. "Isn't it tiring and disillusioning to always see everyone's lies?"

I shrugged. "Untruths are often diplomacy. It's what produces a polite society."

"Wow." He sat back, shaking his head. "Just wow."

"Do you need a moment and a hanky or will you bloody well tell us what connection there is between the president, Benoît Faure and your unsavoury characters?" Manny crossed his arms.

"Madame Godard got the president to go to the opera when they were a young couple. He fell in love with the art and started supporting it in whichever way he could. For the last two years, President Godard has donated a substantial amount to the Opéra National du Rhin."

"Let me guess." Manny's top lip curled. "Benoît Faure was also a huge opera lover and his name is also on the list of donors."

"Benoît Faure and more than a dozen other individuals who are quite well known to law enforcement."

Manny's *frontalis* muscle drew his eyebrows towards his hairline. "More than a dozen?"

"Apparently, mafia-types like dramatic music and singing that could separate bone from marrow." Lucien's top lip curled.

"No singing could ever manage such a feat." What a strange thing to say. "Your expression leads me to believe you don't enjoy opera?"

"Not at all." His disgust was another honest expression. "Give me good old rock and roll any day. Bruce is king."

I knew of no current king with that name and dismissed the comment. "Are there any other connections between Benoît Faure and President Godard?"

Lucien's tension returned. "Faure supported another two charities the president is a patron of."

"Well, what do you know." Manny uttered a sound of derision. "Criminals donating to charity. What is the crime world coming to?"

I pointed at Manny's face. "I can see that you are being sarcastic, but I don't understand."

"Sorry, Doc. I'm just thinking that criminals will never cease to amaze me. I would be willing to bet supermodel's shoe collection that what those fools call supporting a charity is just another way of laundering their blood money."

"Francine would not be pleased to know that you're wagering her shoes." My best friend, our IT expert, had recently entered into a romantic relationship with Manny. Theirs was not a logical match. They shared very few interests and argued all the time. What confounded me even more was the enjoyment they both derived from those heated disagreements. I'd witnessed on more than one occasion their pupils dilating and their lips becoming fuller with arousal as their voices rose in a fight over something I considered inconsequential. Despite their growing affection for each other, I was quite convinced Francine would take umbrage at Manny's use of her precious shoes.

"That's how convinced I am of this fact, Doc. My hide will stay intact on this wager. Those criminals are using charities to clean their dirty money. And now the president is connected to them." Manny looked at Lucien, one eyebrow raised. "Don't you people check out these charities before you let the president associate with them?"

"Of course we do. None of these men, including Benoît Faure, ever put their names to anything. They used their companies to support the opera house and the charities. Those companies all checked out. These men are smart enough to run the companies through some kind of proxy. Their names are seldom on the letterheads."

"I would like to return to the topic." I enunciated my words slowly. "Why should we look into this case?"

"There are a few other details that concern the president. He wants the best on this case so it can be solved as quickly and cleanly as possible."

"Don't insult me with practiced compliments." I thought about his nonverbal cues when he'd relayed the case to us. People seldom realised how much they revealed with only a few muscle contractions. I preferred replaying an interview on the twelve monitors in my viewing room, but my memory was sufficient for now. "There is something about the crime that has you confused and worried. Not the crime? The crime scene? Aha. What is it?"

"Shoot, Doctor Lenard. It feels like you're in my head." Lucien touched his temples, the fear around his eyes slight, but familiar. People didn't enjoy feeling vulnerable when they no longer had deception as a tool to soften harsh words or to maintain a level of privacy.

"The crime scene, Privott." Manny straightened.

"The murderer tattooed Benoît Faure while he was still alive."

"How the hell did he get the criminal to lie down for that?"

Lucien shifted in his chair. "The coroner found traces of Sevoflurane in Faure's system."

"Isn't that the anaesthetic gas thieves are now using to dose owners of a house and rob them blind while the poor rich people are sleeping it off?" Manny asked.

"It's reportedly one of the gases used. There wasn't any trace of this gas around Faure's mouth, so the theory is that the murderer released it into the air. Obviously he was wearing a mask so he could get his tattoo work done while Faure was under."

"The theory that gases are used during burglaries is greatly disputed." I found it hard to believe people wouldn't wake up from the potent smell before it had any effect. "This theory can only work if the dosage was right for Benoît Faure and it was administered correctly."

"All things which can be googled, Doc." Manny shrugged. "I have no expertise on this topic, but I reckon that in a small hotel room, blowing that stuff in someone's face might just do the job."

"The crime scene technicians said much the same. And since the murderer was planning on killing Faure in any case, he only needed to worry about his victim not waking up while he was busy with his artwork." Lucien took a large smartphone from the inner pocket of his suit jacket and swiped the touchscreen a few times. He winced slightly when he got to the photo he was looking for and handed the phone to Manny. "It's a crude job, definitely not professional. The coroner said it was done perimortem, but he was killed very shortly after."

Manny swiped the screen a few times, his brow pulling down in a deep scowl. He looked at me, the screen of the smartphone tilted so I couldn't see it. "Doc? It's a crime scene photo of a dead man."

Everything in me rebelled at taking the phone and looking at the photo. It wasn't normal for any human being to process as much death as we had done in the last three years. Homicide detectives, paramedics, police officers and medical examiners often developed myriad coping mechanisms allowing their consciousness to register the corpse they were looking at not as a human being, but rather as a case. The average neurotypical human being usually mourned the loss of a life, even a complete stranger's.

As I was non-neurotypical, death affected me in different ways. It took me down a dark path I didn't want to visit. My mind would grab onto the depravity of human nature and go into an obsessive loop analysing that part of human behaviour.

I touched my little finger to my thumb and focused on the positive emotions associated with that physical act. I'd been training my brain to recall calm, inner strength and control whenever those two fingers made contact. It was an anchor I used to help prevent shutdowns or to enable me to deal with a situation that usually would overload my senses.

I might have taken offence at Tim's desire to have Colin present when talking to me, but at this moment, I truly wished Colin hadn't decided to have breakfast with Vinnie before coming in to the office. Daily, it surprised me how much I'd come to rely on him to be a stabilising factor in my life. His presence alone would have made my finger-anchor unnecessary.

"Doc?"

It took a lot of control to take my eyes off the smartphone in Manny's hands. When I looked at his face, I realised that I must have been quiet for a lot longer than he was comfortable with. I pressed my fingers harder against each other. "I'll be fine. Let me see."

"Are you sure?" He held the phone even further away from me. "I can get supermodel to give you some art-type rendition of this."

"No." My voice was strong. "I will learn much more when I can see the crime scene, not only the tattoo."

Manny looked at me for another second, then handed the

phone to me when I shook my open palm impatiently at him. The little finger and thumb of my other hand still tightly pressed together, I turned the phone over and looked at the screen. It was a close-up photo of a man's naked chest. Specifically, the left side. The skin was leathery from years of sunbathing, the muscles hidden under layers of fat. But it was the tattoo that was the focal point, the skin around it slightly raised and pink, reacting to the needle puncturing the dermis and injecting ink underneath the surface.

It was clear the tattoo had not been done by an artist. What could have been a beautiful wreath of climbing roses looked like it had been drawn by an unsure, unpractised hand. Dark leaves stretched out over Benoît Faure's chest, the stems twisted and weaved together. A rose in the centre of the wreath-tattoo and a second at the bottom were simple in design, but striking. Standing out from the dark stems and leaves, the two red roses had to have significance.

"If you swipe the screen, you'll see the other crime scene photos," Lucien said in an almost whisper.

I glanced up at him. He jumped in his chair when another phone started ringing in his pocket. I considered having more than one smartphone superfluous at best and pretentious at worst. Lucien fumbled finding the smaller phone in his jacket pocket. His *corrugator supercilii* muscles pulled his eyebrows together when he looked at the screen. "Please excuse me. I have to take this."

He got up and left the conference room. After the violent event eight months ago, Phillip had installed security cameras to cover every centimetre of Rousseau & Rousseau. If Lucien was in search of privacy, he would only find an illusion of it.

I returned my attention to the phone in my hand. The screen had turned off and fortunately didn't require a passcode when I turned it back on. Francine would mock Lucien's lack of smartphone security. I'd always been vigilant with my computer security, but the ease with which Francine hacked other people's systems had made me much more paranoid.

"What do you think, Doc?"

"It's time for me to change my passwords again."

"Huh?" Manny's face communicated his confusion. Then he sighed. "I mean, what do you think about this case?"

"Oh." Specific questions were always better. "I have no particular thoughts on this case yet. We have far too little information for me to draw any conclusions."

"Hmph." Manny hated it when I didn't want to speculate. "What do you think about the tattoo?"

"It's most interesting." In a macabre way. "We can look at it in two ways. Firstly, this specific design could have great significance to the murderer. Possibly, it also had some significance to Benoît Faure. We still don't know if Benoît Faure was targeted or whether it was a crime of opportunity."

"That bloody hipster is holding back too much. Don't you worry, Doc. I'll speak to the president and get all the details you need."

"We need. You would be able to speculate much better with more information."

"True, Doc. True. Now tell me what the second way is we can look at this."

"The killer is playing a game. If this is a psychopath, he would derive great pleasure from knowing that we're pursuing some lead that he invented only to waste our time." I lifted my hand to stop Manny. After three years of working with him, I was confident that he was going to ask me whether I thought the tattoo had significance or whether it was a game. "I will not speculate. Definitely not at such an early stage. I will, however, give this tattoo appropriate attention during the investigation, but I recommend that you don't build your case around this."

"Look at the other photos. Tell me what you think about them."

Something in Manny's tone triggered my curiosity. I turned the phone on, but looked back up when Lucien rushed back into the conference room. His smooth control was nowhere in sight.

"Who got killed?" Manny's posture didn't change, but the narrowing of his eyes told me he also noticed Lucien's distress.

"Another damn criminal." Lucien grabbed his phone from my hands and nodded towards the door. "Come on. You're coming with me. You can see this one for yourself."

I grabbed the armrests and hooked my feet around the legs of the chair before I realised what I was doing. "I'm not going anywhere."

"Where's Frey, Doc?" Manny knew why I wouldn't go to a crime scene.

"Breakfast with Vinnie."

"If they meet us there, will that work for you?"

I thought about this. "As long as I don't have to go there in your car."

"There is nothing wrong with my car."

"It looks like a recycle bin."

"It's my filing system and it works for me."

Times like these brought understanding why Francine enjoyed bickering. My hands had relaxed and my feet were already pointing towards the door. I sighed at myself and got up. "We are going in my car. After I speak to Colin."

Chapter TWO

Immense relief relaxed all the muscles in my body when I saw Colin standing at the gate of the large property on the left. He was talking to Vinnie, their postures mirroring. It wasn't surprising. These two men had been best friends for almost two decades.

Vinnie was only a few centimetres taller than Colin, but had the build of one of the wrestlers he liked to watch on television. He was wearing his usual combat pants, boots and tight black t-shirt that showed off his muscular upper body. Colin was a contrast to Vinnie in his designer slacks, linen shirt and Italian loafers.

I pulled into the driveway and stopped in front of the gate, grateful that the twenty-five-minute journey was over. Manny had insisted on going in his car. He'd still been arguing his point when I'd taken my keys and left the office. That was after Colin had reassured me that he and Vinnie would be waiting for me. He'd kept his word.

The moment I turned off the engine, Colin opened my door and held out his hand. "You made good time. Millard isn't here yet."

"We all know he drives like the old man he is." Vinnie smiled when I allowed Colin to pull me out the car. "Hey, Jen-girl."

"Hey." I turned to Colin, not letting go of his hand. "Thank you for coming."

Something must have alerted Colin. He lowered his head and studied me. "What's wrong?"

"I saw a photo of a dead body this morning with a tattoo that was done a short while before the man was murdered, and now I'm going into a house with another dead body which apparently bears great similarity to the other crime scene, and…"

Colin pulled me against his chest, his arms tight around me. I took a shuddering breath, thankful that he'd stopped my run-on sentence. I allowed the familiarity of Colin's body to ground me. His steady heartbeat against my ear slowed my own down until I felt more in control. In my entire life, Colin had been the only person whose touch didn't send me into a panic or a shutdown. Feeling his arms holding me tightly or his hand on my forearm always calmed me. The next deep breath I took was not as tense.

"What's going on here? This is no time for snogging." The annoyed quality in Manny's voice was not genuine enough to hide the undertone of concern.

I pushed away from Colin, but stayed in his embrace. "We are not snogging."

"And if we want to, it's none of your business, Millard." Colin looked down at me. "You're okay now?"

I nodded and took a step back. Colin reluctantly released me, but took my hand and interlaced our fingers. I squeezed his hand.

"Doc? Are you sure you're up for this?" Manny nodded towards the high fence surrounding the property.

I looked at the landscaped garden that could qualify as a small inner-city park. Barely visible from the road was a mansion, five police vehicles parked in front of it. With my free hand, I touched my little finger to my thumb and looked back at Manny. "I'll manage."

"Hmph." He didn't look convinced and gave Colin a look.

It was most irksome when these men acted as if I couldn't function without them. Admittedly, I operated better with them, but my own strength had brought me this far. It would take me further. Yet I knew that their support would make the journey smoother. Only because of this did I decide to reassure them, no matter how exasperating it was. "The moment I'm overwhelmed, I'll leave the crime scene."

"You do that, Doc. And don't wait too long. I'll make sure they video everything, so you can have that as well as the crime scene photos."

"Maybe you can now tell us what we're doing at Léon Blanc's house." Colin nodded towards the house. "Is he the victim?"

"We don't know who the victim is yet." Manny pushed his hands into his pockets. "Privott forgot to mention that little titbit before he took off."

"Who's Privott?" Vinnie crossed his arms, his triceps bulging.

"Lucien Privott is the president's PR guy. He spins any potential scandal until it smells like roses." Colin winked at me. "Figuratively speaking."

"And how the hell do you know this, Frey?"

"I need to know who I'm connected to, no matter how

tenuous that link." Colin's vigilance had saved him on more than one occasion. "Léon Blanc?"

"No, Frey. You first. Tell me how you know whose house this is." Manny might have convinced a criminal he was interrogating that he was suspicious, but his micro-expression revealed his genuine surprise and curiosity.

"Some people have a level of sophistication that is far above your comprehension, Millard. Those people attend the opera, go to exhibitions and support charity events. Those people also meet other likeminded individuals. Léon Blanc is one of those people."

"You haven't yet explained who he is." I wanted to stay on topic and get this over with as soon as possible.

"For you, love, I'll give Léon Blanc's full history." Colin winked at me. "Léon Blanc is the director of the Opéra National du Rhin. He's... what? Why are you and Millard looking at me like that?"

"Doc?" Manny's eyes were wide. "What are the odds of Lucien Privott and his little connection to Faure's murder and now the opera house director being involved in a similar murder all being connected?"

"I have no such statistical data."

"Whoa." Vinnie raised both hands. "Two murders? Connections? You two want to let us in on your secret?"

Manny gave a summary of our meeting with Lucien. While he talked, I prepared myself for the crime scene waiting on the far side of this property. I had not looked at the other crime scene photos on Lucien's phone and thus had inadequate data to truly prepare myself.

"Okay, so the president donates to the opera house,

Benoît Faure also donated to the opera house and now the director of the opera house is dead. Yeah, that smells fishy." Vinnie nodded as if he had concrete proof to support his statement.

"We don't know if the victim is Léon Blanc yet," I said. "It could be someone else."

"Then we'd better get inside and find out everything we can about this bloody mess." Manny walked towards the gate. "Come on. Let's go."

When Vinnie, Colin and I reached the gate, Manny was already talking to someone on the intercom. A few seconds later the ornate iron gates slowly opened. We walked through and they closed again behind us. I didn't mind the walk up the driveway. It was beautiful. Large oak trees provided plenty of shade, the lawn had recently been mowed and all the flowers were in full bloom. Tranquillity prefacing the aftermath of violence awaiting us in the house.

"Privott sent all the crime scene photos to your account, Doc." Manny was maintaining a brisk pace. With us he didn't have to uphold any kind of façade. His posture was alert and his steps confident. It would change as soon as we reached the house. "Supermodel downloaded all of them already and is analysing them."

Since Francine had come into my life and onto our team, I'd no longer had any privacy in my inbox. Francine claimed it was for security reasons that she scanned all my mail before I even had the chance to open it. I'd seen her lie and got her to confess. She was protecting me. I didn't feel singled out since she did that to everyone on our team. With or without their permission.

"It might be a good *and* bad thing that I haven't seen the photos yet."

"Why do you say that, Doc?"

"Good because it won't affect the way I view this crime scene. I will look at it with no bias. Bad because, having the first crime scene as a reference point, I would be able to find similarities and differences much faster."

"Hmm. Makes sense." Manny stopped to talk to a uniformed officer guarding the door. Once we were all vetted, the officer opened the heavy carved wooden door. We stepped into a large foyer. The ceramic floor tiles were probably imported from Italy, but I doubted they'd been as expensive as the Persian carpets scattered across the floor as far as I could see.

A few steps led down to a spacious living area to the right and a kitchen designed for gourmet cooking and entertaining guests to the left. We went to the right. The room we entered was divided into two sitting areas, one with a green leather sofa and two matching chairs. The sofa was facing the large flat screen television against the wall. The other sitting area was furnished with one sofa, three wingback chairs and one settee. None of them matched in style, but the arrangement resulted in an elegant combination of modern and antique.

Strategically placed on the floor were numerous antique coffee tables, kists and, of course, Persian carpets. I wasn't surprised when Colin gravitated towards the side wall, pulling me along with him. Seven paintings decorated the khaki-coloured wall, heavy frames accentuating the beauty of each individual work. It fitted perfectly with the eclectic design of the room, the wall not looking cluttered, the paintings complementing each other.

"Morisot, Cézanne, Degas, Renoir, and Sisley." Colin pointed at each painting as he named their creators.

"This way, thief." Manny walked down a hallway leading to the back of the house. "You can scope out your loot later."

"You're a comedian, Millard." Colin frowned at the Morisot painting before turning towards the hallway. He'd seen something of interest and I intended to question him about it later. I pressed my fingers together and braced myself when we followed Manny into a room to the right.

It was a home office that looked more like an art gallery combined with a library. Two of the three walls had floor-to-ceiling bookshelves, each filled to capacity. The third wall was covered in masterpieces, not leaving much of the wall exposed. Large windows overlooked the garden, heavy curtains pulled away to allow the summer sun to bathe the room in bright light.

A grand piano stood on a Persian carpet, two music stands next to it. The opposite end of the room had a heavy wooden desk, next to it three wingback chairs arranged around a round table. Yet there was enough space for Manny, Colin, myself and two crime scene technicians without the room feeling crowded.

My focus on the furnishings was a weak attempt at avoiding the floor space next to the piano. That was where the two crime scene technicians were busy taking photos. And that was where the murder victim was.

"Jenny?" Colin's hand tightened around mine. "Want to take a closer look?"

"No." I took a deep breath and immediately regretted it. Smells flooded my senses. Books, furniture polish, a faint scent of blood and something else. I sniffed, trying to identify the smell. "Is that ink?"

"Indeed it is." One of the crime scene technicians looked over his shoulder. "The vic got tattooed by the killer."

I stepped closer. Colin followed.

"Let's see that tattoo," Manny said.

"My ink was done by an artist." The technician slapped his shoulder. "This guy's ink was done by an amateur."

I forced my eyes away from his shoulder to look at the body lying on the floor. I blinked in surprise. "Where is the blood?"

"There isn't any." The technician pointed at the left of the victim's exposed chest. "Here's your tattoo."

"What's his COD?" Manny asked.

"Well, I reckon the blunt-force trauma to the back of his skull was this poor unfortunate soul's cause of death. His head is total mush at the back. It definitely wasn't the gunshot." The technician got up. "I'll give you a few minutes. I need the head in any case."

"What head?" Oh, my goodness. "Was someone beheaded?"

The technician stopped dead in his tracks and stared at me. His eyes widened a second before he slapped his forehead. "You must be Doctor Lenard! Heard about you. Hah! Good one, Doc. Gonna tell the boys about this."

He left chuckling and shaking his head. I turned to Manny.

"Why is he laughing? Why are you smiling? A decapitation is a serious deviation from the last crime scene."

"'The head' is a Navy term for the lavvy, Doc."

"The toilet? How odd." I was going to research the origin of that particular term. I'd learned from Manny the term 'lavvy', but still preferred to refer to the toilet by its name.

I groaned at the distraction. It was simply too easy for my mind to lock on to a word or topic and go into an unending loop analysing it. I made a conscious effort to focus on the tattoo that took up a large part of the man's chest. "Is this Léon Blanc?"

"Yes," a soft voice answered from underneath the piano. Covered from head to toe in a white plastic suit, the young woman groaned as she exited on the far side of the piano and got up. "Someone sanitised this crime scene. There's nothing. Not a single fingerprint, not a blood drop, not a hair. Not even a speck of dust. They even vacuumed under the carpets. He definitely didn't die here. This carpet has no traces of blood."

She continued to list all the places they'd looked for blood evidence, but I was more interested in the crude tattoo. "It's his heart."

"Huh?" Manny's shoulders slumped and he grunted when I didn't expand. "Explain, Doc."

I pressed my fingers hard against each other before I let go of Colin's hand and went on my haunches next to Léon Blanc. Making sure not to touch anything, I traced one of the many badly drawn stems of the tattooed climbing rose. "The way it is hidden beneath all the leaves and other branches, I think the killer wanted to disguise it. But it's there. My knowledge of human anatomy is not perfect, but I estimate the outline to be quite accurately above Léon Blanc's heart."

The tattoo was similar to the one I'd seen on Lucien Privott's smartphone, but there were slight differences. This tattoo had three roses—one in the centre of the design and the bottom, as with Faure's tattoo, but Léon Blanc's tattoo had another rose at the top of the design. Another similarity was the dark core of the centre rose. I hadn't had enough time to look closely at Faure's tattoo, but I was sure the dark core on that rose would prove to be the same as this one. A bullet hole. I supposed that was the gunshot wound the technician had referred to.

"This isn't right." I tilted my head, recalling the photo on Lucien's phone. "This wound has little dots around it. The other had a ring around it."

"Good eye." The technician's smile was similar to my childhood teachers' when they'd been pleased with my answers. I'd only received that smile a few times. The technician leaned against the piano. "My name is Isabelle, by the way. I know who you people are. Everyone wants a chance to work with you. I'm so going to brag about this."

"The dots and ring, Isabelle." Manny pointed at Léon Blanc's chest.

"Ah, yes. I wasn't at the last crime scene, but I can tell you now if the wound was circular with blackened, seared skin margins, it means the muzzle of the gun was pushed right against the victim's skin when the trigger was pulled. The heat from the explosion would cause the searing. These dots? That means the gun was held a short distance from the victim's skin when the killer shot him. Until I know what gun was used, I won't be able to tell you the exact distance. But it was less than a metre. Those dots are called stippling, by the way."

"Do you think it means something that he didn't press the gun against Blanc's chest, Doc?"

"I don't know. I don't have enough information." I looked at Isabelle. "Who reported this crime?"

"The housekeeper found him this morning when she came to clean here. She said she's used to Monsieur Blanc keeping strange hours, sometimes sleeping until lunchtime, so she didn't think anything of it when she came in this morning and he wasn't around. I heard her saying this to one of the police guys when I was walking here, by the way. If you want to know anything else, you should speak to her."

I got up, stepped away from the body and slowly turned a full three hundred and sixty degrees, registering as much detail as I could. When I returned to my starting point, Colin was standing in front of the wall with all the paintings, his eyes narrowed as he glanced from one to the other. Everyone else was staring at me. "Where's the computer?"

"We haven't found any electronic devices yet." Isabelle glanced at the empty surface of the desk. "My guess is it's locked in one of the desk drawers. We haven't opened anything yet. Usually we gather evidence before we break open any cupboards or drawers. Since there is no evidence, I'll go ahead and get Luc to jimmy the lock when he comes back. He's good with that."

"If you find the computer, send it to us immediately," Manny said. "Frey, what are you looking at?"

"These pretty pictures on the wall in their beautiful frames are called paintings, Millard." Colin's tone didn't have its usual mocking quality.

I walked closer and stopped next to Colin. I didn't see anything amiss with the artwork. Three of the eleven paintings were by the same artist. Morisot. I was not familiar with this artist's work. None of the clients I'd had access to in Rousseau & Rousseau had ever insured a painting by this artist. I would've remembered. I glanced at Colin's expression. "What's wrong with these paintings?"

"They're forgeries." He stepped closer, his nose five centimetres away from a painting of a nude girl with a yellow headscarf lying in a field. For a few seconds he inspected the artwork, then straightened. "Yes. This is a forgery. A brilliant forgery, but not painted by Berthe Morisot."

"It's a female artist?" Manny joined us and tilted his head. "Never heard of her. Who is she?"

"She was an impressionist painter who died in 1895. She was one of the few great female artists of that time. Édouard Manet was a close friend of hers. They even painted a few works together. She married his brother."

"Huh. Never knew about her." Vinnie pushed away from where he was leaning against the doorframe. I'd almost forgotten about his presence. It took only four strides with his long legs to reach us. He folded his arms and squinted at the paintings. "They're pretty. In a girly sorta way. You think this is related to the murder, dude?"

Colin inhaled to answer, but stopped. He looked at Isabelle, who was watching us. "Did you check the frames for prints?"

"Not yet." She handed Colin a small plastic stepladder. "You can check, but please don't touch."

Colin stepped onto the second step to look at the top of the lower paintings. He huffed and climbed higher. He moved the ladder to inspect all the paintings, then stood back. He rubbed his hand over his mouth, then held his chin in a thinker's pose. "Well, here's another mystery. The frames of the three Morisot paintings are clean as if they were hung yesterday. The Picasso, Degas and Manet have a slight layer of dust like one would expect."

"Did you notice fingerprints?" Isabelle asked.

"No, but it doesn't mean there aren't any."

"Make sure you check every single frame in this house for fingerprints." Manny's *corrugator supercilii* muscle pulled his brow low over his eyes. "Bloody forgeries."

Colin didn't respond to Manny, but handed the ladder back to Isabelle. "Please be very careful when you dust for prints. The Picasso, Degas, Manet here and the Cézanne, Degas, Renoir, and Sisley in the living room are authentic. You wouldn't want to be the one damaging a few million euros' worth of paintings."

Isabelle's hand flew to her mouth. "Are you kidding me?"

"Not at all. That is the approximate value of these paintings. I'm sure there are more in the house, which means you are looking at a much larger sum."

"Luc can dust for prints. I'm not touching those things. Not in this lifetime, by the way." She stepped back and took her camera from the large toolbox standing next to the desk. "I'm better with the camera in any case."

"Would you then be so kind as to take individual photos

of each of the paintings?" Colin waved at the wall. "And a shot of the whole wall."

"And send all those paintings to Rousseau & Rousseau." Manny looked at Colin, both eyebrows raised. "You're one hundred percent sure these paintings are forgeries?"

"Without a doubt. Not one of these pieces was painted by Berthe Morisot."

"That is not possible," a new voice said from the doorway.

Chapter THREE

Everyone turned to the man standing in the doorway. He was average height with dark hair and facial features of a kind I immediately recognised. In his twenties and thirties, he most likely had been fit and had attracted a lot of female attention. As with most people, his fourth decade had brought a bit more weight which gave him a softness that was reflected in his nonverbal cues. This was not an aggressive man.

"You cannot be here, sir. This is a closed crime scene." Isabelle held up both hands as if to push the man out from a distance.

"This is my house." The man looked at Léon Blanc's body on the Persian carpet. The micro-expressions flashing on his face were most interesting, finally settling on sad acceptance. "At least, now it is."

"Who are you?" Manny walked towards the door, Vinnie right behind him.

"He's Léon Blanc's son." I'd seen the similarities in their brows and noses, but the sadness around his eyes and mouth had confirmed my suspicions.

"I'm Sébastien Blanc, Léon Blanc's only son." He didn't offer his hand in introduction, too distracted by his father's lifeless body. His shoulders were hunched with sorrow.

"What happened to him?"

"The crime tech was right." Manny moved to block Sébastien Blanc's view of his dad. "You cannot be here. Let's take this to another room."

Sébastien's jaw moved a few times before he tightened his lips, pulled his shoulders back and looked away from his dad. "Can I first get the authentication papers for the paintings from his safe?"

"No. You cannot touch anything." Isabelle shook her head vigorously.

"Where is the safe?" Manny asked.

Sébastien Blanc pointed to the Picasso painting hanging on the bottom left of the wall we'd been looking at. "There's a hidden button in the desk that will swing this painting open and reveal the safe."

"A good place to keep a safe." I studied the painting and couldn't see any difference from the other paintings. It was the same distance from the wall. The heavy frame didn't look as if had been frequently touched and so it did not attract attention.

"I agree." Colin's smile was genuine. This was his field of expertise as well as his passion. "People always look for a safe in the centre of a wall space. To the left and the bottom is not the first or even second place anyone would look for a hidden safe."

"Where is the button?" Manny walked to the desk. "You stay right there and tell me what to do."

"It's the handle of the second drawer on the left." Sébastien waited until Manny stood in front of the drawers. "Twist the handle forty-five degrees anticlockwise."

Manny's body stiffened a second later. "It clicked."

"That means you can push in the centre part. That will remove the magnetic lock from the painting." No sooner had he said this than a soft click sounded next to me and the painting swung away from the wall.

Colin's smile widened. He grabbed two latex gloves from Isabelle's toolbox. By the time he stood in front of the painting, his hands were protected. He touched the bottom of the frame with one finger and pulled the painting until it revealed the safe behind it. "State-of-the-art Paragon 7775 Deluxe Safe. Not easy to crack."

"We won't need your skills today, Frey." Manny walked around the desk, stopped next to Colin, but looked at Sébastien. "We're going to get the code."

"Of course." Sébastien gave Colin the thirteen-digit code.

With sure hands, Colin entered the code, enjoyment still evident around his eyes and mouth. A snick sounded in the silent room before Colin turned the handle and opened the square door. His eyes widened and his *masseter* muscle slackened in shock, leaving his lips slightly agape. "Hmm."

"What?" Sébastien stepped closer. "Is it empty? Please don't say that. All Dad's most important documents were there."

Colin stepped away to reveal a neatly organised, yet deep space in the wall. His eyes weren't on the three full document folders or the stacks of hundred-euro notes that had to add up to at least a hundred thousand euros. They were on a small black box. He reached in and took it out with the same care I'd seen him take when handling an original masterpiece.

Manny leaned closer, preventing me from seeing the box.

"What the bleeding hell? Frey? Are those real?"

"No way to tell with the naked eye, but if Monsieur Blanc had them locked up, then I would assume yes."

"Dude." Vinnie shifted from one foot to the other, stretching his neck to see what Colin was staring at. "What is that?"

Colin turned towards us and tilted the box just enough for us to see through the glass cover. "Diamonds. Lots of diamonds."

Sébastien reared back, his eyes wide. "I didn't know Dad had diamonds. I swear. I don't know anything about this."

Manny took the box from Colin and held it for Isabelle to photograph. "Log this and everything else in the safe. We're taking the diamonds and folders with us to the living room."

It took seven minutes for Manny to remove the contents of the safe and Isabelle to photograph each item. We left the cash in the safe, but took the folders and diamonds to the living room. Manny wasted another five minutes loudly berating a young officer for allowing a stranger into the house. Sébastien's lips thinned at being called a stranger, but he didn't interfere. He sat down heavily on one of the wingback chairs, the gravity of the situation evident in his nonverbal cues.

Colin sat down next to me on one of the sofas, Vinnie choosing to stand at an angle behind Sébastien. Manny was last to join us. He sat down in the second wingback chair and rested his elbows on his thighs, his hands dangling between his knees. "Firstly, please accept our condolences."

"Thank you." Sébastien showed no appreciation. Instead

he narrowed his eyes. "You still haven't told me what happened to my father."

"I understand you have a lot of questions, but first we need our questions answered." Manny's gentle tone and uncommon sensitivity would've been surprising when I'd first met him. After working with him for three years, I knew that he was a master at reading each person and adjusting his interrogation methods to get the most information in the shortest period. "Are you up for some questions?"

"Yes. I suppose." Sébastien lifted one shoulder. "Although I don't know how I can help you."

"By telling the truth." I pointed at his shoulder. "Your nonverbal cues just revealed that you are not convinced of your statement that you can't help us. That leads me to surmise that you do in fact have information that could be of great assistance in solving your father's murder."

Sébastien's eyes widened. "I don't know anything about the diamonds."

"That's true. But you know something else." And I wanted to know what he was hiding.

"We'll get to that soon, Doc." Manny leaned towards Sébastien, his expression sympathetic. "Why don't we start with basic information about who you are."

"Like I said, I'm Sébastien Blanc, the only son of Léon and Diane Blanc. I'm a paediatrician. I work at a hospital and have a small private practice. All of this information you can find with a minimal search on government databases."

"Your mother?" Manny asked.

"Died when I was four years old. My dad never remarried. He was married to his job. I was raised by a succession of nannies. When I was old enough I was shipped off to boarding school and any holidays were spent in camps that were carefully planned to fill up the whole holiday." His *risorius* muscles twisted his mouth in what laymen called a bitter expression. "I grew up without any parents. That influenced my career choice and also my decision to work only in one city. I've been married for seventeen years and my three children see me every day. I go to all their conce… You don't need to know any of this, do you?"

"We don't yet know if your information is relevant, so I have no answer to your question." I did however value all data. "Anything you tell us will give us a better understanding of your father. Sometimes the seemingly inconsequential can be key to solving a mystery."

"Who are you?" Sébastien tucked his jacket firmly in place. "I've introduced myself, but I don't know who you are. Are you with the police?"

"I'm Colonel Millard." Manny nodded towards me. "That is Doctor Genevieve Lenard and these are our colleagues. We are working with the police to solve your father's murder. Now can you please tell me why you came here this morning?"

"My dad didn't answer his phone. That used to be the norm, but the last few weeks he's answered every time I called him." Sébastien looked at the ceiling. "That and I had a strange feeling."

"A strange feeling?"

Again he lifted one shoulder. It indicated that the speaker wasn't convinced of what he or she was saying. It could imply deceit or in this particular case I believed it to be awkwardness. "It was just a strange feeling. Appears it was a premonition of sorts."

"Why did you phone your father?"

"He's loaning paintings for an exhibi... Oh, God." Sébastien pressed the heel of his hand against his right temple. "That's going to cause all kinds of complications."

"What are you talking about?"

Sébastien waved at the paintings against the wall. "As you can see, Dad collected paintings from the nineteenth century. I used to joke that he had a love affair with ol' Berthe. He loved her works more than all the others. Altogether he has seven of her artworks. And they're real." He pointed to the documents Colin was perusing. "You'll find all the paperwork there. Anyway, I organised this exhibition to raise funds for new equipment for the hospital. The gallery that is hosting this has been able to get a few private collectors to loan one or two of their paintings. There will be over a hundred and fifty works on display. A Manet will be auctioned off on the last evening and a percentage of the sale will also go to the hospital."

"All the papers are here." Colin put the folders on the coffee table. "But I can tell you now those paintings are not the original Morisots."

"It's not possible." Sébastien enunciated each word slowly.

"Could he have ordered forgeries to display at home while he stores the originals in a safe location?" Colin asked.

"No. Never. He is..." Sébastien swallowed. "He was so proud of his collection. He loved each brushstroke."

"And you say it's only Morisot's paintings that are forged?"

Manny looked at Colin. "All the others are the real deal?"

"I had a very quick glance, but yes." Colin got up and walked to the wall. I followed him, curious. He pointed at the Renoir. "Undoubtedly authentic." He stepped to the right and leaned closer to a Degas. "Also the original." Then he stepped in front of the Morisot painting. "This is a fantastic reproduction. And it's not man-made."

"Explain." Manny was standing behind us.

Colin glanced over his shoulder, then looked back at the painting, his head at a slight angle. "Remember the case we had with the 3D-printed guns? Yeah, well, 3D printing has come a long way since. This painting was printed layer by layer. Hundreds of layers."

"A 3D printer made this?" Manny stepped closer, his face pulled in a tight squint. "Did it print the whole thing, frame and all?"

Colin made a rude noise. "Must you be so ignorant? It only printed the pretty picture, Millard. The canvas and the frame were made in the traditional manner."

"What about the quality of the paint?" I had learned from Colin that the greatest forgeries came from people who knew how to recreate paint that had the same chemical structure as the original. The canvas and the aging process of the painting played as important a role in convincing the experts as the artistic skill in reproducing the artwork.

"We'll need to test this in a lab, but from what I can tell, the colours are a perfect match." Colin leaned back, still looking at the painting. "I remember studying this painting at an exhibition in 2002. What really got to me then was Morisot's use of loose brushwork. The small scale of her work, the sense of spontaneity that came from her works. If we ever find the original and compare, these brushstrokes will be an exact match."

"So, how does this work?" Manny pushed his hands in his trouser pockets. "They scan the original and print it?"

"Pretty much. Very recently a company started offering services to museums reproducing masterpieces. This is all done on the up and up." Colin looked at me. "Legally. They use a top-of-the-range 3D scanner under the supervision of museum officials to scan the original painting. Then they produce a draft for the museum experts to approve. That way the museum can make sure the colours are an exact match. Once they give the go-ahead, the company will 3D-print that painting to produce an exact copy."

"What do the museums want a copy for?"

"To sell." Colin raised both hands. "Legally. It has a marking that the museum and this company agree upon that identifies the painting as a certain number in a limited series. It also marks it as a reproduction. The museums have the opportunity to make money and art-lovers have the opportunity to have a very real-looking masterpiece hanging on their walls for a fraction of the value of the original work."

"Hmph." Manny thought about this for a few seconds, then turned to face Colin fully. "Who do we go to here in Strasbourg if we need it?"

Colin's smile was genuine. He was amused. "I'll reach out to my contacts. I know of three people who have equipment that could produce this quality."

"Why the hell do they need equipment like that?"

"Is this relevant?" I didn't want Manny to go on yet another rant about criminals using technology that sometimes saved lives to destroy lives.

"I suppose not." Manny waved everyone back to the sitting area. "Okay, Sébastien, can you think of any reason why there would be forgeries on your father's walls?"

"I'm still not convinced they are forgeries." Sébastien stared at Colin. "Who are you? How can I trust your quick analysis of a painting to be true?"

"Oh, you can trust his analysis." Manny's *levator anguli oris* muscles caused his lips to twitch. He was not complimenting Colin's skills. "If he says they're forgeries, they are. But since you are not completely convinced, we will have them tested. In the event that they are indeed forgeries—"

"Which they are," Colin said.

"—do you have any thoughts about it?" Manny ignored Colin, not taking his eyes off Sébastien.

"No."

"You're lying." I pointed at Sébastien's neck. "You touched your neck, your blinking increased and a few other blocking cues. All indicators of a person being deceitful."

"Are you some kind of body language reader?" His question came through thinned lips. He was angry at being exposed, being vulnerable.

"I'm one of the top nonverbal communication experts in the world. Now tell us what you suspect."

Sébastien looked down at his hands, his breathing erratic. We waited in silence for almost a minute while he composed himself. He interlaced his fingers and held his own hands in a tight self-comforting grip. "My dad is… was… a complicated man. He was friends with people I only recently discovered are not the amicable uncles I'd known growing up."

"What friends?" Manny asked.

"Serge Valois and Audric Daniau." Sébastien's smile held no humour. "I see you recognise those names. Yeah, I didn't know they were mobsters when I met them the few times I was at home during school holidays. I always thought they were Dad's friends from school or university. Then I saw an article in the newspaper a few weeks ago exposing Uncle Serge's illegal activities. My God. All these years and I'd thought he was one of my dad's best friends. I never suspected him to be a thief and murderer."

"Can you provide us with a list of your dad's friends?"

"Sure." Sébastien looked at the little black box on the coffee table. "Do you think those diamonds were a payment for something illegal? Are those blood diamonds?"

"They look like usual white diamonds in a round brilliant cut." I frowned. "I have no knowledge of a blood diamond category."

"Diamonds that are mined in conflict areas, usually by slaves or children, are called blood diamonds, love. The money from those diamonds most often goes to fund war, and the environment and circumstances of the mining are always horrid." Colin picked up the box and stared through the glass cover. "There's no way to tell without my loupe eyeglass."

"You know, I thought about this." Sébastien nodded as if confirming an internal statement. "I wondered what I'd do with this huge mansion when my dad dies. With his valuable collections. I think I'm going to sell it all. I'll donate all the proceeds to charity."

"Why would you do that?" Manny's question was more polite than I would've phrased it. The guilt on Sébastien Blanc's face made me suspicious.

"I have no proof of this, but I don't think my dad lived a clean life."

"What does that mean?" The house appeared clean enough, so I assumed Sébastien Blanc wasn't referring to hygiene.

"I think my dad was friends with bad people and might have gotten himself involved in bad things. Illegal things. Dad was born into a family with enough money to live very comfortably, but not enough money to afford these paintings. Did you know he paid over two million dollars for the Degas? That's money that my dad's inheritance and his job would not have been able to afford. So where did he get it all from?"

"We hope to find those answers." Manny's words might have sounded sympathetic, but I saw the determination in his tight jaw and lips.

"You might want to start at the opera house. Those people are worse gossips than a bunch of old ladies. And they're all up in each other's business. They'll tell you a lot more about my dad's private life than I can. I'm sure by now you know we weren't close. I had no idea what he did in his private time or who he did it with."

"We'll need you to be available if we have any more questions."

"I'm at a medical conference for the next two days, but it's here in Strasbourg. If you need me and I don't answer my phone, just leave a message. I'll help you any way I can." He snorted a humourless laugh. "Most people would take time off. My dad just died and I… I feel relieved, impatient to get to work and guilty because I feel relieved and want to work."

Manny looked at me and I nodded. Sébastien Blanc was telling the truth. Often the death of a loved one brought great relief when it ended complicated relationships.

I wondered if there was any footage available of his father giving an interview. It would be fascinating comparing him to Sébastien. From the last twenty-three minutes, I surmised that this was a case where nurture had indeed had a stronger long-term outcome than nature, especially since his parents hadn't had much input in his childhood years. I wondered if I would see the same honesty in Léon as I saw in Sébastien's nonverbal cues. Or the clear lack of practice whenever he attempted to tell an untruth.

"Doc?" Manny's tone held a quality that warned me he'd been talking to me and I'd not paid attention.

"I'm listening."

"Good. I want you and Frey to go to the opera house and talk to those people. I need to ask a few more questions here and get cracking on what we already have. The criminal stays with me. He'll scare all those sophisticated opera people."

Chapter **FOUR**

"Daniel." I was surprised but pleased to see the leader of the GIPN team standing in front of the Opéra National du Rhin, the opera house in Strasbourg. We frequently worked with his elite team of France's equivalent of SWAT. They'd proven themselves to be the best GIPN had to offer in every respect.

Daniel's smile lifted his cheeks, the corners of his eyes crinkling. A genuine smile. "Good to see you, Genevieve. Colin, you ready for Friday night?"

"Not as ready as Vinnie." Colin shook Daniel's hand. "He's been watching YouTube videos of pool championships to prepare."

Daniel laughed. "Those firefighters really pissed him off last month."

Despite Vinnie's strong dislike for law enforcement, he'd become friends with Daniel's whole team, often joining for training sessions. He'd drawn Colin into their tight social circle, especially for the monthly billiards competition against one of the local fire departments. Colin's skill had been honed playing snooker, but apparently he had found it easy to adjust to the different rules of pool. Daniel and his team had been ecstatic when Colin had joined their team. The firefighters not so much.

"That is what happens when someone insults Vin's aunts." Colin shook his head. "Those guys should've known better."

I'd had enough of their small talk. "Why did Manny phone you?"

"I'm your arm candy." Daniel winked at me. "That means I'm only here to look pretty."

"You're not pretty." I inspected his medium height and his posture that hinted at a military background even when he was relaxed, like now. He shaved his head, his olive-coloured skin shining in the summer sun. His square jaw and strong facial features were softened by the compassionate expression he always wore. "I suspect most women would find you very handsome. You are too masculine to be described as pretty."

His dark skin warmed with colour as he laughed. "Coming from you, that is a huge compliment. Thanks, Genevieve."

Colin put his arm around me and pulled me in for a quick sideways hug. "You've just made this man's day, love."

I frowned at Daniel and shook Colin's arm from my shoulder. "Looking pretty will not assist us interviewing people in the opera house. Why are you really here?"

"Manny thought having a uniform around would help with authority issues."

I thought about this. My social skills were not good. If I had to, I could interact at a level that made people comfortable, but it was exhausting and would not necessarily help us. People revealed different information when they were uncomfortable. When relaxed, they might lower their defences and allow information to slip out, but when uncomfortable, those secrets usually revealed themselves through nonverbal cues. My speciality. Colin's speciality was putting people at ease. Together we made a good team, but without Manny we lacked the important law-enforcement element. "It was a prudent decision."

"Why, thank you. I'm glad to be here. I don't get enough opportunity to use my negotiation skills." The preparation each GIPN member received ranged from intense physical training to ongoing weapons instruction. But it was the psychology training that everyone hoped would prevent situations from turning into a gun battle. My first meeting with Daniel had shown him to be an astute observer. Within less than a minute with me, he'd known to adjust his communication. An admirable skill.

"Did Millard give you background on the case?" Colin asked.

"A short briefing. I don't know much about the first case though."

"Neither do we." I wasn't pleased with it. "All the information was sent to our system. I'll ask Francine to forward it to you."

"Manny already got Francine to do that. I suppose you also haven't had time to read any of it."

"We were just introduced to the first murder when we were called out to Léon Blanc's." Colin pointed at the opera house. "And now we're here. Jenny reckons it's better to see everyone's first reaction to the news. Else we would be in the office reading up on the other case."

"She's right." Daniel looked at me. "You're right. We can tell a lot from the first few seconds of someone's reaction to bad news. Do you think we should get Colin to tell them the bad news and you and I will observe?"

"No. Your uniform would serve well in giving us the authority to question them. If you introduce yourself and share the news, we might get even stronger reactions."

We discussed our approach for a few more minutes before climbing the stairs to the heavy doors. The Opéra National du Rhin was a beautiful building. The six tall pillars on the outside were a mere introduction to the splendour of the inside. The theatre itself was elegant and richly decorated. The quality of the productions presented here rivalled those of the larger houses.

Daniel held the door open for us to enter first. The moment we stepped into the foyer I wanted to smile. Like Pavlov's dogs, I had been conditioned to associate this space with beauty, peace and music that could inspire the darkest soul. It was a pity I'd had to come here under such unpleasant circumstances.

"You must be the police officers we were told to expect." A petite woman walked towards us, her high heels noisy. "I am Jane Dubois, office manager to the director of the theatre, Monsieur Blanc."

People revealed volumes about themselves with their outfits, their nonverbal cues and the way they introduced themselves. I wondered why it was so important for Madame Dubois to be known as an office manager and not a personal assistant or even secretary. Prestige might be her motivation, if I were to judge her by her designer outfit and expensive shoes. Her medium-length hair would need at least thirty minutes of styling each morning and her makeup another ten to fifteen minutes. This was a woman who took great care not to look her age.

Daniel stepped forward, assuming the role of authority. "Daniel Cassel. Thank you for making this meeting possible, Madame Dubois."

"Oh, call me Jane." Her blinking increased and her pupils dilated as she shook Daniel's hand. "If you'll follow me, I'll take you to Monsieur Blanc's office."

She showed no interest in Colin or in me, her flirting subtle, but aimed solely at Daniel. As we walked through the hallways, Daniel used her chatty attention to build rapport with her. By the time we walked into the carpeted reception area, Jane Dubois was mirroring Daniel's body language. She walked to a closed door and opened it. "You can wait in Monsieur Blanc's office while I get you something to drink. Unfortunately, Monsieur Blanc is in a meeting that is running late. He should be here any moment, though."

I was about to confront her about this outright lie, but a subtle headshake from Daniel had me pulling my lips between my teeth and biting down. Daniel walked past Madame Dubois into the office. "Thank you so much, Jane. My colleagues and I would all appreciate green tea if you have any."

"Of course we have green tea." She fluttered her eyelashes. "Please make yourself at home. I'll be back with your tea in a few minutes."

Without waiting for Colin and me to enter the office, she smiled widely at Daniel and walked back towards the hallway. Colin chuckled and walked to the open door. "Seems like being pretty has its advanta…"

I'd seen it a millisecond before Colin had registered it and stopped talking. I stepped deeper into the office and like in Léon Blanc's home office did a full three-hundred-and-sixty-degree rotation, taking in every detail of this room. "It is an exact copy. With the exception of the art on the wall, everything is exactly the same."

"An exact copy of what?" Daniel looked around.

"Léon Blanc's home office." Colin's eyes were wide. "Jenny, if we measure this, do you think everything will be in the same places?"

"This room is larger." Not by much, but it made this feel like a chamber concert hall whereas the home office was too small for that. I'd never seen anything like this. "Why would he want to replicate a space with such detail?"

The windows were not as big as in Léon's house, but the curtains were the same, drawn open, letting bright sunlight in. I stepped closer to the bookshelves. Another difference. These were not the same books as he had at home. It would make sense to extend one's library if one had space to do so. Duplicating it would seem a waste of space and opportunity to collect more books.

Daniel was standing next to the grand piano, swiping across the screen of his smartphone. He pointed his smartphone at the Persian carpet under his boots. "That's where they found him. I'm looking at the crime scene photos Francine has uploaded and this is the spot."

Colin walked to the desk. "I wonder how much everything is the same."

I joined him just as he twisted the handle of the second drawer and pressed in the centre. A poster for Verdi's opera

Aida swung away from the wall, its placement similar to that of the Picasso painting in the house. Like the other posters on the wall, this one was framed in a beautiful wooden frame, making the poster seem more like an artwork than an advertisement for an opera.

"How interesting." Daniel walked to the poster, pulled it further away from the wall, but then closed it again. "Mademoiselle Dubois is coming back with our tea. Let's first break the news and get a read on her before we delve into that safe."

"I don't want tea." I walked to the small round table and sat on one of the wingback chairs. "Why did you order green tea for all of us?"

"It usually takes a bit longer than pouring coffee from the pot." His last words were a whisper. The clicking of Jane Dubois' heels announced her entrance to the reception area. Daniel remained standing next to the table, his face already friendly and open. He stepped forward when Jane entered the office and took the tray from her, making her blush. "Let me take that for you."

Daniel placed the tea on the table, but made no attempt to serve anyone. Colin sat down next to me and put his hand on the back of my chair. The brush of his fingers against my back was comforting. "Please join us, Jane."

"Oh, I couldn't." She said this to Daniel.

"I insist." He pulled out a chair and held it until she sat down. "We would like to ask you a few questions."

"You have me intrigued." She picked up the teapot and poured hot liquid into the fine white cups. "I only received a phone call from the police to tell me that three people would be coming and that we needed to give you our full co-operation."

"And you've been very kind to us." Daniel accepted the cup she handed him, putting it on the table. He pulled out the last chair and placed it so he was facing her when he sat down. "Could you please tell us where Monsieur Blanc is at the moment?"

She touched her pearl necklace and twisted the pearls. "Like I said, he's in a meeting."

"He's not. We know that." Daniel's tone was not accusing. It was reassuring. "When was the last time you saw him?"

"Last night. Why? Where is Léon? Has something happened to him?" She clutched her pearls.

"When was the last time you spoke to him?"

"Last night when he left." The muscles in her throat tightened from tension, causing her voice to come out strained. "He left earlier than usual and told me that he was going home to meet with someone. He looked stressed. Please tell me what is happening."

"Did he tell you who he was going to meet?" Daniel was using typical police interview techniques, answering a question with a question. Getting the most information from someone superseded relieving the distress they experienced when not knowing what was happening.

"No. I only manage his professional schedule. Sometimes he meets sponsors at his home or hosts small dinner parties or concerts there. For those I make all the arrangements. He never asks me for anything when he sets up private meetings." Jane clenched her fists on her lap. "Why are you asking all these questions? What is wrong? Where is Léon?"

Regret flashed across Daniel's face. "I'm sorry to tell you, Jane, but Monsieur Blanc was found dead this morning."

Colour drained from her face, her hand flying to cover her mouth. A tortured sound escaped from her lips and she pressed her hand harder against her mouth. Her eyes begged Daniel for something, I assumed to tell her that he was lying. People didn't want to believe bad news.

It was clear that this woman had great affection for Léon Blanc. Watching tears fill her eyes and spill over onto her cheeks, I was willing to posit that she might even have had romantic feelings for him. There was no doubt in my mind that this news came as a shock to her. She'd had nothing to do with Léon's death and most likely had not wished him dead either. If we were looking for suspects, we'd better move on.

"Do you know of anyone who would want to harm Monsieur Blanc?" Daniel asked softly.

Jane shook her head without removing her hand. Another strangled sound made it past her lips and hand. Tears were now streaming down her cheeks, her face drawn in an expression of extreme distress. The shock was too great for her.

"Is there someone we can phone for you?" Daniel moved a bit closer, putting his hand on her shoulder. She jerked under his touch, but didn't respond. Daniel sighed and looked at us. "I didn't expect this."

Colin got up. "I'll find someone to take care of her and show us where the other people are."

The five minutes we waited for Colin to return was spent productively. Daniel contacted his team to assist after he ordered an ambulance. I used the time to walk around the eerily similar room. Upon closer inspection, I noticed the differences in the Persian carpets, but they were negligible. The posters on the wall were placed in almost the same spaces as the paintings in the house, the differences in size making it hard to replicate exactly.

I was looking at Léon's collection of autobiographies of great opera singers when Colin returned with a woman around the same age as Jane. They couldn't have been more dissimilar. The newcomer was wearing clothes that no longer had distinct colours, her hands rough, her nails clipped short. The smell of cleaning agents led me to the conclusion that Colin had brought the cleaning lady to help Jane.

The moment she saw the distraught woman, she rushed to the table where Jane sat unmoving. Jane's eyes appeared vacant, tears still running unchecked down her cheeks. She had gone into a state of shock that required medical attention.

"Oh. Madame Dubois." The cleaning lady took Colin's chair and sat down next to Jane, pulling the weeping woman against her ample bosom. "Don't you worry. I'll take good care of you."

"I've called for an ambulance." Daniel got up. "Please stay with her until they arrive."

"We're here, boss." Pink, Daniel's IT expert, walked into the room. "Hey, Genevieve. Colin."

The next six minutes were spent organising Daniel's team to guard the office until the crime scene technicians arrived. They took control of communicating with the paramedics when they arrived, allowing us to follow another staff member to the rehearsal room. Pink was with us, carrying his tablet. He'd suggested recording the moment Daniel shared the news of Léon Blanc's demise. Even though the quality of the footage might not be brilliant, it would be a great reference to return to.

The sounds of Verdi's *Rigoletto* reached us long before we arrived at the double doors. This opera was considered by many to be the first of many Verdi masterpieces. It also had several popular arias that were often recited at concerts or used in films and other media. We stood in silence, waiting until the quartet sang the last heartfelt notes of *Bella figlia dell'amore*.

Classical music made sense to my brain. The structure, the beauty of the sounds it produced was soothing to the chaos that often erupted in my mind. Similarly, I found solace in classical jazz, whereas the easy sounds of smooth jazz and Fado relaxed me, but didn't bring order to my thoughts. Classical music felt like a cooling balm on a burn. I revelled in the moment for another second after the tenor finished the last note.

"You can go in now." The small man who'd brought us here opened one door.

The conversational buzz that had followed the end of the aria stopped the moment Daniel and Pink walked into the large room. Police uniforms tended to have that effect. Colin and I followed them.

"Ladies and gentleman, if I can have your attention for a few moments, please." Daniel walked to where the conductor was talking to a violinist. Pink stood next to the door, his posture relaxed as he held up his tablet to record the crowd. The room was large enough to host the orchestra and choir as well as the soloists. The choir was seated at the back of the room, the orchestra in front. The soloists were between the two groups, three of them seated, the others standing.

Everyone turned to the front, their expressions ranging from annoyed to curious. I positioned myself in the front left corner. It gave me a complete view of everyone. Colin was standing on Daniel's other side, his eyes roving over the crowd of people.

"I'm Daniel Cassel with GIPN. It is my very regretful duty to inform you that we found Léon Blanc dead in his house this morning. His death is being investigated as suspicious and we would greatly appreciate any information you could share with us to help us understand this sad situation."

The reactions were telling. The most prominent first reaction was shock. A few people followed their initial response with a shrug or other nonverbal cues indicating their lack of interest. Maybe later, I would view the footage Pink was recording, but these people were not the ones we were looking for. It was three of the soloists who grabbed my attention.

A tall, blond man was not successful in immediately hiding his intense grief. It lasted for only a few seconds before he covered it up with superior acting skills, but his professional sadness did not convince me. Another was a short man sitting in the soloist section, his chair slightly away from the others. The intense hatred that flashed over his features was alarming. More curious was that he made no attempt to show sadness. He crossed his arms, his nostrils flaring, his *levator labii superioris* muscles curling his top lip.

The third was a woman who'd been standing next to the choir section and was helped into a chair when her legs gave way under her. Her face bore the same pain as Jane Dubois'. Had Léon Blanc been romantically involved with many women? I made a mental note to ask Sébastien about his father's romantic interests. It was not unknown for people in the arts to have numerous partners, but be committed only to their art—their true love.

"Please phone us if you have any information that you think could help us solve this horrid crime." Daniel's expression held the right combination of authority, empathy and professionalism. "Or speak to us while we are here today."

There was a moment of silence before one of the men who'd shrugged shifted in his chair. "How is this going to affect opening night? It's this Sunday. Will everything still go on?"

"Unfortunately, I can't answer that for you, sir." Daniel pointed towards the hallway. "We'll be in Monsieur Blanc's office for the next hour or so if any of you would like to speak to us."

I walked to Daniel and pointed at the soloists. "There are three people we need to speak to."

"The tall, blond guy and the woman who almost fainted." Daniel waited until I nodded. "Who's the third?"

"The man with glasses, wearing jeans and a white designer shirt." Colin took my hand. "Right?"

"Yes. There might be others, but I won't know until I

review the video. Those three's reactions were significant though."

"Want me to bring them to the office, boss?" Pink put his tablet in one of the side pockets of his uniform. "I emailed the video to Francine."

"Bring them in separately, please, Pink. Start with the lady. I don't know how much longer she'll be coherent." Daniel nodded towards the woman, silently sobbing against the shoulder of another choir member.

We left the rehearsal room and didn't speak until we reached Léon Blanc's office. Colin let go of my hand and walked straight to the wall safe. Nicolas, another member of Daniel's team, was standing in front of the poster, making it hard to see that it was not flush against the wall like the other posters. He stepped aside. "Gonna show us how to break in to this safe, mate?"

The corners of Colin's mouth lifted slightly. "Step aside and let the pro show you how it's done."

Nicolas laughed and moved away from the wall. Colin pulled the framed poster to reveal the safe behind it. He glanced at Daniel. "Do you have any gloves handy?"

Daniel reached into one of his uniform's many side pockets and pulled out two purple latex gloves. "Never leave home without them."

"Thanks." Colin took both, but only put one on his right hand. With his index finger he entered the thirteen-digit code Sébastien had given him for the home safe. It opened with a soft snick. "How can one person be so dumb?"

"Why was that dumb?" Daniel asked. "And how did you know the code? Did you see some imprint on the keypad?"

"He's not *that* good." Manny walked into the office, his eyes widening as he took in the room. "Bloody hell. This really is the same as the house office."

"Okay, you guys are going to have to tell us what's going on here." Nicolas looked from Manny to Colin to me. "It's like walking in halfway through a movie."

Manny briefed them on our meeting with Lucien and the crime scene in Léon's house. I didn't listen. I was more interested in the contents of this safe. The home safe had revealed diamonds and cash that few people would have in their homes. Colin put the second glove on before he reached into the safe and placed the contents on the table where Jane had been. I assumed she'd been taken away by the paramedics. I was relieved to no longer be a witness to her pain.

"What do you have there, Frey?" Manny pointed at the individual items, not giving Colin a chance to answer. "Music books, more stacks of cash, more documents, three passports."

"Are all three his?" Daniel asked.

Colin opened one passport after the other and held up the last. "They're empty. And they look real. All that is needed is for the data pages to be completed."

"What the bloody hell was this man up to? Why would he need three empty passports?"

"Oh, I can think of many uses." Colin paged through the second one. "It's not that hard to get almost perfect data pages done. That would give anyone freedom to go wherever they pleased."

"You start talking like that and I want to reach for my cuffs." Manny lifted both eyebrows. "It sounds like you're planning an escape."

"You don't carry cuffs, Millard. And if I wanted to, I'd be gone before you could find those rusted cuffs in the back of your panty drawer."

Their bickering had yet again veered away from pertinent facts. It also gave me an almost obsessive need to know why Manny would use rusted cuffs, why he would have those in his drawer and whether or not he wore panties. These questions would soon overtake my mind until I could think of nothing else. That was why I loathed straying off topic.

"I've got Chantal Paquet waiting in the reception area, boss." Pink stood in the doorway. "She's very close to a breakdown."

"Thanks, Pink." Daniel glanced at the passports in Colin's hand. "Give us a minute, will you?"

"Sure thing, boss."

"Put those things away, Frey." Manny waved at the table, then pushed his hands in his pockets, his shoulders hunched. "We'll take them with us when we leave, but we don't want to distract anyone with all that cash lying around."

Colin picked up the three music books, cash and documents to put in the safe and Pink went back into the reception area. Hearing the soft murmurs of Pink and Chantal Paquet did nothing to stop the questions looping in my mind. Eventually, I just couldn't hold it in anymore and the words erupted from my lips. "Do you wear panties?"

Silence followed my question. The supratrochlear artery on Manny's forehead became more prominent as his face turned a dark shade of red. Colin snorted, which triggered suppressed laughter from Daniel. Manny's breathing became heavier and his lips tightened to a thin line. "No, Doctor Face-reader. I do not wear panties. Now could you please get your mind back on this case and do what you do best?"

"I'm trying to, but I have more questions. What about rusted handcuffs? Why would you keep those?"

Colin chuckled again as he pushed the *Aida* poster against the wall. "I'm sorry, love. I was just giving Millard a hard time. I'm sure he doesn't keep his rusted cuffs in his panty drawer."

"Does this mean he has rusted cuffs?"

"Stop!" Manny was still looking at me, but his warning was aimed at Colin. "Doc, I don't have rusted cuffs, I don't have a panty drawer and I don't have any panties."

His micro-expressions surprised me. "You're lying. Why are you lying?"

"Bleeding mother of Mary, Doc." Manny's face turned an even deeper shade of red. He walked closer to me, his chin lowered, his voice low. "Those are supermodel's panties and this is now the end of this discussion. Does that bloody mind of yours now have all the answers it needs? Can we now interview the choir member?"

I didn't know why he was so angry telling me that Francine had left some underwear in his home. Everyone knew they spent many an evening together. I blinked a few times. "I have no more questions for you."

"Well, thank the saints." Manny walked to one of the chairs and fell into it. "Where's Pink and that choir member?"

Chapter FIVE

Chantal Paquet's eyes were bright with unshed tears. Her arms were tight around her waist, hugging herself and keeping her emotions contained. Slight tremors shook her small frame every few seconds and she was biting down hard on her bottom lip.

She was sitting at the table next to me, Manny still slouched in his chair. Colin and Daniel were standing by the piano. Both had changed their body language to blend into the background. Pink was standing guard at the door.

"How long have you been in the choir, Chantal?" Manny was gentle in his tone and expression. Being harsh with this woman would not render any results.

"Twelve years." Her jaw moved a few times as she struggled to keep her composure. "I've known Léon since university."

"You studied together?"

"Yes. We both studied music at the same university. He was brilliant. Everyone knew he would go and do great things." The expression around her mouth and eyes indicated self-mocking. "I became a music teacher at a school in a small town and conducted two youth choirs. Nothing big, but those years were great."

"Did you stay in touch with Léon during that time?"

"Oh, yes. We were two peas in a pod at university. I was already engaged when we met, so there was never any romantic nonsense between us. Léon, Antoine and I had so much fun in those years. Antoine… oh, God. I have to tell my husband." Her breathing became erratic. She clenched her jaw and closed her eyes until her breathing evened out. "Antoine always said Léon was the brother both of us never had. We were at his wedding, we are Sébastien's godparents. Oh, God. Sébastien."

"He knows. We've already talked with him."

"They had such a hard relationship." She shook her head. "No, not hard. There was nothing bad about their relationship. I suppose I would say that they didn't have a relationship. This is one of those cases where the parent simply didn't bond with the child. I never picked up any hatred between them, just indifference. Léon wasn't really the family kind of person."

"Did he have a lot of friends?"

"Oh, yes. He was very social. But his friends were almost exclusively professional. After all these years, I think Antoine and I were the only people who really knew Léon."

"Did he have any relationships after his wife died?"

"A few affairs, but nothing that would ever reach the point where it could be called a relationship. Many women were madly in love with him." Her head tilted towards the reception area. "He wasn't interested. His one and only passion was this opera house. He lived and breathed it."

"Can you think of anyone who would've wanted to hurt him?"

"No." Her answer was immediate and true. "He instilled

respect and admiration wherever he went. People might not always have loved or liked him, but all I ever heard about him was how much people respected what he did."

I thought of the deep anger I'd seen on the short man's face. I wondered how well Chantal really knew Léon Blanc. Did he show his true self to Chantal and her husband? Or did they only see the part that he knew they would accept?

"Could you give us any insight into his financial situation?"

"I assume you will find all this out in any case." She bit the inside of her cheek, behaviour common when people were uncomfortable. "This is personal information, but I hope it will help. He inherited money from his grandfather about forty years ago. The last twenty years he's been getting better and better with investments. He was so proud of making his money grow. He and Antoine would spend hours talking about stock markets and investment opportunities. He believed in dual currency investments. That was where he made most of his money. Antoine said he didn't know how Léon did it. It almost seemed impossible."

Manny glanced at me and I nodded. She was being truthful. It didn't mean that she was telling the truth though. We would only know how Léon came to have all that cash in his safes once we analysed his financials.

"Has Léon mentioned anything troubling him in the last while?" Manny asked.

"No." She frowned. "Wait. He didn't mention anything, but a few weeks ago something strange happened."

"Can you remember exactly when?"

"Hmm. It had to be three months ago. It was the day of

Antoine's birthday. Léon couldn't come for dinner that evening and told me to come to his office and get Antoine's birthday gift before I went home. When I walked into the reception area, I heard Léon shouting at Jane. She's his personal assistant. Léon never shouted. It shocked me so much that I stood there and listened for a few seconds."

"What was he shouting about?"

"It didn't make sense. He was asking Jane who'd opened his desk drawer. He was furious."

"Why didn't it make sense?"

"Léon had an open-door policy. Everything in his office was available to the staff and the crew. Even the stuff in his drawers. He didn't have any secrets and welcomed everyone into his office. That's why it surprised me when he was shouting so loudly at Jane."

Chantal clearly didn't know Léon as well as she thought. He had secrets—secret safes, three empty passports, lots of cash and diamonds in his house safe. I wondered what secrets in his private life we would uncover. I thought of Jane Dubois' extreme reaction to the news of Léon Blanc's death. "Was Jane one of the women Léon had an affair with?"

"Oh, no. She was the best personal assistant he's had in years, but he had no interest in her. He told me once that she tried a few times to seduce him, but he wouldn't have any of it. Like I said, his true love was this place." She waved around the room, moving her arm away from her self-comforting hug for the first time. Her composure faltered. Her *mentalis* muscle caused her chin to quiver and one tear rolled down her cheek. Her arms wrapped around her torso again as she stared at her lap, attempting to regain control over her emotions. It took her a few seconds. "I don't know anything more. Please. I need to phone Antoine."

Daniel came forward with a business card. "If you think of anything else, please let us know. Even if you think it is unimportant."

She stared at the card for a few seconds before inhaling deeply and grabbing it from Daniel's hand. Immediately her arm went back to the self-hug. "May I go now?"

"Of course." Manny got up when she jumped out of her chair. "Thank you for your help, Chantal."

From our short encounter, I deduced that she was generally a very polite and kind lady. Not now. She stormed out the room without another word. The realist in me wondered how much her trauma would be exacerbated once we uncovered the truth behind the cash, passports and diamonds in Léon's safes. I considered questioning Antoine for more information about Léon Blanc. I immediately dismissed the idea. We would have no way of knowing how much of that information would be the truth or Léon presenting himself in the best light.

"Well, that was interesting." Manny sat back down. "Doc?"

"She cared deeply for him."

"Romantically?"

"No. She was being truthful the whole time."

"Think her husband was jealous and killed Léon Blanc?"

My frown was immediate. "That would be gross speculation, totally unsubstantiated."

The corners of Manny's mouth twitched. "Hmm."

"Don't tease me." I leaned back in my chair.

"She said Léon shouted about someone opening a drawer." Colin looked at the desk. "Could it be that someone knew how to open Léon's secret safe and took something from it? Maybe he was killed because of something inside it."

"Then it had to be something mind-blowing." Daniel frowned. "To forgo three empty passports and all that cash? Had to be something very powerful."

I thought of the three music books that were locked in the safe with the cash and passports. Locking music books away with such incriminating valuables made me curious. But it would have to wait. I looked at Daniel. "Who's next?"

He stepped towards the door just as Pink came in. "I've got Gustave Victore. Can I bring him in?"

"Thanks, Pink." Daniel returned to his place next to the piano. Colin nodded at him and turned to watch the door.

The short man walked into the room with long strides. His arms were slightly away from his body, his forearms showing, his hands in tight fists. The complete opposite nonverbal cues to Chantal. "I hope you people can give me answers. We need to know what is happening with *Rigoletto*. Will the roles remain as is? Opening night is only four days away. We can't change it. Yves Martin is coming."

"Who's Yves Martin?" I asked before I could stop the irrelevant question.

"Only the most important critic in the whole of Europe!" He walked to the wall of posters and pointed at the one for Verdi's opera *Nabucco*. "See this? Yves Martin made this opera the runaway success it was. If it hadn't been for his review in *Le Journal du dimanche*, it would have been just another production of *Nabucco*. But no. He was here on opening night and it was his review that made it a sold-out show for the whole season. The whole season!"

"Monsieur Victore." Daniel stepped out from behind the piano, his posture no longer harmless. His chest was broadened, his right hand resting on his holstered gun. "Please take a seat. Now."

Gustave glared at Daniel in the type of staring challenge typical of alpha males wanting to assert their superiority. Daniel didn't change his posture or the authority in his expression. He simply maintained his nonverbal cues. After almost a minute it had an effect on Gustave. He briefly lowered his gaze before he stomped to the table. He might have conceded, but it was clear he resented this as much as the inconvenience Léon's death was causing him and his career plans.

"What has your knickers in such a knot?" Manny's question didn't make sense to me, but it did to Gustave.

His top lip curled and his nostrils flared. "I told you. We need *Rigoletto* to continue."

"There's more." I stared at his face. "Your concerns go deeper than just the opera."

"Concerns? Hah! You should call it what it is. A grudge." He put his fists on his hips, his jaw jutted. "Yes, I was majorly pissed off with Léon. Have been for three years."

"Enough to kill him?" Manny asked.

"Are you really as stupid as you look? Well, I am not. If I killed him, I wouldn't tell you I had a grudge against him. I don't know when he was killed, but I've been in Paris for the last four days. I only arrived in Strasbourg this morning at nine. I'll give you all the places I've been and all the people I've been with so you can check. I didn't kill that twat."

"Hmm. Want to tell me why you've been carrying a grudge against Léon for the last three years?"

"Because that cretin has been giving lyric tenor roles to spinto tenors!" Gustave threw his hands in the air and looked from Manny to Colin to Daniel, ignoring me. "You idiots don't know what that means, do you?"

"Please. Educate us." Manny did nothing to correct Gustave's low opinion of his intellect.

"A lyric tenor, like me, has a warm voice with a full and bright timbre. Our voices are strong and can easily be heard over an orchestra. A spinto tenor's voice is too dark for these roles." He put his fists on his hips again. "But no! It didn't matter than I was perfect for the roles. Not only are my acting skills fantastic, my voice is the only voice in a radius of two hundred kilometres that could do justice to these roles."

"So who did he give these roles to?"

"That prissy Julien." Gustave flapped his hand as if dismissing Julien. "Sure, Julien has an okay voice. And maybe he can act. But there is no way he could ever be Alfredo. Verdi wrote that role for me."

"That's not possible." What an absurd thing to say. There was absolutely no possibility that Verdi, who had written *La traviata* to be performed in 1853, could have had knowledge of Gustave's voice a hundred and fifty years in the future. Gustave looked at me and immediately glanced away. Something about me was making him uncomfortable. I didn't care. "Despite your resentment, you are distressed by the loss of Léon Blanc."

"Of course I am." He looked at Manny as he spoke. I wondered if he treated all women with the same imperiousness. "He was the heart and soul of this place. Do you know that our salaries are the best in France? Job security in this industry is not an easy thing to come by. Léon believed in paying for quality. We have the best equipment, costumes and stage designs of all the smaller opera houses. Only the Grand Théâtre and Opéra Bastille have better stuff than us. But they get a lot more money from stupid Godard and his idiot government. Léon made sure we weren't dependent on any moronic politician for our salaries. Most of the money for this place comes from dedicated individuals with a true appreciation and understanding for the importance of our art."

"Do you know who these benevolent individuals are?" Manny asked.

Gustave crossed his arms over his chest. "I'm not sure if I can share that information with you. I'd rather not break the trust that was placed in me. You will just have to do your own work and get permission to see that information."

Manny nodded slowly as if considering Gustave's words. But I'd seen Manny's hands forming fists in his trouser pockets. "Well, then I suppose we will have to do our own work. Thank you for your help."

"Help." Gustave got up, shaking his head. "People are right to think you police people are incompetent."

"Have a lovely day, sir." Manny's smile was not friendly. He waited until Pink closed the office door behind Gustave. "And up yours too."

"What an arrogant prick." Daniel wasn't one to swear or insult people. Gustave had really aggravated the men.

"Doc, I don't know about you, but I think this jackass is too full of himself to kill anyone."

"He was being truthful when he said he hadn't killed Léon. I couldn't attest to him being too full of himself though."

"Typical tenor." Colin shrugged when we looked at him. "I read an article written by a psychologist who categorised most tenors to be arrogant, but in constant need of reassurance."

"I find it hard to believe that one could generalise a demographic by the timbre of their voice." I was most definitely going to research that. But only after we'd found Léon Blanc's killer. And Benoît Faure's.

Pink opened the door, came in and closed it behind him. "You guys and lady finished venting about that horse's ass? Can I bring in the last man? His name is Julien Travere."

Daniel looked at Manny and me. "Ready to speak to the man who's stolen all the roles despite being a mere spinto tenor?"

"Hmm." Manny scratched his stubbled chin. "Two men with strong reactions when hearing that Léon Blanc died, one angry because the other one is favoured. Bring this Julien Travere in, Pink. Let's hear what he has to say."

Pink opened the door wide and looked into the reception area. "Please come in, Julien."

The tall man walked into the room and immediately I felt ill at ease. Most people were terrible liars, unable to control their nonverbal cues and easily revealing their deception.

Some people had noteworthy control over their reactions and could convince even the most astute observer of their lies. But then there were actors. A few actors who had won numerous acting awards did so by method acting. They would study the character they were about to play until they were able to think and behave as that character would've done.

Looking at Julien Travere as he walked in and sat down at the table, I saw appropriate levels of sadness, concern and anger at Léon Blanc's death. But these emotions were too perfectly expressed. Micro-expressions were named such because most emotions didn't linger on our faces for more than a fraction of a second. They often revealed those emotions the person was consciously or unknowingly trying to hide.

I leaned back in my chair, needing to observe Julien to see if he was trying to hide something. It would require more than my usual analysis to separate genuine emotions from those carefully expressed to mislead.

"Thank you for speaking to us, Julien." Manny rubbed his cheek, bringing attention to his two-day-old beard. He used the same tactic whenever he interviewed arrogant men. His shoulders were hunched, his expression communicating boredom with the task at hand.

"No problem. I will do anything I can to help find out who killed Léon." Julien rested his hands lightly on his thighs, his fingers splayed, relaxed.

"Good. Good." Manny nodded. "Do you know of anyone who would've wanted Monsieur Blanc dead?"

"Honestly? No." He was telling the truth. "I knew Léon a

bit better than most of the singers here. He didn't have enemies. People respected him, even if they didn't like him."

"Can you give us examples of people who didn't like him?"

"Directors from other opera houses. They were insanely jealous of the success Léon had with this opera house. We never had problems with unions, singers or orchestra members striking or any of the other problems they have. Even when some of those houses have more funding than us, they always have problems with their staff."

"What makes the staff here so different?" Manny asked.

"Léon. He treated everyone with the greatest respect. And that respect was returned in spades. Everyone here loved him."

"Even if they didn't get the roles they wanted?"

Julien's lips thinned and his nostrils flared. "Gustave. He was going on about me getting the role that Verdi wrote for him, right? It's all just sour grapes. He doesn't want to accept that his voice needs additional training. You haven't asked me, but no. He wouldn't have killed Léon. Not over a role. He's too lazy. If he really wanted a leading role, he would do a lot more voice training and apply for roles in other opera houses."

"You say that you knew Léon Blanc better than anyone else. Why is that?"

Julien's chin rose as he looked down at us. "I suppose he knew that he could trust me. We shared a passion for bringing quality classical music to the people of Strasbourg. He's maintained an incredibly high standard here for more than twenty years. Something that people noticed. He was well known throughout Europe for having the secret to a successful opera house. Many times, other opera house directors invited him to consult and help them correct managerial or production mistakes. Or deal with problematic staff. He was a master at all these aspects of running an opera house. A great businessman. A great man. He always said he lived and loved here. He would also die here. '*Quel detto un eco eterno in questo cor lasciò*.'"

"'Those words left in my heart an eternal echo.'" This Italian quote sounded vaguely familiar, but I couldn't place it. "From which opera?"

"Verdi's *Il trovatore*. One of Léon's favourites. Did you know that Léon loved all Verdi's work? This opera house has done every one of Verdi's twenty-eight operas. Even the lesser-known ones. All because of Léon."

Manny cleared his throat. "Do you know of any problems Léon might have had?"

"What kind of problems?"

"Personal? Financial? Romantic?"

"Léon was a wealthy man." Julien raised both shoulders. "I don't know how wealthy, but he did well for himself. So I don't think he had any money troubles. He wasn't in any relationship and I can't think of any personal problems he had."

"What do you know about his romantic life?" I needed more context to accurately interpret Julien's discomfort when he'd mentioned Léon's relationships.

Deep anger flashed across his face a millisecond before he arranged his expression once again into appropriate sadness.

"Not much. Everyone here knows that he lived for this place. This was his only true passion."

"Do you know Sébastien Blanc?" Manny asked.

"Léon's son? I met him twice. No. Three times." He was telling the truth. "They weren't close. Do you think he killed Léon?"

"We don't have any suspects at the moment, Julien." Manny got up and waited for Julien to join him. "Would you be available if we need to ask any more questions?"

"Any time." He held out his hand and shook Manny's. "You can reach me on my cell or home phone or even email me. Anything to help."

Pink ushered Julien out. We were silent for more than a minute.

"Well, Doc." Manny stretched his shoulders and sat down. He didn't slouch. "What did you think of *that*?"

"He's hiding something."

"Yeah. I got that. But what is he hiding?"

"I don't know." I winced when the corner of Manny's mouth lifted. "You were asking a rhetorical question."

"You're not happy about something." Colin walked to me and put his hand on my arm. "What's bothering you?"

"He exhibited too many conflicting nonverbal cues. For some reason he felt the need to conceal his true feelings and act sad, angry and worried. I saw those emotions come through as genuine as well, but then he would hide them and replace his true body language with something similar, but rehearsed."

"Do you think he killed Léon?" Manny scratched his jaw. "He doesn't look like he could fight his way out of a wet paper bag, never mind kill someone with a blow to the back of the head."

"Why…"

"Ignore the wet paper bag, Doc. All I'm saying is that he doesn't look physically strong enough to have overpowered Léon."

I thought about this. "We need more information from the autopsy. Someone doesn't have to be very strong to cause another person to lose their balance, fall and hit the back of their head."

"True." Manny leaned back in his chair. "I still don't see him doing it."

"Do you guys agree that there's something off with him though?" Daniel spoke for the first time.

"He's an artist." Manny smirked. "We can't be surprised when they're eccentric or weird."

The ringtone of a phone drew everyone's eyes to Colin's jacket pocket. He took his smartphone out, his eyes widening slightly before he swiped the screen. With the exception of greeting the caller, Colin said nothing. He made a few noises to indicate he was listening, but didn't even say goodbye before he ended the call. He looked down at me. "Want to go find out more about forging masterpieces with a 3D printer?"

Chapter SIX

After all this time, it still fascinated me how much I'd come to trust Colin. Even his driving. Vinnie's skill at the wheel was acceptable, but I'd only once been a passenger in Francine's car. She'd taken perverse pleasure in breaking all speed limits and waving at irate drivers when she'd cut them off. Manny, on the other hand, drove either too slow or at a speed that brought blackness to my peripheral vision.

I leaned back against the seat of Colin's SUV and took a contented breath. We had left behind the chaos of emotions and death. I was curious about this new branch of 3D printing. "Who are we going to speak to?"

"Gunter." Colin's expression softened. "I met him when he was still creating awful forgeries and convincing people with no idea about art that those were the real thing. He chose his targets well and didn't even have to put much effort into persuading them that they were making the best investment of their lives."

"What changed? Why is he no longer forging artwork?"

"He had a come-to-Je…" Colin smiled. "He had a life-altering experience."

"Your smile is smug. Did you report him to the authorities?" I shook my head. "No, you wouldn't have done that. What changed for him?"

Colin chuckled. "I told his mother."

"Why does this give you so much enjoyment? Is she a terrible person? Did she punish him?"

"Oh, did she ever. She didn't speak to him for two months, didn't cook Sunday dinners for six months and made him renovate her kitchen, both bathrooms and the garage before she would even acknowledge his presence."

"I'm not clear why this was life-altering for him." I wasn't close to my parents at all and as an only child, I had no family connections to speak of. That made the relationships I had with Colin and the others hard for me to navigate. "Was it because she is a controlling person or because they are so close that he didn't want to risk his relationship with his mother?"

"The latter." Colin turned down a side street. "They are a family with five children and are very close. Gunter is the youngest and the only son. He's always been treated like a prince. I think he got away with a lot of bad behaviour for a very long time without any consequences. His eldest sister is a doctor, the next a lawyer, the next a psychologist and the fourth a teacher. Whenever he had any difficulties, someone would bail him out."

"Literally?"

"Sometimes. But most of the time it was figuratively. He was spoiled as a child and never finished any of the courses he started at university. He started the forgeries as a lark when he was in his late twenties."

"When did you find out about him?"

"Seven years ago. He had just turned thirty. After that event, his mother and sisters gave him an ultimatum. Either he went back to university to study something that would give him a stable job, or got a job, or start a business with all the knowledge that he had accrued."

"As far as I know 3D printing wasn't readily available seven years ago."

"It was actually already well-developed. Nothing like we have today, but additive 3D printing was gaining ground."

"Additive? As opposed to subtractive 3D printing?" I would never have thought to define printing as such.

"Yup. Ten years ago, it was common to have a block of metal, plastic or other material and the printer would shave off parts until it was a copy of the original scan." Colin slowed down and turned in to a property with single building on it. Under a shade net, six cars were parked, another four parking spaces open. Colin turned the SUV into one of the spaces, parked and turned to me. "He used the knowledge he got from studying business and marketing, combined that with everything he'd learned about the art world and started a printing business.

"At first he was only producing high-quality conventional prints of masterpieces. It was only around 2009 that 3D printers became commercially available. Gunter was smart to wait a few years until the technology had time to improve before he bought his printer. The first printers were pricey, so it made even more sense to wait a while. And when he bought his printer, he immediately started experimenting until he reproduced an exact copy of a Van Gogh."

"Was he planning on selling it illegally?"

"Why don't you ask him?" He pulled up the handbrake. "We're here."

I waited outside the car while Colin retrieved a box he kept under his seat. That was where he kept fake glasses, moustaches, caps, jewellery and other things to be consistent with whichever alias he was using. I studied him when he got out the car. He walked towards me with a slight limp, squinting through black-framed glasses. His mouth seemed fuller and when he smiled, I winced. "Those teeth are really not a healthy colour."

"Why, my dearest, as a professor of art history, spending money on anything as frivolous as teeth whitening would be an utter waste of time." His accent was more British than Manny's. He winked at me and held out his arm. "Shall we?"

I glared at his arm and started walking towards the building. "Your clothes are too trendy for this role. If you don't care about your teeth, you will also not be wearing Italian loafers or that expensive fitted shirt."

"You're forgetting my Etro trousers." Colin fell in next to me and took my hand. "I can say that you are the reason that I'm dressing better now. You know, like Francine is getting Millard to buy better clothes."

"I don't like lying. I'm not good at it." I stopped.

Colin walked another step before he turned to me and pulled me closer to him. Gone was his accent and any playfulness. "Then let me. You don't have to say anything you're not comfortable with."

"Professor Henry Vaughn! Is that you?" A large man rushed towards us, his face turning red from the exertion. "It is! You lowlife tattletale!"

I took a step back and away from Colin when Gunter

grabbed Colin in a tight embrace and slapped him hard on his back.

"Good day to you too, Gunter."

"Man, it's good to see you." He slapped Colin one final time and stepped away to look at me. "Did this ugly mutt tell you how he did the worst thing anyone could do to another human being?"

I thought of our cases in the last three years. "He hasn't told me anything about a murder, human trafficking or torture. As far as I know, he's never committed any of those crimes. Right?"

Colin took my hand again and squeezed when I looked at him with wide eyes. "No, love. I haven't done any of those things. He's talking about me telling his mother about his forgeries."

"Oh." I turned back to face Gunter. "It is not the worst thing anyone could do to a human being."

Gunter stared at me with wide eyes. "Wow. Like, really. Wow. You're the female version of my one brother-in-law. He takes everything so seriously."

"Allow me to introduce Doctor Genevieve Lenard." Colin's shoulders moved slightly back, pushing his chest out. "She's my partner."

"Like your business partner or your sweetheart partner?"

"None of your damn business, Gunter."

"Well, I'll be." Gunter folded his considerable size into a bow, then rose with a red face and a wheeze. "You must be a goddess to have tamed this no-good prof. Can't wait to know everything about you. Come on. Let's get out of this terrible heat. It's supposed to be the beginning of autumn.

I swear, each year is getting hotter and hotter. I'm a total believer in global warming. I feel it. Well? Don't just stand there. Let's go inside."

He reached towards us and for a moment I thought he was going to push us to the building. He didn't. He slapped Colin once on the shoulder, laughed heartily and led us to the only entrance. At the glass doors he stopped, opened them and waved us inside. "'Enter,' said the spider to the fly."

Colin chuckled and followed me into the empty foyer. The desk in the centre of the room was unmanned and looked unused. There was a sofa that also looked as if no one ever used it. Air-conditioning made the room uncomfortably cold. The change in temperature was enough to take my mind off the strange spider-phrase Gunter had used. I made a mental note to ask Colin about it. Now wasn't the time. I was more curious about what lay beyond the doors leading from the foyer. "Is the noise coming from the printers?"

"The drumming?" Gunter shook his head. "No, that sound is coming from real, honest-to-God drums. We have a drumming session every week and you arrived towards the end of it."

"Drumming?" Colin's eyebrows lifted. "You surprise me, Gunter."

"Hey, you've got your ladybird who seems to be getting you to dress better. I've got my ladybird looking after my spirituality." His face contracted into an expression of pain. "From next week, she's putting me on a detox diet. I'm still trying to convince her kale is an invention by pharmaceutical companies to make sure we don't get enough nutrition so we get sick and use their medicine. She's not buying it yet."

"Can we see the 3D printer?" I realised my impatience with his inane conversation had made my tone harsh. I took a deep breath. "Please."

"Totally like my brother-in-law." Gunter leaned a bit towards me. "You're just much, much prettier. Prof here chose well."

"Enough goofing around, Gunter." Colin shifted to put his shoulder in front of mine, shielding me from Gunter. "We have a few questions about your new and very successful business."

Gunter's smile was wide and proud. "Bet you never thought my forgery days would come in so handy. How about that, huh? Well, follow me."

He entered a code in the keypad next to a side door, then pressed his middle finger to be scanned. This was a smart security measure. Most people used their thumbs or index fingers for the security system. The middle and ring fingers were uncommon choices. The moment the door opened, the drums became much louder. Assuming the people beating out the rhythm were amateurs, I was quite impressed with how well they were keeping to the beat.

Gunter's smile broadened and he walked with wide strides towards the drums. He might not be excited about his new diet, but he loved the drumming. The hallway was short, two small rooms on each side. I peeked into one that looked like an office. The desk was littered with piles of papers, flowing over onto the floor. I looked away with a shudder.

At the end of the hallway was another door. Again Gunter went through the security protocol. This time, when the door opened, the drumming overwhelmed me. I clutched at

Colin's hand and stood frozen on this side of the door. I could not enter. As irrational as it was, it felt like the sound was beating me into the earth. With each new beat, I felt the weight of it on my head and shoulders, pushing me down. I pressed my thumb to my ring finger. It didn't help. The weight of the sound was going to push me through the tiles, through the concrete foundation, into the ground and beyond.

"Jenny. Love." Colin's voice made me feel lighter. I grabbed onto that. "Come back to me. Listen. The drumming has stopped. Gunter isn't here. He's inside. He said I just have to knock on the door and he'll open for us. Jenny?"

I opened my eyes. And groaned in embarrassment. I was sitting on the floor, my knees pulled up to my chest, still rocking. I took a few deep breaths before I could stop rocking and focus on Colin's arms around me. He was sitting on the cold tiles next to me and had pulled me between his legs into a full embrace. I took another deep breath. "I'm okay."

"Was it the drums?"

I nodded. "How long have I been in a shutdown?"

"I don't know." He glanced at his watch. "Maybe five minutes. Not too long."

"What did you say to Gunter?"

"That you're sound-sensitive."

"Did he believe you?"

"I don't care." He lowered his brow to make sure I was looking at him. "As long as you're okay."

"I'm okay. The floor is cold."

"This whole building is freezing. I'm surprised those people could get their muscles to work enough to hit the drums." Colin smiled and helped me up.

I rolled my shoulders a few times to loosen the tightness brought on by the shutdown. This one had come as a surprise to me. Usually, I had some warning when I was exposed to too much stimulation or emotions and a shutdown was looming. I had never been this close to such overwhelming rhythm and therefore hadn't expected anything like this. Now I knew. "Can we finish this quickly?"

"Absolutely. Vinnie is cooking risotto with his special truffle recipe and I'm hungry." He knocked three times on the closed door and stood back.

Four seconds later the door opened wide, Gunter's large frame filling the space. "All well? Good. Good. Sorry about the sound, Genevieve. May I call you Genevieve?"

"Yes. Can we see the 3D printer?"

"Right to business." His jovial smile returned and he stepped away from the door. "Come in and I'll show you how the big kids play."

Colin and I followed him into a large room. In contrast to the office next door, this room was immaculate. I counted six different printers, each placed a good distance from the others. Each printing station had a small desk, a filing cabinet and two large bins. Along the far wall was a long worktable where prints were carefully stacked either on top of the counter or between hardboards underneath it.

We walked to the printer in the centre of the room. The printer head was moving over a canvas, adding another layer of colour and texture. For the next five minutes we didn't speak at all. Colin walked around the printer, inspecting it and the painting from every angle. I stood in one place and marvelled at the technology. After his third time around the table, Colin stopped next to me. "This is incredible work, Gunter."

"Thank you, Prof. Coming from you it really means a lot."

"I see that you added a logo above Rembrandt's signature."

"That's the deal. If I don't do that, it is a forgery and I could go to jail. Adding the museum's logo makes it one of the limited editions the museum has ordered to sell."

"How does the scanning work?" Colin asked.

Gunter pointed towards the other side of the room. "We use two cameras and fringe projection in a hybrid scanning system to capture over forty million 3D, full-colour points per shot. This gives us microscopic detail of the brushstroke type and length, the topography of the painting and much more. We can see the details of the styles used by masters like this Rembrandt, Monet and Sisley."

"Then you print it." Appreciation was clear on Colin's face. "Ever tempted to print a copy or two without the logo?"

Gunter laughed. "Plan to tell my mom again?"

"Maybe."

"No, Prof. I'm done with that life. It's a good feeling to know that I'm making my own way in life." His smile turned shy. "It's also nice to have my sisters and mom so proud of me."

"You're telling the truth." There was no sign of deception anywhere in his nonverbal cues.

"Of course I am, Genevieve. The prof telling my mom is the best thing that ever happened to me. I still hate him for it." His warm smiled aimed at Colin belied his words. It confused me, but I decided that it wasn't important.

"Do you know anyone else who would print forgeries with something of this calibre?" Colin pointed at the 3D printer still humming along.

"Where? Here in Strasbourg? France? Europe?"

"Strasbourg." I had no concrete evidence that the criminal who had produced those paintings was from this city, but logic dictated that it was better to start closer to home.

"Hmm. Let me think." He pressed his index finger to his lips and looked at the ceiling for a few seconds. Then he snapped his fingers. "Antonin! Yeah. He would do it for the right price. But his printer is not as good as mine. The quality will be good, but not as realistic as my products. These frigging printers are expensive, as well as the scanning process. You know how much this baby cost me? Huh? I'll tell you. The price of that brand spanking new E-class Mercedes I wanted to buy. Had to choose between my dream car and this babe. Guess who won? And I can tell you, Antonin the Gambler doesn't have that kind of money."

"Anyone who might have that kind of money?" Colin asked.

"Hmm. Maybe Marcelle. But she's too impatient to do it right. It takes forever to get it to the right quality. Yeah, she's also not a good candidate. And I don't think her printer is up to snuff either."

"Whose is?" Colin asked.

"The only other printer as good as mine belongs to the University of Strasbourg. No idea why they need a printer."

"If a university is well-funded, they often are the first to try out new technology." I wished all universities had funding for the best equipment. "It could be that the engineering department want to test the quality of 3D-printed parts for bridges, planes, cars and other structures. The medical faculty could test it for printing limbs, ears and heart valves to only name a few."

"Wow." Gunter leaned a bit back, staring at me. "Just wow."

Colin snapped his fingers in front of Gunter. "Stop making eyes at my partner."

"Sorry, Prof. She's just so... amazing." He pulled his shoulders back. It pushed his wide girth forward. "But you don't have to worry. I have my own amazing girl."

"I'm glad for you, Gunter." Colin gestured at the room. "About all of this too."

"Thanks, Prof." He shifted and glanced at the painting. "Anything else I can do for you?"

"Yes. Please phone me if you think of anyone else who could be forging masterpieces with a printer like yours."

He looked at Colin for a few seconds. "I'm not asking what this is about, but I think I know. You're going to find that person's mother and blab to her as well, aren't you?"

Colin laughed. "Yes. That's exactly what I'm going to do. Now promise me you'll let me know if you think of anyone else."

"I'll promise only if you promise to visit more often."

"That's an easy promise to make." Colin held out his hand.

Gunter grabbed it and pulled Colin into another tight embrace. "My brutha from anotha mutha."

It took another ten minutes before we were on the road. Gunter was a warm individual with clear affection for Colin. His reluctance to let us leave was endearing to Colin, but unwelcome to me. I wanted to have some form of normality to this day. My day had started with its normal routine of turning on my computer and going through my emails. But nothing since had fitted into the daily rhythm I preferred.

This busy day had had no routine to it and I was feeling the unsettling effects of it. Routine made me feel safe and this late in the afternoon, I needed some form of that predictability. I wanted to go to my viewing room, turn off my computer and make sure everything was in its right place.

The ringtone from Colin's phone paused the relaxing Melody Gardot music we'd been listening to. Colin pressed the answer button on the steering wheel. "Yes, Francine?"

"Hey, you. Is Genevieve with you?" My best friend's voice came over the SUV's sound system. It was very hard for me to interpret people's communication by words and tone of voice alone, but her tone made me frown.

"I'm here. What's wrong?"

"Nothing." She forced her tone to sound light and happy. "Where are you?"

"You are lying. Why are you lying?"

"Dammit, girlfriend. I can't even get one by you when you're not looking at me." She paused. "I didn't want to worry you until you could see everything and put it into context."

"See what?" Colin's hands tightened around the steering wheel.

Another pause sent a shot of adrenaline through my system. Despite Francine's tendency to seek a conspiracy theory in every small detail, she seldom overreacted when it came to important issues.

"Gallo sent Genevieve another email." The anger in her tone made Marcos Gallo's surname sound like a swear word.

I had never met this man, but he'd become a part of my life since our last case. Four months ago, he and his childhood friend had murdered another friend, kidnapped a law enforcement official's family members, stolen millions of euros' worth of jewellery and helped two prisoners escape. One, Raul Fernandez, Gallo's friend, had been in prison just outside of Strasbourg. He had died shortly after the escape. Arnaud Brun, the other prisoner, still remained at large.

"How many emails is that now?" Colin asked.

"Nine. He's been sending an email every Wednesday for the last two months." I had come to dislike Wednesdays.

"Yeah," Francine said. "This one is just as angry as the others. He's not about to forgive you for his bestie's death."

"Please don't use that word." Even though I accepted that language constantly evolved, it was hard for me to embrace the new words entering our vernacular. Francine enjoyed calling me her 'bestie' and then patiently listening to my diatribe about proper English. "And don't distract me. What did Gallo write this time?"

"'The family is the first essential cell of human society. You took that essential cell from me.'" Francine sighed. "These quotes are so banal. This one comes from Pope John the twenty-second."

"Similar to the others." Each of his previous emails had

contained some trite quotation about family, followed by a sentence about how I'd taken his family from him. "He thinks he's intimidating me."

"I don't know why he's picking on you," Francine said. "I was the one who fought with Fernandez and saw him slip and fall to his death. Not you."

"In his eyes that action proved your strength. A person like Gallo would look for the weakest person in a group and target him or her. He wouldn't have to be as good as he is with computers to find out that I'm on the autistic spectrum. A man like him would see that weakness and exploit it."

"You're not weak." Colin glanced at me, his expression severe. "Don't you ever say that again."

"You didn't listen to what I said. And you're reacting emotionally. I didn't say that I was weak. I said Gallo would see my autistic spectrum disorder as a weakness and exploit it."

"Doesn't matter." Colin's lips thinned even more. "I don't like hearing it from your lips."

This kind of reaction used to confuse me. It had taken me a surprisingly long time to recognise it for what it was. I put my hand on his thigh and squeezed. "Thank you."

He glanced at me again, this time longer. "You're the strongest person I know, Jenny. The strongest."

"Totally agree with him, girlfriend. Now tell me where you are and when you're coming back."

I pulled my hand back onto my lap. "We're on our way to the office."

"Should be there in another ten minutes," Colin said.

"There are too many variables to be that certain about our

estimated time of arrival. You don't know what the traffic…" I took a deep breath. "It's not important. Francine, have you been able to get any useful information from this email?"

"Another email address. We now have nine emails and nine email addresses."

"Your breathing and tone has changed. Have you found something more?"

"You bet your sassy butt I did. An IP address."

"Where did you track it to? Strasbourg?"

"Nope. Ecuador. Gallo keeps moving."

Marcos Gallo was wanted in eight countries. In some it was for the fraud his two companies had committed, in others it was for intimidation, torture and murder. Internationally he was wanted for being part of the 2010 heist that had stolen five paintings from the Paris Museum of Modern Art. We had recovered four of the five stolen paintings, but Braque's *Olive Tree near Estaque* was still missing.

"And he'll continue moving." Colin turned into a side street to avoid the traffic that usually congested the street in front of our office this time of the day. "All that money he took from his accounts will fund his escape for a long time still."

"Did your new search into Arnaud Brun give you any new information?" I had been irrationally hopeful when Francine had told me she'd entered new search parameters to look for the escaped prisoner. Brun had been Fernandez's cellmate and had been responsible for some of the logistics of their escape. We'd looked into his conviction and I still shuddered to think of the type of man who was now free amongst unsuspecting civilians.

Arnaud Brun had been convicted of organising dog fights as well as unregulated fights between men. Both types were to the death. He'd been doing it for almost a decade before the police had found enough evidence to arrest and prosecute him. To everyone else, he'd appeared to be an upstanding citizen, training women and young people in self-defence from a small studio in Strasbourg. Most of his income had been derived from training bodyguards and VIPs in self-defence, whereas training women and young people was to solidify his reputation as a caring, community-oriented individual. It had proven not to be the case. This man deserved to still be incarcerated.

A loud sigh sounded through the SUV. "Sorry, girlfriend. He's still out there living the life of a free man. Vinnie has printed out a new batch of wanted photos."

Colin chuckled. "He's going to need a new dartboard if he keeps this up."

Vinnie had been pinning Brun's wanted poster to his dartboard and using it for practice. I considered it most barbaric, but Vinnie had told me it made him feel good. Odd. "Where is Vinnie now?"

"At home, cooking. And working off his frustration." Francine laughed. "He was so pissed off when Manny ordered him to oversee the logging and transport of the diamonds, music books and paintings. He kept mumbling that he's a man of action, not a babysitter."

"Are the diamonds, paintings and books in Rousseau & Rousseau or in our team room?" Vinnie, Phillip, Colin and

Daniel had made sure Rousseau & Rousseau in the next-door building was secure, but I liked having the evidence in our team room, which spanned the whole top floor of the building.

"The team room. Vin even got easels from Phillip to put the paintings nicely on display for you, Colin."

"Fantastic."

"Did they find a computer in Léon Blanc's offices?" I had found the lack of computers in his workplace odd.

"Yes, they did." The jingling of Francine's bracelets sounded through the SUV. "Each desk had a laptop hiding from plain view in one of the drawers. I've gone through one already, looking for things not related to music and found nothing. Nada. Zero. Zip."

"That's a pity." Colin stopped at the red light. "We're another three minutes out. Then we can talk more."

"Well, hurry. I'm ready to go. I have to make a quick stop before digging into Vinnie's risotto."

Chapter SEVEN

I stared at Nikki from across my dining room table. The young woman who shared the large apartment with Colin, Vinnie and me was used to being under my scrutiny. Usually she rolled her eyes or stuck out her tongue when she caught me doing it. Not now. My eyes narrowed. "What's wrong?"

"Nothing." Her smile was forced. I didn't tell her she was lying. I just continued staring at her until she dropped her face in her hands. "Don't look at me."

"What's wrong, punk?" Vinnie picked up the salad bowl and dished up a second helping of the delicious broccoli salad he'd made.

Colin and I had arrived at the office to find Francine ready to leave. She'd received a phone call that the new pair of designer sandals she'd ordered had arrived and she couldn't wait another second to collect them from the store. A moment before the elevator doors had closed she'd promised to tell us about her new findings.

I'd taken my time shutting off my computer and making sure everything in my viewing room was in its exact place while Colin had looked at the paintings and other items brought from Léon Blanc's house. Fortunately, he hadn't lingered when I'd been ready to go home and hear about Francine's discovery.

For the last twenty minutes though, I'd been too distracted by Nikki's odd behaviour to remind Francine to tell us about the new information she'd found.

"Doc is right." Manny put his knife and fork down and frowned. "You're all squirrelly. What have you done?"

"Oh, my God!" Nikki threw her hands in the air and glared at everyone around the table. "You're all ganging up on me."

"Because we're worried, Nix." Francine bumped Manny with her shoulder. "Right, handsome?"

"Worried she's been under the criminal's influence for too long and has now broken the law." Manny lowered his brow. "Did you steal something?"

Manny's accusation had the desired effect. Nikki burst out laughing. "You are all too much."

"Well?" Manny folded his arms. "Did you? Steal something?"

Discomfort flashed across her face a second before she pulled her shoulders back. "I hope so."

"What?" The word burst from Manny's lips as he straightened in his chair. "You better start talking right now, little lady."

Nikki laughed again, this time much more relaxed. "I hope I've stolen a heart. Nothing criminal."

"Are you talking euphemistically, Nikki?" My eyes were wide, my hands balled in fists around my cutlery. "Stealing a human organ is most definitely criminal."

"Oh, Doc G. I'm like totally talking metaphorically." She shuddered. "I can't even imagine the organ-stealing thing.

Urgh. Why did you have to go and put that thought into my head?"

"Someone's heart?" Francine pushed Manny back so she could see Nikki better. "Spill. I want all the deets. Now."

"Explain the metaphor first." Anxiety tightened my throat, my words a whisper.

"Surely you've read about stealing someone's heart in one of your gajillion books, Jen-girl." Vinnie nodded towards the large bookshelves in my reading area, but kept his eyes on Nikki. "I also want to hear the details, little punk."

The panic when I'd understood Nikki's declaration literally had temporarily disallowed further interpretation. It took a millisecond to make the connection. I turned to Nikki. "Someone is in love with you?"

She blushed. "I think so."

"Ooh!" Francine clapped her hands, her bracelets jingling. "Deets, girlie. Deets."

"He's one of the art dealers at the gallery." Nikki worked at an art gallery in the afternoons during the summer holidays.

"Why are you so nervous?" It worried me.

She glanced at the front door. "When I heard everyone would be here for dinner, I invited him too. I want you to meet him."

"That's a wonderful idea." Francine turned to Vinnie. "Better set another place."

"He'll be here in another twenty minutes. And only for coffee." She swallowed and looked at Vinnie, Manny, then Colin. "I know how you guys can be. Please be kind to him."

"It's a big step for you to bring him here, Nix." Colin leaned towards her. "This serious?"

"I hope so. I like him."

"I don't like this." Manny's lips were in a thin line. "Who is this man? You said he's an art dealer. Exactly how old is he?"

"He's twenty-six." Her look was pleading as she focused on Manny. "He's a really nice guy."

"And six years older than you. What else do you know about him? What is his surname? Did he even go to university? Does he still live with his mommy in her basement?"

"Oh, stop it, grumpy." Francine put her hand over Manny's mouth. "You're scaring Nikki."

Manny pulled her hand away from his mouth. "Get off me, supermodel. Nikki should know that any man crossing that threshold is going to be investigated by all of us."

"I know this." Nikki swallowed again. "He also knows this."

"What have you told him about us, Nix?" Colin was the only one around the table who was exhibiting any form of calm. Francine's eyes were wide with excitement, Manny was glaring at Nikki, Vinnie had gone quiet in a concerning manner and I was trying hard to keep my heart rate and breathing at a normal level.

"I told him that you were insurance investigators. The same thing I tell all my friends. It's still okay, right?" She looked at Colin.

"Yes, it is." Colin had come up with a simple solution to explain our employment to her friends. She didn't often entertain her friends in our apartment, but we knew most of her friends. It was only logical that they would ask about our careers. She'd been very concerned about compromising our safety or breaching confidentiality by sharing that we were a specialised investigation team that worked for the president of France.

Colin's suggestion that Nikki tell her friends we were insurance investigators was simple, elegant and very close to the truth. It was also something I was comfortable sharing with Nikki's friends, since I'd started as an insurance investigator at Rousseau & Rousseau nine years ago.

"Name and surname, Nix." Francine took her tablet from her handbag. "We need to calm these men down before your boyfriend comes through that door."

Nikki looked at the tablet and sighed. "Rainier Labelle."

I considered Nikki's decision to introduce this young man to us. To an outsider we were an intimidating group of people. Vinnie's size and the vicious scar down the left side of his face were usually enough to scare people to the other side of the street. He didn't mind the effect he had and often used it to his advantage.

Despite Manny's preference for slouching and creating the false impression of absentmindedness, numerous times I'd seen his gaze unsettle people we'd interviewed. Francine wasn't intimidating in the traditional sense, but her hacking skills would expose every secret someone had taken care to hide. I knew I unnerved people as I observed their nonverbal cues.

Francine entered the name into her tablet, then swiped the touch screen a few times. "Hmm."

"Hmm, what?" Manny leaned over to look at her tablet. "Is this Rainier Labelle a criminal?"

"No. It's not that." She frowned and tapped a few times on her tablet. "It's about Benoît Faure."

"What about him?" Manny leaned even closer, then scowled when his phone rang. He took the device from his trouser pocket and swiped the screen. "Millard. Yes? Hmm. What? Why the bloody hell didn't he…? That pretentious little… Yes. Make sure you do that. Thanks, Daniel."

Everyone sat motionless, staring at Manny. Francine was the one who broke the silence. "What did Daniel say?"

"Faure has been under investigation for the last two years already. And bloody Privott knew about this."

"Why didn't he tell us?" I asked. "We could've had more information that might have helped us make faster progress."

"Oh, believe me, Doc, I plan to ask that little hipster this question."

"How did Daniel find out about this?" Colin asked.

"He didn't." Manny glanced at Francine's tablet. "Pink did. He checked their police database and found the investigation hidden behind a few fire fences."

Francine slapped his shoulder with the back of her hand. "They're called firewalls and you know it."

"Why would the police hide an investigation from their own?" Vinnie folded his arms and leaned back in his chair. "Unless they want to keep this information from someone or someones inside the department."

"Well, if Benoît Faure was as involved in organised crime as is alleged, it would make sense." I looked at Francine, who was back to tapping and swiping her tablet screen. "What did you discover about him, Francine?"

She looked up, her smile genuine and crinkling the corners

of her eyes. "Scandals. Delicious, huge, fabulous scandals."

"Supermodel." Manny sighed tiredly. "Just tell us."

"I set my system up to scour the interwebs for any mention of Faure. It must have found this while we were eating, because there was nothing…"

"Supermodel!"

"Okay, okay. Calm down or I tell them what you did last night."

Manny gasped and leaned away from Francine, his lips a thin line. "Work, supermodel. Talk about work."

"You're too easy to rile. You know I would never tell them about that thing you did with…" She burst out laughing at Manny's outraged expression and blew him a kiss. "I found an article about Benoît Faure. It was published ten days ago and is a full exposé of the man."

"Personal or professional?" I asked.

"As far as I can see, everything. It's talking about his business connections with people I'm sure handsome here will want to arrest." She scrolled down the article. "It also reveals his children's details, their careers, his grandchildren, even where they shop. Ooh! He has a thing for nurses' uniforms. There's a few online receipts of his purchases. And let me just say these uniforms will cause heart attacks in hospitals. And, oh, this is disgusting. He likes honey in his coffee. Who drinks honey in their coffee?"

"Who wrote the article?"

"Dion Gravois." She frowned, lifted one index finger and tapped on her tablet for almost a minute. "Hmm. Well, isn't this just interesting."

"Care to share with the class, supermodel?" Manny asked when Francine didn't elaborate.

"Oh, yes. Of course. Dion Gravois is an award-winning investigative reporter. The stuff I'm seeing here all points to a man who is a really good journalist."

"Who does he work for?"

"No one." Francine's eyebrows rose. "That's the coolest thing ever. Until three years ago he was working for the French Euronews station, before that *Le Canard enchaîné*, a satirical newspaper known for their investigative journalism. He's written articles for the *Economist*, the *Wall Street Journal*, the *New York Times* and other very reputable publications. Some of his articles have led to arrests, further investigations and loads of resignations from officials."

"Where did he publish the article about Faure?" It was hard to ask only one question, but I knew Francine didn't respond well to being bombarded.

"On his blog. This is so interesting." She shifted in her chair with excitement. "He left *Euronews French* three years ago, was silent for about sixteen months and then started this blog. Although, I must say, it looks more like a news website and it is really well-designed. And it looks good on my tablet."

"Does he say where he got this information about Faure?" I didn't care about the user-friendliness of his blog.

"Hmm." She scrolled some more. "Not that I can see at a glance. You can read this... hah. Of course you're going to read this. Maybe you will catch something, but I'm not seeing him talking about his source here."

"I need to talk to him." He could give me more information

about Faure, which might help me understand the differences between Faure's murder and that of Léon Blanc. The discrepancies were bothering me greatly. With all the events of today, I hadn't had enough time to process all the information I'd gathered. Or to analyse it and pinpoint the issue that was causing me mental distress.

"I'll organise that, Doc. I'll get him to come to Rousseau & Rousseau tomorrow."

"Hmm." Francine put her tablet flat on the table and worked on it with both hands. "I can't locate any metadata for his blog."

"And?" Manny asked.

"And it's very curious. I can see how much traffic he has to his blog and it is a lot. What I can't see is where his blog originates from. Either he is really good with hiding his online presence or he has help."

"Is that a good or a bad thing?" Nikki asked.

"In my world it is both." Francine shrugged. "I have no idea why he would want to cloak his presence. Why have a public blog if you're trying to hide?"

"He's an investigative reporter," Vinnie said. "Maybe he's pissed off so many people with his exposés that he's received threats and he's taking precautions."

"Good point, big guy, but…"

"Benoît Faure was killed three days after the article was published," I interrupted Francine. "Is there any connection? Can you trace who read the article?"

"I can, but the traffic to Dion Gravois' blog is huge, so we might land up with thousands of IP addresses." She winced. "And IP addresses aren't always useful. Not when people are reading the articles while surfing the web on a café's Wi-Fi or a hotel's or a shopping mall's."

"Check it, supermodel."

"Will do. And I would love to ask him a few questions when you bring him in tomorrow."

"We'll see about that."

A ping on her tablet drew Francine's attention back. We watched as she scrolled and tapped. Her smiled grew wider. "Your Rainier Labelle is quite a handsome devil, Nix."

"What did you find?" Vinnie rested his elbows on the table, staring at Francine's tablet.

"Lots of information. But firstly"—she looked at Manny—"he doesn't have a criminal record, has never been interviewed by the police and doesn't live with his mommy."

"What a relief." Manny's expression did not support his words. I wondered why he was being sarcastic.

"He has a business degree and minored in art history. Seems to be perfect for his job." She turned her tablet for us to see. "And he's not hard to look at."

The photo on Francine's tablet appeared to be from a social networking site. Rainier was laughing at something or someone to the left of the camera. He had dark hair and strong features, and his laughter was genuine. A photo was impossible to analyse for nonverbal cues. In that millisecond when someone's body language was captured, many other factors were at play that were not captured in the photo. Was he laughing at or with someone? Who was with him? What was the context of their conversation? Their relationship? All these questions replaced the questions I'd had about Faure.

"I don't like him." Vinnie crossed his arms again and shook his head. "Nope. Don't like him."

"How can you say that?" Nikki's shoulders dropped, the corners of her mouth turned down. "You haven't even met him yet."

The doorbell rang and Nikki jumped up.

"Seems like you're going to meet him now." Francine didn't look away from her tablet.

"Search deeper, supermodel." Manny got up to join Nikki at the door. "Doc always says we need as much data as possible to make an informed decision."

"He's telling me to hack." Francine's whisper was loud enough to reach Manny, but he didn't react. Like him, I also didn't approve of hacking into people's private lives. But there had been times in the last three years where I'd struggled with the ethics and morals of my stance. It felt like a lifetime ago when I'd strongly believed that everything in life was black and white, right and wrong. No longer. The knowledge that hacking into someone's email, bank account or social network profile could save the lives of many had me questioning the right a criminal had to privacy.

I got up from the table to break the hold these distressing thoughts were taking on my mind. I didn't want to spend another night unable to sleep, sitting on my sofa and trying to find a middle ground.

The door opened and the man from the photo stood in the doorway. Nikki stepped forward, grabbed his hand and pulled him into the apartment. "Come in, Rainier. Everyone is so excited about meeting you."

That wasn't true. The expression on Manny's face was

anything but excitement. It was suspicion, watchfulness and fear. I saw the same on Vinnie's face.

Rainier kissed Nikki on her cheek and held out his hand to Manny. "You must be Colonel Millard. I'm really pleased to meet you."

Manny shook his hand. The micro-expression of pain on Rainier's face told me what I'd expected—Manny was crushing his hand. Rainier was handling it well though. He didn't lower his gaze, but he also didn't challenge Manny's authority. His demeanour was that of an alpha male. He was standing confidently, his jeans and t-shirt making him look more relaxed, but no less self-assured. Yet he was respectful of Manny's position of power.

Nikki slapped at both their hands and rolled her eyes. "You men are all the same. Come on, Rainier. Meet the others."

The young man nodded at Manny and followed Nikki to the table. I stood frozen, completely out of my depth. From Nikki's expression and her prior nervousness, I knew how important this was to her. I didn't want to do anything that could cause her distress, but I didn't know how to act. Any new people I met were usually suspects or someone helping us in a case. I didn't socialise other than with the group of friends that were currently in my apartment.

Colin got up and stood next to me. He put his left arm around me and pulled me against him while holding out his right hand. "Pleased to meet you, Rainier. I'm Colin."

"And you must be Doctor Lenard." He shook Colin's hand, but didn't offer to shake mine. Nikki must have told him about my intense dislike of being touched. Well, being touched by anyone except Colin. Rainier's smile lost some of its honesty. "I've been looking forward to meeting everyone."

I nodded. There was nothing I could say. I hadn't known about his existence until a few minutes ago. Nikki had been in love before. The first time I'd worried about her behaviour. She'd constantly checked her smartphone, then run to her bedroom to continue some chat with the boy. That had lasted three weeks. For a while she'd had no romantic interest in anyone until another young man had caught her attention. That relationship had lasted two months. Nikki hadn't agreed with the way he'd treated a disabled person in a shop and had ended it immediately.

I studied Rainier. For some reason Nikki was more invested in this relationship than the others. I wanted to support her, but didn't know how. So I did what I was best at—I studied him.

Vinnie pushed his chair back, making sure it scraped loudly on my wooden floors. He knew how much the potential damage to my wooden floors irked me and never did it. I wondered what his strategy was. If it was to get Rainier's attention, it worked.

Rainier looked towards Vinnie. Then his eyes stretched. Clearly Nikki had not been successful in conveying Vinnie's size. And Vinnie was making himself more conspicuous. He pulled himself to his full height, pushed his chest out and walked towards Rainier offering his right hand.

Rainier stared at Vinnie's hand for an indecisive second before taking it. Again he winced as Vinnie's hand tightened around his.

"I'm Vinnie."

"I'm really pleased to meet you." Rainier's expression was in conflict with this statement. Vinnie scared him.

"We'll see about that." Vinnie let go of his hand and turned his back on Rainier. "I'm making coffee."

Francine hadn't left her seat, still swiping and tapping on her tablet. I didn't like the anger pulling at the corners of her mouth. Still not knowing how to act in this situation, I refrained from asking her whether she'd found more articles on Faure or if it was information on Rainier that had her breathing hard through her nose. She put her tablet on the table and stared at the younger man.

He stared back at her. "Francine? I'm Rainier."

Francine got up and stood next to Manny, her expression of suspicion and dislike mirroring his. "Who's Sabine Fournier?"

"Who?" To an untrained eye, his immediate reaction would've seemed innocent. I didn't have an untrained eye. The bobbing of his Adam's apple as he swallowed and his hands disappearing behind his back told me he was worried. The quick widening of his eyes told me he'd recognised the name. Still I didn't say anything.

"Answer the lady." Manny's eyes narrowed. "Who's Sabine Fournier?"

"Am I supposed to know her?" He glanced at Nikki. "I don't know who they're talking about."

Vinnie came from the kitchen carrying a bread roll and a large knife. He stood next to me, tapping the knife against the bread roll. "Jen-girl?"

I didn't know what to do. Nikki's emotional welfare had

become a priority in my life. Most times I didn't know how to handle that priority and often I failed in protecting her from my own uncensored words.

"Doc G?" She looked at me, trust clear on her face. "What's happening?"

I waited until she prompted me again with an impatient look. I wanted her to be sure she wanted an answer. "Rainer is lying. He knows this Sabine Fournier and the mention of her name aroused him."

"Jesus!" Rainier took a step back. "What is this? An interrogation? Nikki, I thought you were introducing me to your family."

"I was." Nikki turned to him, her chin quivering. "What is Francine talking about?"

"You take their word over mine? I said I don't know this Sabine woman."

I recognised the look Nikki gave Rainier. I'd seen that expression on my own face when I'd rewatched a recording of an interview where the suspect had said something incriminating and I'd been convinced of his guilt.

"I take their word over anyone's, Rainier." For a second, Nikki's chin continued to quiver, but she pulled her shoulders back. "I would like for you to leave now."

"Are you kidding me?" He took a step closer to Nikki. "One question and you're giving up on me?"

"Sometimes it's all it takes." Her words came out as a whisper. It felt as if someone had plunged Vinnie's knife into my heart.

Vinnie put the bread roll on the table, the knife still in his right hand. He took a step closer towards them and held his left hand out to Nikki, not taking his eyes off Rainier. "You heard what she said. Colonel Millard will see you to the door."

"You are…" Rainier looked sincerely baffled. "You don't even give a person a chance to explain anything? You just throw people out of your home?"

Nikki took Vinnie's hand and stared at Rainier, hurt evident around her eyes and mouth.

"You had three opportunities to explain." I sighed when he continued to look confused. "Francine asked you once, Manny once and Nikki once. You chose to lie, not explain."

"This way." Manny took Rainier by the elbow and steered him to the front door. "Another word and I'll make sure you are under legal scrutiny for the rest of your miserable life."

I didn't pay attention to Rainier's answer. My concern was Nikki. She was hugging Vinnie's waist, her face pushed against his torso. Standing this close to him made her look small. Vulnerable. "Nikki?"

She raised her head, her eyes shiny with tears. "I really liked him, Doc G."

I saw it in her expression. She needed me. It took mentally writing three bars of Mozart's Piano Concerto No. 1 in F major before I moved away from Colin's embrace and opened my arms. She let go of Vinnie and threw herself into my arms.

I pushed away the panic that was building in me and closed my arms around her. She exhaled a shuddering sigh and rested her head on my shoulder. She wasn't crying. Not like the first time we'd met, shortly after her father had been killed. She was just holding onto me, needing the human closeness of someone she trusted.

While we stood like that for one minute and forty-seven seconds, Vinnie returned to the kitchen. Francine was leaning against the dining room table, guilt evident in every facial muscle contraction. Manny had locked my front door and was standing next to Francine. When he glanced at her, I saw pride and deep affection. No one spoke until Vinnie brought a tray with coffee, cookies and a disturbingly large slab of chocolate. "Let's take the party to the sofas."

I relaxed my arms around Nikki to give her the opportunity to step away, but she shook her head against my shoulder. "Another minute."

"Five seconds." Because I couldn't last another minute of this close proximity without going into a shutdown. I felt her cheek contract as she smiled against my shoulder.

Four seconds later she lifted her head and leaned back. I dropped my arms next to my sides. She did the same, but still stood close to me. "Thank you, Doc G. I needed that."

"I know." I lifted my hand and with the tip of my index finger touched her left temple. "You are a very smart and strong woman. You need to learn to trust yourself and rely on your own strength."

Tears filled her eyes and I quickly pulled my finger away. I searched her face for evidence that my words had exacerbated her emotional pain. She laughed softly and wiped the tears with the back of her hand. "That was very sweet. Thank you, Doc G."

"Oh." The relief that I hadn't said the wrong thing was

overwhelming. I didn't know what to say next. "Vinnie made coffee."

She laughed again and walked to the sitting area. Manny and Francine were on one sofa, Vinnie in his usual wingback chair and Colin on the other sofa. I sat down next to him, Nikki on my other side. She grabbed a cookie and pushed it in her mouth. I grimaced, especially when she looked at Francine and spoke past the food in her mouth. "So? Who's Sabine Fournier?"

Again guilt flashed across Francine's face. "I'm so sorry, Nix. I really didn't want for you to get hurt."

"I know."

"I checked out his social media profiles and stumbled across another account in his name."

"You hacked into his private Facebook account?" Manny shook his head.

"Hey, you asked me to." Francine raised both hands. "Fine, you didn't say it in so many words, but I know that's what you meant. Anyway, Rainier has a few other girlfriends he's staying busy with."

"Girlfriends? As in plural?" Vinnie slammed his fist into his thigh. "I knew I didn't like that dude."

"Yup. I found three other accounts he's using specifically for his girlfriends. He was chatting with one an hour before he came here."

"That bastard!" Vinnie got up. "What's his address?"

"Sit down, Vinnie." I looked at Nikki. "You suspected this, didn't you?"

She blinked a few times and waited until her chin stopped quivering. "I really, really, really liked him. But something was off. He even asked me to move in with him, but it didn't feel right. Proves I was right."

"You should learn to trust your observations more." I softened my tone. "I'm sorry that you're disappointed."

"Oh, well. That's life." She grabbed another cookie. "Now I have an excuse to eat cookies and finish the ice cream in the freezer."

"Next time, come to me first, Nix." Francine lifted her tablet. "I'll get you all the down and dirty before your first date."

"Maybe. I don't know. Maybe I don't always want to know everything."

My eyebrows rose at that statement. How could anyone not want to know as much as possible? Knowledge was power. This experience should've taught Nikki that. Now that she knew Rainier was not monogamous, she could make an informed decision.

This was exactly why I was so frustrated with this case. We had so little information. I needed to know more. I needed to know who Dion Gravois' source was. I needed to know if there was any connection between the article and the murder.

Colin squeezed my hand to bring me back to the present. For the next hour, I forced myself to relax and spend time with my friends. When Manny and Francine left, and Nikki took a container of ice cream to her bedroom, I was relieved. For the first time today, I had time to analyse the vast influx of information I'd absorbed since I'd stepped into the conference room this morning.

Chapter **EIGHT**

"Ooh, yay!" Francine turned towards the team room and waved at Vinnie and Colin when they stepped out of the elevator. They had taken the opportunity to fit in an early-morning training session with Daniel's team while Francine and I scoured through the data we had. Both men looked relaxed and were freshly showered.

Colin walked towards the paintings Vinnie had arranged on the far side of the large open space of the team room. Vinnie followed him. "I put the diamonds in the safe. It just felt wrong to leave them out here in the open. It's like an invitation, ya know?"

"You did good, Vin. I would've done the same." Colin stopped in front of the Morisot painting.

"Are all these really fake?" Vinnie waved at all the paintings. "That's just insane."

"No, they're not." Colin pointed to his left. "This Picasso is the real deal. But this Morisot? A very good reproduction. No, a brilliant reproduction."

"You can study the paintings later." Francine tapped her dark purple nails on my desk. "Come here. We found something."

Vinnie's smile was wide. He was always happy after a good training session with the GIPN team. He followed Colin into my viewing room and stopped next to Francine. "What's cookin', good-lookin'? Missed me?"

"Like a fly misses a spider." She rolled her eyes.

Colin leaned over and kissed me. "Got a lot of work done?"

"Yes. I studied the video Pink took when Daniel announced to the opera singers Léon Blanc was dead." I shrugged. "I didn't see any other person acting suspiciously, so Francine and I pursued other leads. I haven't had time to look at the documents or music books from Léon Blanc's safe, but it's been a very productive three hours."

He sat down next to me. "Can't believe it was that long. It felt much shorter."

"Because we had fun." Vinnie's smile widened even more. "My man here pissed Pink off like you can't believe."

I frowned at Colin. "You shouldn't alienate Pink. He's been very helpful."

"Vinnie exaggerates."

"As usual," Francine added. "So what did you do to Pink?"

"He stole Pink's smartphone three times without the dude even noticing. Pink was too busy on his tablet or with something else." Vinnie chuckled. "And he changed all Pink's ringtones. Classic!"

"I might've gone too far with the ringtones. But Pink got all huffy about his devices." Colin smiled at Francine. "Much like you."

"Yeah. You touch my devices and I'll change the security codes to all your offshore accounts." Francine's threat was made in jest, but I saw the truth behind it. Concern replaced the playfulness around her mouth. "How's Nikki? Genevieve says she's fine, but I find that hard to believe. Breakups are the pits."

Vinnie snorted. "Seriously? You don't believe Jen-girl?"

Francine and I had had this discussion as soon as the elevator doors had opened this morning. After seven minutes of repeating myself, I'd come to the realisation that she didn't need to be convinced. She needed to be reassured. I hadn't been able to do that.

Francine shook her head. "Of course I believe Genevieve. I'm just wondering if she's missing something."

"My opinion?" Colin raised both eyebrows and waited until Francine nodded. "Nikki was looking for an excuse to break up with Rainier. You heard her say that she suspected something was wrong. Maybe she just didn't want to be the one to take the step."

"That little hussy!" Francine put her fists on her hips. "She used me to break up with him? I'm now the resident breaker-upper by proxy?"

I jerked. "Breaker-upper isn't a word."

"I'm making it a word." Francine slammed her fist on my desk. "And I'm making that little minx pay for making me feel so guilty."

When Francine was like this, there was no reasoning with her. I pressed my lips together to stop myself from pointing out yet again that no one could make you feel anything. It was our choice how we reacted to situations.

"We found another article." I wanted to share our findings with Colin. "Another exposé about an alleged organised crime leader."

"It's positively delicious! So many scandals." Francine wriggled in her chair, her mood restored.

"He was also murdered."

"Who was murdered?" Manny asked from the elevator doors.

"Tell us first what Lucien said." Francine had wasted at least fifteen minutes this morning speculating what excuse Lucien Privott would give Manny for not sharing that Benoît Faure had been under investigation. Manny had set up a secure video call with Lucien in Rousseau & Rousseau's conference room and had spent more than two hours there. I was also curious.

"That bloody hipster." Manny pushed his hands into his trouser pockets. "It took a bleeding hour of shouting before he would admit that he was scared of appearing incompetent."

Francine nodded slowly. "That makes sense. He does appear incompetent for not catching on that Faure was bad news. And for not registering that Faure had a connection to the president through the opera house and other charities."

"His reasoning is flawed." It amazed me how often people were unwilling to admit to mistakes. "Had he told us immediately that Benoît Faure was under investigation, we could've had better context for Faure's murder. By not telling us, he revealed his incompetence."

"That's exactly what I told him." Manny lifted his chin towards the twelve monitors against the wall. "Now tell me about this murder."

"When we spoke to Sébastien Blanc, he said that he'd lost respect for his father's friend when he'd read an article about this friend's illegal activities. When we discovered that an article had been written about Faure before his murder, I was curious to see if there was any connection between Faure and this friend."

"Because of Léon Blanc. He's the common denominator. Good thinking, Doc."

"And we hit pay dirt." Francine lifted both fists into the air. "Pay dirt, baby!"

I ignored Francine's display of victory. "Serge Valois, the friend Sébastien was talking about, was murdered twenty days ago. Three days before his murder, an article was published revealing his illegal activities as well as information about his private and professional life."

"Serge Valois." Manny scratched his head. "I remember Sébastien talking about him. A man with serious crimes to his name. As far as I can remember, he spent some time in prison."

"He did." I had researched this man while Francine had been busy with a more illegal activity. "He was fifty-nine when he was murdered and had been to prison three times, but never longer for nine months. He was convicted for tax evasion, extortion and the last one was for attempted murder."

"Who did he try to kill?" Vinnie asked.

"His wife." I frowned when Vinnie laughed. "Domestic violence is no laughing matter, Vinnie."

"Oh. Yes." He sobered. "Sorry. I didn't know he beat her. I thought he put out a hit on her."

I didn't want to argue that neither was humorous. "They'd had a disagreement about their business and he had beaten her so badly that her children convinced her to press charges. Typical in these cases, this had been going on for years and she'd never reported it before."

"What business did they have?" Colin asked.

"He had a successful catering business that started as a small restaurant and now supplies many exclusive food stores with baked goods. His wife inherited the business, but had been running it with Valois since the beginning."

"Did she kill him?" Manny asked.

"When the police investigated Valois' death, they immediately suspected the wife and children. But all of them had solid alibis, so the case is still unsolved."

"Not that the police are making any effort to find the killer." Francine glanced at her laptop. "They haven't added any new information to their case files in the last two weeks. It seems like they're quite content to let the murder of a wife-abusing, law-breaking criminal go cold."

"Holy hell, supermodel. You hacked the police files?"

"You weren't answering your phone."

"Then you should have asked Daniel. He would've sent those files to you in a jiffy."

"But it's not nearly as much fun."

Manny glared at Francine, the supratrochlear artery on his forehead prominent. "Well, that's just great. You had fun and now I have to go and make nice with that police captain so he will legally give us the files."

"You won't have to make nice. He doesn't even know I hacked their system." Francine's top lip curled. "Seriously. They have to update their firewalls and other security protocols. It was too easy. I didn't even have that much fun."

Manny clenched his jaw and closed his eyes as if he was praying. After a few seconds, he looked at Francine. "Well? Tell me what you found."

"He was murdered in Paris. In a hotel. Just like Faure. The hotel is a bit more upmarket, but also has a reputation for being available by the hour."

"Show them the photos." That had been the only reason I was able to tolerate Francine's illegal manner of acquiring the files. I had learned a lot from the photos.

Crime scene photos replaced everything else that was on the monitors. Francine pushed her laptop towards me. "Just click if you need to show a specific photo."

"That one will do." I pointed to the one in the bottom left monitor. Looking at the photos analytically had helped soften some of the panic that rose every time I saw the dead body. "Valois was positioned the same as Faure. On their backs, their arms next to their torsos, their chests exposed."

"To show the tattoo." Francine pointed at the photo above. "See? The same as with Faure and Blanc."

"Not the same." I stared at Francine's computer. I didn't like using other people's devices. An American university's research had shown that the average computer keyboard contained four hundred times more bacteria than the average toilet seat. I had to remind myself that Francine was pedantic about keeping her computers clean. And it wasn't a public computer. I pulled it closer and soon had the photos of the three murder victims next to each other. I zoomed in on the tattoos. "There are many similarities between the murders, but also differences. The basic tattoo is the same on all three. The same crude creeping rose design."

"I see it." Colin leaned closer to the monitors. "Valois' tattoo has only one rose, Faure's has two roses and Blanc's has three roses."

"I posit that it denotes the order of the murders. Valois was killed twenty days ago, Faure eight days ago and Léon Blanc two days ago. The similarity is that each rose has a bullet hole through its centre. Valois was shot once, Faure twice and Blanc three times. All post-mortem."

"No blood," Vinnie said.

"There was minimal blood found at the first two crime scenes and no blood at all in Blanc's home office. All three men had been dead before they were shot." Something I was grateful for. It made the crime scene photos a little less gruesome.

"What is their COD?" Manny asked.

"Valois and Faure both died from manual strangulation. Blanc suffered a fatal brain haemorrhage from the blunt-force trauma to the back of his head. The medical examiner also found an injection site at the base of his neck, just inside his hairline. He tested it and found unmetabolized midazolam."

"One of those roofie-type drugs?" Vinnie asked.

I frowned. "This drug has nothing to do with roofs. It is used to treat acute seizures and to induce sedation. In Léon Blanc's case it was injected post-mortem. The other two men both had Sevoflurane in their systems, but it was administered perimortem. It incapacitated them."

"When did you speak to the ME, Doc?" Manny looked worried.

"I didn't. Daniel did. He sent me the findings this morning.

Apparently, this doctor is one of the best in his field. He became suspicious and asked Daniel about the case. Daniel told him about Faure's death and the doctor immediately looked at the autopsy report."

"So what is his finding?"

"That Léon Blanc was dead before he was tattooed." It bothered me. "Just another difference between his death and the other two. Another difference is that the Léon Blanc's gunshot wound had stippling around it, the other two circular seared margins. The gun had been pressed against Valois' and Faure's chests when they were shot, but had been a short distance from Léon Blanc's chest."

"Hmm. You're onto something here, Doc." Manny counted on his fingers. "Blanc wasn't killed in a hotel, he was tattooed after he was dead and also wasn't gassed. Are you sure this Valois was gassed?"

I nodded. "It was in that coroner's report that Serge Valois had Sevoflurane in his system."

"Bloody hell." Manny rubbed both hands over his face. "It seems we have a serial killer on our hands and this is his signature."

"Sevoflurane is expensive and you need a licence to buy it."

Vinnie snorted. "Wanna bet that I can get you enough of that gas to sedate all the opera singers in about ten minutes flat?"

"Is it that easily available on the street?" Manny asked.

"Old man, anything you want is available on the street. It might cost you a bundle, but it can be delivered as soon as you need it."

"Holy Mary. What a mess." Manny scratched his jaw.

"Let's get back to the article on Valois. Who wrote it?"

"Dion Gravois," Francine said before I could answer. "It was also published on his blog."

"Where the bleeding hell is he getting all this inside information on these criminals?"

"I tried to get past his internet security, but it's solid." Francine interlaced her fingers and stretched out her arms. "Doesn't mean I'm giving up. No, siree. I'm gonna crack this baby if it's the last thing I do."

"What have you found on Dion Gravois, supermodel?"

"Now that question I can answer." She pulled her laptop back. A few seconds later, a photo and three different documents appeared on the monitors. "He's quite a hunk. Those blue eyes could make a girl swoon."

"Supermodel!"

She winked at Manny. "Dion Gravois. Thirty-seven years old. Born in Lille to an engineer father and a teacher mother. Top student in his school. Studied journalism and political sciences in Paris. Graduated top of his class. While at university, he worked for *Parti de Gauche*, the democratic socialist party, writing their speeches and press releases. After eighteen months at *Parti de Gauche*, he quit. Personally, I think he got sick and tired of all the conspiracies and decided to expose them rather than write clever press releases spinning scandals into fairy tales."

"Supermodel." Manny sounded tired.

"Fine. Fine." She flicked her hair over her shoulder. "I have a reason for my theory, just so you know. After *Parti de Gauche*, he went to work for *Le Canard enchaîné*, known for their investigative reporting. He worked his way up to editor within four years and spearheaded many investigations into politicians and other high-powered officials."

"Married? Children?"

"No to all of that. He was also an only child, so he isn't even an uncle." She frowned. "I didn't find a lot of info on his personal life. Looking at the output of his writing, I don't know if he has a private or social life."

"His finances?"

Francine slapped her hand over her chest. "Be still, my beating heart. Did you just ask me if I illegally looked into an innocent citizen's finances?"

Manny stared at her until she giggled.

"I don't know so much about the dude being innocent," Vinnie said. "I mean, he wrote articles about two of the dead dudes, so he must be connected to them somehow."

"I'm not so sure, Vin." Francine dropped her hand, her expression thoughtful. "I've read through some of his articles and it's really good stuff. He's been exposing crime and injustice for the last eleven years. I can't quite see him changing his mighty pen for a sword."

"I haven't seen any mention of swords." I moved towards my laptop. "Where did you find that?"

"Sorry, girlfriend. I'm talking about the pen being mightier than the sword."

"Oh. Yes." I sat back in my chair. "I don't agree that we can assume innocence merely from reading Dion Gravois' articles. We have far too little information about him."

"And his finances are normal for a man who's running his own business," Francine said. "I've managed to find his business account and a private account, but that doesn't mean he doesn't have more accounts. I haven't been able to break through the security around his email and his website. As soon as I'm in, I'm sure I'll find all kinds of treasures."

"What did you learn from his finances, Doc?" Manny frequently grew weary of Francine's wild theories.

"Francine is right. Those two accounts are consistent with someone who doesn't have salaried employment. His business account shows that his blog is doing exceedingly well. Most of his income is from advertising. He also gets a substantial income from YouTube."

"He has a vlog there," Francine said.

"A what now?" Manny scowled.

"It's a video blog, oh ancient one. Although this is much more like the quality of a TV news report. Each article he writes is supported by high-quality video footage of interviews and evidence of the conspira—"

"His expenses are what one could expect." I also grew weary of Francine's love for outrageous theories. "I didn't see anything that made me suspicious."

"Those two accounts could only be for show." Manny closed his eyes tightly for a second, then looked at Francine. "I want everything you have on this guy."

"Ooh! I get to snoop." She affected a happy shudder. "And it's ordered by his highness."

"How many articles did you read?" Colin smiled at Manny's annoyance.

"I didn't read any articles, Frey."

"I wasn't asking you, your highness."

"Oh, bugger off." Manny pushed his hands into his pockets and took a step back.

Francine laughed. "Genevieve and I only looked at his blog half an hour ago."

"We haven't had enough time to go through all the articles. To answer your question, we read four articles. Dion Gravois is a good writer." I had been impressed with the detail of each report. They were intelligently written, logically presented and factually sound. I'd checked the first two for accuracy and couldn't find any flaws in his article. The video accompanying the Serge Valois exposé had been illuminating to watch. I'd learned more about the journalist than Valois.

Dion Gravois was a confident and well-spoken man. He spoke with authority and believed in everything he reported. There was no sensationalism or exaggeration in his presentation of facts. And the only times I caught possible deceptive nonverbal cues were when he talked about his sources. I understood the need journalists had to protect their sources and didn't count his deception against him. Very seldom did I enjoy meeting new people. I was looking forward to meeting this man.

"Jenny?" Colin touched my forearm and smiled when I looked at him. "Where did you go?"

"Nowher…" This was not the first time he'd asked me this question. I should've known he didn't mean it literally. "I was thinking about Dion Gravois."

"Anything you need to share, Doc?" Manny was no longer standing by the door. While I'd been lost in my thoughts, he'd moved to stand next to Francine.

"I would like to meet him."

"Good. He's coming in this afternoon. We can grill him

then." Manny snorted when my eyes widened. "Grill means ask questions. I'm not a cannibal, Doc."

"I know that." But it was an odd expression. My next question to Manny was interrupted when his phone rang. He took it from his trouser pocket and answered. He didn't speak much and finally said, "We'll be there in fifteen minutes. Don't let them move anything."

"I don't want to go." The words left my mouth before I could stop them. I'd seen the expression on Manny's face while he'd listened to whoever had phoned him. I knew what was waiting for us.

"Unless you're going to go into a total shutdown, you better get yourself together, Doc. We have ourselves another murder and it was discovered less than an hour ago."

I really didn't want to go. It was nothing but my intense aversion to the change in my routine that prompted this. My curiosity, on the other hand, was strong enough to make me nod tersely. If this murder was similar to Valois' and Faure's, it would give me an even better baseline to compare against Blanc's murder. His was the anomaly. And it was usually the anomaly that provided the most important information.

Chapter NINE

I studied the couple waiting with us at the hotel's elevator. The man appeared to be in his late forties, the lady in her late twenties. His attire was characteristic of a businessman in mid-level management. His suit was not bespoke like Phillip's, nor were his shoes from any designer label. His receding hairline fitted his expanding waistline. This made it so much more interesting to study the woman with him and the dynamics between them.

The high quality of her short skirt and tight top that allowed for a generous view of her cleavage did not add class to her demeanour. Her affected interest in her much older companion and the overwhelming smell of her perfume made it easy for a person to draw a conclusion. I didn't like stereotyping people, but most people fitted so well into a category, it was hard not to.

She leaned against him and ran her hand down his sleeve. His shoulders straightened, he pulled in his stomach and his chest puffed out. He put his arm around her back and pulled her flush against him. She giggled just as the elevator doors opened.

A businesswoman stepped into the foyer without making eye contact with any of us. The man and woman walked into the elevator and turned to wait for us. I shook my head and held Colin back when he moved to join them. There was enough space for another four people, but I didn't want to be in such a small space with the overpowering scent of her perfume.

Manny waved the couple on. "We'll get the next one."

The man gave Manny a knowing smile and pressed a button on the side wall. The moment the doors closed, tension I hadn't even realised was there left my shoulders. Colin squeezed my hand. "What's wrong?"

"I think he's renting a room by the hour."

"You can bet your book collection he is, Doc." Manny shook his head. "Not even discreet about it either."

"Why should he be discreet?"

Manny only snorted and pointed at the second elevator when it opened. I was immensely relieved that we didn't have to go into the first elevator. The residual smell of the woman's perfume would've resulted in me mentally writing a Mozart concerto until I could breathe unperfumed air again.

We made the ride to the fifth floor in silence. Situated on the border of the old town, the hotel had six floors and seventy-three rooms. It was neither large nor small and didn't belong to any chain. It surprised me that rooms were rented out for carnal purposes. Reasonably priced accommodation in the old town was hard to come by. I would've thought the hotel to be fully booked. "Until yesterday, I didn't even know hotels rented out rooms by the hour."

"Not all of them do, love." Colin followed me into the hallway when the elevator doors opened. The thick carpet was much thinner in the centre from years of foot traffic. The walls were freshly painted. The artwork on the walls looked like cheap reprints of impressionist artists. Colin pointed at one painting. "Hotels that have these horrid Van Gogh prints all over their walls are the kind that would do it."

"What does the print have to do with renting rooms by the hour?"

"It indicates the quality of the hotel." Colin glared at the framed reproductions. "Although this is not the worst I've seen."

"Many years ago, I investigated a murder in a hotel like this." Manny looked at the door number to his left and continued on. "The receptionist had been renting out rooms for an hourly fee without the manager or the board knowing. Sometimes the manager does it, sometimes it's the receptionist, but they always have clients. Ah. Here we are."

The door opened almost immediately when Manny knocked on it. Daniel's muscular frame filled the door. He looked at his watch. "You made it in fourteen minutes."

"Only because Millard wasn't driving." Colin had ignored Manny when the latter had suggested taking his car. Colin had walked to his SUV and Manny had followed, complaining the entire ride to the hotel.

"At least I keep to the speed limit, Frey."

Daniel smiled and stepped to the side. "Better come in. This is not pretty."

I stopped mid-step. "What do you mean? Is there a lot of blood?"

"Nope. It's just not pleasant looking at an old body when it's naked and dead." Daniel's smile dimmed. "It looks almost the same as the previous crime scene, Genevieve. Very little blood. It almost doesn't look like a crime scene."

I swallowed and mentally wrote the first two lines of Mozart's Violin Sonata No. 11 in E-flat. On a deep inhale, I walked past Daniel into the room. The smell of blood wasn't nearly as strong as the ink and a sickly sweet smell. The room had to be one of the more expensive ones on offer. The king-size bed, sofa and small table left enough space to easily walk around. But it wasn't enough space for all the people inside the room.

Two crime scene technicians were collecting evidence on the other side of the bed. Colin and Vinnie walked towards them and Manny was going through the pockets of a man's jacket draped over a chair. I stepped back and bumped into Daniel.

"Oops. Sorry about that." He leaned to the side and looked at my face. "Everything okay?"

I shook my head. Colin glanced at us, then quickly made his way back to me. "Jenny?"

"Too many people." My breathing was erratic.

"Why don't you wait in the hallway for a minute while we make space for you?" Colin's touch on my forearm snapped me out of the paralysis that had overtaken my legs.

Without even a nod, I walked back to the hallway and wrapped my arms around my torso. I despised crowded places. One of my greatest joys was that internet shopping had become easily accessible. Not having to brave bodies bumping into me while I was looking for clothes or food was one less stressor in my life. The hotel room would've been spacious for two people. But six people in there with me was simply too much.

The two technicians walked past me and I recognised the shorter one the same moment she recognised me. "Oh, hi, Doctor Lenard! I hoped we would meet again, but not like this."

"Hello, Isabelle."

She came to stand next to me, looking into the open room. "It's very similar to the other one. Léon Blanc, right? Yeah. That was his name. Léon Blanc. The difference is that this one doesn't have any blunt-force trauma to the head, by the way. So, what do you think?"

"You talk too much, but your voice isn't irritating." She had a gentle alto that was soft and sounded like she laughed a lot.

She blinked a few times and laughed. "Um, thank you?"

I was going to ask her why she was uncertain about thanking me. And why she was thanking me in the first place. But Manny, Vinnie and Daniel came into the hallway and Colin stood in the doorway. "Ready?"

I wasn't ready to look at another dead body, but looking at it within the context of the room would give me more information than looking at it from a photo. Colin must've seen the decision in my expression and walked back into the room. I followed him.

Isabelle was right. This man's body was positioned in exactly the same way as Léon Blanc's. As if resting on his back, he was lying at an angle to the bed, his legs straight, his arms next to his body. I glanced around the room. Nothing seemed out of place. The bed cover didn't look as if anyone had touched it or leaned on it. There was no evidence of a struggle or of someone being tattooed while sedated.

I forced my eyes back to the body on the floor. The man's shoes were the same quality as Phillip's and Colin's. Expensive. His black trousers also appeared to be of high quality, as did his leather belt. I flinched slightly when I looked at his torso. His skin was saggy, as if he'd lost a lot of weight too quickly and his skin hadn't had time to keep up. He was also very pale, as if he hadn't been in the sun for a few years.

I glanced at his face. I estimated him to be in his late fifties, early sixties. Again, I caught myself cataloguing less important information to avoid looking at his chest. I touched my little finger to my thumb and stepped closer.

Down the centre of his chest was a healed scar that indicated heart surgery. The branches and leaves from the tattoo on the left of his chest covered some of the scar. Carefully placed between the branches were roses. Four red roses.

The fourth victim.

I pressed my fingers harder together and leaned closer. In the centre of each rose was a hole. I didn't like to speculate, but wouldn't be surprised if the autopsy confirmed those to be bullet holes. This was indeed the same killer.

I straightened, countless questions swirling through my mind. "Did he also have a criminal history?"

"Oh, yes," Manny said from the door. "And then some."

"Who was he?" Colin asked.

"Claude Moreau."

Colin stiffened and turned to the door. "Claude Moreau of Moreau Exclusive Transport Services?"

"The one and only." Daniel was looking over Manny's

shoulder into the room. "He made sure the rich and famous got to their destinations in style."

Colin turned to me. "We're talking about private jets, armoured limousines and luxury yachts. Nothing is too outrageous for his clients."

"What kinds of crime was he involved in?"

"The usual," Daniel said. "He's been convicted of fraud and tax evasion, but investigated for all kinds of other crimes. Extortion, bribery, punching a politician in his manly parts and a few others."

"More similarities." And more differences between Serge Valois, Benoît Faure, this Claude Moreau and Léon Blanc.

"Three out of the four victims have criminal backgrounds." Daniel scratched the back of his head. "Could it be some vigilante handing out his own form of justice? Someone who wants to get rid of all the leaders of the criminal underworld?"

"Would you classify Valois, Faure and Moreau as organised crime leaders?" I didn't care for any of his other speculation. This was more important.

"Definitely."

"Mind you." Manny leaned against the door, his expression thoughtful. "The last few years these guys have been very quiet. Or am I just out of the loop?"

"No, you're right," Daniel said. "Pink has been checking them out and he's also surprised that those three have not been visibly active in the last seven or eight years."

"But why has Faure been under investigation?" I still hadn't had time to look through that case file.

"The Paris Police Prefecture opened a cold case squad and

his was one of the cases they reopened. It was not for any new crimes. Those were crimes they couldn't pin on... prosecute him for nine years ago. I suppose some rookie detective thought it would be cool to take down a renowned mobster."

I stepped away from the body and took my smartphone from my handbag. Two swipes and one ring later, Francine answered. "Hey, girlfriend."

"Did Dion Gravois write an article about Claude Moreau?"

"Who are you speaking to, Doc?" Manny took a step into the room, but stopped when I took a step back. "Supermodel?"

I nodded.

"Put her on speakerphone, love." Colin sat down on the sofa.

I did as he suggested and held the phone in front of me. "You're on speakerphone, Francine. Manny, Daniel, Colin and I are here."

"Hello, one and all!"

"Was there an article on Claude Moreau?" I asked again.

"Yes. I just found it hidden on Gravois' blog. Why he would hide such a delicious exposé, I have no idea."

"What do you mean it was hidden?" I asked.

"The other articles were published on his main page with links all over the place. He linked them to his Facebook page, his Twitter feed and a few other places. Not this article. He didn't publish it on his main page, but put it in a subpage where it was quite hard to find."

"Why would he do that?" Daniel asked.

"I intend to ask him that." Manny looked at his watch. "He should be at Rousseau & Rousseau in another hour. That bloody journalist has a lot to answer for."

I agreed. I was curious about this man who had written such well-researched articles. As with the beginning of all new cases, I felt the frustration of having an overwhelming influx of information with little to connect it. I tilted the phone towards me. "Francine, we need to go through the hotel security footage to see who entered this room."

"I already requested the videos," Daniel said. "This hotel only has cameras in the foyer and over the outer doors."

"And I've requested the videos of the hotels where Valois and Faure were murdered." Manny leaned towards the phone. "You should already have received those, supermodel."

"Not yet, handsome. Did they send it to my email address?"

"No, my address. But I know you snoop around all the time, so I'm surprised you haven't seen it yet."

"I don't snoop." Her tone was a pitch higher. "I filter."

"Call it what you will. Make sure you do your thing with those videos. Maybe we can catch a break. If one person appears on all three videos, we have a lead."

"I'll get right on that. Any more questions?"

I looked at the men. They shook their heads. "Not now, Francine."

"Genevieve, can you take me off speakerphone for a sec? I want to talk to you."

I frowned at the device in my hand, tapped the small

speakerphone icon and lifted the phone to my ear. "What's wrong?"

"I spoke to Nikki just now. She sounds weird."

"Explain 'weird'." To me, Nikki often sounded strange, but that was when she was being her typical self.

"I don't know. I'm worried about her. Is she handling the breakup okay?"

I wished I could see Francine's expression. I knew there was a lot more behind her questions, but couldn't determine what without reading her nonverbal cues. "What is really your concern? Do you still feel guilty?"

She groaned loudly. "It feels like I stole someone's Christmas."

"That's not possible. You can't steal a religious holiday." I turned away from the men. Their expressions were distracting.

"It means that I feel really, really, really, really bad for causing her break-up."

"You didn't cause it." I took a moment to organise my thoughts. Nikki was usually the one who needed reassurance from me. It appeared that the earlier comfort Francine had drawn from Colin's words no longer alleviated her guilt. I sighed. Reassurance meant repetition. I greatly disliked repeating myself. But I valued my friendship with Francine more. "Nikki suspected something was wrong in her relationship with that man. She wanted... maybe needed confirmation from us. That gave her the confidence to end it. Stop feeling guilty. It's an unproductive emotion and you have a lot of research to do at the moment."

The men behind me snorted and Francine made a sound that sounded like a combination between a cough and laugh. "Yes, ma'am. I'll get back to work this very moment."

"We've been friends for three years, Francine. You don't need to call me ma'am." I paused. "You can call me Doctor."

Her laughter over the phone was as loud as the men's. Three months ago, she'd also responded to a strongly worded request of mine by calling me ma'am. It had bothered me and Colin had explained the reference. He'd also suggested the retort that was now causing everyone mirth.

"Ooh. When Vin comes back from getting info on the other owners of the 3D printers, I'm totally telling him. And Nikki. She'll love it." Francine sighed happily. "That was the best ever. I can't believe you made a joke."

"It wasn't my joke. Colin suggested it."

"Don't care. It was great." She sighed again. "So funny. Okay. I'm getting back to work now. Bye-bye, my favourite best friend."

I ended the call and turned back to the room. The dichotomy of the situation was disconcerting. To my left on the floor was a dead man, murdered by a serial killer for reasons unknown. Next to and in front of me were three men, their expressions relaxed from laughter. I glanced back at the body. It was hard to enjoy the one moment in my life I had managed to entertain people and make them feel better by telling a joke. "I want to leave."

"You've seen all you needed to, Doc?" Manny stepped into the hallway.

"I have." I didn't consider our trip to the hotel a waste of time, but the lack of evidence of a struggle or insight into

Claude Moreau's personal life made it less useful than being in Léon Blanc's house. More time spent here would be imprudent. I would be more productive reading other articles on Dion Gravois' blog before he came in to be interviewed.

Chapter TEN

Dion Gravois was a tall man. Even taller than Vinnie, but
without the muscle mass. He was sitting in the conference
room chatting to Phillip about insurance fraud and how
prevalent it was in all sectors of the industry. He tried to
maintain an appearance of confidence and relaxation. He
wasn't successful.

For the fourth time since I'd joined them, Dion pushed
both hands down his thighs as if to smooth his brown
trousers. People only did that when they needed to soothe,
calm or comfort themselves. His chequered shirt and wire-
rimmed glasses added to his scholarly look.

I'd been busy reading one of his articles when he'd arrived.
The in-depth research he'd done on the strategic appointment
of board members to a pharmaceutical company with
government ties had interested me and I'd chosen to finish
reading it before joining Phillip and Manny in the conference
room. Francine had put the feed of the conference room
security cameras on one of my monitors and I'd seen Manny
slumping in the chair to Phillip's left. He didn't say anything,
appearing bored.

Phillip, as always, was the perfect host. He'd put Dion at
ease within the first few minutes and had kept the younger
man engaged in conversation. By the time I'd joined them,

I'd been able to establish a baseline for Dion's nonverbal cues merely from catching glimpses of their conversation on the monitor.

"But someone needs to hold those people accountable." Dion pushed his glasses up the bridge of his nose. "The affluent get away with too much too easily."

"I fully agree with you," Phillip said. "That is why I have two dedicated teams working daily to make sure all claims are legitimate."

Dion looked around the conference room, trying to be casual. But I saw his interest in the original masterpieces hanging on the walls. His casual inspection stopped briefly on each one as if cataloguing them. "Two teams. Isn't that overkill?"

"Maybe, but I can't risk the reputation of my company by trying to cut corners." Phillip looked at me. "I've not once regretted employing any of my investigators."

Dion's gaze followed Phillip's. "I didn't know you were working for Rousseau & Rousseau."

"I'm not." I pressed my lips together to prevent myself from revealing my current employment status. Manny had repeated himself three times, telling me that he would decide when we would reveal the true purpose of Dion's visit and our roles in the investigation.

Dion's eyes narrowed. He glanced at Manny, then at Phillip. I saw the exact moment that he came to a decision. "Why am I here? I know you didn't invite me to write some exposé about insurance fraud."

"We invited you here to talk about the articles you've

written on your blog." Manny sounded indifferent. "You have quite a lot of impressive exposés there."

"Who are you?" Dion didn't look intimidated by Manny.

"Colonel Manfred Millard." Manny shrugged. "The same name I gave you when we met."

"You know that is not what I'm asking." Dion looked at me. "And why is a world-renowned nonverbal communications expert here? Are you going to check if I'm telling the truth?"

"I'm already doing that. So far you've been mostly truthful in everything you've said. Your pretence of—"

"Doc, not now." Manny shifted in his chair. "Gravois, tell us how you choose the tales you write about."

"They aren't tales, Colonel." Dion's *orbicularis oris* muscle tightened his lips. "These are investigative reports."

"Well, pardon me." Manny didn't look apologetic.

"We are truly interested in how you come to decide which story you're going to cover." Phillip leaned towards Dion, mirroring his body language. "Surely there are plenty of scandals that you can expose at any time. Including some insurance fraud."

"I will tell you about my selection process if you tell me why I should share anything with you. Who are you people? Are you investigating one of my reports?" Discomfort, concern, determination and relief all flashed over his face. "If you have credentials, you better show me now or I'm leaving."

Manny's expression softened ever so slightly with respect. He took his hand out of his trouser pocket and handed Dion a business card. "Phone any of your sources to verify me."

Dion turned the card over and studied it for a few seconds. "What about Doctor Lenard and Monsieur Rousseau?"

"Don't worry about them. Just phone and give them the details on that card." Manny straightened. "I recommend phoning the head of GIPN or the president's office. You can speak to Lucien Privott."

Dion's eyes widened. "President Godard's director of public relations?"

"The one and only." Manny's top lip curled. "He's expecting your call."

It took Dion a few seconds to come to a decision. He got up. "Please excuse me for a few minutes." He left the conference room, his phone already in his hand.

"What do you think, Doc?"

"About what?" I wished people would be more specific.

"About this journalist, missy."

"He didn't lie during his conversation with Phillip. But he is hiding something. He's also trying to appear relaxed, but he's not. He's worried."

"He bloody better be. We're looking at him for these murders."

Dion Gravois didn't look to me like a murderer, but I knew never to judge anyone by their appearance. From the short time I'd observed him, I hadn't noticed anything that could point to some form of psychopathy. He came across as a highly intelligent and neurotypical man who was suspicious of us. Under the circumstances, very normal.

Two minutes later, he returned to the conference room, looking even more suspicious. He sat down slowly, not making eye contact for a few seconds. When he looked up, he addressed me. "Can I rely on you to be honest with me?"

"Yes."

"Only to some extent." Manny gave me a warning look. "None of us can share sensitive information with you."

"I understand." He looked at me again. "Why am I here?"

"You wrote articles about Serge Valois, Benoît Faure and Claude Moreau. We need to know more about that."

He closed his eyes, his head falling back. Relief. "I don't know who you people really are. All my sources told me is that I should give you my full co-operation, that you are the best in your field. I don't even know what field this is. I'm just glad someone is looking into this."

"What is 'this'?" Manny asked.

"When Serge Valois was murdered three days after I published the article, I put it down to bad luck. As a matter of fact, I only learned about his death two weeks after he'd been found in that hotel. The police seemed relieved that a criminal was off the streets and didn't make much of an effort to investigate. For some reason they'd also managed to keep his death low-key." He took his glasses off, rubbed the bridge of his nose and carefully put his glasses back. "But the second murder? Benoît Faure? That was when I knew something was off. Three days after my article, he lands up dead in a hotel room. That's too many coincidences in my world. I really don't want to ask, but is Claude Moreau also dead?"

"Yes." I took note of the deep regret settling around his eyes and mouth. "Why are you feeling guilty?"

"Did you kill them?" Manny's tone was confrontational, his gaze piercing.

"Maybe." Dion took his glasses off again and rubbed his eyes. "I don't know."

"How can you not know if you killed someone?" It didn't make sense. "Were you drugged? Do you have memory loss?"

His laugh held no humour. "No. That's not what I mean. I don't know if my articles are the reason these men are dead. I didn't kill them. Not with my own hands."

"Did you order their murders?" Manny asked.

"No." Dion shook his head. "No. I would never kill anyone. My whole life's work has been to expose people who prey on the weak. People who get away with myriad crimes. I want to hurt them, but not physically. I want them to feel, to understand on a financial and reputation level the damage they've done to their victims. But to kill them? Never."

"He's telling the truth." There had been no deception markers in his nonverbal cues, only deep concern.

"Now tell us how the bleeding hell you got to write about those three criminals."

"Like every good journalist, I have a Tor email account."

"Again with that bloody dark net, deep web, Tor business." Manny frowned. "Do you advertise your account to everyone?"

"Not exactly. Sometimes I receive information that could lead to a good investigative report. That would be when I give this email address to my sources. They can email me anonymously and I can get as much information as I need."

"So, where would I get your Tor email address?"

"It's hidden a few steps into my blog. My main contact page gives my normal email address. There is small print at the bottom of that page with a link that will give you my Tor email address. I don't want that inbox clogged up with hate mail, so I made it hard to see."

"Do you get a lot of hate mail?" Manny's question was interesting, but I didn't know if it was pertinent.

"Like you wouldn't believe. People would stand behind a politician even when the evidence is clear that he's a paedophile, or a clergyman who's involved in an underground gambling ring. Those supporters love to send me all kinds of threats. I've even received a few offers to pray for my soul."

The hate mail might be an avenue to explore, but I didn't consider it useful information at the moment. "Do you know who sent you the email about Valois, Faure and Moreau?"

"No." Dion shook his head. "I don't often get emails to my Tor address. So when I got that email, I was delighted and perplexed. It was cryptic to the point where I almost didn't take it seriously."

"Cryptic how?" Phillip asked.

"It gave me a link to a YouTube recording of an opera and told me to install an extension to my Chrome browser and watch the opera. If I took action, they would send me more." He cleaned his glasses and put them back. He was hiding something. "I have a special computer I use for these kind of things. It has no connection to my everyday work in case someone tries to hack my life. Anyway. I installed the extension and watched the first ten minutes of the opera. Nothing happened. I was in the middle of another report and decided to shelve this."

"What opera?" This was peculiar. I was most intrigued.

"Verdi's *Il trovatore*." Dion winced. "I'm not a big opera

fan. Those ten minutes were bad enough. I didn't want to sit through more than two hours of melodramatic music in the hopes of learning something. I just put it down to some idiot wanting to infect my computer with a virus."

"Was there a virus attached?"

"No. I had it checked from all sides and the extension is fine. The YouTube video is a normal video, nothing fancy."

"So when did you watch it?"

"After I finished the report I'd been working on. I hadn't heard anything else from this mysterious person, but was curious if there was something after the ten minutes. Needless to say, there was. A treasure trove of information." His expression lightened the same way Francine's did when she was talking about a new scandal in the news. "As the opera continued, subtitles appeared with facts about Serge Valois' business dealings and personal life. There were links to a Tor account that held printable files to support all these claims. I checked all of them and the ones I could verify all proved to be true. Can you imagine my utter joy? An exposé on the notorious crime lord Serge Valois was handed to me on a platter.

"I decided to break it up in three parts and published it like that. The first part promised more to be delivered the next day. It is a great marketing strategy. By the time I published the third part I had over eight hundred thousand hits in one day."

"Explain hits." Surely he didn't mean physical.

"Visits to my blog. I can see how many people view my blog or view one article. It makes it easy to see which articles are successful and which not." Regret and shame were visible around his eyes and mouth. "I was so excited about the spike in visitors. So when I got the next email with a link to a YouTube video, I immediately watched that opera."

"What opera?"

He looked up and left. Remembering. "Verdi's *Falstaff*."

"Were all the operas Verdi?"

"Yes. They're not too hard to listen to once I got used to it." He pushed his glasses up his nose. "So I watched the opera and lo and behold, loads of dirt on Benoît Faure. I immediately got to work on that article."

"Before you continue." I held up my hand. "What happened after you published the three articles on Serge Valois?"

"I got a lot of mail congratulating me on outing a very bad man. I also got a few threats, but I didn't pay attention to those. After years of receiving threats, I've learned which ones to take seriously. I did, however, set up an alert for any news about Valois. It didn't surprise me when the police announced an investigation the day after my third article. But then I received the next opera and I didn't check again what happened with Valois.

"It was a few days before I published the first article on Faure that I checked my alerts and saw that Valois had been murdered. Like I said before, I didn't really make much of it." He lowered his chin. Shame. "The thought did cross my mind that he got his just deserts."

"But you didn't think it was connected to your article?" Manny asked.

"To some extent, I suppose I did. Maybe one of the many people he had wronged in the past had decided to get revenge. But I didn't think further than that. I should've. I'm much smarter than this."

"When did you realise that there was a connection?" I asked.

"Like with the first three articles, I also set up an alert when I published the articles on Faure. I checked the news more carefully and knew something was very wrong when, three days after the last article was published, Faure was found dead in a hotel room."

"Then why did you publish the article on Moreau?" It didn't make sense to me.

"I didn't have much of a choice." He swallowed and pushed his hands down his thighs. Twice. "The day after I published the last article on Faure, I got another email with a link to another opera. I didn't want to alert whoever was sending me the emails that I suspected something was wrong, so I told them that I was busy working on an article about a crooked politician and would get to the opera later. Almost immediately, I received a reply saying that I had better publish an article about Moreau or I could become the next news story."

"Why did you take this threat seriously?"

Dion crossed his arms and leaned back in his chair. "I really don't want to tell you."

"But you are going to." I saw it in his expression.

"Dammit. Yes." Again he rubbed his thighs. "These arseholes did hack my system. But not through the Chrome browser extension. I don't know how they got in, but they did. They knew the names of all the sources to three of the exposés I'd written. If they revealed those names, the people who had risked their lives, their livelihoods to help me would lose everything. I didn't know what to do."

"And what is the death of a known criminal weighed against the life of a whistleblower?" I saw the evidence of that hard choice on his face. "You chose to protect your sources."

"And caused the death of another human being." He shook his head. "I never set out to have this result."

"Then why didn't you report it?"

"Their threat included a detailed report of my internet use, my phone calls and my whereabouts. They've been watching me and said they would reveal my sources the moment they suspected I was speaking to the authorities." He looked around the room. "That is why I'm here. A visit to an insurance company wouldn't raise any red flags."

I studied him. "You suspected we wanted to talk to you about the deaths."

"Honestly? I didn't know what to expect. Or suspect. But I hoped that was why I was invited here. Someone needs to investigate this."

"There's an urgency in your nonverbal cues that leads me to believe you have more information."

"Spill it, Gravois." Manny leaned forward. "What else have you got?"

"First tell me what you have."

"Why?" I asked just as Manny's scowl intensified.

Dion pushed his glasses up. "Do you think the murderer is escalating?"

"Do you know who this murderer is?" I countered.

"No." He turned to fully face me. "See the truth, Doctor

Lenard. I don't know who this person or these people are. And I really need some answers from you."

I was satisfied with what I saw. "I do see an escalation in the murders. Thirteen days passed between the first and second murder, seven between the second and the third and only one day between the third and fourth murder. So yes, something has triggered an escalation."

"Wait." Dion sat up, his eyes wide. "Four murders? I only wrote articles about Valois, Faure and Moreau. Who's the fourth person? I don't know anything about this."

"Doc?"

"He's being truthful." I wasn't surprised. Nothing in his behaviour so far indicated that he was in any way complicit in these crimes. I looked at Dion. "Léon Blanc was murdered some time in the early hours of yesterday morning."

"Léon Blanc? The director at the Opéra National du Rhin? What does he have to do with any of this?"

"We would also like to know that." Manny relaxed back in his chair. "What do you know about him?"

"Not much. A few of my investigations into the high-flyers who laundered money set me on the trail of their donations. Most people trying to hide money donate to charities to divert attention. Of course I checked out all the charities and even exposed one or two as fraudulent, only there to wash blood money. Anyway, the opera house came up a few times as the recipient of donations."

"Not Léon Blanc?"

"No. I've not seen any donations made to him personally. I only know his name because I checked out the management board and he's the director. Why? What do you know?"

"Not enough." Manny was truthful in his answer, even though it wasn't a direct answer to Dion's question.

I'd been observing the tall man and something was bothering me. "Why did you ask me if the murderer is escalating?"

"Like you said, the murders have been closer together."

I stared at him. "Do not insult me by lying, Monsieur Gravois. I will see each untruth. Why did you ask?"

He closed his eyes and fiddled with his glasses. "After my first article, I received the next opera two days later. After the second article, I received the opera the next day. I didn't reply to that email immediately. I first wanted to see if there was any news about Faure."

"Then you read he was murdered and you refused to write about Moreau."

"Well, we know how that turned out. I wrote about Moreau and published all three instalments three days ago. I thought hiding them in one of my sub-pages might help, but, well, we know how that turned out too. An hour after I published, I got an email with more YouTube links."

"Links?" I tilted my head. "Plural?"

"Yes."

"How many operas do you now have?"

"In total, I have ten."

"Have you watched them all?"

"No." He looked away and shook his head. "I don't want to. I don't want to write another article and cause another man's death."

"What about your sources?" I asked.

"I don't know." The pain of his internal conflict was in the lines around his mouth and eyes. "I'm hoping you can solve this before anything happens to them. Before this person or persons has the chance to hurt anyone else."

"Will you give us full access to your accounts? Your email? Your computer?" I knew Francine would force her way into all of these without his permission, but I would prefer to have his agreement to go through his secrets.

He shook his head and looked at the ceiling. "I can't do that. You will see all my sources. I can't risk that."

"What did your contacts tell you about me when you phoned them?" Manny asked.

"That you are discreet and that I can trust you. Why else do you think I've told you everything I know?"

"Do you trust your contacts?"

"Completely." There was no hesitation in his answer. I wondered who he'd phoned.

"Then give us access."

Again he shook his head. This time with less conviction. "I have to think about it."

"You can't take too much time weighing up your options, Gravois. If there's been only one day between two murders, who knows what will happen tonight?"

"Technically, there were eight days between two murders." I ignored Manny's glare. "I don't believe Léon Blanc's murder was planned. I think it was a crime of opportunity or passion. It lacks the same level of planning that went into the other three murders."

"The three murders are connected to my articles." Dion frowned. "Then where does Léon Blanc fit in?"

"I don't know that yet." Frustration made my tone harsh.

"I run a multimillion-euro business, Dion." Phillip's calm confidence lowered the tension in the room. "And I trust these people with every single cent. I've spent my life building a reputation of honesty and above-board business dealings. I trust them with my reputation. As a matter of fact, I trust them with my life. I can give you my personal and professional guarantee that your sources and all your personal data will be safe in their hands."

"I don't know." Dion still wavered, but I saw his desire to trust Phillip's statement. "Give me a few hours to make a few more calls and think about this."

"We can do that." Phillip looked at Manny. "We will do that."

"I've been told that you have a top-level hacker on your team. Please wait until I've made my decision before you gain unlawful access to my life."

"I can live with that." Manny glanced up at the camera in the corner of the conference room. I wouldn't be surprised if Francine had been trying again to hack Dion's blog while we'd been talking. Manny's look became pointed as he addressed the camera. "We won't hack or snoop. Not tonight."

Dion glanced at the camera and grunted. "You people are as bad as all the other Big Brother-types."

"No, sir." Phillip's shoulders stiffened. "The security you will see in and around Rousseau & Rousseau is for our, and now your, protection."

A half smile pulled at one corner of Dion's mouth. "I'm now under your protection, am I?"

"Yes." Manny's answer was immediate and true. "You continue to co-operate and we will do right by you."

Dion got up. "My experience has taught me that I should never trust such statements. For everything there is a price and usually that price is much higher than initially thought. Yet I have this ridiculous gut feeling that I should trust you."

"What you call a gut feeling is a combination of reasoning, observation, life experience and expected outcome." I truly didn't like people referring to an organ when they were making decisions. "If this feeling has served you well in the past, you would be wise to heed it."

Dion's smile was genuine. "I like you, Doctor Lenard."

I didn't know how to respond to that. I didn't know him well enough to return the sentiment. So I remained silent. That caused his smile to widen. He nodded his farewell and left.

Manny was asking me questions, but I was already replaying everything Dion had told us in my mind. If there were ten operas to watch, I would've liked to avoid waiting even another hour to start watching them.

I didn't have a choice. Dion Gravois needed to assure himself that he was making the right decision by allowing us into his digital world. Until then, I needed to go over the evidence and data we already had, do more research on the current murder victims and read more of the articles on Dion's blog.

Chapter ELEVEN

"Printing textured copies of masterpieces?" Roland Gagneux, mechanical engineering professor and vice-head of the engineering department at the University of Strasbourg, inhaled sharply, his cheeks reddening in excitement. "Man, I would love that."

I looked around Professor Gagneux's office. Like most offices given to professors, his was spacious. There was a front area which most other professors used for their receptionists. The second room could have been his office. It wasn't. This space in no way resembled an office.

It reminded me of the garage I had seen when I'd walked past the television three nights ago. Vinnie and Nikki had been watching some horror show about people cleaning out their homes after years of hoarding. It had taken quiet time in my bedroom and mentally writing three pages of Mozart's Sonata in C major to relax my throat muscles and prevent the panic that had been surfacing.

Since entering this office, in what felt like the aftermath of a grade-four tornado, I'd already mentally rewritten those three pages. Now I was writing Mozart's String Quartet No. 1 in G major in order to stay calm while surrounded by such utter chaos.

Despite most people fitting into a stereotype, there were always exceptions. Professor Roland Gagneux was one. Nothing about the man communicated academia. His jeans were old, torn and thin over his thighs from years of wearing. His hands were calloused, ungroomed and the skin stained like the hands of mechanics or carpenters who used wood stain to treat the timber.

Colin adjusted his bowtie. "If I may be so bold as to ask, what have you printed with your 3D printer?"

I hated when Colin was in disguise. It made it hard to concentrate on the discussion when I was constantly concerned about revealing his true identity. Today he was dressed as Professor John Dryden, a persona he used whenever he was visiting the University of Strasbourg. This disguise had taken him twenty-seven minutes to perfect. Leaning heavily on his cane, Colin now looked like a retired gentleman of means.

"Oh, man, we printed all kinds of shi… oh, sorry, Doctor Lenard." Professor Gagneux's smile was apologetic. "Um. We've printed a lot of stuff. Let me think. Last week we scanned and printed all the parts of a jet's fuel system. Two of the parts were a bit wonky, but we fixed it and got it to work. Together with the medical faculty we've also printed and stress-tested a spine implant. Thirteen hours later, it was still functioning as good as new."

I stopped listening to the long list of things his department had printed and focused on his nonverbal cues. Some people had more expressive faces than others. Professor Gagneux's face was on the far end of the scale. I could see every emotion, every thought being processed in his mind.

When Colin had insisted we visit Professor Gagneux before we went to the office this morning, I had been most displeased. Again my routine was being upended. Watching the uncensored emotions flit across the professor's face made me glad that I had conceded to Colin's entreaty. This man was a fascinating and entertaining case study.

At breakfast this morning, Vinnie had confirmed that Antonin and Marcelle indeed both had 3D printers able to produce passable reproductions of masterpieces. But Gunter had been right. Neither was printing art. Antonin was printing guns and Marcelle was trying to get into the legitimate production of car parts. Colin had immediately gone into our bedroom and started putting on his Professor John Dryden disguise while convincing me that we simply had to go to the university.

Once I'd conceded, he'd made a phone call, grabbed his jacket and cane and hobbled to the front door. We'd arrived at the university to Professor Gagneux's enthusiastic welcome. It had taken mere minutes to realise that the person Colin had called must have given Professor Gagneux the impression that the fake Professor John Dryden was interested in donating generously to the engineering department. I loathed deception.

"We do great work here, Professor Dryden." Roland Gagneux's sincerity increased the discomfort I felt with Colin's disguise. "I would be honoured if you and Doctor Lenard would spend a few hours with us in our workshop. We're getting the printer back from the medical department today, so we can start playing around with it again."

"Our time is unfortunately already spoken for, Profe—"

"Oh, please. Just call me Roland. I've never felt like a professor."

Colin's smile was slightly obscured by the ageing makeup he'd used, but it was genuine. "Thank you, Roland. We really would've loved spending more time with you and your students, but we have to leave."

"Such a pity." His disappointment was real. "If ever you have a few free hours, just give me a shout... no, don't even give me a shout. Just show up. You are welcome here any time of any day."

"That is exceedingly kind of you." Colin offered me the crook of his elbow. "Shall we, my dear?"

I glared at his arm and walked to the door. I was conflicted about what I wanted to escape more—the chaos of this room or Colin's deception. He made some apology for me which was immediately dismissed by Roland.

I didn't wait for Colin and walked through the gardens towards the SUV. I needed time to analyse my impressions, because those were all I had. The chaos and Colin's deception had so distracted me that I'd not registered any important information Roland might have shared. His nonverbal cues had been my only source of pleasure in the last thirty-seven minutes. It was also the only information I was leaving with.

I reached Colin's SUV a few minutes before him. He took his time, not once breaking the character he was playing. He walked slowly to the vehicle and pressed the remote control to unlock the doors. He even grunted as he sat down in the driver's seat and twisted to put his cane on the back seat. I got in and stiffly fastened my seatbelt.

When I looked up, Colin was studying me. "Will you forgive me?"

"It's not about forgiving you. It's about accepting that deception is part of who you are. I don't know how to do that. I don't know how to reconcile my trust in you with your exceptional deception skills."

"So you're not angry with me?" Concern filtered through his makeup.

"I'm distressed, not angry."

"Aw, Jenny." He touched my cheek, his movements no longer hindered by age. "I never meant to cause you any suffering."

"Why are you apologising now? You seemed accepting of my anger."

"Anger is okay. Distress is not. I don't like doing something that pisses you off, but it will happen from time to time. Causing you anxiety? No. I don't want that between us."

I pressed my little finger to my thumb and took a few deep breaths while organising my thoughts. "This is *my* challenge. You are already doing a lot to fit in with my preferences and behaviour. Learning how to deal with my cognitive dissonance about your deception versus my trust in you is for me to face. It will help me grow."

His expression softened. "Gods, I love you."

"I know." I didn't only see it in his nonverbal cues. I saw evidence of his emotional commitment to me in his everyday behaviour. I shifted in my seat. Speaking about other people's nonverbal cues and emotions came easily to me. Speaking about my own was never easy. Not even with

Colin. But I knew how important it was for him, so I inhaled slowly and placed the palm of my hand over his heart. "I love you too."

The *orbicularis oculi* muscles around his eyes relaxed even more, his *levator anguli oris* muscles turning the corners of his mouth into an affectionate smile. He pressed my hand hard against his chest. "Thank you."

For a few seconds we sat in silence, staring into each other's eyes. I didn't know what he was seeing, but what I saw reinforced my trust in this man. That thought led me back to the catalyst of this conversation. "I've been wondering if the person sending Dion the operas is indeed the killer or whether we should be looking for two different people."

Colin's eyebrows shot up, then he laughed. He lifted my hand and pressed a light kiss on my knuckles. "That's the thought that follows your love declaration?"

"Yes." I frowned and pulled my hand back. "Is that inappropriate?"

He chuckled again and started the SUV. "No, love. It's perfect. Now tell me why you're thinking we may be looking for more than one person."

I crossed my arms, realised what I was doing and carefully put my fists on my lap. "I don't have evidence."

"You have a feeling?" He was enjoying this. Too much.

"Don't be smug. You know I don't believe in your gut feelings. This is a suspicion my brain is alerting me to because my subconscious has registered something that has not yet filtered through to my consciousness." I needed Mozart. I needed to find out the rationale behind this impression. I reached for the radio and set it to play Mozart's Symphony No. 9 in C major.

Colin's smile was knowing. Whenever I listened to Mozart while we were travelling, he knew not to speak to me. We made the journey back to the team room in silence, only the sounds of the orchestra filling the vehicle and soothing my mind. Listening to any of Mozart's compositions was as if someone was easing the knots and tangles out of a bundle of strings until they hung unencumbered next to each other.

By the time the elevator doors opened to the team room, I was relaxed even though I hadn't found the reason I was suspecting more than one person involved in these crimes.

"I've been waiting for hours." Francine stood in front of the elevator doors, her hands on her hips. "Why did it take you so long to get back here? Have you heard anything from Dion Gravois? Has he given you access to his email yet?"

I staggered back into the elevator. "Dion Gravois doesn't have my phone number. He has Manny's."

"And I keep telling supermodel that," Manny said from his desk. "But as usual she doesn't listen to me."

Francine threw her hands in the air and stormed back to her desk. "I can't stand this waiting around. I'm a woman of action."

Colin took my hand and pulled me into the team room. "Let's hear what's bugging the woman of action."

I reluctantly followed him. Vinnie was lounging on the sofa in front of the windows, amusement evident on his face. I straightened my shoulders, took my hand out of Colin's and walked to Francine's desk. "Why are you more melodramatic than usual?"

"Because I'm not allowed to do what I want to." The glare she gave Manny communicated great displeasure. "That horrid man won't let me hack."

"This horrid man is trying to keep your law-breaking butt out of jail." Manny slumped into his chair. "I gave Gravois my word that we would give him time to decide whether he would legally give us access."

"But he's had the whole night and half of the morning already. When is he going to make up his mind?"

"When he's ready, supermodel." Manny looked at me. "I got Phillip to send him another email this morning, urging him to rush his decision."

"Smart move, Millard." Colin leaned against Francine's desk. "Phillip can persuade an Eskimo to buy ice if he sets his mind to it. And yes, Jenny, it's a silly metaphor."

I thought about it for two seconds and decided I didn't need to understand the metaphor. "Has he answered Phillip's email?"

"Nope." Manny scowled at Francine. "*She* made me phone Phillip five minutes ago to make sure. He told me again that he would immediately forward any correspondence he receives from Gravois."

"I still say we just hack our way in and get what we need." She tapped on her wristwatch. "It's not like we have loads of time before another murder."

"If we go by pattern, Dion would first have to publish another article before there would be another murder. And that murder would be three days after the article is published." I hoped Dion wouldn't give in to the pressure to protect his sources and publish another article.

"How long are you willing to wait?" Colin asked Manny.

"I say we give him until tomorrow morning." Manny glanced at Francine. "Then we can consider alternative options."

It was a pity. I had been looking forward to watching the operas, analysing the clues and looking for patterns. There was, however, still a lot of other research that had to be done. I looked at Francine. "Have you found any links between the finances of Léon Blanc and the other victims?"

"Nothing direct. The only commonality in their finances is the donations to the opera house. But that is from their businesses to the opera house's account. Not one personal donation was made. And no donation was made directly to Léon Blanc."

"What did you learn at the university, Doc?" Manny asked.

"Professor Roland Gagneux has no sense of order. It's inconceivable that anyone can work in such a cluttered environment." Renewed panic pushed against my chest at the memory of that office space.

"Did he say anything about the printing?" Manny looked at Colin. "About the forgeries?"

"He's aware of forged 3D renderings of masterpieces, but insisted that neither he nor anyone in his faculty would ever do something like that." Colin took off the jacket he wore when he pretended to be Professor John Dryden. "The 3D printer is under strict control. Only he and the heads of other faculties are allowed to use it. Otherwise it can only be used while under their supervision. That piece of equipment cost the university a pretty penny, so they're quite pedantic about who's working with it, when and where."

"Doc? What was your take on this Professor Gagneux?"

I blinked a few times. I'd missed most of what the professor had said, but I would've immediately registered conflicting nonverbal communication had there been any. "He was being truthful in everything he'd said."

"Everything?" Manny looked sceptical.

I thought back. "Whenever Colin asked him a direct question, his answer was honest. You must remember that people might be telling what they believe to be the truth even when it is not. He was not being deceptive, but his answers might not have been the truth. Unless we confirm everything he'd said, we won't know if he'd been misled about something."

"And when Frey didn't ask him a direct question?"

"He was honest in everything he presented."

"Jenny won't say it, but I will." Colin smiled at me. "Roland Gagneux is extremely smart, but he comes across as the son of a mechanic when he's actually the son of a judge."

"The dude's dad's a judge?" Vinnie asked. "That must suck."

"Yup. His father discouraged him from asking the university for the 3D printer because so many legal cases were pending. This technology is still new and there hasn't been much precedent set for scanning and printing parts for a car and selling it. Printing guns is still not illegal, but the gray area is vast and his father was worried that some student might print something that could land Roland on the wrong side of a lawsuit."

I couldn't recall that fragment of the conversation at all. I took a deep breath and reminded myself that Colin was astute not only at reading people, but also understanding all the subtle nuances of the conversation. He would've caught anything worth pursuing further.

"So, getting dressed up all pretty was a colossal waste of time?" Manny lifted an eyebrow while looking at Colin's outfit.

"You're just jealous that I will still be handsome when I'm old while you're just… well, you just look old." Colin's laughter joined Vinnie's when Manny pushed himself out of his chair. "You're too easy, Millard. And no, I don't think it was a waste of time. Roland will be a good contact to have if we need more information."

"My life was so much easier before I started working with a bunch of criminals," Manny grumbled as he sat down again. "Tell them what you unearthed about Brun, supermodel."

"Oh, yes!" Francine perked up. "Since I'm not allowed to get into the good stuff, I went looking into Arnaud Brun's history. That bastard needs to be back behind bars."

"Obviously you don't know where he is, else Manny would've been there to arrest him." I agreed with Francine that the escaped prisoner should be returned to prison. "What did you find out?"

"More background info. I was thinking we might look for him in places the authorities haven't searched yet. Maybe a childhood friend or family member."

"Your expression indicates he doesn't have any of those."

"Not that I could find." She wiggled her fingers in the air. "And you know how good these fingers are at searching out hiding places."

"He has no contact with anyone from his past? At all?" Colin asked.

"Nope. And I'm not surprised. Arnaud Brun grew up in the worst situation possible. He was born to a mixed-race mother in the immigrant area in Paris. Already his mother wasn't well received, so he would've been even more ostracised because of his heritage."

"How do you know this?" Was she speculating? She knew I didn't approve of that.

"I managed to find a few sealed police reports on him. He started breaking the law at quite a young age." The corners of her mouth turned down. "After reading more about Brun, I wonder if he isn't a product of his circumstances."

"What circumstances?"

"All this info is on the system, so you can go through it yourself. But the picture that I've managed to paint is that Brun grew up without a father in one of the poorest and most crime-ridden areas of Paris. For the first few years of his life, his mother worked in various offices as a receptionist, but then something happened. I don't know what, but she started receiving monthly welfare payments and I couldn't find any more employment records for her. Brun was around nine when that happened.

"The police reports I read about him don't make for happy reading. It seems like his mom got into drugs and he was pretty much left to his own devices. A few times he was caught stealing bread or medicine when he was sick. By some miracle he finished school and went directly to the army. In my very expert opinion, I think that he was already screwed up by the time he joined the army. They just gave him the tools to legally live out his love for violence."

"When did he leave the military?" Vinnie asked.

"The question you should ask is how." Francine paused the way she did when she wanted to add drama to her stories or theories. "I'll tell you how. He was in Gabon, deployed as part of the *mission de presence*, the troops who ensure the safety of French nationals in Gabon. It took his superiors months before they discovered that Brun and three others were hosting organised fights between the locals for payment. These people were so desperate for money, brothers would fight brothers just to get a measly five euros.

"Some of France's peacekeeping forces already had such horrid reputations for raping and plundering around Africa that the army made this go away quietly by discharging him and the others. And before you ask, I did check out the other three. Two are dead, one by his own hand and the other in a skiing accident. The other one is living in Guadeloupe, retired on a Caribbean island."

"I rechecked the investigative reports that led to Arnaud Brun's conviction." Manny nodded at his computer. "He was very successful with his self-defence training and had a really good reputation. The police would never have suspected him if it hadn't been for the gym wristband they found in one of the victims' belongings."

"You're not telling the story right." Francine lifted her hand to stop Manny from talking. "I'll tell the rest of it. Five years ago, the police recovered the remains of a homeless man buried deep in the woods south of Strasbourg. The body was found by students. That weekend they decided to do some illegal camping and get high. Being young and stupid, and most likely already high, they didn't check the weather report. Nonstop rain spoiled their weekend and also washed away a layer of top soil. When they decided being wet wasn't much fun and hiked back to their cars, they literally fell over the decomposing body of this man. Instant sobriety."

"The investigators were good." Manny nodded slowly. "Bit by bit they discovered that Brun had been up to his old tricks. He would get homeless men to fight against each other. The winner would get a share of the pot for the night. The loser would be buried in the woods."

"All the fights ended in someone's death?" It was horrific.

"Yes. That's why that bastard needs to be back behind bars." The corners of Francine's mouth turned down. "And someone needs to throw the key far, far away."

The ringtone of Manny's smartphone sounded through the team room. Francine sat up, her eyes on him as he picked it up from his desk, swiped the screen and lifted it to his ear. "Millard. Yes?… Hmm… Hold on a sec, I'm putting you on speakerphone." Manny tapped the screen and put the phone on his desk. "Continue, Monsieur Travere."

"Oh. I'm on speakerphone." A melodious male voice cleared his throat. "Well, hello, everyone. This is Julien Travere. I'm *the* tenor at the Opéra National du Rhin. And please call me Julien."

I remembered the tall tenor we had interviewed in Léon Blanc's office the opera house. He had given us a performance then and I could hear in his voice he was giving another performance now.

"We remember, Julien." Manny's tone was polite, his expression not. "You said you had some information we might find useful?"

"Yes, indeed." A dramatic sigh reached us. "We deeply mourn Léon's death. We miss him every day."

"The information?" Manny sounded less polite.

"I've been thinking about the horrid way Léon died. I haven't had a good night's sleep since we heard the news." Another deep sigh, followed by another clearing of his throat. "During my sleepless nights, I thought about Léon's life. Then I remembered that a few weeks ago a rumour did the rounds in the opera house that Léon had a new romantic interest."

"Do you know who this was?" Manny asked.

"Sadly, no. But I thought it might help you. Maybe it was this person who killed Léon. I shudder to think that anyone would have wanted to hurt a man as noble as he was. *'De' corsi affanni compenso avrai, tutto il futuro ne ariderà.'*"

"'We shall make up for all our heartache, the future will smile upon us.'" I recalled the last time he'd quoted lyrics. "Is this also from an opera?"

"*La traviata.* Alfredo's words as Violetta fights for her life." Julien Travere paused. "Is that you speaking, Doctor Lenard? After you visited the opera house, we discovered that you were world-renowned in your field. It's such an honour to speak to you."

I desperately wanted to see his face. I wanted to determine if that last sentence was the true reason for this phone call. I wouldn't be surprised if he'd only phoned to speak to someone he considered famous. The affectation I heard in his voice and the pleasure when he was put on speakerphone confirmed my initial impression that he revelled in attention.

"Is there any more useful information you can give us about Monsieur Blanc's romantic interests?" I phrased my question carefully.

"Oh, how I wish I could give you more. I really want to see justice done." A deep inhale. "I've been through bad relationships, but never one where I feared for my life. I'm so lucky to have someone now who shares my dreams and who wants to see me live to my full potential."

"We're all happy for you." Manny didn't look happy. At all. "If you can think of any more information, please let me know."

Julien Travere started to answer, but Manny swiped the screen and ended the call.

"What a douche!" Francine stared open-mouthed at the phone on Manny's desk. "Did he really just phone to get us to ooh and aah over him?"

"He exhibits many symptoms of narcissistic personality disorder." I still wished I could've seen his face, but the short conversation had revealed a lot. "When we spoke to him, he showed a strong sense of entitlement and a grandiose sense of self-importance. Today's hint at his relationship was to feed his need for admiration and reveal his fantasies of ideal love. I suspect he also hoped we would admire his perspicacity in telling us about Léon Blanc's alleged new romantic interest."

"Yeah, that." Manny pushed the phone away from him. "What do you make of it, Doc? Think there's truth to it?"

I thought about what Julien Travere had said. "I don't

know about truth. What was telling was the lack of pronouns when he talked about this person. He didn't indicate whether it was a woman or a man."

"Oh, my God!" Francine clapped her hands. "You think Léon Blanc was a closet gay?"

"I don't think anything other than people will automatically say 'he' or 'she' unless they're hiding something."

Francine's computer pinged. She glanced at it once, then swung around to face it. "Ooh! Ooh! Dion sent you an email, handsome."

"And you're already opening it." Manny's tone was wry.

"Of course." She was quiet for a second, then her shoulders dropped. "He's sending us all the links to the operas and the extension we need to install to watch them. But he's still deciding about letting me into his accounts."

Chapter TWELVE

Rigoletto held the sack above his head, ready to throw it into the river when the tenor voice of the Duke stopped him. The sounds of *La donna è mobile* filled my viewing room. Spread across nine of my monitors was the stage of La Scala, the tenor gently putting the sack on the floor in front of him. I sat unmoving as Rigoletto opened it and found his gravely wounded daughter.

With amazing voice control, the soprano awoke briefly to beg Rigoletto to forgive her and the Duke, whom she continued to love despite his infidelity. She died in her father's arms and his final cries of agony were intensified by the full force of the orchestra.

I stopped the video and took a deep breath. Without exception, this had been the most rewarding part of any investigation I'd been part of until now. This was the third opera from Dion Gravois' list I'd watched and with each my mind had calmed more. It was not Mozart, but Verdi's mastering of the romantic opera was inspiring.

"Eight years ago I saw Anna Netrebko sing Gilda in La Scala." Phillip's voice held a measure of awe. I turned in my chair. He was standing by the doors. I hadn't heard him enter my viewing room. After fifteen minutes of watching the first opera, Vinnie had begged us to close the glass doors that separated my viewing room from the team room. It made my room soundproof, which meant no one in the team room would hear the wonderful music. Phillip stared at the monitors. "I think this is a recording of that performance. It was magnificent."

"I must admit that I haven't heard anyone equal Anna Netrebko's interpretation of this role." Colin's legs were stretched out in front of him, his posture and expression relaxed. He'd joined me not because of his interest in the case, but because he wanted to watch the operas. "Except maybe Maria Callas."

"Oh, yes." Phillip pulled the third chair away from my desk and sat down. "That woman had a voice straight from the heavens."

"A true gift." Colin nodded.

"So how many operas have you watched so far?" Phillip asked.

"*Rigoletto* is the third." I faced the monitors and looked at the final scene that I'd paused. At the bottom of the screen were two lines of text. I'd already noted everything down. "We've gathered an incredible amount of information."

"We decided not to watch the operas that Dion had already watched," Colin said. "The ones that gave him the info on Serge Valois, Benoît Faure and Claude Moreau. We've just watched operas about Émile Roche, Nicolas Denis and Stéphane Guillory."

The glass doors whooshed open. "Is it safe to come in?"

I frowned at Vinnie. "Why would you think there was any danger in here?"

"Danger to my eardrums, Jen-girl." Vinnie walked into the

room and glanced at the monitors. "Those people can separate bone from marrow with their voices."

"That is impossible." I registered the expression on his face. "You're making a joke."

"Kinda." He shrugged. "I really don't enjoy this music."

"I got the deets on the new people." Francine walked into my room, waving her tablet. "I've already put them on the system."

"Then I say we take this to the table." Vinnie turned to the door. "I made lunch."

I wanted to remain in my viewing room to watch the next opera. Not only to gather more information, but to surround myself with the beautiful sounds of Verdi's works.

"You need to take a break, Jenny. Stretch your legs, eat, let your brain breathe a bit." Colin got up and held out his hand. "Come."

I got up without taking his hand. "A brain doesn't breathe. The flow of oxygen to any organ is not termed breathing."

"Then your brain needs to have a flow of oxygen outside of this room." He winked at me. "And your stomach needs some of Vin's food."

My viewing room was on the far side of the open space. Manny's desk and Francine's computer station were a few feet from the glass doors to my room, giving them a view into my work space. Vinnie didn't have a desk. He spent most of his time in the team room sitting on the ugly sofa he'd placed in front of the window. The round table was on the other side of the desks. Manny was already sitting at the table, knife and fork in his hands.

"Hungry, old man?" Vinnie tried to make his smile mocking,

but he couldn't hide the pleasure seeping through.

"Just hurry up, criminal." Manny shook his cutlery. "The food's getting cold."

"It's already cold." Vinnie pointed at each dish. "My auntie Helena's pasta salad, a selection of cold cuts, a mixed bean salad that's a bit spicy and my auntie Teresa's curried carrot salad. She never told me where she got that recipe. It's definitely not a family tradition. Curry is not something she used often, but this was always my favourite."

"Everything is your favourite." Francine sat down next to Manny. "You really should put more cumin in the pasta salad, Vin."

"Don't start with me." Vinnie glared at her. "I'll ban you from my table."

"You don't own this table." Now that I was seated at the table, I was glad for the break. I was hungry. "Colin paid for it."

Colin had not only bought the building that housed our workspace, he'd also renovated it and furnished it to suit our needs. Vinnie's only contribution had been the unsightly sofa.

"Then I'll ban the spice-fiend from Colin's table."

The bickering continued until everyone's plates were overflowing with Vinnie's food. Manny was already halfway through his first helping. "Tell us what you got from the operas, Doc."

"*Rigoletto* revealed astonishing details about the life of Émile Roche, *Nabucco* about Nicolas Denis and *Otello* about Stéphane Guillory."

"Colin forwarded all the links and other details to me

while they were watching the operas and I've been doing my own digging." Francine pointed at the pasta salad with her fork. "Really great, Vin."

He narrowed his eyes. "What? No more spice suggestions?"

"Nope. This is really good."

He looked at her, then around the room. "Are you punking me?"

"The subtitles provided us with the information." I wanted to talk about this fascinating case, not listen to Francine and Vinnie's bantering. "After each revealing statement, there is a link that leads to a Tor website with photos, receipts or other tangible proof corroborating the allegations."

"We have evidence against all three of these men?" Manny put his knife and fork down. "Do you have any idea what this means?"

"They can be prosecuted." It was obvious.

"Not only that, Doc." Manny leaned back in his chair. "I have seen Émile Roche's name more times than I care to remember. Memos sent around all the law enforcement agencies, looking for evidence to nail this guy. Until a few years ago, he was considered the Don of the Dons."

"What does that mean?"

"All the other organised crime leaders looked to him as a role model."

I thought about this. "They followed his example? Was he the leader of leaders?"

"In a manner of speaking. There were rumours of crime bosses going to him for business advice, following his guidance on investment and getting their dirty money clean." Manny straightened and pulled the bean salad closer. "What did you find out about Émile Roche, Doc?"

"I have evidence that he bribed a government official to get a multimillion-euro construction contract for highway repairs in the west of France. There are two more bribery cases, two situations of gross intimidation and evidence that points to three offshore accounts that are not registered to any of his companies." I looked at Francine. "Did you get information on his background?"

"Did I ever." She tapped on her tablet lying next to her plate. "Émile Roche is sixty-nine, was born in Paris and moved to Strasbourg thirty-four years ago. He's been married for forty-three years to Margot and has three children. Two sons and a daughter."

"There was information about them in the opera." It had been during the second act. "Both sons are lawyers, the daughter an accountant. The subtitles were about the seven grandchildren's schools and that Émile Roche had donated to those private schools to ensure a place for his grandkids."

"Ooh, I peeked into Émile Roche's children's lives and saw the schools the grandkids are going to. Do you have any idea how much they're paying per year in tuition?" Francine's eyebrows were raised. "The price of a seven-week cruise with unlimited spa treatments."

"They are also some of the most prestigious private schools in France." My parents had sent me to one of these internationally renowned institutions. The school hadn't been able to cater for someone like me. After a few unsuccessful placements in other private schools, I'd been home-schooled. I looked at Manny. "You said that he had been known as the leader of leaders until a few years ago. What happened? Is he no longer respected?"

Manny's eyes widened. "That's a bloody good question, Doc. As far as I know, there hasn't been any shift in power, but I'll have to check with Daniel or the organised crime unit about this. What I do know is that I haven't seen his name or any of the other three's in the last six or seven years."

"The same as Claude Moreau." I looked at Francine. "Can you check the six names we have now and see when last they were mentioned in a police report?"

"Which six names, girlfriend?" She picked up her tablet.

"The three victims—Serge Valois, Benoît Faure and Claude Moreau—and the three opera names—Émile Roche, Nicolas Denis and Stéphane Guillory."

"Not the opera dude?" Vinnie asked.

"He's the anomaly. These six men all have connections to organised crime, Léon Blanc doesn't." I thought about this. "Francine, can you also check if the three men from the operas have connections to Léon Blanc or the Opéra National du Rhin?"

"Will do." She continued tapping with one hand while lifting a forkful of bean salad to her mouth. "It will take a few minutes."

It took twenty-five minutes. By then we'd finished eating and I wanted to go back to watching the next opera. Colin and I had had a good system while watching. I'd noted important details and my thoughts on a notepad, while Colin had put names, details and links on his laptop and sent the information in batches to Francine to verify. The next opera was *Don Carlo* and the beauty of the music in this work made me even more eager to return.

Colin had convinced me not to start watching because I would get lost in the music. His words. I'd conceded and agreed to have a cup of coffee while waiting for the results of Francine's search. She'd taken her tablet to her station and continued working on the two computers she had there.

I took the three music books that we'd found in Léon Blanc's home office safe and went into my viewing room. Colin was once again studying the paintings, giving me the opportunity to quietly page through the books. I sat down at my desk and put my coffee mug on a thick red felt coaster.

All three books were professionally bound, but consisted of only handwritten music sheets. I paged through the first book and didn't recognise any of the music. I had enough knowledge of classical music to be confused by the time I paged through the second book. None of the music made sense. It didn't fit in any of the typical classical music eras and simply didn't make sense at all.

There was no harmony between the music written in the treble clef and bass clef or the chords in the individual clefs. The rhythm was wrong and there was no musicality to any of it. Even the sometimes harsh and dissonant sounds of the modern era in classical music still had a format to them. This lacked all musical elements.

"You were right." Francine knocked on her desk to attract my attention. "Hey, girlfriend! You were right."

"Right about what?" I wondered if I should yet again ask everyone to be more specific in their communication. I put the music book down and walked to her desk.

Francine swivelled in her chair to face me. "All six of those crime bosses have donated to the Opéra National du Rhin. All of them through their companies, not one personal donation, and nothing to Léon Blanc's account. The opera director still looks as clean as a whistle."

"I've told you before whistles aren't clean. You shouldn't use that expression."

She smiled. "Léon Blanc still looks innocent of any wrongdoing."

"There's no bloody way he's clean." Manny got up from his desk and walked to Francine's. "Six different criminals donating to his opera house, three empty passports and all those diamonds? There has to be something. Find it, supermodel."

"Sir, yes, sir." She winked at him. "Want to hear about everyone's police files?"

"You want me to ask?"

"Beg." She pouted and fluttered her eyelashes. "I want you to beg."

"Supermodel."

She chuckled. "I've looked at all the databases we have access to and couldn't find any new cases filed against any of them. Except Benoît Faure. There is the reopening of Faure's cold-case file. That happened two years ago. And then the renewed interest after Dion's article. Further back than that I found that the Lille police prefecture opened an investigation into an aggravated assault charge against Nicolas Denis six years ago. Nothing since. For anybody. Have these men all gone into hiatus?"

After three years of working with Francine, I knew her behavioural patterns. "What else did you find?"

"I'm going have to start becoming unpredictable."

"It will require a lot of planning and effort to be unpredictable. Usually, people fall back into a pattern which means their unpredictability becomes predictable." I put my hand over my mouth. It was most vexing when a sentence would throw me off topic and onto another line of thought. "Your other findings?"

"I checked the info Colin sent me. The investments, the properties, Nicolas Denis' art collection, Stéphane Guillory's vintage car collection, Émile Roche's wine collection, it all checks out." She gave Manny a flirtatious look. "I snooped into their finances and couldn't find any questionable activity in their business or private accounts. It seems like they're living within their means with no red flags anywhere."

"Except the donation to the opera house."

"Except that, yes."

I started counting on my fingers. "These men are from different cities. They have different business interests. Their families don't share many similarities."

"Are we comparing?" Francine lifted her hand and copied me. "None of them have the same lawyers, but all of them have the best lawyers France has to offer. The same goes for accountants. They have not been criminally active in the last five years—at least not that any law enforcement agency is aware of. Want to know what I think?"

I closed my eyes and sighed. "Not really, but I know you will insist on telling me."

"See?" She looked at Manny. "I told you she loves my theories."

I bit down on my lips to prevent the denial from bursting forth.

"Stop torturing Doc." Manny lowered his brow. "I can still return the tickets to that ridiculous fashion show you want to go to."

"Spoilsport." She turned back to me. "My theory is that all these men were simultaneously abducted by aliens. The brain probing they underwent was similar to a religious experience and when they were returned, they changed their evil ways."

Not bothering to respond, I got up and walked to my viewing room. Aliens? If Francine was going to share an outrageous theory, she could do much better than resorting to fictitious abductions by extraterrestrial beings. I sat down and looked at the photo of Émile Roche on the far left monitor. This picture was taken at a charity function three years ago—allegedly two years after he'd stopped his criminal activities.

Evidence of a hard life was in the deep lines around his eyes and mouth. His light blue eyes were in contrast to his suntanned skin. His hair was cut short on the sides and a bit longer on top. He still had a full head of hair, the gray coming through strong on the sides. In this photo, his smile was genuine, his nonverbal cues relaxed. He was happy.

"Jenny?" Colin sat down next to me. "Francine apologised."

I glanced at Francine in the viewing room. She winked at me. I frowned. "You shouldn't apologise when you're not contrite."

"But I love aliens!"

I turned away from her and faced Colin. "I think the operas are a list."

"A list for what, Doc?" Manny walked into the room and stood behind Colin's chair.

"A murder list."

"Like a hit list?" Manny nodded. "I've been thinking the same. Someone is playing vigilante. They got these names and this info from God knows where and are now ridding the world of these men. The question is, what is the killer's motivation?"

"I think a more important question is who will be next." If this was indeed a hit list. "We need to watch the other operas so we can have more informed theories."

"Not now, love." Colin pointed at his watch. "It's twenty to six. If we watch another opera, we won't get out of here before nine. We—you—have been at it the whole day. Time to take a break."

I stared at his watch. It couldn't be this late. We'd just had lunch. I looked at the clock on my computer and confirmed that it was indeed twenty to six. "I don't want to stop now."

Colin's expression turned calculating. "You don't want to stop what? Investigating?"

"I don't trust you when your expression becomes devious. What are you planning?"

He chuckled. "The exhibition that Léon Blanc lent his art to is opening tonight and Sébastien sent us an invitation. I thought we would go. You know, interview some people and look at the art. It's a soft opening, so we won't even have to get changed. The gala event is the last night."

I leaned forward. "Your pupils dilated and more colour came into your face when you talked about the art. Your motivation is not the investigation. It's the art."

"Guilty." His smile was wide. "But if the thought of speaking to Sébastien gets you to join me, I'll consider this a win."

"Go, Doc." Manny walked to the door and stopped just outside my viewing room. "You said yourself that the pattern of murders shows escalation, but we don't know when the killer will strike next. Since Gravois is not writing another article, we have no way of knowing who the killer will target next. Each opera is what, two hours long? You still have another four to go through. Nah. Go to this exhibition and see if you learn something there. Then go home and sleep. Tomorrow will be time for more crazy singing."

Chapter THIRTEEN

I parked two cars away from Colin's SUV. Only when Colin had reminded me had I remembered he and Vinnie were meeting with the GIPN team tonight to challenge the fire department in a pool contest. We'd stopped at my apartment to pick up my car after leaving the office. I had no interest in pool and preferred to return home after visiting the exhibition.

My door opened the moment I turned off the engine. Vinnie was standing next to my car, tapping his foot. I got out and pressed the remote control to lock my car and turn on the alarm. "Why are you impatient?"

"I don't want to be here." Vinnie shook a fist at Colin, who was waiting for us by his vehicle. "He made me come to this shindig."

I looked at Vinnie's size. "It can't have been by physical force."

"Worse." Vinnie walked next to me as we made our way to Colin. "He threatened to pull out of the championship."

"I didn't know it was a championship. Is this an organised competition with prizes?"

"Only in Vin's dreams, love." Colin took my hand and kissed my temple. "It's a friendly competition between two departments."

"Friendly, my ass." Vinnie rolled his shoulders. "This is a match to the death."

I gasped and Colin pulled me closer. "He's being hyperbolic in a very crude way, love. Vin, you should know better."

"Sorry, Jen-girl." He didn't appear contrite. "I just really want to kick those losers' butts."

"How is that related to your reluctance to be here?"

"Reluctance? Hah. Try evasion." His nose crinkled. "I'm not the type to stand around galleries writing poetry about a drop of paint on a canvas."

"This is an exhibition of nineteenth-century art, not modern art. I doubt there will be anything resembling the art you've just described."

Vinnie grumbled under his breath, but I wasn't paying attention. We'd arrived at the entrance of the gallery. The Gerome Art Gallery was in the city centre and finding parking nearby was so unlikely that we'd decided beforehand to use the parking area usually utilised by office workers during the day. It was a block away from the gallery, but not known to people who didn't frequent this area.

People milled around on the wide pavement in front of the gallery. Some stood with wine glasses, others with small plates with *hors d'oeuvres*. This time of the season, daylight was fading, the sun hovering just above the horizon. The light from the gallery spilled over onto the pavement, together with the streetlights, creating a different atmosphere. More festive.

A few people stopped to stare at us as we neared the doors. Vinnie grabbed a glass of red wine from a passing waiter's tray and held it out to me. "Here you go, Jen-girl. I'm not going to be drinking this stuff."

"Neither am I." I leaned away from the glass of wine. "I don't know the level of hygiene maintained by this catering company."

"Vin, you might want to tone down your frown. And attitude." Colin took the glass of wine. "You're scaring the natives."

Vinnie chuckled and looked around. "I can pick my teeth with these puny people's bones."

"Ignore him, love." Colin steered me into the gallery. "Vin's not going to pick his teeth. Or use anybody's bones."

I followed him into the large open space. In the centre was a thin wall running the length of the room, serving no other purpose than to provide more hanging space. The wall didn't even go all the way to the back of the room. Every wall had careful lighting, showcasing paintings from Paul Cézanne, Camille Pissarro, Alfred Sisley and Pierre-Auguste Renoir. Those were the artists I recognised. I was sure there were many more represented on the walls.

I glanced behind me. Vinnie was still at the door, smiling at people who dared look at him. His smile wasn't genuine. Or friendly. I wasn't used to this behaviour. "Why is Vinnie being churlish?"

Colin inhaled to answer, then changed his mind. "What do you see, love?"

I took a moment to study Vinnie's nonverbal cues as well as those of the people around us. Those who were staring at Vinnie communicated interesting combinations of fear and curiosity with their expressions and body language. A few people stopped at the door and turned back to the street when they saw him. I took a mental step back and saw the reason. "Vinnie is dressed like someone in the armed forces and these people are all wearing designer clothes. His stature and the incorrect conclusions they are drawing are scaring them."

"He's having fun playing it up." Colin sighed. "And he's punishing me for bringing him."

"Then why did you?"

"I'm punishing *him*." Colin smiled when I frowned. "He volunteered me for this pool thing after I told him I wasn't keen on going."

I looked at him for a few seconds. "Yet you agreed because you don't want Vinnie to lose his standing with his GIPN friends."

He leaned in, kissed my cheek and turned to face the wall. "This Degas is a beautiful example of his obsession with the figure. He loved not only showing the various dress styles, but the many human forms."

"You're avoiding an emotional moment." I swallowed when I realised I shouldn't have verbalised my observation. Colin had avoided it because he didn't want to admit to or talk about the lengths he would go to for the people he cared for. I looked at the painting Colin was inspecting with unusual interest. "There's too much pink."

"A girl after my own heart," Vinnie said from behind me. "That's why she's my favourite. Not you, dude."

"Oh, put an *hors d'oeuvre* in it, Vin." Colin moved to the next painting. "Try to appreciate the beauty in this room."

"I only see old biddies. Apart from Jen-girl, there aren't

many beauties." He chuckled when Colin scratched his ear with his middle finger. "Aw, dude. Don't flirt with me like that. Not in front of your girl."

The corners of Colin's mouth twitched as he stepped to the next painting. When his muscle tension increased, I went and stood next to him. "What's wrong?"

"This painting."

"It looks like it should be in one of these old biddies' living rooms, together with their collection of stuffed poodles." Vinnie joined us, his bantering not as light-hearted as before. "Apart from that, what else is wrong, dude?"

Colin leaned closer, but the red cord in front of the wall kept him fifty centimetres away. He tilted his head a few times to look at the painting from different angles. When he straightened, his lips were in a thin line. "This Renoir is a forgery. A 3D-printed forgery."

"Please lower your voice."

We all turned to face the man who'd spoken behind us. Colin held out his hand in greeting. "Sébastien. Thank you for inviting us."

"You were rather insistent, Professor Dryden." He shook Colin's hand, but his expression communicated great distrust. "I asked around like you'd suggested. People at the university and the museums highly recommended you. An old you. A gentleman deep in his seventies."

Colin nodded. "My father. We share the same name, passion and education. He still has experience over me, but his eyes have been failing him lately and more frequently he's turned to me for confirmation on his work."

I pulled my hand from Colin's and stood closer to Vinnie.

The ease with which Colin changed roles was highly disconcerting. Such was his deception that Sébastien relaxed, the distrust being replaced with mere wariness. "Does that mean that your opinion of this painting can be trusted?"

"If you don't trust anything else about me, you can trust my word when it comes to art." Colin was completely truthful.

"This is not one of Dad's paintings." Sébastien's voice was lowered, concern pulling his brows together. "How naïve of me to think that someone only forged the Morisots."

"This is not your world, Sébastien. Your job is to help the sick. My job is to know all the various forms of art crimes. Don't be too hard on yourself." Colin mirrored Sébastien's posture and tone. "Do you know whose painting this is?"

"Not offhand. I can check if you want me to."

"Please. That would be a great help."

Sébastien took only a few steps before he returned. "Could you please have a look around the whole exhibition and make sure the other works are authentic? Especially the Manet that we're going to auction next week."

"It will be my pleasure." Again Colin was being truthful. He waited until Sébastien was too far to hear us and held out his hand to me. "I'm sorry, love. Will you walk with me?"

"Is this going to take long?" Vinnie followed us, not even looking at the art.

"Do you want to go sit in the car?" Colin's tone was different. Like that of a parent rebuking his child. The humour around Colin's eyes and Vinnie's chuckle alerted me to a jest I didn't comprehend.

"You're so going to owe me for this." Vinnie sighed heavily

and stopped next to us as Colin paused to inspect a landscape by Alfred Sisley. Typical of the era, the style made the meadows next to a body of water appear more tranquil. The woman in the foreground of the painting appeared as unrushed as the two people behind her.

"Each era in art has its own charm, but the impressionists really managed to make ordinary life look beautiful and soft."

"An illusion." I pointed at two tracks in the mud. "This painting doesn't depict the difficulty they must have had walking through the mud in a meadow during the spring season."

"That is part of the charm of the impressionist era. These artists were considered radicals by their peers. They broke all the rules set by the academics of that time. Instead of painting in a studio, they painted real-life scenes in the outdoors." Colin moved to the next painting. "This Morisot is a great example of the short, broken brushstrokes they used. This beautiful scene of the man in front of the yellow field shows how she used vibrant colours that were not mixed and not smoothly blended or shaded."

"Wait." Vinnie put one hand on his hip and stared at the painting. "Didn't you say this artist dudette Morisot was friends with Monet and Degas?"

"Somebody listened to the teacher. Give the boy a gold star." Colin chuckled at Vinnie's annoyed expression. "Yes, Vin. Morisot had a close friendship with many of her peers. Her sister was painted by Degas, and she married Eugène Manet, the brother of her good friend and colleague Édouard Manet. And she was good friends with Claude Monet."

"Huh. A Monet and a Manet."

"People often confuse the two artists. Especially since they painted in the same era."

"Wasn't it hard for chicks in those days to paint?" Vinnie gave one of his insincere smiles to the lady next to us, who frowned at his use of sexist terminology. "I mean, those days only men got to do this kind of work. Right?"

"She was not the only prominent female impressionist artist. Mary Cassatt was an American artist who lived in Paris. While there, she took part in four impressionist exhibitions. Breaking into the art world was always harder for women, but these ladies were so far ahead of their time, the critics had to take note." Colin's demeanour changed when he talked about art. He became more animated and had more colour in his cheeks. Of all my friends, he was the most self-contained. Francine never attempted to hide her emotions behind fake expressions and neither did Vinnie. Manny's deceptive nonverbal cues had a language of their own, easy to interpret. Colin's emotional experiences seldom surfaced higher than micro-expressions. Similar to Phillip, he seldom lost his temper or revealed his displeasure in anything more than a flash of emotion.

But when he talked about art or artists, he used his hands while describing the texture of the brushstrokes. His face, his entire body, relaxed as he got lost in his explanations. I understood that pleasure.

Colin's impassioned monologues were always entertaining. Unlike my explanations. My pleasure came from talking about details. It was easy for me to forget to take note of people's nonverbal cues when I got into the fine detail of a topic. Usually, I realised too late that my audience was bored and only listening out of politeness. That was why I appreciated Manny's impatient reminders to summarise.

We reached the Édouard Manet that was to be auctioned. Vinnie and I remained silent while Colin studied the painting of a couple in a rowboat from as many angles as he could while remaining outside the red cord. He straightened and pinched his chin. "I'm ninety percent sure this is authentic. Without a much closer look, I won't be completely convinced."

"Could it be printed?" I asked.

Colin shook his head. "Definitely not. If this is a forgery, it was done by hand."

"Can we go now?" Vinnie sighed again. "We've been here for hours."

"It's been twenty-five minutes." I frowned. "You're being purposely obstinate."

"I'm being purposely bored." Even his sighs were exaggerated.

"Jenny?" Colin was standing in front of an Armand Guillaumin painting.

I frowned again at Vinnie for distracting me and joined Colin. I recognised his expression. "Is this also a 3D-printed forgery?"

"Yes." He tilted his head and was quiet for another few seconds. "We should let Millard know."

Vinnie lost his fake boredom and took out his phone. "I'll do it outside. Away from these old biddy paintings and old biddy people. Annoying the old man will be much more fun than this."

"He actually likes art," Colin said as Vinnie walked out. It was fascinating to watch people stepping out of the way after only a peripheral glimpse of the large man walking towards them. The purpose and confidence in Vinnie's strides unconsciously registered with everyone and they reacted before they'd even seen Vinnie's outfit.

"Could we speak in private, please?" Sébastien was standing behind us, clutching a few sheets of paper in his hand.

"Lead the way." Colin frowned at the open concern on Sébastien's face. He took my hand and we walked to a back room. It was a small office with a medium-sized desk and a lot of paintings leaning against the wall.

Sébastien closed the door. "Is the Manet real?"

"I couldn't do a very close inspection without attracting attention, but from what I saw, I'm ninety percent sure the painting is the authentic Édouard Manet."

Sébastien sat down heavily in the only chair in the room. "What a relief. It took me months to get this fundraiser thing together. We desperately need a mobile X-ray unit and an infant ventilator. The hospital simply does not have the funds for both. We've spent a lot of money upgrading the computer system to centralise all the information. Another huge portion of this year's budget went to renovate the maternity ward. The last time anything was done there was in 1987. At least our ward was built in 2005. It's just our need for equipm... You don't need to know this."

"Maybe not." Colin's tone and empathetic expression were genuine. "But it helps us understand your circumstances better."

Sébastien gave Colin a half-smile. "Thanks. I'm just so relieved that we can go ahead with the auction. After this thing with my dad, I've arranged for extra security. I'm willing to spend that money to ensure the safety of these works."

"That was a wise decision." Colin nodded at the papers still clutched in Sébastien's hand. "Did you find the owner of the 3D-printed Renoir?"

"Yes, I did." He smoothed out the papers on the desk. "That painting belongs to Nicolas Denis."

"Why are you scared?" The nonverbal cues I was seeing on his face were more interesting than the revelation that this painting belonged to a man whose secrets had been revealed through an encrypted opera.

Sébastien's Adam's apple bobbed as he swallowed. "He was also one of my dad's good friends. I remember him visiting a few times during my childhood. They've been friends for years. The same as Serge Valois. What was my dad involved in? Has he somehow involved me? He was the one who arranged for many of these paintings to be loaned to the gallery for this fundraiser."

"Take a deep breath." Colin's advice was prudent. Sébastien's face was white, his fists crumpling the papers. "We don't know how your father is connected to any of this. Not yet. That is what we're trying to establish. You should concern yourself with entertaining your guests out there and making sure you get enough money for your X-ray machine and ventilator."

"Can we have a copy of that list?" I was following Colin's lead. If he wasn't going to pressure Sébastien into revealing the name of the owner of the second 3D-printed painting, then I wasn't either. But I did want to see the list.

Sébastien stared at the crushed papers in his hand. He made a half-hearted attempt to smooth them out, then shook his head and handed them to Colin. "You're sure about the Manet?"

"Not one hundred percent, but enough to tell you to go ahead with the auction."

His shoulders dropped as he exhaled loudly. "Thank you, Professor Dryden. Thank you."

We left him behind in the small office. I suspected he needed a few moments to regain his composure. It took Colin another fifteen minutes to inspect the last of the paintings in the exhibition. There was no more 3D-printed art hanging on the walls.

Vinnie was waiting outside for us, leaning against the wall and tapping on his smartphone. He put it in one of the many pockets in his black combat pants and straightened when he saw us. "So? Do we know whose paintings were forged?"

Colin nodded at my handbag. "The Renoir belongs to Nicolas Denis. The Guillaumin belongs to Louis Masson."

"Hmm. Another connection for you, Jen-girl." There was no evidence of interest in Vinnie's nonverbal cues. He looked at Colin. "Are we done? Can we go? We have another ten minutes before they start without us."

Colin laughed and shook his head. "Let's go, big guy. I'll win and you can make sure the fire department guys know that they're losers."

"That's the first nice thing you've said to me all day."

Vinnie grabbed Colin around the neck in an awkward sideward embrace. "But I still love you, dude."

Colin punched Vinnie in the stomach. The latter's breathing didn't change, even though the punch had been hard enough to raise my eyebrows. Vinnie released Colin and whistled happily. Colin pulled his shirt back in place and took my hand as we walked to the parking area. "Promise me you'll go home now."

"Why?" I had hoped to go back to the office and watch another opera while Colin and Vinnie were playing pool.

"Because I know you're thinking about going back to your viewing room and working. I want you to take a break, go home, read a book, chat with Nikki, relax."

We stopped at Colin's SUV and I turned to face him. "I would get equal enjoyment from watching another opera. It will save us time tomorrow."

He lowered his brow. The parking area wasn't brightly lit, but there was enough light for me to see the fine wrinkles in the corners of his eyes. "Go home. Relax."

"I can't relax when I know there is more wor..." I pulled away from him, my eyes narrowed. "You want me to wait because you want to watch the operas as much as I do."

His smile was wide. "You saw that, did you?"

I waved my index finger around his face. "It's around your eyes and mouth."

"Do you also see my concern?" He waited for me to study his face. "I do want to watch the operas with you, but more than that I want you to go home and rest."

"Hurry up, you two!" Vinnie slapped the roof of the SUV. "I wanna go kick some firefighter ass."

"Get in the car and shut up, Vin," Colin said without taking his eyes off me. "Jenny, promise me you'll go home."

I thought of my laptop at home and its connection to our system. I might get some work done at home. "I'll go home."

"And promise me you won't work too much at home. Have some fun with Nikki. Or read a book." He leaned in until his nose touched mine. "I know you're going to work. I just don't want you to overdo it."

"Fine. I won't." It didn't take much to understand his motivation. "Thank you for caring."

"You know I do." He moved in another two centimetres and kissed me.

The light kiss turned more passionate until Vinnie knocked on the roof of the SUV. "Yo! Dude! This is not the time. We need to go."

Colin smiled against my lips. "He's going to drive me crazy tonight."

I stepped away, but not out of his embrace. "You pretend to be inconvenienced, but you're also looking forward to it."

"Don't tell him." Colin opened the driver's door. "See you later, love."

I stepped back and watched them leave. The emotion in my chest was warm and comfortable as I walked the short distance to my car. The car park was not as full as when we'd arrived. I suspected a few of the vehicles were those of visitors to Sébastien's exhibition. I hoped he made enough money to acquire the equipment he needed. It was clear to me that he felt strongly about his work and was one of those doctors who built a reputation befitting his caring profession.

I pressed the remote control to turn off my city car's alarm and unlock the doors. My mind was already fixed on the search terms I would use while looking into Émile Roche, Nicolas Denis, Stéphane Guillory and the names on the list in my handbag.

Only when I closed the driver's door and reached up for the safety belt did I notice the male body in the passenger seat.

Immediate darkness entered my peripheral vision as I turned to see who was sitting next to me. The moment I recognised the light blue eyes, the darkness took over and I escaped into the warm safety of a shutdown.

Chapter FOURTEEN

"Doctor Lenard, I mean no harm. If you'd look at me, you'd see." The gravelly male voice held no censure, only concern and patience.

The cognitive dissonance I experienced was torturous. On the one hand I wanted to escape back into my shutdown. On the other, I was curious to find out why Émile Roche was in my car, sounding worried about me.

Instead of giving in to my curiosity, I took six minutes to mentally write the first two pages of Mozart's Piano Concerto No. 19 in F major. By the time I reached the *sforzandos*, I felt better prepared to confront this invasion. I opened my eyes and groaned. My legs were pulled tightly against my chest, my arms locked around my knees. It took another two bars of the concerto to get my arms to relax and to lower my legs.

"Please know you are not in any danger." Émile Roche's voice was low, regretful. "I truly mean no harm."

I turned in my seat to face the older man. There was enough light from the street and the parking area to clearly see his expressions. For seventy seconds he sat there allowing me to study his nonverbal communication. I could find no malice in his relaxed posture or in his face. Around his eyes and mouth was evidence of guilt and grave concern. I didn't know if it was for me or someone else.

He was wearing dark linen trousers, his legs stretched out as far as my smaller car would allow. Had he been confrontational, his feet would have been flat on the floor, his leg muscles tense, ready to take action. His fingers were interlaced, his hands resting on his small paunch. Not an open gesture, but also not aggressive. His hands tightened slightly the longer I studied him. He was feeling vulnerable under my scrutiny.

"Why are you here?" My voice sounded strained, my words harsh.

"I need your help, Doctor Lenard." He shifted in his seat, turning towards me. "Do you know who I am?"

"Émile Roche. What help do you expect to receive from me?"

"Nothing you're not willing to give." Everything in his posture, his expression communicated his discomfort with asking for help. Yet I didn't feel threatened, especially when his expression softened. "My oldest son's second daughter is on the spectrum. A few minutes ago, you reminded me so much of her. What a treasure she is. This new year is her second at university. She's going to become a physicist. She's that smart. When she starts talking about science, I feel like a stupid old man. We're so proud of her."

I continued to stare at him. What he'd just shared provided me with valuable information. It gave me a baseline from which I could judge all his other communication. I didn't draw any comfort from his understanding of autism. He was in my car. Uninvited. "What help?"

"Just like my Danielle. No small talk." The corners of his eyes crinkled with a warm smile. Then he grew serious. "I have gathered a few of my... colleagues. We would like you to join us for a short meeting."

I lifted my hand to stop him. "Why do you have contempt for your colleagues?"

His boisterous laughter filled the small space of my car. "You are exactly what we need. I've done my research on you, Doctor Lenard. I know that you will see past all our bullshit. You'll see the truth behind all these idiots waiting for you. And just so you know, I include myself in that category. Why do I hate those idiots' guts? I've known most of them for many years. I know their dark side, their ethics. There's not much to respect there, Doc."

I jerked when he used Manny's moniker for me. It didn't feel right. "Call me Genevieve or Doctor Lenard. Not Doc."

"Forgive me." Again his expression softened when he looked at me. "I would be honoured to call you Genevieve."

"Who are these people who want to meet me? And why?"

"They are men with similar careers as mine."

"Are you referring to your construction businesses or to the many crimes you've committed?"

He cleared his throat. "That last part."

"Why do a group of criminals want to meet me? What kind of help can I provide?"

He blanched at my use of the word 'criminals', but pulled his shoulders back and lifted his chin. "It's come to our attention that a few of our colleagues have been killed. We learned that you're on the team investigating these crimes and we're hoping to speak to you about the investigation."

"I can't." I leaned back against my door. Not because I was concerned about Émile Roche attacking me. I was terrified of my lack of deceptive skills. What if they asked me a question that I answered before I considered the confidentiality involved?

"Please look at me and read me." He waited until I focused on his face. "We will not be asking you about your investigation. We will not ask anything of you, except to listen. And I personally guarantee your safety. These men have no desire to harm you, only a need to protect themselves and those they love."

"Why can't you talk to me here?" I didn't want to leave the relative safety of this parking area.

"Because those men are on the verge of taking actions that might jeopardise everything they've worked for." He paused. "I also think you need to see them for yourself. You can read them and see their sincerity. Or lack thereof."

It was his last sentence that got my attention. "You're using me to assess them. I don't appreciate being manipulated."

He winced. "Forgive me, Genevieve. Some things are such an established habit that it's really hard to just come out and say things as they are."

"You should practice honesty more often. Especially for your granddaughter."

"You're right." He lowered his chin, his expression imploring. "Would you do me the honour of trusting me enough to let me take you to meet these men?"

My life no longer only included me and my interests. I thought of Colin and how he would react to this man in my car and my willingness to trust that he did indeed have no intention of harming me. Colin would be livid. I didn't want to be the cause of it and the thought of Vinnie and Manny's reactions sped up my heart rate.

Yet I continued to study Émile Roche. There would be so much I could learn from these men. If they'd taken it upon themselves to gather and ask for my assistance, they must have identified a pattern in the deaths of Serge Valois, Benoît Faure and Claude Moreau. The need to know what they'd discovered and use the data to tighten my analysis was overwhelming. "I will be safe?"

"You have my word. It might not mean much to you, but to me my word is my honour. Without my honour I am nothing." He was completely truthful.

With a single nod I turned to start my car. Later I would face Manny's, Vinnie's and Colin's wrath. I might even be able to ease their anger if I were to learn enough valuable information. But I knew without any doubt that phoning Colin or Manny would destroy the slim chance I had to acquire that information.

It didn't escape me that Émile Roche's attempt to win my trust was continued as he stayed relaxed in the passenger seat. He could've suggested we take his vehicle or could've insisted on driving. He didn't. He was telling me about his grandchildren, interrupting himself every now and then to quietly give me directions as I drove through the streets of Strasbourg.

We arrived at an exclusive restaurant in one of the affluent suburbs and I turned into the driveway. A man waved me towards a covered parking area. There I parked next to a luxury town car, similar to the other eight parked vehicles.

We got out and walked to the main entrance. As we reached the stairs, Émile stopped. "Genevieve, I know I have no right to ask this of you, but I hope that you could refrain from revealing what you learn about us to each other."

"Be more specific."

"If you read my body language and see how much I loathe Bénédict Herriot, please don't reveal that. Bénédict knows I don't like him very much, but he doesn't know the depth of my disgust with the way he treated his sister eighteen years ago. He lost my respect forever with that stupidity." He glanced at the open door. "The men are very nervous that we would learn too much about each other tonight. They want to speak to you, ask for your help, but still keep their secrets."

I thought about the right way to address this neurotypical concern. "Would it reassure you to know that I take no pleasure in idle gossip? My main concern is to do my job. If anyone confesses to a crime while talking to me tonight, there is a great possibility that I will reveal that to my team and that person might be prosecuted for the crime. But I'm not interested in petty grudges and scandals."

He chuckled and shook his head. "Well, you just put me in my place. I suppose eighteen years is a long time to hold a grudge."

"Are you reassured?" Or did he not understand what I'd said?

"Completely." He tilted his head. "In my life I've learned to never trust anyone. Danielle was the person who taught me there were still some people worth trusting. And you,

Genevieve, might be the second person in the last four decades I'm tempted to trust."

I nodded. How else was I supposed to respond?

He smiled again and stretched his arm out towards the door. He followed me up the stairs and into the foyer. When the *maitre d'* saw Émile, he straightened even more and nodded subtly. Émile led me to a private room at the back of the restaurant. He opened the door and moved aside for me to enter. I immediately recognised the quality of the voices when speaking in a soundproofed room. Interesting.

I pressed my little finger to my thumb and entered the room. All conversation stopped. In the centre of the room was a long table seating six men. One glance told me they were all alpha males. Warriors. A second, more observant, look around the table brought darkness to the edges of my vision. I froze, closed my eyes and wrote another three bars of Mozart's Piano Concerto.

When I opened my eyes, Émile was standing at the head of the table, giving everyone a warning glare. I looked at the man seated at his left. He'd lost some weight since the photo on his file had been taken, but it was Nicolas Denis. The man sitting furthest from Émile was Stéphane Guillory. I wondered if the other three men would complete the list of ten men represented in the operas sent to Dion Gravois.

"Doctor Lenard, I would like to introduce you to these men." There was no evidence of the gentleness Émile had exhibited in the car. Towering over six other organised crime leaders was a hard man, someone I would be loath to cross. If I hadn't seen the micro-expressions of concern and protectiveness when he looked at me, I would've thought the forty minutes I'd spent with him in my car had been a lie. He pointed at Nicolas. "From Lille we have Nicolas Denis, next to him is Louis Masson from Paris, across from him Stéphane Guillory from Toulouse, next to him Yves Patenaude from Marseille, then Bénédict Herriot also from Paris and to my right Albert Satre from Nice."

It was immediately clear Nicolas Denis and Yves Patenaude didn't trust me. The other four men exhibited both interest and concern. Louis Masson's posture relaxed as he leaned back in his chair, confident. "It's a pleasure to meet you, Doctor Lenard. We're hoping you can help us."

"I don't know how." I resisted the urge to cross my arms tightly around my torso.

"Please sit down, Doctor." Émile was treating me with professional courtesy. The flash of possessiveness I'd seen in his expression made me wonder if his past had made him reluctant to share a relationship he'd built with a strategic person. Especially with men he would consider rivals.

I sat down across from him at the other end of the table. There was a chair between me and the men. It gave me an irrational sense of safety.

"Permit me to tell you a little bit about ourselves," Louis Masson said. "Stéphane Guillory, Émile Roche and I are in complete agreement about inviting someone as esteemed as you to aid us in this situation we're facing."

I stared at him. "Your smile is social, insincere. Your compliment was manipulative and your use of language clumsy, as if you don't usually speak like this. Don't manipulate me."

Émile laughed, Stéphane Guillory looked uncomfortable and the two men who showed great distrust looked pensive. Louis Masson's eyes were wide. "Ain't you a peach. I don't know how you do your woo-woo stuff, Doctor, but Émile had me completely sold when he said you ain't police."

"I don't know what woo-woo is." It wasn't the question foremost in my mind. "And no one has told me how you expect me to help you."

"Let me be very clear." Yves Patenaude knocked on the table. "I don't want you here. I suggested we handle this in-house. Like we used to do."

"And go back to the bad old days?" Stéphane shook his head. "I'm not entirely comfortable with it either, Yves, but we know Doctor Lenard's reputation. She's not going to try to screw us over."

"Are you?" Nicolas Denis' gaze was direct and confrontational. "How do we know you're not going to reveal everything we say to you today to some vindictive bastard who wants to throw us all in jail? Or even worse, destroy our businesses or take over."

"You have no such guarantee. The same as I don't have a guarantee that you won't harm me." I took my time to assess the seven men. "What I see is overwhelming concern, bordering on fear. It made you reach out to someone you don't know for help. What has elicited such anxiety in men who are reputed to be ruthless and fearless?"

"We fear for the safety of our families, Doctor." Yves Patenaude's top lip withdrew from his teeth in a display of aggression. "Some bastard is revealing details about our families that could put their lives in danger. I want to find the fucker and put a bullet in his brain, but I'm willing to try your way first."

"What way is that?" I still had no idea what they expected.

"What you see here are men who have been working hard for the last six years to put a distance between our businesses and our families." Émile raised his hand when Nicolas inhaled. "We can't expect her to trust us if we don't trust her, Nico."

Louis Masson put his hand on the table, unconsciously reaching out to me. "We know the connection between all of us and the deaths of Serge Valois, Benoît Faure, Claude Moreau and Léon Blanc. We'll share that with you if you can stop the flow of information about our private lives."

I thought of Dion Gravois and the operas he'd received. "Are you referring to the articles published on Dion Gravois' blog?"

"Yes," Émile Roche said. "I had some of my people hack his computer. We found nothing. Then I sent some people to look through his house. We also found nothing. We don't know where he's getting his information from."

"Your last sentence is not truthful." Did they know about the operas?

Émile bowed his head. "Forgive me. Let me explain. We know where the information originated, but we don't know how this blog-writing idiot is getting this information."

"It's putting the lives of our families at risk." Stéphane's fists rested on the table, his elbows away from his body, his expression contentious. "If that Gravois fucker publishes an article that talks about my grandchildren's school, he will wish he was never born. I've busted my ass to keep those kids safe. They know nothing of this part of my life and I never want them to. My daughter recently had a baby who's very sick. I don't want it public knowledge which hospital is treating the little one and for what."

I thought about privacy and secrets. "Why is it so important to keep your lives private?"

"Does she know who we are?" Yves asked Émile. "I thought you said she'd know more than us?"

"She knows." Émile Roche dismissed Yves with a flick of his wrist and looked at me. "Doctor Lenard, we have not always followed the law. We've done very bad things. But our children and grandchildren should not be punished for the sins of their fathers and grandfathers. The few men you see in this room are a small representation of our business."

I lifted my index finger to stop him. "When you say 'business' are you referring to the fraud, tax evasion, bribery, extortion, intimidation, drug traff—"

"Uh. Yes." Émile shifted in his chair. "That's the business I'm talking about. And that's the business our grandchildren don't know about. We are only a few people who are in this business. And, if I may say so, we've been very successful. There are factions, newcomers, who would love to destroy us and take over our reputations. An article with such private information would give them the ammunition to do so."

I studied him closely while he spoke. Then I looked around the table. Even though there was still some hostility coming from Nicolas and Yves, I saw glimmers of hope. These were men who had been successful at avoiding prosecution for many crimes. They were hardened criminals even though my initial research into the names from the operas had revealed no violence. The vast majority of their crimes had been white-collar crimes with the exception of trafficking marijuana.

My studies had given me academic knowledge, but the last three years had given me a much better understanding of the criminal mind. I realised, and respected, the difficult step it had been for these men whose lives were built on suspecting everyone to trust me. "I'm part of a team. I share everything I know with them. Our team was established to solve crimes and make sure those who committed said crimes are prosecuted. I have never been in a situation like this, but I know that the police and prosecutors often negotiate with criminals when they co-operate or provide valuable information. I cannot negotiate or promise you anything but to do my job. And the case I am working on is to stop the murders of criminals like you."

"Do you really have to call us criminals?" Yves asked, his mouth pulled in an expression of distaste.

"It is what it is." Émile Roche shrugged. "Please continue, Doctor Lenard."

"My team will be enraged that you met with me like this. If you want to avoid prosecution, you have to provide me with information valuable enough to present to them." My throat tightened slightly at the thought of Manny's, Vinnie's and especially Colin's anger.

"And you said you don't negotiate." Émile's smile was warm. "We can give you everything we know. In turn all we ask is that you and your team work as hard as possible to prevent this threat from coming close to our families."

Again I took my time studying all the men around the

table. They were all in or close to their sixties. Their clothes communicated quality and luxury, their body language communicated ruthlessness and determination. Nicolas and Yves were exhibiting less hostility now, all of them waiting for me to respond. "For the moment, we've halted any more articles from being published. To be clear, we were able to get Monsieur Gravois to agree to that. I cannot guarantee that someone else won't publish any more articles."

"Do you know where Gravois has been getting his information?" Émile asked.

"Not yet." It worried me, but it worried the men much more. I thought of everything I'd learned so far and looked at Louis. "You included Léon Blanc when you said you knew what connected all the murders. How does Léon Blanc fit into the murders of men like you?"

Louis' lips thinned and the other men's nonverbal cues turned resentful. I wished for a camera to record this for later assessment as I watched the glances they gave each other. Fascinating.

I rested my hands on my lap and listened as Louis Masson started talking.

Chapter **FIFTEEN**

My front door swung open as I lifted my key. Colin stood in the doorway, his face pale. He searched my face for something, heaved a shuddering sigh of relief, then searched my body. A second later, he grabbed me and pulled me into a crushing embrace. He breathed as if he'd run upstairs, his face buried in my hair. "I've never been so worried in my life."

"Get her in here, Frey." Manny's voice sounded strained.

Colin didn't let me go. I had been expecting anger, not this level of concern. Guilt settled heavily on my mind that I was the cause of Colin's distress. I didn't attempt to move away, allowing him the comfort he derived from holding me. When he did release me, he held my face between his hands. "Are you okay? Did he do anything to you?"

"I'm well." As uncomfortable as it was for me, I looked him in the eye. "I'm really well. Nobody did anything to me."

"Then you'd better start explaining, missy." Manny sounded closer. "Get inside, Frey."

Colin stepped back and I looked into my apartment. It was seventeen minutes past midnight and all the lights were blazing. I frowned at the many people looking at me. "Why is everyone here?"

"Why?" Manny stepped closer. "It's the middle of the bloody night, you disappeared without a trace and you're asking why we called on every single power that be to find you?"

I leaned back. "I didn't ask that."

"We'd better get inside so you can tell us what happened, love." Colin locked the door behind me and put his hand on the small of my back.

Everyone stared at me with varying levels of concern and relief. Vinnie was hovering nearby, Nikki was standing next to Francine, her arms wrapped tightly around her body. Phillip was in the sitting area, his hair messy as if he'd pushed his hands through it, his tie askew. In the kitchen Pink was standing next to Daniel, both men in their uniforms, their expressions dire.

I walked deeper into the room, but didn't get far. Vinnie stepped in front of me. "What the fuck, Jen-girl?"

Without warning he lifted me in one of his strong hugs. I closed my eyes and wrote a few more bars of Mozart's Piano Concerto No. 19 in F major. I could only tolerate Vinnie's touch because I knew how much he needed it. He put me down and stormed to the kitchen. Pink and Daniel got out his way as he opened the large container of his homemade cookies. It was a strange atmosphere. No one spoke, but their nonverbal cues shouted at me. Everyone had questions, but didn't ask.

I looked at Nikki and knew my discomfort was going to continue for the next few hours. I lowered my chin and made sure she was looking at me. "I'm fine, Nikki."

"They couldn't find you, Doc G." Her voice was thin.

"Francine tried to track your car's GPS and your phone, but couldn't find it. You were gone. Gone."

"I'm here now."

"Can I hug you?" She didn't move away from Francine, her arms tightening around her own torso. I held out my arms and she rushed forward. Like the previous night, she held me tight, her head on my shoulder. "I was so scared. Manny was swearing all the time and I was sure Vinnie was going to break everything in the kitchen. Colin wasn't speaking at all. He was so quiet."

I didn't know what to say. Clearly my academic knowledge of how the neurotypical brain processed difficult situations wasn't serving me well. I had thought I would face their anger. Not this level of distress. I now understood Colin's preference to cause my anger and not emotional anguish. I winced at the guilt weighing down my mind. "I'm fine, Nikki. I'm well and I'm here."

"Then you'd better sit down and start explaining what happened, Doc."

Nikki released me, but stayed close to my side. We walked to the table and I sat in my usual seat. It was a relief when the others sat down as well. My apartment didn't feel as crowded. Vinnie brought a tray with a large plate of cookies and mugs for everyone. "Coffee's coming."

"Speak." Manny's lips were tight, his posture rigid.

"Émile Roche was in my car waiting for me when we left the gallery."

"What the fuck?" Vinnie stormed back from the kitchen. "He was there? We drove away while that motherfucker was waiting for you in the car?"

"He didn't harm me." I saw Vinnie's outburst for what it was. "You didn't fail in keeping me safe, Vinnie."

"Like hell I didn't." He punched his chest. "It's my job to make sure nothing happens to you. Tonight something did happen and I was right fucking there!"

Nikki's eyes widened, her face growing pale. Colin saw me looking at Nikki and leaned forward. "Take a breath, big guy."

Vinnie glared at Colin, but noticed when Colin tilted his head towards Nikki. Vinnie stormed around the table and gently rested his hand on her shoulder. "Sorry, little punk."

"'S okay." She lifted her shoulder to push his hand against her cheek. Immediately some of the tension in Vinnie's muscles eased.

"Doc?"

This was going to be difficult. I told them about Émile's appeal for help, but didn't get far into recounting the last three and a half hours. Manny slammed both his hands on the table. "Holy, bloody hell, Doc! You willingly went with that criminal to meet more criminals?"

"Yes."

Manny pushed himself out of his chair and leaned over the chair, glaring at me. "Aren't you supposed to be a genius?"

"I am."

His nostrils flared, colour flushed his cheeks and the supratrochlear artery stood out on his forehead. He pushed his chair back and walked towards the front door. Knowing this behaviour, I waited. At the door, he turned around and stormed back, shaking his index finger at me. "You're a stupid genius. Stupid! Of all the hare-brained things to do.

Trusting a criminal like that? Have you no sense of preservation?"

"I do." I inhaled to continue, but Manny didn't give me a chance.

"You do? You do?" His repeated question ended in a shout. "You do *not*. You don't understand self-preservation. If you did, you would never have gone anywhere with him. You would've phoned Frey, the criminal, me, Francine, anyone. You should not have gone with him."

The open space of my apartment was deadly quiet when Manny ended his outburst. Nikki was hugging herself again. Vinnie was rigid in his chair. I didn't know how I was going to reassure him that he had not failed to keep me safe. Daniel and Pink didn't exhibit the same level of personal offence, but their nonverbal cues led me to believe they shared Manny's opinion. Francine was focused on her tablet, avoiding eye contact. The glimpses of fear hidden behind her anger tightened around my chest. Phillip looked tired. Tired and relieved.

Colin hadn't moved. I turned to look at him and blinked in shock. He was failing at keeping his fury hidden. He'd shifted away from me, his right arm resting on the table, creating a barrier between us. He wasn't looking at me. He always made eye contact. Not now. He was clenching his jaw, shaking his head, his lips tightly pressed together.

It surprised me that I longed for his touch. I put my hand on his and waited until he looked at me. At first he stared at our hands. I didn't often initiate physical contact. When he looked at me, I inhaled sharply. "I never intended to cause you such fear."

"What did you expect, Jenny?" Colin turned his hand over and held mine. "Francine tried to reach you. When she couldn't, she looked for your car and managed to find one video grab of you driving and Émile Roche in the passenger seat, followed by two dark SUVs. They'd disabled all the street cameras, your car's GPS, your phone's GPS, everything. Then she phoned us. We had no way of tracking you. Why didn't you phone me? Even if just to say you were okay?"

I closed my eyes for a second. "I apologise. Phoning you wasn't an option."

"Please explain to me what you were thinking." He shook his head, the anguish of the hours of worrying still visible around his mouth and eyes. "I'm trying to understand your reasoning, but I'm coming up short."

I organised my thoughts. This explanation would be pivotal in regaining his and everyone else's confidence in me. "I'm one of the best nonverbal communication specialists in the world. I don't trust my ability to do and say the right things in my relationship with you or with Francine, Nikki, Vinnie, Manny or anyone else. I don't trust my ability to maintain any of these relationships. I simply don't have the emotional skill set to intuitively know what to say, when and how to say it. But the one thing I trust about myself is my ability to accurately read people.

"What I had observed in the car before I agreed to go with Émile Roche had given me enough confidence that he would not harm me. I forget to consider your emotions when I make decisions. But you forget that my mind observes, analyses and gives me feedback with very small margins of error, all within seconds. Émile had revealed that he'd researched me. He would never have risked exposing himself and the others to my scrutiny if he didn't truly need my help."

"He could've lured you there to kill you," Manny said.

I shook my head, not taking my eyes off Colin's face. Of everyone, I needed his regard the most. "I had established a baseline very early on. A miniscule percentage of the population is adept at deception for long periods of time. Julien Travere is one of the best I've seen at masking his true emotions, yet I've been able to see beyond that. Please trust me that I made an informed decision.

"You are more intelligent than Manny, Francine and Vinnie. You reason things out before making decisions, yet many of your decisions are emotion-based. Mine aren't. The decision I made to go with Émile was based on the information he had provided me through his body language—a manner of communication that he is not proficient at using for the purposes of manipulation."

Colin stared at me. It took a lot of willpower for me to maintain eye contact. The seconds stretched out, yet I waited patiently for him to consider what I'd shared. His blinking increased as it did when people processed information. With a sigh, he leaned closer to me until our foreheads touched. "We're going to have to discuss a way to do things differently if ever another situation like this comes up. I never want to relive the last three hours."

"I deeply regret causing you any distress." My voice was low. "I understand now why you prefer that I'm angry."

"Frey might be all soft on you, but I have not forgiven

you, Doc." Manny tapped with his index finger on the table until I looked at him. "You can't run around with criminals like that."

Daniel snorted, then pretended to cough. "Pardon me."

"This is not the same, dude. We are not criminals. Not like those lowlifes." Vinnie's fists pressed against his thighs.

I looked at Vinnie and again around the table. "I truly apologise for causing all of you such anxiety. It was never my intention. If you are able to move past that for a moment, I can tell you what I've learned in the last three hours."

"It better be bloody good, Doc." Manny slumped back in his chair.

I told them about the six men who'd been waiting for me when Émile had taken me to the restaurant. I looked at Francine. "Three of the men who'd been exposed by the operas have been killed, the three men whose names I'd learned yesterday from watching the operas were there tonight and I suspect the other four names in the operas will be Yves Patenaude, Louis Masson, Bénédict Herriot and Albert Satre."

"We'll check it tomorrow." She nodded, her usual exuberance not present.

I swallowed. "I find myself disproportionately in need of hearing you propose a ridiculous theory. Your micro-expressions are confusing me. I don't understand the withdrawal I'm observing."

Francine tapped on her tablet for a few seconds before looking at me. "I sometimes wish I could expect normal things from you. I suppose I mean neurotypical things. Then at least I could be angry when you don't deliver. Now I feel guilty because I'm so angry that you hugged Vinnie and Nikki and not me. I know how uncomfortable it is for you, but it often feels like all I do is worry about your comfort. What about a time like tonight when for a few hours I thought that I'd lost my best friend? Instead of being happy that you're here and hugging it out, I have to keep my distance because you don't like being touched."

The intensity of her emotions affected me. A few times I'd seen her unconsciously reach for me only to pull her hand back. Unwelcome tears filled my eyes. "I never meant to be selfish. Or to cause you such emotional pain. I can never be what you term 'normal'. But I can learn from this experience and remember to also offer you physical comfort."

She lowered her head and covered her eyes with one hand as she huffed a humourless laugh. It took three seconds before she looked at me again. "How about I tell you what I need? Then I won't feel snubbed and you won't have to worry about remembering who to give physical comfort?"

"I like your proposal about informing me of your needs." I frowned. "But your expression tells me I shouldn't have used the term 'physical comfort'."

"Yes, you should never use that term again." She leaned towards me, some of her usual humour returning. "It's a hug. Spelled H-U-G. Hug. That's what we do. We hug."

"Noted." I would later ask Colin why 'physical comfort' was an offensive term. Was it impersonal?

"Oh, for the love of Pete. Can we hug later? All this lovey-dovey nonsense is driving me bonkers." Manny caught Francine's hand as she slapped his shoulder. He looked at me. "I'm still waiting for the big revelation, Doctor Face-reader. Having ten names of organised crime bosses simply isn't doing it for me."

"Léon Blanc is the keystone connecting everyone." I was still feeling the rush of excitement that I'd first felt when Émile and Louis had shared the full role of the director of the Opéra National du Rhin. "Two years after he took leadership at the opera house, he realised they were facing bankruptcy. By that time, he'd already made friends with Émile and had met a few other men who were involved in illegal activities. He started cultivating these friendships. He introduced these men to people in legal businesses, creating a delicate network of legal businesses benefitting from illegal businesses, but in such a way that there was never any evidence of fraud.

"Léon Blanc would put one of the criminals in contact with a real-estate developer who needed a cash infusion to finish a project. The criminal would invest in the project with the understanding that he would receive his investment plus ten percent after five years. The real-estate developer would put the financing down as a private investment and get great financial gains from completing the project on time and above standard."

"Blood money would be washed and a businessman would get rich." Manny's top lip curled. "They're all bloody criminals in my opinion."

"That was only one part of the networking Léon was involved in." When I'd first heard all these details, I'd marvelled at the social engineering skills Léon Blanc had shown. "Over the years, he built powerful relationships with the criminals. He became their friend, their confidant. Many years and numerous experiences had shown them that they could trust him with more personal information.

"They even started trusting him with business decisions. Upon his recommendation, they invested in art, expanded their portfolios and even financed a few technological start-up companies.

"What they didn't know was he kept meticulous records of every conversation, every confidential bit of information they'd shared with him. When he'd gathered enough evidence to put them in prison for life, he would approach them and invite them to donate to the opera house. Nobody spurned his invitation.

"He was never interested in their illegal operations, just their money. When Émile considered leaving behind his fraudulent practices, Léon encouraged him. He even helped him secure a few legal contracts with the understanding that Émile would continue to generously donate to the opera house."

I had everyone's undivided attention. Pink's mouth was slightly agape, Daniel's eyebrows were raised. Colin was staring at the ceiling the way he always did when he was thinking and Manny was rubbing his chin. "So you're telling me that all these exposés are coming from Léon Blanc's little black book?"

"I don't know where he kept this information," I said. "All seven of the men I'd spoken to tonight were convinced that Léon would not have revealed any of it. He never used that information against them except to get funding for his opera house. It was his insurance to continue adding quality productions to their repertoire. It was an interesting contradiction. He used their secrets against them to fund his opera house, but he'd also helped them in so many ways that they spoke of him with high regard."

"And all of these crime bosses are trying to go straight?" Manny asked.

"By going straight, do you mean becoming legitimate in their businesses?" I waited until Manny nodded. "Yes. Only Albert Satre looked less convinced of his success in maintaining his legal business dealings. The others all came over as strongly committed to putting distance between their families and their crimes."

"Bloody hell." Manny rubbed his hands hard over his face. "Do they have any idea who might want them dead?"

Vinnie snorted. "Those dudes? I reckon there's a long list of pissed-off people who wouldn't mind seeing them gone."

"I asked them." Their reactions had been similar to Vinnie's. "But they haven't been able to pinpoint one person or even persons all the men have in common."

"What I don't get is how these badass dudes walked into the hotel rooms." Vinnie scratched his head. "I mean, they've been looking over their shoulders since the first day they did someone in. Why did they go to those hotel rooms without their bodyguards, without first checking the place out?"

"The men were adamant that Serge Valois and Benoît Faure never went anywhere without two bodyguards. Apparently Claude Moreau only had one bodyguard, but would often take another two with him. The men refused to believe those three would've entered their hotel rooms alone." Émile had repeated himself a few times to convince me of this fact. "I asked them to locate the bodyguards. Maybe they could help us find some answers."

"But"—Manny rubbed his chin—"if the murderer used that Sevofloride gas to knock the victims out, it would also have knocked out the bodyguards. He could've killed them too and dumped them somewhere."

"It's Sevoflurane and your theory is sound." I'd thought the same. "But I suggest we wait until we hear from Émile whether they were able to make contact with the bodyguards."

"You said Léon advised them on investing in art." Colin looked away from the ceiling to face me. "Did you ask about that?"

"I did. I thought about the Morisot, and the Renoir and Guillaumin at the exhibition. I asked them to each compile a complete list of the paintings they own. Émile didn't allow them to ask me why I wanted it. He made them promise to send the lists tomorrow."

"Hmm." Colin looked up at the ceiling again for two seconds. Then he straightened in his chair and looked at Manny. "We need to get all the art from the houses of Serge Valois, Benoît Faure and Claude Moreau. I'm sure we'll find 3D-printed forgeries there."

"What's your theory, Frey?"

"I don't know if any paintings were replaced or when, why or by whom." He glanced at me. "It's a gut feeling."

"I'll get on that." Daniel tilted his head towards Pink. "We'll get those paintings in the team room tomorrow."

"Thanks." Colin leaned back in his chair.

"Bloody hell." Manny grunted loudly and pointed his

index finger at me. "You did a very stupid thing tonight and you and I have not finished our conversation about this. You can thank your lucky stars that you left there in one piece and came away with all this information. Now we need to find Léon Blanc's proverbial black book so I can arrest all those bleeding criminals."

"I told them you would want to arrest them." I could still see their expressions. "Without Léon Blanc's records they are convinced you would have insufficient evidence to arrest them. With the records, they expressly asked me to remind you that they were the ones who informed you about the records. They also insisted I remind you of the lack of any cases pending against them in the last five to six years."

"Holy Mother Mary, Doc. You want me to let these men walk free?"

"I didn't say that. I merely relayed their message."

Manny huffed and slumped back in his chair. "I want to hear the whole story again. Every detail from the moment you opened your car door until you arrived back here."

His request wasn't born from distrust. It had been too much information for him to process all at once. I knew he needed the retelling so he could solidify the information and also have more time to decide what action he wanted to take against Émile and the others, if any. I would recount the last few hours and hopefully avoid the conversation Manny had alluded to. The emotionality of the conversations since I'd arrived home had tired me.

I wanted to focus on all the new information. And I wanted to watch the last four operas.

Chapter SIXTEEN

"It all checks out." Francine's eyes were wide, her expression delighted. "This is at least five of my biggest fantasies all coming true at once."

"We haven't yet confirmed all the details." I couldn't accept her sweeping statement about all the details we'd received through the other four operas. Verdi's *Falstaff*, *La traviata*, *Aida* and *Il trovatore* had indeed completed the list, providing us with details on the lives of Yves Patenaude, Louis Masson, Bénédict Herriot and Albert Satre. It had been a fascinating morning watching the four operas. "We still have to finalise the analysis of the opera house's finances. And your search into Léon Blanc's finances also isn't complete."

"Don't ruin my moment of glory, girlfriend." She stretched her arms towards the ceiling. "The gods and goddesses have granted me this joyous moment of having loads of dirt on loads of bad guys. And to top it all off, we've got ourselves a good guy blackmailing them all. Ah, it's too delicious for words."

I was too tired and too focused to respond to Francine's enjoyment. I had only managed to sleep four hours. When I'd woken up for the third time, I'd realised it would be senseless to attempt to rest when all my mind wanted to do was solve this mystery. By the time I'd come out of the shower, Colin had made coffee and had insisted on joining me when I came to the office.

We hadn't yet discussed his displeasure with the decision I'd made to trust Émile. Knowing Colin, I was certain he was forming his arguments and working through everything he wanted to tell me. There would be plenty of time for emotional discussions later. Our time now had to be used to find out who had sent the operas to Dion Gravois, find out if it was the same person who was killing people named in these operas, and hopefully prevent any harm coming to another person trying to move away from their life of crime.

"Do you have any actionable information, Doc?" Manny walked into my viewing room. He'd been gone the whole morning.

"Not yet." Frustration made my answer terse. "We're now looking at the Opéra National du Rhin's finances. It would appear—"

"Would appear, my sexy tush." Francine turned to face Manny. "Hey, handsome."

The muscles around his mouth and eyes relaxed marginally. "Supermodel."

"A man of few words." She winked at him. "Genevieve here doesn't want to admit that we've found proof that these ten men have been donating monthly to the opera house."

"What's wrong with supermodel's proof, Doc?"

"Hey! You're supposed to be on my side." She turned away from him and continued working on her laptop.

"We've established a pattern of monthly payments from

businesses associated with the men from the operas to an account the opera house uses for fundraising."

"They've admitted to paying Léon Blanc's blackmail money into an opera house account." Manny frowned. "I can't see why you don't want to confirm the connection."

"We've only confirmed donations from businesses associated with eight of the men. Francine's still working on Bénédict Herriot's donations and Yves Patenaude's."

"These guys are pretty good at covering their tracks." Francine continued to work on her laptop. "No wonder they haven't been successfully prosecuted for most of the crimes they committed."

"Did you learn anything important from the operas, Doc?" The quick contraction of Manny's *depressor anguli oris* muscle around his mouth conveyed his dislike for the music.

"A lot of incriminating information as well as details about their families, their holiday homes, private investments, art and other collections, but nothing that helped me determine who's gained access to this information or has been sending it to Dion Gravois."

"How're you doing on getting into Blanc's computer, supermodel?"

"Working on it." She briefly raised both hands and shook them. "Only two hands, handsome. Only two hands."

"You've had his laptops for three days already."

"Gotcha!" She winked at him. "I double-checked both laptops the day before yesterday for anything that didn't have to do with music. The few files that were on his laptops were all librettos and music for operas, drafts for posters and the like. Nothing incriminating. The financial data on his computers is exactly the same as we got."

"You found more." I recognised her expression.

"I found something." She wiggled her nose. "But I don't know what I've found yet. There is something odd in the coding."

"And you're going to start talking conspiracies." Manny glared at her.

"It could be alien script." She lifted both shoulders, attempting an innocent look. Manny grunted.

"How was your meeting with Lucien Privott?" I'd received an annoyed voice message this morning from Manny that he was meeting Lucien. I didn't know whether he'd been irritated because I hadn't answered my phone or because he'd had to meet Lucien.

Manny's top lip curled. "That bleeding annoying hipster. I can't believe I had to fly to Lyon just to hear him say all the things he'd said before. Twerp."

"You flew to Lyon?" Francine swung around. "You should've told me. I would've loved a pastry from the little bistro close to *Parc de la Tête d'Or*."

"Why do you think I didn't tell you?" Manny raised one eyebrow. "I wanted to get back here as soon as possible. I didn't want to go traipsing around the city park looking for your cute little shops with your cute little somethings."

"You should've taken me with you, old man." Vinnie was leaning against the doorway. He'd been on his sofa the whole day, guarding. "I would've scared Privott into saying something useful."

Manny lifted one shoulder. "It wasn't a complete waste of

time. He said the president's team had done an in-depth forensic audit of the president's finances, especially his donations. They didn't find anything that could implicate the president in any illegal or unethical behaviour."

"Why did he need to meet you in person to relay that information?" I narrowed my eyes when I noticed Manny's micro-expressions. "Why are you feeling self-satisfied? What did you do?"

"Privott wasn't the one who'd insisted on seeing me in person." One corner of Manny's mouth twitched. "He expected me to return his call. Not to show up at his hotel."

"Ooh!" Francine's smile was elated. "Why the subterfuge?"

"That bloody idiot has been phoning me seven, eight, ten times a day. When I'm not answering his calls, he's leaving bloody messages." Manny placed his fists on his hips. "I'd had enough. He's just a little lackey trying to play a power game with me."

"And you went there to intimidate him." My eyes widened when Manny's expression became even more pleased with himself.

"I went there to tell him to back the hell off." Manny pushed his fists in his pockets. "I think he got the message. Especially when I gave it to him in front of a dozen military officials he'd been briefing."

"Smooth, old man." Vinnie smiled. "Smooth."

Manny grunted, but I'd seen the quick, yet pleased, smile relaxing the tension around his eyes and mouth. "Where's Frey?"

I looked towards the team room and realised that I hadn't

seen Colin in a while. Had I been so focused again that I'd lost track of his whereabouts?

"He went to speak to some people about the 3D printers." Francine looked at me. "He knew you didn't hear him when he told you he was going out."

"Oh." What else could I say? "Did he say when he'll be back?"

"He phoned me five minutes ago to say that he's coming in with Jane Dubois." Manny glanced at the elevator doors. "He didn't give me an exact arrival time."

"He couldn't have phoned you five minutes ago." I glanced at the clock on my computer. "You've been here for eight minutes. That means he would've phoned you while you were standing here."

"Doc." Manny sighed. "I only meant that he phoned me a while ago. I don't know exactly how many minutes ago."

"Then you shouldn't state it was five minutes."

Manny turned around and walked towards the team room. "I've got emails to answer."

"Well done, Jen-girl." Vinnie pushed away from the door. "Man, I like it when you put the old man in his place."

It hadn't been my intention to offend Manny or 'put him in his place'. I just truly abhorred incorrect statements or Francine's love for broad generalisations. I shook my head and turned back to face my monitors.

At some time in the morning when Colin and I had been watching the operas, Francine had joined us. As usual, she'd set up her laptop to my left. As Colin and I had made notes of the details revealed on the operas, she'd put the data in her system to confirm the information.

When we'd started looking into the financial details of Léon Blanc and the opera house, she'd stayed next to me, claiming it was just as fast working here as at her station. I marvelled at the speed her fingers flew over the keyboard as she typed in some code. She reached for the mouse and clicked a few times.

I returned my attention to consolidating the information about the ten men while Francine continued her work. For the next sixteen minutes we worked in silence until I felt a hand on my forearm. I glanced down then up into Colin's face. "I didn't hear you."

He smiled. "When? Now or when I left?"

"Both times."

"Thought so." He sat down. "Jane Dubois phoned Daniel this morning, saying she was ready if we had any more questions. Daniel and I met her at the opera house and brought her in. Apparently, she doesn't drive and her husband had some brunch meeting with friends. She's waiting in the conference room next door when you're ready."

I looked at my notebook and the lists I'd made. "I'm ready."

Vinnie insisted on joining us in Rousseau & Rousseau's conference room. He ignored Tim's greeting as we walked through the reception area. "I know this woman is fragile and all. I'll just stand outside the room."

"We're safe here, Vinnie." I would have to ask Colin how I was going to reassure Vinnie that he hadn't failed in keeping me safe. When Vinnie didn't answer, I stopped in the long hallway and waited for him to look at me. I could only think of one thing to do. "But it would make me feel good to know you're outside the door."

Vinnie lowered his head to be closer to my height. "You're not a good liar, Jen-girl. But it's very sweet that you're trying."

"Then stop acting as if you did something wrong. I find it most stressful to find ways to convince you that it was one hundred percent my decision to go with Émile."

"I should've seen him in your car."

Realisation illuminated my understanding. "You feel guilty that you were too absorbed in your obsession with winning pool against the firefighters. You only had that goal in mind, nothing else."

"And when you say it like that, it really doesn't make me feel better."

This was difficult. Manny and Colin had stopped a few feet ahead of us, waiting. Colin's patient nonverbal cues didn't surprise me. Manny's did. That was also why I knew this moment was important. I sighed. "How many times have I forgotten about you when I become hyper-focused? Nikki and Francine have both pointed out to me how rude I can be when my mind is obsessed with solving a mystery. Do you hate me for it?"

"Of course not."

"Then don't hate yourself for being human. I've done the same thing. I'm human."

"But you're not like me." He lowered his head even more, his voice soft. "You're special."

The awe, admiration and affection in Vinnie's nonverbal cues robbed me of a response. Moments like these I wished

I hadn't such a dislike for touch. So I did the best I could. I kissed the tips of my fingers and lightly touched them to his cheek.

Some of his guilt and worry was immediately replaced by relief. How my touch was more successful in convincing him I wasn't angry, I had no idea. I held my fingers there for a few more seconds before I moved away. "Jane Dubois is waiting."

"I'll be right outside the door." He walked towards the closed conference door and positioned himself next to it. "You holler and I'll be there."

I nodded and reached for the door. I didn't look at Manny or Colin. The pride and love I'd glimpsed when I'd turned away from Vinnie had overwhelmed me. I needed to be focused on the case. Emotionality was always an unwelcome distraction.

I opened the door and walked into the large conference room. At the head of the table, Phillip and Daniel were talking to a visibly tense Jane Dubois.

"Doctor Lenard." Phillip's smile was warm. He always made me feel welcome. "Madame Dubois has been telling me the most interesting stories about the opera house. Such a rich history and she's been there for long enough to have a few really good tales."

"I'm glad you could join us, Madame Dubois." Manny walked past me and held out his hand. "Thank you for coming in."

She shook Manny's hand, then hid both hands in her lap. "Thank you for bringing me here. I didn't have the courage to brave the traffic or public transport getting here."

"No problem at all." Again Manny showed sensitivity to this woman who clearly needed it. Phillip was doing the same, his nonverbal cues communicating empathy and confidence. Daniel was in his uniform, seated a few chairs away from Jane, his posture not attracting attention at all. Colin and I sat down next to Daniel, Manny next to Jane. "Have you thought of anything you could share with us?"

Her colour increased. "I don't like gossiping at all. I like it even less when it is about people no longer here to defend themselves."

"I can give you my word that nothing you say will be considered gossip, Jane." Phillip leaned towards her. "These people are trying to find Léon's murderer. Even the smallest hint of something could lead them to find important information."

Manny shifted in his chair, seeming relaxed, but I noticed the impatience pulling at his mouth. "We would appreciate anything you can tell us. Maybe you can tell us more about Léon's private life."

Manny's manipulation of the conversation paid off. Jane's blush intensified even more. "Léon was an amazing man. For a short while I'd even had stupid ideas about him. I'm really happily married. I suppose I was just drawn by his passion. He was so passionate about the opera house, the singers, the orchestra, the repertoire, everything. Listening to him talk about Verdi was like listening to Verdi's best friend telling his life stories. It was amazing."

I thought of the seven operas I'd watched in the last two days. "What more can you tell us about Léon's love for Verdi?"

"Oh, he didn't just love the music, he also loved every detail of Giuseppe Verdi's life. From Verdi's first job as the official paid organist at a local church at the age of eight to his first opera written and performed in 1839 to Verdi's interest in politics influencing his music and the audience responding to a *Nabucco* chorus with nationalist fervour.

"In the time I worked for Léon I learned so much about Verdi. Léon loved all his music, but he used to say it was the operas where Verdi had left his mark on the world. Léon loved that he could play a role in sharing the beauty of Verdi's operas with people. He would sit for weeks with the design team planning the set and costumes. It had to be perfect. He would settle for nothing less."

"His love life?" Manny prompted.

She blushed again. "Yes. That. I just want to say again that I don't like talking about Léon like this."

"Noted." Manny barely hid his exasperation.

"About eighteen months after I started working for Léon, rumours did the rounds that explained why he never…" She swallowed. "Why he never showed an interest in me."

"Did these rumours imply he was homosexual?" Phillip's tone was respectful.

She nodded. "I never saw him with anyone, male or female. If he was gay, he'd hidden it well. No one I ever spoke to had seen evidence of it. Those were all just stupid rumours."

"But you had your own suspicions?" Manny asked.

"I started watching him more closely. He never looked at a beautiful woman the way other men look at women. My husband is the most faithful, wonderful husband and even he looks at a sexy woman with some level of lust. Léon never did. But a glimmer of that lust would shine through when he was looking at a sexy man. But these are just my impressions. I never, ever saw him behave anything but professionally and courteously to everyone."

Manny, Phillip and even Colin asked her a few more questions, but she had no more useful information to share. As they ended the meeting with her, I wondered if Léon's sexual preference had any bearing on this case. Had his murder been a hate crime that had been covered up to fit the pattern of the other crimes? That would mean the murderer had known Léon and had also known about his secret. And it would mean the murderer had been close enough to Léon to have gained access to all the incriminating information Léon had used to fund the opera house.

"Jenny?" Colin touched my forearm. I looked up, surprised to see Pink talking to Manny. Vinnie was seated at the table. Daniel and Phillip were still in their chairs, talking about art. I'd missed Jane's departure. Colin squeezed my arm. His eyes were wide with excitement. "Pink brought all the art from Valois', Faure's and Moreau's houses. Francine is setting it up in the team room."

"Hey, Genevieve." Pink waved at me.

"Are any of the paintings 3D-printed?"

Pink smiled. "I'm good with computers, not analysing art. That's Colin's field."

"And that's why I would like to go to the team room." Colin got up and held out his hand. "Shall we?"

"Francine told me to first tell you my findings from the hotel videos," Pink said.

"What hotel videos?" Manny grunted. "Bloody hell. I forgot about those. Why do you have findings? Supermodel was supposed to go through the hotel videos."

"She decided to delegate." Pink smiled. "And I don't mind. I watched all the footage from the hotels where Valois, Faure and Moreau were murdered. Nothing. I went over those babies twice and didn't see anyone who acted suspiciously."

"Are you trained in nonverbal communication?" I doubted he would notice any alarming body language without training.

"Not at your level, no." Pink nodded at Daniel. "We all receive quite intensive training in recognising body language that could lead to all sorts of crimes. I got ninety-seven percent on my test."

I tightened my jaw to avoid reminding him about the three percent possibility of making a mistake.

"I trust him, Genevieve." Daniel took a step closer to his team member. "Pink watches out for this kind of stuff when we're in the field. He's not once called it wrong."

I nodded. "Very well, then. Let's go to the team room."

"At last." Vinnie got up. "I'm starving for some snacks with coffee."

"Um, Phillip? Sirs?" Tim stood in the doorway looking very nervous. "There is a very loud and very angry man downstairs shouting at security. He insists on speaking to Doctor Lenard."

"Who is it, Tim?" Phillip asked.

Tim lost some colour in his face. "Émile Roche."

Chapter SEVENTEEN

After the initial outburst in the room, Tim's expression turned even more fearful. "I don't think we should let him in."

"Oh, let him in." Manny's expression was alarming. He looked far too eager to welcome Émile. "Daniel and I would just love to speak to him."

Tim took a step back when Vinnie got up, his top lip pulled up, baring his teeth. "Let him in. I get to speak to him before the law gets him."

Tim leaned to the side to see past Vinnie and addressed his question to Phillip. "What should I do?"

"I think it is up to Genevieve." Phillip looked at me. "Would you like to speak to Monsieur Roche?"

I thought about it. Émile had revealed a level of research last night that I had not yet shared with my team. His IT expert had managed to uncover a lot of information on us that I felt concerned about. I still needed to speak to Manny and especially Francine about it. But Émile had learned through that information how strong our co-operation with GIPN was. He would not have come here and risked being confronted by law enforcement if it had not been important. "I would like to see him. But only if you assure me that no one will confront him."

"You can't expect us to welcome him with open arms after what he did to you last night, Doc." Manny pushed his hands in his pockets.

"I don't expect anything from you except to listen to what he has to say. And not to confront him." I looked at Vinnie. His fists were pressed against his hips, his nostrils flaring. "Please, Vinnie."

"You're asking too much, Jen-girl." He pulled his seat out and sat down. "For you I'll do it, but I won't like it."

"Bring him up, Tim." Phillip pulled at his cuffs when Tim hurried down the hallway. "I suggest we all sit down before someone does throw a punch."

The tension in the room was uncomfortable. No one spoke, most eyes focused on the hallway. When we heard muted footsteps coming towards the conference room two minutes later, the tension increased even more. Tim reached the door first, but stood aside to let Émile enter. I lost interest in the abject fear on Tim's face when I saw Émile's expression.

I got up and walked around the table towards him. "What happened?"

"Why don't you answer your phone?" His *frontalis* muscles pulled his eyebrows up and in. His lips were colourless. Fear. "I've been calling you nonstop for the last two hours."

"I would watch my tone if I were you." Vinnie's voice was quiet. He was standing right behind me. Colin had moved around the table to stand next to me. Daniel and Manny were both out of their chairs, Daniel's hand resting on his holstered weapon.

"What happened?" I asked again. The anxiety visible on Émile's face was pressing against my chest.

"They took Yves' grandkids. The bastards kidnapped two toddlers." He didn't even acknowledge the threat of the other men in the room. Instead he leaned closer to me. "You said Gravois wasn't going to publish any more articles."

Manny glanced at the security cameras and I knew Francine would be checking it immediately. Phillip got up and walked towards Émile. "My name is Phillip Rousseau and this is my business. I would consider it a great courtesy if you would sit down and calmly explain what happened. As you can see, you don't have many friends in this room."

"I don't need your friendship." Émile looked back at me. "Only hers."

"If you want her help, you will need to tone down your aggression towards us."

"I don't work without them." I lifted my hands to include the men surrounding me. "I've asked them to be polite to you. You should do the same."

Émile stared at me for a few seconds, then pressed the palms of his hands against his eyes. A few deep breaths later, he lowered his hands. "Forgive me. We are all raging mad that Yves' grandkids are missing. I've sent my best guys to assist him in their search for the idiots stupid enough to make this move."

"Please. Take a seat." Phillip gestured at the chair Vinnie had vacated.

Émile nodded and sat down. Everyone returned to their seats except Vinnie. He stood against the wall behind Émile, his arms folded over his chest, his eyes not wavering off the man looking at me. "Yves phoned me this morning ready to go to war. He's been the most volatile of all of us, the least committed to keep his business as far away from his family as possible. But he has been trying. After so many years working to go legit, this business has now come right into his home."

"When did they take Yves' grandchildren?" I asked.

"This morning around nine o'clock. His daughter-in-law went to the shops with the kids before she dropped them off at kindergarten. She wanted to buy them both some chocolate to take to school. The shop's security cameras show how three SUVs followed her into the parking lot, boxed her in and took the kids from the car." His jaw protruded, his lips thinned and the *orbicularis oculi* muscles around his eyes tightened as his breathing grew louder. "Her screams nearly did me in, Genevieve. Yves is losing his mind and wants to kill anyone in his way."

"You said something about articles being published." I'd discovered that neurotypical people could seldom relay a story logically when they were emotionally distraught.

"Yes. Late last night a story was published about Yves. It gave even more details than the articles about Serge, Benoît and Claude. Louis has two masters degrees and he says that this last story was not nearly as well written as the others. I don't give a crap. All I care about is that another infodump made its way onto the internet and has now put the life of innocent people in danger. That three-year-old boy and five-year-old girl have nothing to do with Yves' business."

"Has he received any phone calls?" Daniel had taken his

hand from his weapon, concern visible on his face. "Any ransom demands? Anyone claiming responsibility?"

"Did he ever." Émile still only looked at me. "The kids were taken by some gangster idiot who wants to build street cred by getting Yves to hand over whatever is left of his... business."

"Name?" Daniel took his smartphone from one of the many pockets in his pants.

"Abélard Belamy." Émile glanced towards Daniel, then turned to face him and smirked. "Don't bother looking for him. You'll have to collect his parts from all over the globe. If you ever find him."

"Have you already located him?" I asked. "The kids?"

Émile nodded. "While I was waiting downstairs for you, I got the call. The kids are safe. Those who haven't sent their families away are doing so now. Those who have are sending their families to different locations. It took everything I had to convince Yves not to start a street war."

"Yet you killed Abélard Belamy." Manny slumped in his chair, looking bored.

"I didn't say that. And you will not catch me admitting to any crimes, so don't even bother trying." He looked at me again. "Why didn't you answer your phone?"

"The better question is why do you have her number?" Manny asked, still appearing bored.

"I gave him my number." I hoped that I was able to convey censure with my look at Manny. I returned my attention to Émile. "I apologise for not answering your call. My phone is still in my handbag, which is closed in one of my cabinets in my office."

"Just in case you think you're special, she does that all the time." Manny shrugged. "Bane of my existence."

Émile's expression softened as he looked at me. "Just like my Danielle."

"If you've found the kids and you know who took them, why are you here?" I was certain there was more to his visit.

"To tell you to answer your phone." He ignored Manny's rude coughing. "And to ask you who the f… hell is Marcos Gallo?"

I stared at Émile in shock. "How did you come across that name?"

"I have really good people working on computers. When Yves phoned about the article, I put my people on it. They traced the story through God knows how many IP addresses and found one in Venezuela. I might not be as smart as my Danielle, but my memory is really good. I would've remembered if I'd had any business dealings with a Gallo in Venezuela. So tell me, Genevieve, who is this Gallo? And why is he still alive?"

"Doc, don't say a word." Manny sat up and looked at Émile. "She can't talk about an ongoing investigation."

"Genevieve?" Again Émile didn't acknowledge Manny.

"We investigated Marcos Gallo in a previous case. Until now we've had no reason to suspect any connection between him and these murders." I pressed my lips together to organise my thoughts before I revealed too much.

"It is clear to me that you trust Genevieve." Phillip waited until Émile looked at him. "Would you trust her to find the connection between Marcos Gallo and the murders of your friends?"

I was glad it was Phillip who was speaking to Émile. Manny exuded far too much hostility and Daniel communicated distrust with his hand staying close to his holstered weapon. If anyone could deal with Émile, it was Phillip.

"If I don't push for more information, will I have your word that you'll do everything you can to stop this before any more children are traumatised?" Tension returned to his features. "Those little ones are going to need therapy, but Yves' daughter-in-law is going to need years of it to get over her kids being forcibly removed from her car."

Manny got up. "You have our word, Roche. I can't promise you that your day won't come though. Waiting in Doctor Lenard's car was not a good move to make. You better watch your back."

Émile dismissed him with a single chuckle and turned back to me. "With all the drama that went on today, no one has had a chance to write up those lists for you. I'll get mine to you later today. The others promised to do the same."

I pointed at his face. "You have more information, but don't want to share it because of Manny's threat."

"You can really tell that from my face?"

"Your glances at Manny and the following contempt around your mouth tells me you didn't appreciate his threat. The calculation and doubt when you look at me lead me to that conclusion."

He nodded slowly. "You're right. On both counts."

"I don't care that you don't like Manny. I only care about any pertinent information you can share. And how that information can help us stop any more murders."

"Only because I like you," he said after three seconds. He

shifted a bit to half-turn his back on Manny. "We've done what you asked and tried to find Serge, Benoît and Claude's bodyguards. They're missing. All of them. They've been missing since the murders of their bosses."

I closed my eyes. I had hoped my suspicion would come to naught. I didn't care that these men had ventured into the darker side of the criminal world. Already there were too many victims and I had naïvely hoped there wouldn't be more. I touched my little finger to my thumb and looked at Émile. "I'm sorry."

He sighed heavily. "Yeah. We also think they're dead. We just don't know where to look for their bodies."

A familiar niggling started in the back of my mind. On a deeper level, my brain had made a connection that still needed to filter through to my consciousness. Thinking more about it would not help, so I focused on Émile's nonverbal cues. "You have more information. Hmm. More important than your findings about the bodyguards."

"God help those who have to face you in an interrogation room." Émile looked proud as he smiled at me for a second. Then his expression turned serious. "When we decided six or so years ago to straighten out our paths, a few others also showed interest in doing so."

"How many?" I asked.

"Four others. One lasted only three months before he dropped out because of a very lucrative drug deal he closed with some Nigerians. Two others lasted a year before they also dropped out and one latecomer lasted all of three weeks before he realised it wasn't for him."

"Their names?" I thought about Phillip's skilled way of working with people. "Please."

Émile chuckled. "The drug guy is Mainard St Pierre, the other two Hamon Gage and Leroy Villeneuve. The pussy who only lasted three weeks was Arnaud Brun."

Shocked silence filled the conference room. It felt like a lightning bolt when the niggling connection blasted into my cerebral cortex—the thinking part of our brains. I looked at Daniel. "Look for the bodyguards in the woods south of Strasbourg."

He took his smartphone from a side pocket in his pants. "Any specific location?"

"Cross-reference it with the locations where they found the homeless men who died while fighting in Brun's organised contests."

"Holy hell." Manny fell into his chair. He rubbed his hands hard over his face a few times, then glared at Émile. "If you want to win some points with us, you will give us as much detail on St Pierre, Gage and Villeneuve as you can. It would be great to at least arrest someone today."

"I'll get the info to you," Émile said to me. I didn't know what Manny would have to do to win Émile's favour. "Yves and Nicolas are still talking about taking things into their own hands. The last few years have been the years that I've worked the hardest, but they are also the years I've been the most relaxed. I don't want us to return to the bad old days. Please, Genevieve. Find these bastards revealing all these hurtful secrets and stop them."

I didn't know how to respond. I always did my job the best possible way. With Manny, Vinnie, Colin and Francine on my team, I'd become even more efficient and successful in solving crimes. "We're already working on this. I don't want to see anyone else murdered because of these secrets."

"That's all I'm asking." He got up. "I will leave you and your protectors to it then. Where's that little fella? He can show me out and maybe I can get him to pee his pants this time."

"I'll see you out." Vinnie pushed his chest out to make himself look even larger. He pointed at the door. "Leave."

Émile didn't move. His expression was pleading as he looked at me. "Please stay in touch. If your protectors won't let you share details with me, please just let me know if and when you're making progress."

Thankfully he didn't wait for me to respond. I couldn't make such a promise. As it was, the expressions of the men in the room warned me of hard words to come. The room was quiet for three seconds after Émile left.

"You gave him your bloody phone number?" Manny was leaning on the table, the supratrochlear artery on his forehead visible. "What else did you give him, missy? Your bloody home address and a key to the front door?"

"Francine keeps my phone safe from intrusions." I'd had to listen to those conversations during numerous lunches Francine and I had shared.

"I don't care what the bleeding hell supermodel does. Don't ever give anything to a criminal again." He swung towards Daniel when the larger man snorted. "This is not a laughing matter."

"Will it appease you to know that I never willingly put my life in danger?" I asked. "Or the lives of those I care for?

Or the lives of anyone. I don't want to be the cause of harm at all."

"Appease? Do I look like that little Lucien Privott with his hipster beard and knowledge of calming herbs? No, missy. I don't need you to *appease* me. I need you to bloody well listen to me."

"I found something! I found something!" Francine ran into the room holding her laptop in front of her. She stopped next to Manny and looked around the table. "What did I miss?"

"I don't know." I didn't know whether she'd watched both the visits from Jane Dubois and Émile Roche on the security feed. "Did you see the part where Émile said that Arnaud Brun had also tried to stop his illegal activities, but only lasted three weeks?"

"What?" She put her laptop on the table and sat down. "Oh, my God. That makes even more sense. All of this is totally coming together."

"Why? What did you find?" At last we were finding the keys to put all the disjointed pieces together.

She pointed at herself with both index fingers. "Who's your queen? Huh? Queen of all technology?"

"Supermodel." Manny slapped his hand on the table. "I do not have the patience today."

"Well, pardon me." There was no contrition visible on her face. She pressed a few keys on her computer and turned it for me to see. "Remember the strange code I saw on Léon Blanc's laptops? Well, I transferred his entire system to mine, did a full analysis and voila! Do you see it? Isn't it just too shocking for words?"

I looked at the screen filled with unending lines of code. "What am I looking at?"

"Marcos Gallo's signature. I got him, baby! I got him."

"What do you mean you got him?" Daniel looked up from where he was texting on his smartphone. In our last case, he'd been instrumental in providing contacts with his counterparts in Brazil. He was equally invested in seeing Gallo incarcerated. "Do you have his location?"

"Not at the moment." She lifted both shoulders. "Sorry."

"But you have something else?"

She took a deep breath as if to prepare herself for a long speech. "I found this code in Léon's computer and traced it to an email he received three months ago. I then sent an email from Léon's email account. I made it a general appeal for funding for the opera house and made it look like it was sent from an emailing service that sends mass emails. I'm hoping Gallo will open the email. He doesn't even have to click on any of the links I provided. Just opening the email will trigger a virus that will wait for him to use one of the email addresses he's used before to send Genevieve those awful quotes. Then I'm in his system and can track him wherever he is. As long as his computer is switched on."

I had many questions swirling around my brain. "What is the connection between Gallo and Léon?"

"Wait!" Francine lifted both hands to stop me. "I'm not finished yet."

"Then get to it, supermodel."

"I noticed a prior attempt to hack Léon's system. That happened about a week before the email was sent to his private email address. I can't be sure, but it looks like someone tried to upload the virus manually."

"Hmm." Manny rubbed his chin. "What the hell is the connection between Gallo and Léon? Doc?"

"I asked that question earlier." I shrugged. "I still don't have a satisfying answer. We now know that Brun is connected to Léon through the organised crime leaders, but we're missing a stronger connection between Léon and Gallo, and Léon and Brun. There's also Gallo's connection to Brun through Raul Fernandez."

"Asshole." Francine touched her neck. She'd almost suffocated when Fernandez had grabbed her cloak during a struggle. "May he not rest in peace."

"Bloody hell. This is making my head hurt." Manny grunted. "We have more information, but a million more questions."

I knew Manny was being hyperbolic, so I didn't correct him about the unknown number of questions. I did, however, agree with him that it certainly felt like our questions outnumbered the bits of information we had. "Francine, did you find any of the secrets on Léon's computer?"

"Nope." Her shoulders sagged. "I looked in every nook and cranny, but didn't even find a hint of a scandal. I'm beginning to think he kept all his secrets on old-school good ol' paper."

Another niggling started. Had I seen those documents somewhere during our investigation? Léon's book collections in his home office and opera house office? Or were they hidden somewhere in his desk or piano or in the seats of the antique chairs?

"Dude." Vinnie walked into the conference room, his smartphone in his hand. The excitement on his face took my focus off the documented secrets. "Ilbert just SMSed me."

"Good." Colin sat up. "I asked him to send you a message when he had some answers."

"Who's Ilbert and what answers did he give?" Manny looked from Colin to Vinnie and back.

"Ilbert is a source you don't need to concern yourself with at the moment." Colin raised both eyebrows as he faced Vinnie. "What did he say?"

Vinnie looked at his phone's screen. "'Activity at university. Rumours about Prof. G. Nothing else anywhere else.'"

"Hmm." Colin frowned. "If he's talking about Professor Roland Gagneux, I have a hard time believing it."

"Do you trust this Ilbert?" Manny asked.

Colin thought about it. "Yes. He wouldn't send me on a wild-goose chase." He looked at me. "He wouldn't give me false or useless information."

"Then you'd better go check out this Professor Gaggley." Manny looked at Vinnie. "Go with them. Make sure Doc doesn't hand out more house keys."

"I did no such thing. And the professor's surname is Gagneux." I was more concerned about Ilbert's SMS than Manny's mistake. I couldn't reconcile any illegal activity with the man I'd met. The worst quality I'd observed about him had been his utter failure at organising his space. At least with this visit I knew what to expect and could mentally prepare myself. I got up and looked at Colin. "I want to speak to him. He might be the link between Gallo, Léon and Brun."

Chapter EIGHTEEN

Something was causing Professor Roland Gagneux great distress. He was not the same jovial man we'd met two days ago. The *orbicularis oculi* muscles were tense around his eyes, the *depressor anguli oris* muscle pulling the corners of his mouth down. He glanced at the hallway behind me, Colin and Vinnie and swallowed. "I'm glad you accepted my invitation to come back."

We had decided it best not to phone ahead, but rather arrive unannounced, as Roland had suggested during our first meeting. It was a Saturday afternoon and Colin had been convinced the professor would be here. Apparently Roland had mentioned that he loved coming in on the weekends to do his preparation work for the week. Yet another piece of information I'd missed by being distracted.

After a visit to his office, we'd located him in a thankfully very neat workshop that had the look of a warehouse.

"We couldn't resist the opportunity to visit you again, Roland." Colin leaned heavily on his cane and took a step deeper into the workshop. Long workbenches were placed equidistant from each other. Different types of equipment were on each workbench, but there was no clutter in sight. It was a relief to have one less distracting factor. I could focus on the professor.

"Please come in." Roland walked back into the workshop and stopped at the first workbench. The workbenches were in the front of the extremely large space. Behind them were numerous machines I knew nothing of. Close to the front of the room was one closed side door, another about halfway into the room. There was no one else in the workshop. Roland glanced at the closest side door. "What can I do for you, Professor Dryden?"

The fear flashing across Roland's face grabbed my attention. Colin's disguise as the ageing professor no longer held any interest. Nor did Vinnie's insistence on staying close to me at all times. I walked into the workshop, Vinnie right behind me. We stopped next to Colin. He took his time to answer. "We wanted to find out a little more about the work you do with that fancy 3D printer of yours."

Another micro-expression of fear was followed by regret and deep sadness. When Roland glanced at the side door for a second time, I took a step towards him. "The person you expect to come through that door is causing you a lot of fear. Who are you expecting? Who are you scared of?"

Roland's reaction was immediate. For a moment I thought the masculine man was going to cry. He didn't. He regained his composure, walked to his large wooden desk and leaned against it. He took a few uneven breaths and rubbed both hands over his face. His hands rested over his mouth as if to prevent words from being formed. When he spoke it was through his fingers. "I don't know what to do."

"What's wrong, Roland?" Colin also stepped closer. "Maybe we can help."

Roland looked at Vinnie. "You might be the only one who can help."

"Then tell me what I can do." Vinnie didn't move, but his muscle tension increased.

Roland stared at Vinnie for a few seconds, then looked at Colin. "How can I think about hurting my own flesh and blood?"

"You mentioned a sister," Colin said. "Is that who you're talking about?"

"No." His laugh was without humour, his accompanying expression hopeless. "Valerie is the sweetest thing. No, it's not her. It's my brother. Ever since I can remember he's been getting himself into trouble. And all I seem to do is enable him. I thought this time he was going to get his act sorted out. My dad and my sister warned me, but I didn't listen. I'm such a sucker. I believed all his sob stories about having this new mission in life and making things right."

"Are you expecting your brother?" I asked when he glanced again at the side door, then at the two large cabinets flanking the door.

"My half-brother." Roland's shoulders sagged. "I wish I'd known about him earlier. I only learned about him three and some years ago. Then it was too late. He was already into all kinds of shit."

"Why didn't you know about him before?" I didn't find it strange that he would trust us with such personal information. Often it was much easier to talk to complete strangers than to share one's difficulties with loved ones.

Roland gave a half-laugh. "My dad was apparently quite a naughty bugger when he was younger. When my mom died six years ago, he took a full year to recover from her loss. Not that he really recovered, but at least he was able to function again. Mom was an angel. She kept all of us on the straight and narrow, including my dad.

"One day he invited my sister and me for lunch. There he announced that he'd had an affair with a receptionist in one of the first legal firms he worked in. As soon as she fell pregnant, he dropped her like a hot potato. He gave her a bunch of cash, made sure the legal firm paid her a generous severance pay and fired her. Within a few months, he got himself another job and forgot about her. Many years later, he was a judge when a case crossed his desk and he recognised the name.

"This woman was being prosecuted on drug charges. The same woman who had borne his child. It was already too late to intervene. But he started keeping tabs on his son. My half-brother. When my mom died, he thought it was time to confess his crimes and hoped that together we could help my half-brother."

"Help him with what?"

"Getting his life sorted out." Roland made a rude sound. "No sooner had we learned about his existence than he landed in prison. And he had the audacity to blame us for it. I can understand some level of anger aimed at my dad, but what did my sister and I ever do to him?"

My mind raced as disconnected pieces floated together to form a picture in my mind. An uncomfortable tension settled in my stomach as I came to a conclusion. "You grew up in a life of privilege. Your half-brother had to fight for everything he accomplished."

Guilt settled on every centimetre of Roland's face. "You have no idea how right you are. He's had to fight. And it's the fighting that brought all this trouble to my door."

"Who is your brother, Roland?" Colin's eyes narrowed and I wondered if he'd come to the same conclusions I had.

The side door opened and a well-built man walked into the workshop.

For a second I thought I was going to shut down. I had not seen any evidence in our investigation that could have led me to connect the man walking towards us with Roland. I pushed Mozart's String Quartet No. 2 in D major into my mind, held my breath for two seconds and slowly exhaled.

The initial panic receded and I focused on the combination of extreme anger, hate and pain on Arnaud Brun's face. There was little physical resemblance between the two siblings. Even with Brun standing next to Roland, I would never have said they were half-brothers.

"My big brother is talking about me."

His voice brought the darkness back to my peripheral vision. I pressed my little finger to my thumb and focused on the nonverbal cues of the man who'd escaped prison four months ago. I couldn't afford to be distracted. Not after I'd noticed the cues of intent on Brun's face. When Vinnie took a step closer, I held out my hand to stop him. I didn't know what Brun was planning, but I didn't want to trigger him into action.

Colin fumbled with his cane and put his hand in his suit jacket pocket. He searched around his pocket for a while before coming out with a handkerchief. He wiped his brow and looked at Arnaud Brun. "And who might you be, sir?"

"Ask her." He pointed at me. "She's been trying to put me back into prison."

"This is Arnaud Brun." Roland swallowed and tried to look less fearful. "My half-brother."

"The half-brother you didn't want." Bitterness made Brun's voice harsh.

"I never said that, Arnaud. Never. All I said was that I didn't want all the trouble you've brought Dad and Val."

Brun's *zygomaticus minor* muscles pulled his top lip up. "Yeah. That's what you say, but I see the way you look at me. The way all of you look at me. Your dad threw us away so he could be with his oh-so-holy family."

"Have you been making 3D-printed copies of masterpieces?" I didn't want the emotionality of discussing family issues to escalate. Already Brun's colour had heightened and his muscle tension had increased.

"Yeah. And it took you police types forever to even figure it out."

"How long have you been doing this?" Roland looked devastated. "I gave you the key to this workshop because I thought you were making the furniture you told me about."

Brun's laughter was cruel. "I can't believe you fell for that. Like I would ever use the carpentry work I did in prison to start a furniture business. I had bigger things planned with the skills I learned in prison."

"Like plotting revenge on Serge Valois, Benoît Faure and Claude Moreau?" I asked.

"Those fucking bastards!" Brun stepped away from Roland. His arms were away from his body, his legs apart, his face as tense as his body. He inhaled loudly through his flared nostrils. "One misstep and they turned their backs on me. When I joined their little network, they told me we would be like brothers supporting each other through the change. Since I didn't even know then that I had a brother, I thought it would be good to have a support system. Like hell! They only cared about their reputations."

"What happened?" Colin fiddled in his pocket again. His smartphone was in that pocket and I hoped he was phoning someone for help. For now I could keep Brun occupied by talking to him. Something he appeared to need.

"A contact I'd been working with for many years asked me to organise one final fight. That was after I announced I was retiring from the fight scene. But the money he offered was spectacular. It was going to be my nest egg. Little did I know that I was going to need all that money to pay for my legal fees. The fight had just started that night when the police descended on us like a bunch of starving vultures. I lost all credibility I had on the street and I also lost my freedom.

"My precious little family wasn't there for me during the trial. My so-called brothers turned their backs on me. I'd broken their stupid code and they made sure I knew that they had zero tolerance for such shit. I was totally alone." The corners of his mouth turned down as he nodded. "But I survived well in prison. I scared the shit out of the other prisoners and no one touched me. I even made a friend. The only true friend I've ever had and your fucking team took him from me!"

His last words echoed through the workshop. I'd known Brun and Raul Fernandez had been cellmates and had been friendly, but I hadn't known the depth of their friendship. Despite the hatred and aggression Brun was communicating, his nonverbal cues revealed great loss and pain.

"You loved him." The memory of his affection for Fernandez was clear on his face.

"Not at first." The bitterness returned. "I was straight when I went to prison. Not even in the army did I ever consider batting for the other team. Gays made my skin crawl. But Raul was different. He wasn't one of those pansies. He didn't walk around with weak wrists and sing about fashion and flowers. He was a man like me. It was luck that brought us to the same cell."

Next to me, Vinnie and Colin stood unmoving, yet I knew Vinnie would spring into action at any moment. Colin's disguise was only that. He would be right beside Vinnie.

"I didn't know any of this." Roland's sadness was deep and sincere. "You know we only learned about you five years ago. I would've been there for you. I really would've."

"What? Like now?" Brun waved towards us. "You got the cops involved. They are here because of you."

"No." I made sure my tone was firm. "We are here because of you."

Colin leaned forward, resting on his cane. "In the homes of Serge Valois, Benoît Faure, Léon Blanc and Claude Moreau we found 3D-printed artwork that replaced the originals. Did you take those original paintings?"

Those paintings had arrived in the team room shortly before we'd left for the university and Colin hadn't even had time to look at them. I trusted that he had a strategy in lying to Brun and looked closely at his reaction. If I weren't an expert in noticing micro-expressions, I might have missed the brief softening of his expression. "No. I didn't take the paintings."

"Then who did?" I asked.

"Someone who has suffered as much pain as I have."

"Marcos Gallo?"

"That sick asshole?" Brun took a step back. A step towards the side door and the cabinets. "Look, he's helped me a lot since Raul died and he even helped us get out. I mean, he did figure out the code that got us all those secrets about the assholes and he was the one who came up with the plan. But that man is fucked up in his head. I don't want anything to do with him. Especially now that my whole plan has been shot to hell."

The heavy, uncomfortable feeling in my stomach returned. I slowed my breathing and pressed my fingers harder together. I prioritised my concerns. "What plan?"

"To make sure everyone gets what they deserve. Including that bitch who killed Raul."

"She didn't kill him. He slipped while he was trying to kill her. It was his fall down the ravine that killed him." I was being bombarded with information from his micro-expressions, my mind rushing to keep up with processing everything.

"I don't care!" Brun took another step back. "If it wasn't for her, my Raul would still be here and I wouldn't have to hurt someone else."

His nonverbal cues when he referred to 'hurting someone else' immediately alerted me. "You fell in love again."

"No one can ever replace Raul. No one!"

"Yet you've come to care for someone else." And this person might play a very important role in this case. "Who is it?"

"Why? Do you want to kill him as well? No. I will not let you close to anyone else." Brun glanced behind him. "I was doing well on my mission. I was getting those bastards back for betraying me. Then you stopped the articles. I'm going to make sure Gravois suffers for talking to you and not publishing any more articles. I'm going to make sure everyone suffers. Everyone! Today, all their secrets will be revealed. And soon the others will get what's coming to them."

"What others? Do you plan to kill more people?" I felt cold. Inside and out.

"I wish *I* could." The regret around his mouth was genuine. "You have no idea what a turn-on it was to put my mark on those fuckers. Did you know that climbing roses can be real hardy? Like me. They survive all kinds of weather and hardship. Even betrayal. I don't have thorns to protect myself, but the army did teach me how to press on a man's throat and watch the life slowly drain from him."

"And Léon Blanc?" My voice was hoarse. There was no remorse visible on his face. A cold killer. "Did you also enjoy tattooing him? Strangling him?"

He blinked a few times. "Yes, Blanc as well."

I knew manipulating him would trigger him to act on whatever he was planning, so I asked him a straightforward question. "How did you get those men to the hotel rooms?"

"Stupid fuckers." He wiped his nose on his forearm. "All I needed to do was promise them the name of the person who was giving the information to Gravois. I said I wanted payment and they came with money. Hah. My payment was their money and their lives."

"Arnaud." Roland's shocked whisper got Brun's attention.

"What, little brother? You're surprised that your judge father created a killer?" His smile was cold as he took another step back. "Well, he did. But, I also got a few of his brain cells. And the army taught me some very useful skills. Like how to use gas to overpower the enemy. And how to set up red herrings. I was also smart enough to get Gallo to trust me."

"Did he trust you enough to tell you where he got the code from?" I hoped this was the right question. I needed to know how Gallo found all the secrets.

"The code to all those secrets? I didn't ask." He shrugged. "I don't care. Gallo asked for photos of everything in that pansy Blanc's safes, even the pages of every document. So he got it. I don't know if the secrets were in there or in Blanc's computer he hacked. All I care about is the information that gave me the power to get back at those lowlife motherfuckers."

"Did you break into Léon Blanc's safe?" I didn't know how much longer I would be able to hold Brun's attention. His eyes were losing their focus, his entire body leaning towards the right side of the door. The cabinet.

"Of course I did. I'm a big, bad criminal, remember?" He made no attempt to hide his lie, but it was his other micro-expressions that brought suffocating fear to my throat. I wondered if anyone had received Colin's phone call and whether anyone was coming. There was something very dangerous in that cabinet and Brun was only two short steps from it.

Unconsciously, my right hand reached out to hold him back. I didn't want him to get any closer to the cabinet and its contents. Not after I'd seen the hopelessness in his expression. I desperately searched for more questions, more ways to distract him. I thought about asking him about Léon's safe and the obvious untruth he'd just told. But I was more interested in something else he'd said. "Do you plan to kill your new love interest?"

He jerked. "Never. I wouldn't do that."

"You are concerned about him though."

He was quiet for a few seconds, pain, anger and sadness flashing across his features. Before I consciously registered the final intent on his face, I'd already taken a step back and pulled Colin and Vinnie with me.

Brun pushed his hand into his trouser pocket and came out with a small black remote control.

"I only hope he has the courage to follow through."

I wanted to shout a warning, but Vinnie had already grabbed me around my waist and was throwing me on the floor behind the solid wooden desk. He landed on top of me as a loud explosion blasted through the workshop.

Chapter NINETEEN

"I can't possibly drink this in bed, Nikki." I stared at the tray Nikki had placed on my bed. "I never drink anything in bed."

"Then this is your first. You should like totally have hot chocolate with mini-marshmallows for your first drink in bed." She pushed the tray towards us.

Colin took the third mug on the tray and sniffed the contents. "Thanks, Nix. This is going to be really good."

"Are we having a party in here?" Vinnie walked into my bedroom, holding a mug. His shower had washed all the soot and blood off, but he favoured his left foot. The debris that had landed on his foot would've done much more damage had he not been wearing his usual combat boots.

Of the three of us, Colin had sustained the most injuries. He'd reached the cover of the desk too late and a lot of the flying debris had caused minor lacerations on his left side. There was one particular cut on his side that had needed stitching, but no serious damage had been done. I had a large bruise on my hip where I'd hit the floor, but was otherwise uninjured.

The overwhelming concern for Colin's well-being and the overload of information had sent me into a shutdown a second after the explosion. I'd come out of my shutdown to the chaos of the explosion's aftermath. Daniel and the entire GIPN team had been there and Manny was walking around the workshop barking orders at everyone. The explosion had been rather small. The locked steel doors of the cabinet had offered just enough resistance to minimise the blast that could have been much worse.

I had been greatly relieved when I'd learned that the paramedics had already taken Roland to the hospital. Standing so close to the explosion, he'd sustained serious injuries, but he was not in critical condition.

Vinnie had threatened to kill what was left of Brun for the suicide bombing. Although it was a preposterous notion, I shared in Vinnie's frustration. There were still many unanswered questions Brun could've answered. His death had left us with more unconnected pieces. Manny hadn't cared about my questions or frustration. He'd ordered me home and Vinnie and Colin had fully supported him. We'd returned to my apartment and a worried Francine and Nikki.

Francine had left as soon as she was sure we were safe. Her mouth had an expression of determination I was familiar with. She wasn't going to sleep at all tonight. Instead she would drink more coffee and hack from her computer station in her loft apartment. She'd left two hours ago and I wondered if she'd discovered anything new.

It had taken a lot for me to insist Colin take a shower before me. The desire to wash the explosion off my body had been overpowering. At least I hadn't noticed any blood on my clothes. There had been no way to determine whether the blood on Vinnie and Colin's clothes had been only their own or some of Brun's as he'd been blown apart. I shuddered again at the thought.

After a scorching hot shower, I'd joined Colin in bed, only to have Nikki march into the room with the hot chocolate. She'd put the tray on the bed and sat down before I'd had a chance to object. Now Vinnie pushed against Nikki's shoulder. "Scoot over, punk."

"No." I pulled my legs up and glared at them. "You can't sit on my bed. In my bedroom. We can't drink hot chocolate here."

"After all this time, don't you think it's my bed as well?" There was laughter around Colin's eyes and mouth.

"No. I bought this bed and it is mine." My argument sounded weak.

"Can I at least claim this half of the bed?" Colin pointed to his side with his mug. I wanted to grab the ceramic dish before he spilled hot chocolate on my white bedding.

I blinked a few times and corrected my thoughts. Sixteen months ago, Colin had come home with this set of linen. Ostensibly, the bedding was his. "I don't know how to relate to neurotypical sharing. Technically, certain things belong to you and others to me. That is how I relate to it."

"If I gave you cash for half the value of this mattress, would it make this side technically mine?"

I thought about this. Then I realised that with this argument Colin had successfully taken my focus off Vinnie and Nikki's invasion of my space and my obsessive thoughts about the case. I relaxed against the headboard as I thought about Colin's offer some more. "You would have to pay me much more than that. Half the mattress, half the bedframe and a percentage more if you want to allow these people to continue sitting on my bed."

Everyone burst out laughing. Nikki held her hand over her mouth and her face turned red as she tried to swallow her hot chocolate. It was the first time today that I'd seen Vinnie relaxed. "Aw, Jen-girl. You really know how to make a dude feel special. Hah! I'm now 'these people'."

My intention hadn't been to be humorous, but I was glad that had been the effect. My need to protect my personal space and Colin's white bedding seemed inconsequential against having the people I cared for sitting on my bed and drinking hot chocolate.

I took a calming breath. With Mozart playing in my head, I might be able to give them this moment. I might even enjoy it myself. Yet I couldn't stop myself from watching their mugs the entire time. Just in case a drop might spill.

For the next hour we chatted. I seldom chatted. Chatting required social skills and the ability to talk about things that had little to no importance. I didn't contribute much to the conversation, but strangely found myself enjoying this odd gathering on my bed. I corrected my thoughts—on *our* bed.

The relaxed atmosphere in my room changed when Vinnie's smartphone buzzed. An immediate frown pulled his brows together as he took his phone from his sweatpants. "Fuck it! Dude, lock yourselves in here."

Colin jumped out of the bed and followed Vinnie to the bedroom door. "Who's here?"

I realised Vinnie must have received an alert that someone was trying to enter my apartment. He kept upgrading our security system. Whenever someone rang the doorbell, he received an alert on his smartphone. If someone dared attempt a break-in and triggered any of the alarms, he also received that information on his smartphone. He shook the device as he stopped outside my bedroom door. "That motherfucker Roche."

I got out of bed. "Émile Roche? Is he trying to break in?"

"No, Jen-girl. He's already broken in."

I took a step back. "He's in my apartment?"

"Not yet. He got into the building and is on his way up." He looked at Colin. "Lock this door."

"No." I walked around the bed to where my robe was hanging behind the door. "He's here to speak to me and I won't hide."

"He's not alone, Jen-girl."

Colin took my hand and pulled me behind him. "Who's with him?"

"Some other motherfuckers." Vinnie glared at his smartphone's screen. "They're at the front door."

No sooner had he said that than my doorbell rang. I pulled my hand from Colin's, grabbed my robe and walked to the front door. I didn't get far. Vinnie rushed past me and Colin once again grabbed my hand. "Let Vinnie open the door, love. You might think Émile Roche is harmless, but he really isn't."

"I know he isn't. But I also know he has no malicious intent towards me. Towards us." I allowed Colin to hold me back. I understood Vinnie and Colin's reasoning and thought the caution to be wise.

Vinnie reached underneath the coffee table closest to the front door. When he straightened he had a gun in his hand.

I gasped. I detested all forms of violence. I hated that there was a logical need for having weapons in my home and I hated it even more that I thought Vinnie's hiding place was ingenious. I leaned closer to Colin when Vinnie opened the door, the handgun raised and aimed at the guests at my front door. "What the fuck do you want?"

"I would like to speak to Genevieve." Émile didn't sound concerned with the weapon aimed at him. I couldn't see past Vinnie's body filling the door to confirm what I'd heard.

"What about the other fuckers?" Vinnie seldom used such strong language in front of me.

"We're also here to speak to Doctor Lenard." It was Louis Masson's voice. He sounded annoyed.

I tightened my robe around me and stepped towards the door. "Let them in, Vinnie."

"I'm not lowering my weapon."

"I didn't ask you to." I knew he would never use it unless it was the last resort.

Vinnie stood still for a few more seconds and I was certain he was glaring at them, making sure they saw his intentions. The space available when he took a sidestep was just enough for each man to enter my home sideways if they didn't want to touch Vinnie. He did lower the weapon, but his muscle tension revealed his readiness to act at the smallest provocation.

Émile Roche, Louis Masson and Yves Patenaude walked into my apartment, confident and angry.

Especially Yves. He strode towards me. "They tried to take Stéphane's wife today. She's in hospital so the doctors can stitch up the deep cut she got when she defended herself against a knife attack. This has to stop, Doctor Lenard. What are you doing to stop it?"

Émile looked at me, then at Colin and finally at Vinnie. He stared at the lacerations on Vinnie's bare arms and his shoulders not covered by his white undershirt. He frowned as he looked at the many cuts on Colin's left side. I watched as he processed the information and came to a conclusion. "You were there when Brun blasted the hell out of the university workshop."

"What?" Louis stepped closer and smiled when Colin moved half in front of me. "I'm not going to hurt her. But I would like to hurt the son of bitch who triggered a bomb when she was around."

"None of us sustained life-threatening injuries." I pushed at Colin's shoulder until he moved aside and returned to his position next to me. "How do you know that Arnaud Brun was the one to detonate the bomb?"

"We know people who know things, Genevieve." The expression on Émile's face made it clear he wasn't going to reveal his sources. "It's very interesting though that you are not mentioned on any of the reports. Neither you nor these two men."

Yves pointed at Vinnie. "I know him, but I don't know the pretty one."

Not once had I considered the danger this case would pose to Vinnie and the work he'd put into building and maintaining his reputation as a hard, ruthless criminal. These men could mean the end of the inroads he had made into the criminal community.

Vinnie's nostrils flared. "You don't need to know anyone."

"But I do know you." Yves turned to Émile and Louis. "About eight years ago, he procured a contact for me—the best transporter I've ever worked with. He could move anything from… Yeah. He could move anything."

It had been the warning expression on Émile's face that had stopped Yves. Émile studied Vinnie, then turned to me. "Just as you don't know about us, we don't know about you."

"That doesn't make sense." I waved my hand at the three guests. "You're here. I know your names. Because of the information Léon had gathered, I know a lot of private information. And you know my name and my address."

Émile's smile relaxed his face as well as his posture. "Forgive me for not being clear. What I meant was that we trust you not to run around telling everyone about us. The same way you can trust us to not tell anyone that the big guy who looks like he wants to kill me is actually a sheep disguised as a wolf… a good guy."

I saw the truth on his face, but took my time to study the other two. "Do you give your word to protect Vinnie's identity?"

"I don't give a flying fuck about him." Yves nodded towards Vinnie. "What I care about is keeping my family safe. I think it is now too late to get the cat back into the bag."

"What does that mean?"

"It means that an hour ago, my IT guys found an information dump they traced back to Venezuela." Émile's jaw muscles tightened. "That Gallo asshole from Venezuela put the details of the rest of the guys in one publication online. He didn't even bother to disguise it as an article like the last time. Everything is there. Bénédict's bank details, Albert's wife's weekly salon appointments."

"My children's home addresses, work addresses, email addresses as well as their phone numbers." Louis rested his hands on his hips, his thumbs pointing back. Confrontational. "Émile's guy managed to redirect any traffic to that site, but we don't know who's already seen it."

Vinnie's phone buzzed. With his free hand, he tilted it to glance at the screen and grinned. Four seconds later, Manny and Daniel came rushing through my still-open front door, their weapons raised. They assessed the situation and lowered their guns, but like Vinnie didn't holster them. Manny marched up to Émile. "What the bloody hell are you doing here?"

There was too much aggression in my home. I didn't like it. I cleared my throat. "I will leave if you cannot contain your need to show dominance."

"Are you talking to me, missy?" Manny's scowl intensified.

"I'm talking to all seven men in my apartment. Your alpha displays are distracting. Our time would be used more efficiently if we talked rationally and shared information. That would help me find the connection between all these elements."

"I agree with her." Francine walked into my apartment, her laptop in her hand. "You boys can put it back in your pants for now. Sit at the table so we can talk like adults. I'm sure you gentlemen have done that once or twice?"

Émile, Yves and Louis stared at Francine, their eyes wide and their mouths slightly agape. She was wearing red leather trousers and a black silk blouse that perfectly showcased her figure. Her black high-heeled sandals completed an outfit that would be better suited to a high-end restaurant or club. Not confronting organised crime leaders in my apartment.

She flicked her wrists a few times as if herding them to my large dining room table, her bracelets jingling.

Vinnie half raised his weapon. "You'd better listen to the lady."

Manny was not pleased with Francine's presence in my apartment. He was even less receptive to the other three men's presence. He made a show of putting his weapon into his hip holster and lifting it out to show it was not restrained. He waited for Émile, Yves and Louis to take the seats Francine directed them to before he fell into his usual seat. He slumped in the chair, his gaze never leaving the men. Daniel stood against the window, his hand resting on his holster. Vinnie placed himself between the dining room area and my bedroom directly behind it.

I'd forgotten about Nikki. I glanced at my open bedroom door, but didn't see her. She was a very smart young woman. She knew when to push for inclusion and when it was best to stay out of sight. I was sure she was the one who'd alerted Manny to our visitors and was now sitting on my bed playing some mind-numbing game on her smartphone. But my concern wasn't with Nikki or my guests.

I stared at Francine as she stood next to my dining room table. Something was very wrong. When she'd left my apartment three hours ago, she'd been wearing designer jeans and a t-shirt, her hair swept up. The black silk shirt she was wearing now had three-quarter sleeves that covered most of her arms and her hair had been styled to cover the sides of her face. And she was wearing more makeup than usual.

I walked to her. "What happened?"

"What do you mean?" She put her laptop on the table, keeping her left side hidden.

"Look at me."

"Dammit." Francine turned to face me and I gasped. This close I saw the discolouration under her skin and the swelling on her left cheekbone.

I pressed my little finger to my thumb. Hard. "What happened?"

"I'm fine." Francine leaned a bit towards me. "I'm really fine. I didn't want to tell you because I didn't want you to worry. You've had enough excitement today already."

Vinnie's posture changed, but he didn't move from his place in front of my bedroom door. "What happened, Franny?"

"I was attacked outside my apartment."

Colin stiffened next to me. "You were ambushed?"

"And the two stupid idiots look much worse than me." Her smile was genuine. "Much, much worse."

"Who did this?" I asked, surprised that Manny wasn't out of his chair, shouting at Francine.

"Brun sent them. They were paid half and promised the other half when they finished the job." She glanced at Manny. "They didn't even really start the job."

I looked at Manny. "What really happened?"

"Supermodel kicked the living shite out of the two thugs who thought beating a vulnerable lady is a good idea." His chest puffed a bit before he caught himself and slumped back in the chair, glaring at Émile and the other men. "I was a few minutes behind her and helped her finish the job."

"You killed them?" My voice was a pitch higher from shock.

"No, Doc. I arrested the bloody idiots."

"And I booked them," Daniel said. "That's why we got here together."

"To make sure *these* bloody idiots don't overstay their welcome." Manny scowled at the other men.

I looked at Francine. "Tell me the truth. Are you well?"

"This bruise"—she pointed at her cheek—"and a scrape on my arm is all they managed to do to me. As you can see, I'm dressed for success. I'm so frigging furious that I got jumped. Man, I'm ready to kick some serious digital tush."

I studied her and she allowed me to. After twenty seconds I was satisfied with her answer. But I was greatly distressed. "Brun mentioned you before he blew himself up. He said that you were going to get what you deserved. I just didn't think it meant he would send someone to attack you."

"Hey." Francine lowered her chin to look at me. "It's not your responsibility to keep all of us safe twenty-four seven. As you can see, I'm quite good at taking care of myself. This is not your fault, girlfriend."

Colin put his arm around me and hugged me to him. "She's right, love. This is Brun's fault and the men who attacked Francine's. Not yours."

I blinked a few times. This was a part of friendships and relationships I was not good at. I didn't know how to balance responsibilities. I nodded tightly and turned my attention back to the table and the men. Everyone's intense hostility had been replaced with wariness. We were up against a common enemy. I looked at Émile. "Could you tell me more about the information your IT person found?"

"It was *your* IT guy?" Francine pulled out her chair and sat down. "He's good. If I hadn't had an alert set up, I would never have found that infodump tonight. He did a good job hiding it behind the fake website."

"You also found the information?" I asked Francine as Colin and I took our seats.

"Did I ever. Ol' Gallo is getting sloppy. He didn't even try to mask his IP address this time. Just a straight post from his hotel room." She shrugged. "And I'm sure he won't be there anymore. Most likely has already booked himself into another five-star hotel."

"Why would this Gallo publish this information?" Louis asked. "What have we ever done to him?"

I wondered the same. There was only speculation about his possible motives for doing so and I wasn't willing to voice unsubstantiated theories.

Émile studied Francine. "My guy hasn't been able to remove the information from that site. Can you do it?"

"Already done." Francine's eyelids lowered and she pouted. "This is not just a pretty face, you know."

Émile laughed. "I would never make that mistake."

Manny grunted and glared at Francine.

Louis put both hands on the table and leaned towards me. "I've been wondering about the choices of the articles and murders. Why Serge, Benoît and Claude were chosen first. Why they were killed first."

"You have a theory." It was all over his micro-expressions.

"And it makes sense," Émile said. "You see, not all of us collect art. Léon's obsession with that Morisot painter didn't rub off on all of us. Not on me. I'm more a photography guy. I have framed prints of photos my son has taken when he was in his I-want-to-be-a-photographer phase. He was really good, but when he didn't break into the market after four years, he changed his focus."

"What do your son's photos have to do with the murders?" Manny asked.

"Not the photos," Louis said. "The paintings. I had a little chat with Sébastien and he had some interesting things to tell me about 3D-printed forgeries." He looked at me. "Suddenly, it made sense that you asked us to list all the art we owned. While Émile visited you this afternoon, I got on the phone and found out that only six of us have art that would be worth forging."

"Who?" My mind was racing.

"We know about Serge, Benoît and Claude. Added to the list are Nicolas, myself and Bénédict."

"At Sébastien's fundraising exhibition we discovered that the Renoir painting Nicolas loaned for this cause was a 3D-printed forgery," I said. "As well as your Guillaumin."

Louis shook his head. "I thought something was up with that. Sébastien said that you'd asked for a list of the owners who loaned their paintings. I had a bad feeling about this."

I considered this information. "This afternoon, before Arnaud Brun killed himself with that bomb, he said that all your secrets were going to be revealed. That happened. But he also said that the others will get what's coming to them. I don't know if he was referring to the other six men in your group or someone else. And I also don't know how he would exact that revenge. He's already sent someone to attack Francine. You should be careful."

"Brun is the fucker who killed Serge, Benoît and Claude?" Louis' top lip rose to bare his teeth. "I wish he was alive so I could kill him again."

I glanced at Vinnie, remembering him sharing that sentiment.

"Why did he want to take revenge on us?" Émile lifted both shoulders. "What have we ever done to him?"

"You excluded him and he considered it a personal attack," I said. "And when he was arrested, he didn't receive any support from you, which he also considered to be very personal. Before he detonated the bomb, he revealed that he had a new love interest. Something he said led me to the conclusion that this person is the key to preventing anyone else dying."

"What do you mean?" Émile frowned. "Brun is dead. If he was the killer doesn't that mean the threat is over?"

"No. He planned something that would continue after his death." I'd seen it in Arnaud Brun's expression. "Do you have any recent information on him?"

"I haven't given that man a single thought since we kicked his butt to the curb five years ago." Yves scratched his head. "I'm flabbergasted that he expected support from us and felt betrayed enough to plan this revenge. It seems so far-fetched."

I hadn't had enough time to process everything I'd learned this afternoon. There was no irrefutable connection in my mind yet. I wished for a few uninterrupted hours so I could get lost in mentally writing Mozart's compositions. Since I didn't have that luxury at the moment, I inhaled deeply and faced Colin. "I suspect the next victim will be someone with 3D-printed paintings in their home. Would you be willing to go into these men's houses and inspect their art?"

Manny, Émile, Colin and Louis started talking at the same time. It took seventeen minutes and Daniel's calm intervention before an agreement was reached. The organised crime leaders would only agree to anything if I were to accompany Colin. Manny and Colin would only agree to this if Daniel and Vinnie could accompany us. The levels of distrust rose even more when the discussion turned to keeping whatever Daniel, as a law enforcement officer, saw in their homes out of any reports.

It became far too much for me. I got up and looked at Émile. "Do you have any other pertinent information to share with me?"

The room slowly quietened. "No. That's all we have for now."

"Then you can leave. I need to sleep. Someone will phone you to arrange times for us to visit your homes and look at your paintings." I didn't wait for any agreement. I walked to my bedroom, but stopped next to Vinnie and turned around. "If Brun arranged for someone to attack Francine, he very likely arranged the same for all of you."

Émile snorted. "Let them try. I am so ready for them."

"Don't worry about us, Doctor Lenard." Louis leaned back, his body language confident. "They're not catching us off guard."

I wasn't worried about them. I was worried about Francine. And the rest of my team. I looked at Vinnie and was surprised by his smile. He winked at me. "I've got them, Jen-girl. Nothing will happen to the old man and the spice-fiend."

I nodded and turned to my room. I might not have mastered any skills at friendship, but I'd learned to trust them. Vinnie would make sure Francine was safe. The explosion, all the unprocessed information and the men fighting for dominance were making me long for the solitude of my bedroom. Not that I would be alone. It surprised me that I didn't find the thought of Nikki messing up my carefully arranged pillows distressing. I closed my bedroom door behind me, looking forward to her welcoming smile.

Chapter TWENTY

I studied the paintings. Directly in front of me was an earlier work by Camille Pissarro, to its left a portrait by Francisco Goya and to its right an Alfred Sisley landscape. Colin was confident they were all 3D-printed copies of the extremely valuable masterpieces.

It had taken us four hours to go through the homes of Nicolas Denis, Bénédict Herriot and Louis Masson. Colin had taken his time studying each painting on the numerous walls of these mansions. We'd come away with eight new forged paintings. Back in the team room, Colin had inspected all the paintings from the homes of Serge Valois, Benoît Faure, Claude Moreau and Léon Blanc and had pointed out another seven forged paintings.

"Doc?" Manny's tone held the quality it had after he'd called me a few times. I turned away from the Pissarro and looked at him. He was sitting at his desk. "Where do you think the original paintings are?"

"With the person who stole them." It seemed obvious. "Unless he or she has already sold them on the black market."

"Then who do you think stole the paintings?" Manny tapped with his pen on his desk. It was irritating.

"I don't know." It felt as if the connection was hovering in my brain near my cerebral cortex. I still hadn't had the few hours and Mozart I'd longed for to process the immense amount of information. "Louis, Bénédict and Nicolas asked me the same question this morning. They're furious that they've been robbed."

"I would be too." Colin walked from the Vermeer he'd been studying to stand next to me. "The forged artwork we have in here has a cumulative worth of over two hundred million euros. At least that's what the originals are worth. Not these printed forgeries. It's a great loss to the men who owned them. And to the art world. These masterpieces should never be hidden in some cellar because the so-called owner can't risk putting it on display."

"They should put it on display so someone would notice and report it." Manny continued tapping his pen.

"Stop that." I took a step closer to him. "Why are you nervous?" I narrowed my eyes when I observed more nonverbal cues. "You're not nervous, you're frustrated."

"Of course I am, Doctor Face-reader." Manny threw his pen down and it slid off the table. He glared at where it was lying a few centimetres from his desk. "Bloody hell. We have some looming threat we know squat about. We don't know if Brun was yanking our chains and that bomb was the last of his stupid revenge plan. We don't know whether you are right thinking that he has something planned that will hurt, destroy or kill those other bloody criminals. Or whether his plan, if he had one, will hurt, destroy or kill innocents. We know bloody nothing."

I sympathised with Manny's frustration. It reflected mine. I glanced at Francine at her desk and relief overtook me at seeing her safe and tapping on her tablet screen. I had told Vinnie he was irrational in blaming himself for Émile waiting for me in my car, yet my current internal struggle was the same as his. I pulled my shoulders back and inhaled deeply. Rationally I knew Francine hadn't been attacked because of me. I pondered on the facts surrounding that logic and felt my emotions settle.

I walked to my viewing room thinking about Manny's outburst. I didn't agree that we knew nothing. We knew a lot. We just hadn't received that vital piece of information to connect everything and give us the answer we were looking for. I turned back to the paintings while Manny continued to complain that he wanted to arrest someone and he was tempted to use Léon's information to at least have some joy.

Colin was telling Vinnie about the underappreciated works of Alfred Sisley. The sound of his voice was soothing. I mentally played Mozart's Violin Sonata No. 11 in E-flat while I went over everything we knew. Had I missed some crucial piece of information? Was there something I'd dismissed as unimportant that could be the key we needed? Like fingering through the hanging files in a file cabinet drawer, I ran through all the people we'd so far connected to the case.

Brun's motivation for the murders made sense, even if his sense of betrayal was misplaced. But he'd had no access to the opera house. At least not that we knew about. So who had gained access to all the secrets Léon had kept? And how? I wondered if we should pursue that line and find out if the opera house had security footage for the last six months.

Or maybe I should have another look at the contents we'd

found in Léon's safe. He had after all shouted about someone opening his desk drawer. Maybe the key was whatever had been discovered in the safe. I took one of the three music books and opened it to the first page. I had not actively thought about the books, but the back of my mind had been trying to make sense of the seemingly unmusical arrangement of notes.

I stared at the first page, the connection hovering just out of my reach. Whether it was the music books themselves or a connection triggered by the books I couldn't tell. I turned up the volume of Mozart's sonata in my mind and relaxed into the music.

"Jenny?" Colin's gentle touch on my forearm brought me out of my thoughts. I blinked a few times to come out of my thoughts. I still hadn't solved the music books riddle. An annoying sound came from behind me and I turned to locate it.

Manny was standing next to his desk, scowling at the smartphone Francine was holding out to me. "It's been ringing for the last ten minutes and it's driving me batty. Could you answer that bloody thing, missy?" Manny glared at me. "Supermodel says it's Roche."

I took my phone from Francine and glanced at the screen. It was indeed Émile's name and number flashing on the screen.

"Put him on speakerphone, Doc. I want to hear what he has to say."

I thought Manny's demand was wise despite its rude delivery and tapped the correct icon. "Hello, Émile. You're on speakerphone."

"Why don't you answer your phone?" He sounded most aggravated. "What's the point of giving out your number if you're never going to answer the fuc... the thing?"

Manny snorted, but he was still scowling at my phone. "What do you want, Roche?"

"Louis is with me." He cleared his throat. "I've also got you on speakerphone here and Louis has something you need to hear."

When no one continued to speak, I realised Émile needed a response. "Yes?"

"Hello, Doctor Lenard."

Again the pause. I sighed at the neurotypical need for polite small talk. "Hello, Louis. What do you have?"

"A phone call. Some fucker phoned me half an hour ago threatening my family, talking some shit about finishing it and finishing us. I've already sent my family away and now I have to move them again just to make sure. I don't think this idiot has any idea where my family is, but I'm not willing to take the chance." Louis took a loud breath. "Who is this sicko who is threatening to get me and mine? I swear on my mother's grave—bless her soul—I'm going to hunt down this bastard with his pretty voice and make him suffer if you don't find him soon."

"Stop!" I didn't want to hear about his concern for his family. His tone indicated that he could rant for the next fifteen minutes. I was interested in something else. "Tell me more about his voice."

"His what?"

"His voice." Connections were rushing through my brain.

Louis was quiet for a moment. "He had a modulated

voice. It wasn't raspy like most men I know. You know? Their voices are messed up from all the shouting, drinking and smoking. No, this shithead had a voice that belonged to someone who... I don't know. Maybe he's an actor or something. He sure sounded like one when he delivered his stupid line."

"What line?"

"Some poetic nonsense."

"Do you remember it? The exact words?"

"It made an impression since it really didn't make sense. He said, 'Shall I invoke destruction on the man for whom with love I languish?'"

I staggered as all the disconnected pieces of this case fell into place. The lists I'd made, the music books, my suspicion that more than one person had been involved in committing the crimes, everything came together.

I handed my phone to Colin and waved at Francine to follow me. When I stopped at her desk, she sat down and looked up at me, waiting for instructions. I ignored Émile and Louis' demands to know what was going on and looked at Francine. "How good is your Italian spelling?"

"Passable."

"Search Google for '*Questo fervido amor che oppressa e schiava, a lui che amo pur tanto*' in Verdi opera librettos." I had to repeat it and then fixed two minor spelling errors while Francine typed the sentence into the search box. She pressed enter and zero point three seconds later I had my answer. I turned towards Colin and Manny. "That is the translation from when Aida sings about wavering between her love for her country, her father and Radamès."

"From the opera *Aida*, also composed by Verdi," Francine said.

"What does this mean, Doc? And I'm not asking about the words."

Colin's widened eyes told me he'd also made the connection. "Julien Travere twice quoted Verdi librettos when he spoke to us."

"The tenor with the ego the size of Australia?" Both Manny's eyebrows rose.

I nodded. "The first was when we interviewed him at the opera house just after Léon's death. The second time was when he phoned to hint at a romantic interest in Léon's life."

"Didn't he also hint at his own new romantic interest?" Francine asked.

"He did." Why hadn't I seen this earlier? I thought about our previous cases and technology we'd used. "Francine, could you find any social media accounts in Julien Travere's name?"

"With pleasure, my bestest bestie." Her last words were distracted. She was already putting new terms into her specialised search engine. It took three minutes. "Good Lordy, this man loves his own voice. Pun intended. Look at all these photos and videos he posts on Facebook and Instagram. He's spamming people."

This was exactly what I'd hoped for. Someone as narcissistic as Julien Travere would love the attention he got from every like, share or comment he received on a post. The need for that adulation would override any reasonable sense of personal internet security. All this information was public. "Can you get the metadata from his photos for the last six… no, the last twelve months? Especially the ones in the restaurants and shops. We don't need the photos of his performances."

"Where are you going with this, Doc?"

I flicked my hand backwards at Manny. I didn't want to explain my line of thought at the moment. I watched as Francine gathered this data. "When you're done with his photos, compare it with the metadata of the same type of photos from Léon's social media."

Francine turned to give me a happy smile. "Ooh! Scandals. You know just how to make me happy, girlfriend."

"Just do it." I wanted to see if there was substance to my suspicion.

Five minutes later, my theory was confirmed. Francine clapped her hands and bounced in her chair. "Seventeen restaurants, eleven shops and twelve hotels. There is no way it can be a coincidence that they were in these places at the same time. Especially the hotels."

"When is the last location they shared?" I was still refining my theory.

"Um… four months ago. Huh. That's strange. Before that they were quite busy, about five shared locations a month, some on the same day. Like a restaurant followed by a hotel. Then suddenly nothing."

"Tell us what you're thinking, Doc." Manny knocked on his desk until I turned around to look at him. He pointed his pen at me. "And don't you dare tell me you don't like to speculate."

"We have enough circumstantial evidence for me to posit

that Léon Blanc had a secret affair with Julien Travere. I don't know why, but their relationship ended four months ago, around the time that Arnaud Brun escaped from prison." I winced. "I still don't know how Brun and Julien Travere connect. But if it were Julien Travere who had the affair with Léon, he might have known about Léon's secret safe. He could've been the one who'd used the drawer lock to open the safe and get…"

"Get what, Doc?" Manny got up and followed me when I ran back into my viewing room.

I lifted the music book I'd been paging through. "This. This has all Léon's secrets."

"Doc, you're going to have to slow down and explain like I'm dumb."

"You're not dumb." I waved away his ridiculous suggestion and opened a word-processing document on my computer. I started typing as I explained. "These notes are not music. It's all the secrets Léon Blanc had gathered over the years. See the music sheet? When two staves are combined by a brace, it forms a grand stave. The five lines and four spaces in each stave give us a cumulative eighteen notes. But add the notes just above and below the staves and a few ledger lines and we'll have twenty-six notes. None of the music written is outside those lines."

"What the bleeding hell are you talking about, Doc?" Manny scowled.

"Wait." Colin's eyes were wide as he grabbed another book and started paging through it. "He's only used twenty-six notes on every single page?"

"Yes."

"Um." Vinnie raised his hand as if in school. "The alphabet has twenty-six letters."

I smiled. "And each of these notes is a letter, the chords a word. See? This is what is written on the first line."

Everyone looked at the monitor in front of me. It had the date in Roman numerals and the person Léon had met. Suddenly nothing else was more important than translating the three books. It would be so much fun.

Manny sat down in the chair to my left. "Doc, this is Léon Blanc's black book."

"It's not black, but it is where he wrote all his secrets."

"How long will it take you to change this into readable language?"

"I can write a programme that will translate it quick-sticks." Francine nodded at her computer. "We'll scan the pages and my programme will do the heavy lifting. That way we can go find Julien without wasting more time."

I nodded. "That's a prudent use of time."

"Bloody hellfire." Manny rubbed his hands over his face. "Okay, so now we have all the secrets Brun had. And he told us that Gallo had translated this."

"I don't find that surprising." Gallo was a highly intelligent man. "He wouldn't have had any problems decoding the music. What I don't know is how Julien got the music to Brun or to Gallo. What is that connection?"

"Okay, so we don't know how Brun and Julien connect," Francine said.

"Not yet. But what concerns me more is Gallo's motivation for putting all the organised crime leaders' secrets on the internet. Why would he do that? Émile said that none of them had ever met with or done business with Gallo. So what would be his reason for first getting Dion to publish and now publishing the rest of this damaging information about people he didn't know?"

"To screw with you." Vinnie shrugged when we all looked at him. "You said yourself that he considers you weak. He most likely knows we're investigating this case and is having fun screwing you around."

I marvelled at the need someone had to avenge a perceived wrongdoing. "If we use your theory, it would explain the midazolam found in Léon's system. It was yet another thing that deviated from the other cases and most likely to mislead us."

"That's all well and good, but I'm still wondering about motives here, girlfriend. We know that Gallo's revenge is aimed at you, Brun's revenge was on the ten men he thought betrayed him, but Travere's revenge is for what? Also betrayal?" Francine placed the palm of her hand on her chest. "Unrequited love? Did Léon dump him?"

"I can't speak for Julien Travere's motivation. We don't even know if it is revenge. We haven't investigated him at all." How had I missed that? I had noticed his exceptional acting skills, but put it down to his narcissistic need for attention and his opportunistic use of a tragedy to get it.

Disappointment settled in my mind, but it only lasted for a few seconds. As knowledgeable as I was, I was still fallible. Obsessing about this failure would rob me of the opportunity to find out if Julien was the one who, according to Brun, was going to need courage to follow through whatever Brun had referred to before he'd died. That thought alone led me to many more questions to which I hoped we could get the answers from Julien.

Chapter **TWENTY-ONE**

"At last you're good for something, Frey." Manny looked on as Colin picked the lock of Julien Travere's front door. The top-floor apartment was in a luxury complex only a small margin of Strasbourg's population could afford.

"You're just jealous that I have so many skills, Millard." Colin straightened and pushed the door open. "You may enter."

Manny and Daniel had obtained the necessary legal documentation to allow us access to the tenor's apartment with or without his permission. I had been surprised at the speed the search warrant had been issued, but hadn't questioned it. I was too concerned with what Arnaud Brun might have planned and that Julien might be the one to execute the grand finale.

A few things had taken place before Colin had been asked to pick the lock. I'd insisted on having an Explosive Ordinance Disposal technician join us. I didn't want to experience another blast. I considered it unwise to be impatient to get into Julien Travere's apartment. Especially when there was the possibility of explosives. Manny and Daniel had agreed and Edward Henry, the EOD technician, was standing next to Manny, ready to send his explosives detection robot into the apartment.

"Let's see what we have in there." Edward tilted the tablet in his hands and the robot slowly rolled forward. Francine and Pink were fascinated by the technology and were chatting to Edward as he sent the robot through each room.

Edward was proud as he talked about the lightweight, all-terrain robot not only able to detect bombs, but also able to dispose of explosive devices. Its manipulator arm could lift, move and even dig up suspicious objects and the robot was fitted with day and night cameras and motion detectors. Its first use had been to determine if there had been any explosives near the door. Only when the door area had been cleared had Colin picked the lock.

I was curious what we'd find in Julien's apartment. Any insight into the egotistical tenor might help us prevent whatever Brun had planned. I would also like to know how Brun had been connected to Julien. While we'd been waiting for the search warrant, Francine had written a programme to translate the music books. I had been awed by the speed with which she'd set it up. Vinnie had agreed to scan the pages which were sent directly to the programme.

While Vinnie had been doing that, Francine and I had started working through Léon's finances and tracing payments to shared locations with Julien. We'd found evidence that they'd stayed in fifteen hotels. A few phone calls to these hotels had confirmed they had been in the same bedroom. Francine had clapped her hands in delight when we'd discovered that.

Still lost in my thoughts, I started when the robot rolled out of the apartment. Edward patted it as if it was a pet. "It's clear."

"Let's go see what's in there." Manny lightly touched his hip before entering. He had no need for the holstered weapon. The robot had cleared the apartment of explosives, but Edward would've seen any living beings on his tablet.

Vinnie, Pink and Daniel followed Manny, their postures mirroring his. Edward wished us well and turned towards the elevator at the end of the hallway. Francine absently waved at him, her expression reminding me of those in my university textbooks illustrating the excitement on children's faces moments before they were allowed to open their Christmas gifts. She gave a pretend shudder. "Come on, lovelies. Let's go explore!"

Colin took my hand and together we entered the exclusive apartment. The entrance gave me an idea of what to expect from the rest of the place. Chrome finishings gleamed under strategically placed lights. A tall, thin silver statue of a woman carrying water stood to the right, a small painting hanging on the wall to the left. A light was aimed at it, highlighting the soft colours of the impressionist landscape.

At thirteen minutes after six in the afternoon, the shadows of the late afternoon were a bit too dark to investigate without the aid of artificial lighting. I was glad someone ahead of us had turned on all the lights.

"Ooh! Come here!" Francine's voice came from the right. The heels of Colin's designer shoes sounded loud on the light wooden floors as we walked deeper into the apartment. I didn't like this finishing for floors. It looked clinical and was impractical. The smallest spill or scuffmark would show. My naturally dark wooden floors were much easier to maintain.

We found Francine sitting in a large red hand in the living room. I'd seen those designer chairs before and thought them to have artistic value, but they didn't look comfortable. The wrist served as the base of the chair, the three middle fingers the back, the little finger and thumb serving as armrests. Francine wiggled her behind in the chair and I sighed. "We're not here to test the furniture. Have you found something pertinent to the case?"

She winked at me and pointed to the only wall in the room. Floor-to-ceiling windows gave an impressive two-hundred-and-seventy-degree view over the river and the rest of Strasbourg. Like the hand chair, the white sectional sofa and two matching chairs were also of designer quality. The long part of the sofa was against a light cream wall, a surrealist painting hanging above the sofa.

Colin walked towards it. "That's a Picasso."

"Is it real?" I followed him even though I had no expertise to determine authenticity.

Without breaking his stride or taking off his shoes, Colin stepped onto the sofa to get close to the painting. He leaned down and studied it for nineteen seconds. "It's a fake and it's signed as such. A reproduction that people legally make and sell."

I turned around and looked at the rest of this living area. I was obsessive about cleanliness, yet I wanted to have a home where I felt comfortable sitting down. The seat of the sofa had barely dented when Colin had stepped onto it and Francine was already out of the chair, rubbing her derrière.

It would be an error to look at the carefully placed silver ornaments, the coffee-table books, the white mohair rug and think they didn't represent the person living here. They did. They perfectly fitted Julien Travere's narcissistic personality. He would love to entertain people of importance here, enjoying their admiration of his good taste and their respect for the money he had to have if he could afford this level of decoration. I wondered what his bedroom would reveal and walked towards Manny and Daniel's voices.

They were standing next to the bed discussing the lack of 'stuff'. Unsurprisingly, the spacious room was as carefully decorated as the living area. There was no clutter on any surface, nothing of personal value exhibited.

Combined with the browns, beiges and golds in this room, it should've had a calming effect on me. It didn't. I strongly disliked the chaotic colours and general disorder in Francine's loft apartment, but these muted shades brought a restlessness I wasn't used to.

I seldom felt restless, unless my mind had picked up something that had not yet made it to my consciousness. I walked to the sliding doors that I assumed were for the cupboards and called up Mozart's Violin Sonata No. 22 in A major. With the soothing strings playing in my mind, I looked at the six doors. My wardrobe would fill approximately a third of this space, Colin's possibly half of this space. Francine's walk-in wardrobe was outrageous and overflowed with clothes she wore a few times then grew bored with or declared out of fashion. Her vast amount of clothes would only fill eighty percent of this space. Whyever would a man need this much cupboard space?

"Jenny? Love?" Colin touched my forearm. "Everything okay?"

"How many bedrooms are there in this apartment?" I turned around. Manny and Daniel were still in the room, but were both leaning against doorframes. Manny looked bored. I didn't know how long I'd been staring at the sliding doors.

"We've been through two other rooms." Colin looked disappointed. "We didn't find anything. Not even a computer."

"Isn't there a home office?"

"No." Manny moved away from the doorframe and Francine walked in.

"What are you thinking, girlfriend?"

I looked at the tablet in her hand. "Can you find the blueprints for these apartments?"

"Done and done-r." She sat down on the bed and worked on her tablet.

"What are you thinking, Doc?"

"Did you open these doors?" I pointed behind me.

Daniel nodded. "More clothes in there than in some shops I go to. But nothing suspicious."

"Doc?"

"Got it." Francine jumped from the bed and showed me her tablet.

I looked at it for a few seconds. "Are all the top-floor apartments the same size?"

"Yup. I just checked. They are all three hundred and fifteen square metres."

I turned to the doors. "Someone must open these doors."

"We already did, Doc." Manny walked closer. "What are we looking for now?"

"An entrance to another room. There needs to be another room."

"I think you're right," Pink said from the hallway. "The space here doesn't make sense to me."

"Want to do it with me or wait outside, Doc?"

I didn't know. On the one hand I wanted to open the doors and find the anomaly my mind had picked up. But on the other, stronger, hand, I still had memories of the last time I'd accidentally opened a secret door. I'd put my, Colin's and Vinnie's lives in danger when we'd worked on a case involving biological weapons. I shivered. "I'll wait by the bed."

Manny nodded and waited until I reached the far side of the bed before he opened the first door. Colin started on the other side. They tapped on the back wall of the cupboard and pushed and prodded before going to the next door. Colin found it in the third door from the right. It hadn't taken a lot of searching to find and press the light switch hidden behind a tie rack. He took a step back as the back wall slid open to reveal a large open space.

"Bloody hell, Frey." Manny pulled his gun from his holster and stood in the doorway. "Warn a body before you go and open Aladdin's cave, will you?"

Daniel was already standing behind Manny, his weapon also in his hand. He tapped Manny on the shoulder and they entered the room, weapons raised. I stared into the room with amazement. When Colin had pressed the light switch, he'd opened the door as well as turned on the lights. What I saw was a most unexpected sight.

"Doc. You better get in here." Manny stood in the doorway. "This is bloody messed up."

I nodded and followed Manny into the room. It was an exact copy of Léon Blanc's home office, which was an exact copy of his office in the opera house.

This space was large, but still only about two-thirds the size of Léon's home office. The same heavy curtains were pulled back to reveal large windows overlooking the river. The desk was in the same place. A baby grand piano stood in the place of Léon's large grand piano. The Persian carpets on the floors were different, but so were the ones in Léon's two offices.

The little round table and wingback chairs were not exact copies, but were placed in the exact spots. Bookshelves lined the walls just like in Léon's offices and paintings filled the same spaces. Colin gasped as he walked past me to the wall cluttered with paintings. "Are these...? Oh... Hmm... Oh..."

We watched as Colin moved from one painting to the next, making shocked noises, his hand pressed hard against his mouth. When he turned to face us, his eyes were wide as he dropped his hand to his side. "These are all the original paintings that were stolen." He pointed at the individual artworks. "That's Nicolas Denis' Renoir, that's Louis Masson's Guillaumin, Serge Valois' Paul Cézanne and that, that is Léon Blanc's Morisot. You can see Berthe's human touch in those brushstrokes. That is her work. These are the real paintings."

"I'm counting twenty-one in this room." I'd counted the ones on the other walls as well. "Are all of them authentic?

We only have eighteen paintings in the team room."

"I'll check now." Colin walked to the wall behind the desk and studied those paintings.

"I'm seeing a computer," Francine said from the door. She was looking at the desk. "Can I please play with it? Pretty please? With cherries on top?"

"A request can't have cherries." I found it vexing every time she used this expression.

"I can replace them with chocolates if you'll let me check out that computer."

I looked around. "The room is too small."

Daniel chuckled. "You don't need me in here. I'll go and be quietly freaked out in the hallway. This is too weird for me."

"I'll also leave you to it." Manny lowered his head to look at me. "Call if you need me."

"Such a hero." Francine kissed Manny's cheek as she walked past him. At the desk, she pushed Colin aside to make space as she pulled out the chair. I walked to the bookshelves when she turned on the computer and rubbed her hands together.

The one bookshelf ended against the window, some of the curtain covering the books. This oversight in good design was the main reason I noticed something odd with the curtain. I pulled it back and felt my eyebrows rise. Stacked on the floor were framed photographs. I did a quick count and came to the same number of paintings now hanging in the duplicated home office.

"What have you got there?" Colin asked next to me.

"Photos. I'm wondering if they were hanging in this room before Julien stole the original paintings and hung them here."

"I would really like to know how a tenor got his hands on all these paintings. Do you think he is smart enough to break into six different mafia bosses' homes and replace the paintings?"

"No." I shook my head. "Definitely not."

Colin went down on his haunches to look at the photos. "Jenny, have you actually looked at these photos?"

"Only the ones in the front." And it had raised my level of concern.

"Yeah, well. This is not good. Not good at all." Colin moved to the side so I could see each photo as he laid them in piles on the floor. Every photo was of Léon Blanc. Some photos looked like professional photographs taken for promotional purposes. One photo was taken during a performance of an opera, Léon standing backstage in a tuxedo, his expression happy. The quality of the photo made me think it had been taken by a professional photographer. Four photos were of Léon and Julien together. The angle of the photo made it clear it was a selfie. They looked happy together.

"This level of obsession is most worrisome. If Léon had been the one to end the relationship, Julien's personality would demand retaliation."

"He's the one who killed Léon?" Colin asked.

"He has the motivation, but I have no other evidence to think so. It is very clear that he loved Léon deeply, but his love was not balanced or healthy. Look at the quality of those frames. He spent a lot of money and emotional currency on presenting those photos in the best possible way. The fact that he's replaced all the photos with the paintings he's stolen from men his ex-lover had blackmailed is indicating volatility. Not a good sign."

"Ooh! Ooh!" Francine waved her arms in the air. "Come look at this. Ooh!"

Colin got up and we joined Francine at the desk. On the laptop screen was a paused video image of Julien Travere. "What is this?"

"There was only one icon on his desktop." She hesitated.

"What's wrong with the icon?" I didn't often see Francine hesitate. A shot of adrenaline made it feel as if my stomach was turning.

"He named it 'Open Me, Dr L'." She clicked twice and showed us the desktop. The wallpaper was a photo of Julien performing on stage. In the centre of the photo was one icon, named as Francine had said.

"How would he have known to expect me?"

"He must've realised he was not going to get away with whatever he's been up to." Francine changed the window back to the video. "Want to see what he has to say?"

I nodded.

She clicked on the play button and Julien Travere winked at the camera. "Hello, Doctor Lenard. I bet you're surprised that this video was made for you, right? Well, I had to make it for someone important, someone who would understand."

"What are you watching?" Manny walked towards us.

"The tenor made a video for Genevieve." Francine clicked the pause button. "It's really icky."

"What do you mean icky?" The video wasn't sticky, so I didn't know why Francine found it disgusting.

She twisted around to look at me. "I don't know what you see, but I'm seeing a man who's serial-killer crazy. He's got a shrine-type secret room and he made a video for you. Icky."

"It's an inappropriate use of the word. Disquieting would be closer to what you're trying to convey."

"Nah." She turned back. "Icky."

Manny stood on her other side. "Let's see it, supermodel."

She clicked the play button and Julien continued. "You see, people dismiss me as an egotistical tenor, but they never look deeper than that. No one at the opera house ever spent enough time with me to realise that I'm gay. Personally, I think the men are too damn stupid and the women were in love with me. Maybe not all of them, but there are at least six I can think of who have the hots for me.

"I digress. If you're watching this, it means that you found my haven. Isn't it beautiful? I took such great inspiration from"—he swallowed—"Léon's home office. I loved the layout so much, I just had to have the same. Could you imagine his delight when I showed him this? I suppose the information you found that led you to my haven revealed that Léon and I were together for a blissful ten months and thirteen days. I can in all honesty say I'd never been so happy in my entire life.

"Until the day I showed him my haven. I'd taken months preparing it just so. I was convinced he would love it." Julien's *levator labii superioris* muscle raised his lips in contempt. "It was his birthday and I told him I had a huge surprise for him. I led him blindfolded into my haven. I had fantasies of making love on one of the carpets when I removed his blindfold. That didn't happen. When he saw what I'd spent months preparing for him, he lost his marbles. He shouted and screamed for what felt like hours. Then he slapped me in the face and told me that I was crazy. He slapped me. In the face. The ungrateful bastard!"

I watched the conflicting messages he communicated with his nonverbal cues. The more personal an issue was, the easier it was for someone to slip in their deception. After two minutes of watching him, I was able to distinguish between the pretence and the rage he was trying to hide. It was becoming increasingly difficult for him to maintain his act.

Onscreen, Julien took a shuddering breath. "How could he not see that I'd honoured him in the most wonderful way possible? I'd taken such care with the details, especially the photos. He called those 'fucked-up memories' that he would like to erase from his brain forever." Julien shook his head as if to remove an unpleasant thought. "Now he'll never remember all the great times we had together. Such a pity.

"Surely you understand what I must be going through, Doctor Lenard. As an expert in the human psyche, you must know that the pain of his rejection caused me to have lapses in judgement. I was so overcome by grief that I did things I would never have dreamed of." He touched his neck and I almost smiled at the deception cue he'd not been able to stop. "When I literally walked into Arnaud in the park, I'd been out of my mind with heartache. And suddenly this gorgeous, tall and rugged man looked at me like he wanted to eat me.

"That day in the park we talked for hours and hours and

hours. He told me he was lying low to avoid being found by some people who wanted to hurt him. I told him I'd already been hurt." Julien sighed dramatically and put his hand over his heart. "He put his hand on my thigh and told me that if I wanted, he would go and put the hurt on the imbecile who'd hurt me. That was… romantic.

"I must admit that in my pain I actually considered his offer for a minute. But then I decided against it. First, I told Arnaud everything that had happened between me and Léon. How Léon had never wanted to make our relationship public. Like he was ashamed of me. I told him how I had to sneak around to spend time with Léon and how it made me feel like someone's dirty secret. Sometimes that was fun, but often… it hurt me." His blinking increased and he affected a wounded expression. He took a few deep breaths and shook his head again. "That day Arnaud listened to me like no one has ever listened.

"He let me talk until I felt renewed and then he shared some of his secrets with me. He told me that he'd escaped prison, but that he'd been convicted of something he never did. He told me that he learned a lot of tricks in prison. He'd met a lot of helpful people. He said that those people would help me take revenge on Léon so that he would suffer the same pain I did.

"I knew Arnaud was trying to manipulate me, but I didn't mind. I wanted to show Léon that I could get another man to truly love me and that I could live without him. And I wanted revenge. Arnaud helped me develop a great plan. He helped me see that I needed to invest in my retirement fund. He told me that he knew a brilliant art thief who could steal masterpieces if I knew of anyone who collected such artworks.

"Then I remembered the secret Léon once told me after a beautiful two days in Nice. He'd told me that he had all these criminals' secrets in his safe and that was how he'd been able to fund the opera house. The moment I mentioned one of those names to Arnaud, I knew something was off. Later he confessed that he'd had some inside information that led him to the conclusion that Léon was blackmailing the men.

"Arnaud had been looking for an opportunity to get to them and had wondered if I could introduce him to Léon. He hadn't known about my relationship with Léon, but was convinced the Fates had brought us together. For him to get back at the men and for me to take my revenge on Léon. So Arnaud asked me to photograph everything in Léon's safes. I did. His home and office safes.

"On the one hand I felt a bit guilty that I was breaking the trust Léon had put in me by letting me watch him open these secret safes. But then I reminded myself how ashamed he was of being with me. It made it easier to sneak in and take some photos. I didn't find any books containing those secrets, but Arnaud told me not to worry.

"He asked me to go back and take photos of every page of the music books I'd found and he would get one of his friends to hack Léon's computer. I suppose Léon lied about that as well. He didn't keep the secrets in his safe after all. They were on his computer." Like Brun, Julien also had the incorrect impression of where Gallo had found the secrets. I wasn't surprised that Gallo had been the only one who'd seen the music code.

Julien's mouth twisted briefly before he affected another hurt expression. "When Arnaud got all those disgusting secrets, he used it to find out when those criminals weren't home. That was when Arnaud's thief took the paintings so they could be scanned and printed. His thief replaced all the paintings before these men ever returned home. None of them suspected anything. I must admit it gave me an incredible rush to know I was putting one over on these highly respected businessmen who were actually common criminals.

"Arnaud was such a great help to me. He told me he knew people who would sell these paintings for me and I would be set for life. It was so special to know someone cared about my future. But Arnaud did so much more. He also helped me with sending all those dirty secrets to that journalist and getting his friend, Monsieur Gallo, to help us. Monsieur Gallo was the one who suggested I make this video to"—he smiled—"waste your time. Mind you, it's actually sad that you'll be missing Arnaud's revenge in all its co-ordinated beauty."

"Holy hell." Manny grabbed his smartphone. "Daniel! Get in here!"

Francine paused the video a second before Daniel rushed into the secret office. "What?"

"Get your team ready. We're moving out." He looked at me. "Where am I going, Doc?"

"I don't know. We need to finish watching this video."

"Speculate, missy. Now!"

I loathed doing this. I didn't have enough information to confidently surmise Julien's next step. The expression on

Manny's face was uncompromising. I sighed. "He talks about Arnaud Brun's revenge. We know that Brun's revenge was against the ten organised crime leaders. Julien mentioned a co-ordinated attack. All I can speculate is that wherever the seven remaining men are, their lives are in immediate danger. But it's only speculation."

"Keep watching and phone me if there is a change of plan." Manny rushed out the door, Daniel already in the hallway talking on his phone.

Vinnie stood in the doorway, his weapon in his hand. "I'm not going anywhere."

"Thanks, Vin." Francine winked at him then turned to me and raised her eyebrows. I nodded. She clicked the play button and Julien's smile disappeared.

"When I learned who you were, I became really scared that you were going to figure out my revenge plan on Léon. I wanted him to lose all the precious funds he'd been blackmailing out of these mafia dons. I wanted him to lose their trust. I wanted him to know what it felt like to be betrayed.

"Unfortunately, his tragic death will tonight prevent him from seeing my best performance ever." True sadness pulled the corners of his mouth down for a millisecond. "Despite his betrayal, Léon really was a wonderful director for the opera house. He did so much for my career. '*L'uomo é mobile, qual piuma al vento. É sempre misero chi a lui si affida. Se fiducia gli dai, annientarlo dovrai, e insieme a lui tu devi perir'.*' I think tonight he would've been proud of me."

His only honest expression was replaced by a black screen.

"Is this it?" Francine fervently worked for a few seconds

on the computer until her shoulders slumped. "Yup, this is it. There's nothing else. And when I say there's nothing else, I mean there's nothing else on this computer. At all. This is the only file."

"'Men are as fickle as feathers in the wind. If you rely on him you will regret it. If you give him your trust, you must destroy him, and together with him you must perish.'"

"What are you talking about, girlfriend?"

"This is the translation of those lines. They are from one of the most famous arias in opera. But the quote isn't correct. This aria is about women being fickle and if one trusts a woman, one would be undone, not perish." This wasn't right on many levels. I found it hard to reconcile Julien's story with the conflicting expressions he had exhibited. He'd been careful a few times when he'd phrased certain statements and I wondered why.

"What do you want to do, Jenny?" Colin took my hand. "Should Vinnie take us somewhere?"

"Not yet." I stared at the computer. "I want to watch it again."

Chapter TWENTY-TWO

It was while writing the fifth line of Mozart's Horn Concerto No. 1 in D major that the insight rushed into my cerebral cortex. I froze. A deep, slow inhale calmed me enough to open my eyes. We'd watched Julien's recording three times. The numerous conflicting emotions had made it hard to distinguish between his genuine emotions and those he so expertly acted out.

Francine and Colin were talking softly about the revenge Brun had planned for the ten men and how it fitted in with Julien's own reprisal. I cleared my throat. "Play it once more."

"You're back." Francine smiled and turned back to the computer. "Another show of crazy coming right up."

She clicked the play button and I watched Julien explain his meeting with Brun and their subsequent plans. This time I knew what I was looking for. When Julien referred to the revenge he wanted, his pupils dilated. Exactly the same happened when he quoted Verdi and talked about his performance at tonight's opera.

"Whatever he's planning will take place at the Opéra National du Rhin."

"Should I phone Millard?" Colin took his smartphone from his trouser pocket.

"Yes." I turned towards the door. "We should also go."

"No." Vinnie moved his feet apart and folded his arms across his chest. "I think we should let the old man and Daniel handle this, Jen-girl."

I considered organising my thoughts to convince Vinnie and glanced at my watch. "We don't have time to argue. It will take us twenty minutes to reach the opera house and we might already be too late. If you don't agree with my reasoning by the time we get there, I will not act."

Vinnie's eyebrows rose. "You plan to act. Huh. The old man will have a fit."

"Come on, big guy." Francine was behind me, next to Colin. "We'll leave the officers to guard this place and we can go kick some opera-singing butt. You know Genevieve is never wrong."

"I've been wrong numerous times. Not often, but enough times to have lost count."

Vinnie moved away from the door. "If you're wrong about this, the old man will skin me alive."

"Manny would never do such a thing." I followed Vinnie down the hallway. Colin was talking on his phone, telling Manny to redirect everyone to the opera house.

He ended the call when we reached Vinnie's SUV. "Millard also needs convincing, Jenny."

"Let's go and I'll explain." I got in the back with Colin and fastened my seatbelt. I trusted Vinnie's driving and was hoping he would put his love for speeding to good use. "Vinnie, we need to get to the opera house as soon as possible."

"Why?" Vinnie started the SUV and turned into the street.

"I'm not saying I'm not going to drive like a bat outta hell, I would just like to know why."

"Because the sentence Julien quoted comes from Verdi's *Rigoletto*."

"The opera they're doing tonight," Colin said.

"Yes. And it is from the first part of the third and last act. With twenty-minute intervals between acts, act three should start at nine o'clock." I glanced at my watch again, my heart rate increasing. "That leaves us with only fifteen minutes to get there."

Vinnie changed gears and smiled. "I'll get us there in half the time."

"Wait." Francine fiddled with her smartphone. "I think Manny needs to hear this. I'm putting him on speakerphone."

Manny answered after only one ring. "What have you got, supermodel?"

"Genevieve says Julien is going to act within the next fifteen minutes."

"Holy hell. It will take us another ten to get there."

"The way Vin is driving, we'll be there at around the same time." Francine smiled at Vinnie.

"No." Manny sounded angry. "You're not coming to a potential bomb site."

"I have to be there, Manny." I leaned a bit forward towards the phone, but held tightly onto the seatbelt with both hands. "If any of you speak to him, it will escalate the situation."

"What?" Manny's question boomed through the vehicle. "You want to go into the opera house and speak to that sick puppy?"

I frowned. "I don't know about a sick puppy in the opera house. But if I speak to Julien Travere, the puppy as well as everyone in the theatre has a much better chance of not being caught in an explosion."

It was quiet on the other side for a few seconds. "Doc, you're going to have to do some serious fancy talking to convince me and Daniel next to me that we should allow you into that theatre."

Now was a good time to organise my thoughts. I did so for forty seconds. "Julien Travere is a narcissist. He craves constant attention and validation. If he were a more neurotypical individual who wanted to take revenge on someone he thought had betrayed him, he would've killed that person or he would've destroyed his reputation on social media."

"But he did kill Blanc. Didn't he, Doc?"

"We don't know that for certain yet." I intended to find out. "We watched the rest of Julien's video and he never confessed to killing Léon Blanc. He didn't allude to any of the murders. Back to my point. A more neurotypical person would commit suicide in private or in a park if he wanted to attract attention. The conclusion I've reached is that Julien is not planning suicide per se, he's planning a finale that will leave a legacy. Very much in a style befitting the operas he performs in.

"He wants to be remembered in the biggest way possible, in a manner larger than the man who had betrayed him. Killing the other organised crime leaders would not bring any satisfaction to a narcissist. Blowing himself up in front of an audience of opera lovers—that would give him the eternal acclaim he covets. An operatic ending."

"You still haven't convinced me why you should be the one to talk to him. You're not even good with people."

"And you're not important enough." I was interrupted by Daniel's loud coughing. "He made that video for me. In his mind, I'm the most important person in this investigation. My international recognition and reputation in higher social circles is what attracts him. You're too low on the social hierarchy to catch his attention. He would be insulted if you or any other highly trained individual were to address him.

"I'm not sure what he's planning, but I know that I will be able to retain his focus long enough for you to secure the opera house and keep everyone safe. I know I'm not good with people, but I have the skills to deceive and interact with people on all psychological health scales."

"I don't like this, Doc."

"Don't tell me you're considering this, old man?" Vinnie's tone was harsh as he pulled the steering wheel to turn left. "I'm not letting Jen-girl in there."

"What if Julien has a bomb somewhere in the theatre, Vinnie?" I asked. "He could detonate it and hurt hundreds of people."

"Exactly my point." Vinnie jerked the steering wheel and I tightened my grip on my seatbelt. "You would be one of those hundreds of people."

"But I can prevent it."

"You're sure, Doc? You're completely convinced you will prevent something bad from happening?"

"Of course not." I swallowed. "No one can be one

hundred percent certain of such a thing. All I know is that I am the best choice available to stabilise this situation."

"I still don't like it, Doc." Manny sounded distracted. "Let me talk to Edward and Daniel about this."

He disconnected the call and we drove two blocks in silence. Vinnie was racing through the dark streets, but with skill that gave me a measure of comfort. The jarring sound of my phone ringing broke the silence. I took it from its designated space in my handbag and swiped the screen after a glance. "Hello, Émile."

"Genevieve, you have some problems."

Colin put his hand on my thigh. "Put him on speakerphone."

I tapped the icon. "You're on speakerphone. What problems are you referring to?"

"I'm in the hospital at the moment. And before you get all worried about me, I'm fine. The others are also fine. Brun's idiot goons tried to get to us, but we were ready. I'm at the hospital visiting a certain young journalist who wasn't ready."

"Dion Gravois?" Colin asked.

"The one and only." Émile grunted. "I do not like being in a hospital, let me tell you that. But I heard that the idiot who published those dirty secrets about Serge, Benoît and Arnaud got beaten within an inch of his life. So I thought it would be a good idea to come and see who I owe a large bottle of single malt."

"You're wasting time with small talk. Why did you phone?"

He chuckled. "Forgive me. I phoned because Dion woke up an hour ago after sleeping off some serious painkillers. He had the most fascinating story to tell me."

"Is he there with you?" I asked.

"Lying here, glaring at me because he wants to speak to you."

"Hand him the phone or put him on speakerphone."

"I think I'll turn the speakerphone thing on." It was quiet for a second. "It's on. Speak, little Dion."

"Doctor Lenard?"

"Hello, Dion. Who assaulted you?"

"They said they were sent by somebody Brun. They were supposed to do that yesterday, but I wasn't at home the whole day. When I arrived mid-morning today, they were waiting in my living room. I don't think they know that Brun is dead. I tried to tell them, but they wouldn't listen. He owed them the second half of their payment and they wanted to collect it. Eventually I got them to check the news on my computer. Only then did they believe me. They were supposed to kill me, but just left. I'm pretty beaten up and have five broken bones, but it could've been much worse."

"I'm sorry to hear that." Colin's raised eyebrows indicated he also registered the similarities between Francine's and Dion's attacks. "Is that the reason for this phone call?"

"No." Dion cleared his throat. "I haven't checked my email since last night. I woke up a few minutes before Mr Roche arrived and had a lot of emails, including a very strange email. I thought it might be important because of Léon Blanc's murder."

"And before you ask," Émile said, "he told me because I accidentally sat on his broken leg. He didn't volunteer this information."

I blinked a few times. "Dion, tell me about the email."

"I'll read it to you." It was silent for three seconds, then Dion cleared his throat. "'The hour of punishment hastens on, that hour which will be my last. Like a thunderbolt from the hand of God, the jester's revenge shall strike me from within. If you want to be part of history—see the greatest finale in opera—then you should make use of these complimentary tickets. Bring someone who will also report this greatness.' Um... that was it. Nothing else, except an attachment with two tickets. I think you should go to the opera house, Doctor Lenard."

"Hear that, Genevieve?" Émile said. "Your problems are at the theatre."

"We're already on our way. Do you have any more useful information?"

"Yes," Dion said. "I was curious about the quote and googled it. That strange punishment nonsense comes from the second act of *Rigoletto*."

"Is it ad verbatim the same as the libretto?"

"No. In the original, that hour will be 'your' last, not 'my' last. The last part of the quote is also changed. The original says the 'jester's revenge shall strike you down', where this says 'strike me from within'. Does this mean anything?"

"I don't know." My mind was racing to process this information. "Anything else?"

"Not ye…"

I tapped the red icon to end the call. Each of Julien's quotes had had meaning. I wondered if there was important information hiding in that changed quotation from the opera Julien was currently performing.

"We're here." Vinnie turned onto the paving in front of the opera house. Two black SUV's were already parked there and the GIPN truck was in the side street, blocking any more entrance to the paving from the other side. As soon as Vinnie stopped the SUV, I got out and walked to Manny and the others.

"We have a plan, Doc."

"Julien has the bomb on his person."

"What the bleeding hell are you talking about, Doc?"

I told him about Émile's phone call. "That quotation comes from *Rigoletto*, the opera they are now performing. His earlier reference to perishing, his use of personal pronouns in this last quote and the mention that the strike will come from within leads me to believe that the bomb is on his person. If there is a bomb."

"What do you mean 'if'? Didn't you just try to convince me that Julien is going to blow up this place?" Manny pointed at the opera house.

"You know I don't have concrete evidence to support my conclusions. We are here because I strongly believe in the profile I have on Julien Travere and the circumstantial evidence pointing to this being the location he plans to act out his revenge."

Manny glared at me for a few seconds. "And you still strongly believe that you're the one to speak to this crazy tenor?"

"Yes." I ignored Colin and Vinnie's protests. "How often have I been wrong in a case?"

"Not often and that's what's pissing me off right now."

I was about to point out that he wasn't making sense, but

Edward stood next to Daniel watching me. I didn't have time to argue with Manny. "Act three will start any second now. That is when Julien will sing one of the most popular opera arias, the same one he quoted in the video. I believe that's when he'll act. I need to go inside now."

"Genevieve, would you please wear a Kevlar vest?" Daniel reached into the SUV and came out with a plastic-wrapped package. "This one has never been worn before. It would make me much more comfortable breaking protocol knowing that you have some form of protection."

I looked at the package in his hands and the totality of my insistence of speaking to Julien settled heavily in my mind. Neither Vinnie's objections nor the grave concern on Colin's face had made the potential danger as real as this. "It's never been worn?"

"Not once." His sincere concern for me was evident on his face. I also noted how he remembered my deep aversion to handling or wearing anything that had been used before. The knowledge of the amount of unknown bacteria being transferred to my person would distract me from doing my job.

I wrote another line of Mozart's Horn Concerto and took the vest. It was heavy and suddenly I didn't want to be here. I didn't want to need a bulletproof vest. I didn't want to go into the opera theatre and convince a narcissistic opera singer that he shouldn't hurt innocent people.

It took another two lines of the concerto to remind myself of all the people currently listening to one of the most popular operas around the world. I took the vest from the plastic and lifted it.

"Let me help you." Vinnie stood closer. "I'm quite the expert on how to put these things on."

"Try not to touch me." The words were out before I could stop them. I searched Vinnie's face for signs of offence or hurt and was relieved to find only humour.

"You better be ready for a hug after this, Jen-girl." He lifted the vest and carefully lowered it over my head. He fastened the Velcro straps tightly, but made sure I had full mobility. "I hate that you're going in there. The moment this is over and that fucker is handcuffed or dead, you're being hugged."

"I need a whistle."

"A what now?" Manny blinked in surprise.

"A whistle." I looked at Daniel. "Do you have one that's never been used?"

"I have one, Jen-girl." Vinnie reached into one of the side pockets of his camouflage pants and came out with a red plastic whistle. "I've never used it."

"It's in your pocket and it's not sealed."

"So there's some lint there. At least my spit isn't on it."

I knew I didn't have the time to be particular about this. I vigorously rubbed the mouthpiece of the whistle against my trousers and ignored Manny's questions about my need for a whistle.

"Fine. Don't tell me." Manny's lips were in a thin line. "I'll be the bigger person and tell you about our strategy. Supermodel and Pink are working at jamming any and all signals around this area. If Travere is using some kind of transmitter or mobile phone as a detonation device, he will be in for a big surprise. We'll be in contact, so don't worry that we won't be able to track each other."

"Our second team should be here any second. The two teams will be in the theatre quietly evacuating people."

"Be careful with that." I forced my breathing to slow down. "It might trigger a negative response if Julien sees that you're taking his audience away from him."

"We were thinking of evacuating from the back."

"Good plan."

"I don't want you to walk in there alone, Doc."

"I'm going in there with her." Vinnie stood closer to me. I leaned away. "I don't care what you say, Jen-girl. I'm going in there with you."

"Stay behind her." Manny looked Vinnie up and down. "And for the love of Pete, try to make yourself look a bit smaller."

"We don't have time for more discussion." I walked towards the six pillars and the stairs. "Trust me to do my job and I'll trust you to do yours."

Colin grabbed my arm and turned me to face him. "Jenny."

"This is the best decision available to us right now."

"I know. I don't want it to be, but I know." He lowered his head and pressed his lips hard against mine. "Please be careful. Be very careful. I'll be right behind Vinnie."

The thought of having Colin behind me made me feel both calmer and much more anxious. I didn't want anyone's life in danger, but thinking of putting Vinnie and Colin's lives in danger brought blackness to the edges of my vision.

"Let's do this, Doc."

The second team had arrived and were already at the stairs leading to the doors of the Opéra National du Rhin. Daniel opened one door and let four GIPN members enter the theatre. No one had their weapons raised, but their nonverbal cues would alert everyone as to their purpose in the theatre.

Vinnie, Colin and I entered the theatre's foyer. Immediately the calming sounds of the orchestra affected my tension levels. This was the part where Rigoletto took his daughter Gilda to a crack in the wall to see that the Duke of Mantua, the man she was in love with, was a scoundrel, a womaniser. The baritone singing the fatherly role had a beautiful voice as he refused to be convinced of his daughter's love for the Duke.

I reached a closed door leading into the theatre. Daniel was talking to the usher, who normally would prevent anyone from entering during the performance. Vinnie waited for a nod from Daniel before he opened the door just enough for me to slip through. The beauty of the music as Gilda told her father she loved the Duke was so much more potent inside the theatre. Colin stood next to me and the light from the foyer disappeared as Vinnie closed the door behind him.

I took a few steps forward and absorbed the scene on the stage. The lighting changed to put Rigoletto and Gilda in the shadows. Julien, dressed as the Duke in the uniform of a cavalry officer, entered a wine-shop. His long, loose coat swirled around him as he strutted around the set.

The orchestra started the catchy music of *La donna è mobile* and Julien's voice filled the theatre. He picked up a bottle of wine from a table and sang about the fickleness of women with an arrogance befitting the Duke, which was most likely not hard for him to emulate.

He finished the first part and I forced my legs to move when the strings repeated the thematic melody. I took another step forward, not taking my eyes off his body. From this distance I could only observe his body language, not the micro-expressions on his face. I needed to be closer if I wanted to see more, if I wanted to speak to him, stop him from taking any action.

The music coming from the orchestra pit in front of the stage quieted as Julien's voice projected deep into the theatre. To my estimation, there were only another four bars before the end of this aria. I pressed both my little fingers to my thumbs and walked down the aisle. I knew Vinnie would be behind me and Colin behind him. Halfway to the orchestra pit, people started whispering more and more. We were undoubtedly causing a distraction that no one would welcome during such a stunning performance of *La donna è mobile*.

I reached the front of the theatre and still Julien had not noticed me. He was singing to the upper gallery, the seats which were occupied by the most influential people, especially on opening night.

Julien reached for his coat as he put the bottle of wine down on another table and walked closer to the edge of the stage. When his hand emerged again from under his coat, he had a remote control in his hand.

I staggered forward and grabbed onto the wooden barrier separating the audience from the orchestra pit. I had expected this. I had deduced Julien Travere was planning to detonate a bomb during his performance tonight. Yet blackness pushed into my vision as he slowly raised his hands while working up to the last notes. I held on to the wooden barrier and wondered if this would be the one time I was fatally mistaken in the estimation of my own skills.

The orchestra was quiet as Julien showed off the versatility of his voice with the last notes. I seized the opportunity. I brought the whistle to my lips and pushed as much air into the mouthpiece as I could.

The shrill sound didn't have an immediate effect. The orchestra glared at me until they noticed one of the GIPN members in the orchestra pit making a cutting motion across his throat. They looked at the conductor who held up both hands. They lowered their instruments.

Julien didn't stop singing. He was looking down at me, his hands raised towards the audience as he inhaled to sing that beautiful last note.

"Stop, Julien." I didn't have to shout. It was quiet in the theatre. "Stop and listen to me."

He didn't.

He pressed the remote control.

Chapter TWENTY-THREE

Nothing happened.

"No!" Julien's protracted yell carried through the theatre as he continued to press the remote control. His voice wavered, his shouting ending with an agonised hiccough. "No! Let me have this. No!"

Behind me was the sound of movement. I didn't allow the GIPN teams evacuating the theatre to distract me. I replaced the lingering sounds of Verdi's composition with mentally playing Mozart's Symphony No. 20 in D major. As great a composer as Verdi was, his music had never helped me focus. It had never calmed me. And it had never helped me take note of the smallest details.

"This will not bring back the love you've lost." I didn't raise my voice. I wanted him to have to focus on me.

"Which love?" Julien blinked when strong spotlights were turned on, blinding him to the audience and making him the sole focus on stage. The scant information I had on Julien Travere had revealed a man of average intelligence. He should have been able to conclude that the lights had been turned on to prevent him from seeing what was happening in the theatre. His narcissistic need for being the centre of all attention overrode any sensible thinking. He puffed out his chest and raised his chin to the side, looking wistfully to the top left balconies. "I first lost the love of my life. Then I was lucky enough to find another great love. I even lost him."

Someone gasped behind me. Another spotlight came on, shining down from directly above me. I briefly thought of the wisdom of not allowing Julien to see the audience, putting his attention on me. I wondered if it had been Manny who'd arranged the lighting. It wasn't a fear of being seen and heard by so many people that made my throat muscles tense until it felt like I was being strangled. It was the fear that I would say the wrong thing and put the lives of Colin, Vinnie and everyone in the theatre in grave danger.

I swallowed past the tightness in my throat and considered my words. "Both men adored you. Have you ever considered the possibility that your love for them was too overwhelming? That they felt they would never be able to match the magnificence of your heart?"

Julien lowered his arms, but still held the remote as if he was handing it to someone. "You think so? Because that would make sense. I loved those men. I loved Léon. He was the first man who truly saw the real me. He saw that my voice was made for greatness. Even before we became lovers, he already knew how to bring out the best in me. He offered the best roles to me. He knew how great I could be."

"You're deluded, Julie." Gustave Victore stepped closer to the spotlights, but were immediately pulled back by a GIPN team member. He struggled against the hold as he was dragged away. "You were never that good. You'll neve…"

Julien's lips had tightened when the angry tenor had used a female name to address him. His expression had become even more insulted and resentful when Gustave had continued. He pressed the remote control again. And again. "Why is this not working? This was my final act. I was supposed to be great!"

I didn't know why the remote wasn't working and wished I'd had more time to listen to Manny's explanation of jammers and frequencies. What I did know was how to address a narcissistic personality. "Your portrayal of the Duke was beautiful, Julien. That last note was breathtaking in its purity." I mentally straightened my shoulders and lifted my chin as I prepared to lie. "It was one of the best performances of *La donna è mobile* I've heard. And I've been to seven performances of *Rigoletto*. Gustave is wrong. You are not only good, you are great. I think he's just jealous of you."

"Thank you!" His arm relaxed marginally, his relief genuine. "You understand me. You understand the suffering I've endured under all these envious people who wish they could be as great as me."

"I also understand that Léon's betrayal hurt you deeply."

"How could he do that to me? I was the best thing that had ever happened to him, to this opera house. I was the reason all the shows were sold out." True sadness replaced Julien's arrogant outrage. "I was also the reason he was happy. That's why I still don't understand that he didn't want to make our relationship public. It doesn't make sense."

"Did you ever consider the possibility that he wanted to keep you all to himself? That he was terrified of losing you to someone else if they ever found out how wonderful you were?"

Julien's eyes narrowed and he touched his chin with his free hand. "You know, I never considered that."

"It's also possible that he was scared you would one day discover he wasn't good enough for you and break up with him. Maybe he didn't want to take the chance of everyone finding out that he'd been left by a great man."

Julien's muscle tension lowered even more as he rubbed his chin. "Hmm. Doctor Lenard, you might have something there. A few times in the beginning he said that he couldn't believe how lucky he was to have found me. I think you're right. My God, you're a genius."

"I know." Maintaining this constant deception was exhausting. But I was hearing fewer sounds behind me. I wondered how many people had so far been evacuated. The orchestra pit was empty and dark, the musicians' exit amongst the many instruments having been surprisingly silent. Julien had been so enraptured by my untruths, he had not noticed any of the activities in the theatre. I refocused my body language so it would support my lies. "That is why I also know you didn't mean to kill Léon."

His shoulders dropped marginally and the micro-expressions of genuine grief didn't last long. Again he raised his gaze to his top left, his free hand clutching the material over his heart. "I loved him. More than any opera could convey."

"I believe you." I did.

"I didn't want him to die. I wanted him to come back to me, live out in the open."

"Revealing himself as homosexual would've been a very intimidating step." I noticed movement behind Julien, but couldn't see past the spotlight. "Maybe he didn't feel he had the courage."

"But I was going to do it with him. We were going to stand together."

"What happened the night Léon fell?"

Horror at the memory made him flinch and he shook his head. He pulled his shoulders back and spoke to the audience I hoped was no longer there. "I went to ask him to reconsider leaving me. We were standing in the kitchen like we'd done so many times before. He had poured a glass of wine for me and it fell on the floor. Léon was so upset about his broken crystal glass. He stepped away to get a cloth to clean up the mess and slipped on the wine."

Julien's grip on the material over his chest strengthened as he implored the audience. "There was nothing I could do. Really. I grabbed him, but he was too far. He fell backwards and slammed his head on the floor. Immediately blood started forming a pool around his head." He dropped onto his knees, his hand still holding the remote pointing at the stage floor. "I rushed to him, fell down next to him, but I was too late. I was too late!"

I gave him a moment to enjoy his dramatic performance. "Then you phoned the other man you loved."

Julien lowered his derrière onto his heels and rested both hands on his lap. "I was so confused. I'd fallen in love with a wonderful new man, yet I wanted the man who had left me. Phoning Arnaud felt like such a huge step in our relationship. He didn't judge me once. When I told him what had happened, he just told me I should stay where I was and not touch anything. He arrived twenty minutes later and took control. First, he held me for a long time while I cried over the loss of my first true love. Then he told me to go home and let him take care of everything. That was when I realised I had found a man who was truly worthy of me."

"Yet you lost him too."

Both Julien's fists flew up to press against his chest. "How could the gods be so cruel to one person? I suppose this kind of operatic end to my life would be fitting. I lost my great love and then a man truly worthy of me killed himself."

"As a sacrifice to protect you." I blinked as Daniel and Manny appeared a metre and a half behind Julien. Manny moved his hand in a rolling motion. I made sure to manipulate my expression into only revealing my total focus on Julien. "Did you know he admitted to killing Léon just before he killed himself? He didn't want you to be blamed for that accident. He must have wanted for you to continue being great."

"He did that?" Julien again raised his chin, his expression the exaggerated wistfulness so often seen in operas. "I've been loved by two beautiful men. Men who saw my greatness and sacrificed their lives for it. How could I live with that? How could I live without them?" He raised his hands towards the audience, pleading. "Please let me die. Don't let me suffer through this wretched life alone. Don't let me live another second without their love, without their kind eyes upon me."

"Oh, for the love of all that is holy." Manny grabbed Julien's one hand, Daniel the other. "Put a bloody sock in it."

"No!" Julien struggled against them, his fist closed around the remote. "No! Let me die! Let me die!"

"He's still performing?" Vinnie asked behind me. "The dude is stark raving mad."

Relief made me feel lightheaded. I hadn't realised how tense my muscles were and rolled my neck. Now that I no longer had to keep Julien's attention focused on me, I thought of his grand final performance. Something had registered in my subconscious about his actions that made me feel restless.

Manny and Daniel were trying to keep Julien from moving. Another GIPN member joined them and helped Manny hold Julien still while Daniel carefully opened Julien's robe. Taped to his torso were three small blocks of what I believed were explosives.

Julien glanced up again towards the top left as he allowed Daniel to pull the robe further to the sides. My restlessness increased exponentially. I turned to my right and searched the area Julien had focused on. Against the first balcony, out of the audience's sight, was a digital clock showing the hour, minute and seconds. The red digits showed two-zero-five-nine-five-four. Six seconds to nine o'clock. Julien had been watching the time.

Everything clicked at once. I spoke, but no sound came out. I tried again. "There's a timer on the bomb! It's going to explode in five seconds. Go! Go! Go!"

Manny gave me one look, grabbed Julien and dragged him the last two metres to the end of the stage and pushed him over the edge into the orchestra pit. I just managed to see Manny turn around and run towards the back of the stage. Vinnie had his arm around my waist and was running with me to the first row of chairs. He pushed me down on the floor and I expected his weight to follow me. It didn't. Colin lay down on top of me, his calming voice telling me everything would be okay.

His second sentence was swallowed by the explosion. And my shutdown.

Chapter **TWENTY-FOUR**

"Then I told him I wished he would stifle in his own report and that he might smell of calumny." Nikki giggled when Manny's scowl increased. "It's from an online list of Shakespearean insults. He like totally didn't get it, so I told him he was a whoreson, impudent, embossed rascal and that I never, ever, ever wanted to see him again. I said it in my best Doc G voice."

I tried to give her this moment of triumph, but after the stressful seventeen minutes I'd spent earlier tonight lying to a narcissistic man in order to prevent many people from getting hurt, I simply didn't have the energy to allow such shocking inaccuracies. "Malicious statements don't have a smell, Nikki. Therefore one can never smell of calumny. If you're going to research fatuous insults on the internet, your time will be better spent finding definitions for the wor... you knew what calumny meant? Whyever would you use it in such an inane manner?"

"To see if ever-so-clever Rainier knew." She bumped me with her shoulder. "He didn't."

We were in the sitting area of my apartment, drinking hot chocolate and eating Vinnie's oat cookies. I'd come out of my shutdown two hours after the explosives strapped to Julien Travere's torso had been detonated. I'd still been on the floor between the first and second rows. Colin hadn't been able to move me. A few times in the past I'd allowed Colin to pick me up while I'd been in a shutdown. Not this time. He'd stayed with me while Edward and his bomb squad had gone through the whole theatre to declare it free of any other explosive devices.

The crime scene technicians had still been collecting evidence when I'd become aware of being curled up in a foetal position on the floor. My statement wasn't needed until tomorrow or the day after and we'd come home as soon as I could walk to Vinnie's SUV. At home, I'd spent twice my normal ten minutes in a hot shower before I came out to a dinner of Vinnie's quick pasta dish he made when he didn't have a lot of time to cook.

"So is that Rainier schmuck gone now?" Vinnie rested his elbows on his knees and leaned forward. "Because I'm still wanting to kick some ass."

Nikki's expression sobered. "These men blowing themselves up really doesn't give anyone a sense of justice, does it?"

"It bloody well doesn't." Manny took another cookie. "Criminals should have their freedom taken away, not their lives. Now bloody Brun and Travere don't have to think about all the lives they've ruined."

"Or all the damage they've caused." Colin absently played with my fingers. "It's going to cost the Opéra National du Rhin a lot to fix all the damage to the orchestra pit and stage, not to mention replacing all those instruments."

"Were all the instruments damaged?" Phillip had been quiet during most of our dinner. I'd been surprised when he'd been in my apartment when we'd arrived. He and Nikki had been playing chess when we'd walked in. The unfinished game was now pushed to the side of the coffee table. Phillip had promised Nikki they would finish it after dinner.

"Most of them." Colin had been outraged by the loss of the instruments. "I reckon the cost of the stage repairs might be significantly less than replacing the instruments. A concert-quality violin nowadays costs around thirty thousand euros apiece, a clarinet about the same price. Of course one could buy cheaper instruments, but then it will also sound cheaper. It's going to cost a lot to fix the damage Julien did."

Francine rested her hand on Manny's thigh and looked at me. "I'm just glad you're you, girlfriend. I don't know how many other people would've been able to see past that idiot's performance. Thank you for keeping everyone safe."

"I would not have been able to do that if someone hadn't turned the spotlights on Julien and if Daniel's teams hadn't evacuated the theatre so quietly and efficiently." I didn't say anything about my short-lived attack of self-doubt. It still surprised me and I planned to spend some time analysing it. I wasn't prone to such irrational thoughts. I was immensely relieved I had been able to keep Julien's attention away from the rescue. "Whose idea was the lights?"

"Mine." Manny rubbed the back of his head when everyone looked at him. "What? Doc wasn't willing to listen to our strategy, so I thought it best to follow her lead. Not that she did much different than what we'd planned. We just thought the lights would keep Travere from seeing people leaving during his swansong."

"Ooh." Francine reached up and played with Manny's earlobe. "Look at you using big words."

"Get off me, supermodel." Manny grabbed her hand, put it on her lap and put his over it.

"It was an astute decision." The muffled ringtone of my phone came from my handbag hanging on its usual dining room chair. I sighed. It was past midnight. I didn't want to answer phone calls. Everyone important in my life was in my apartment.

"I'll get it." Nikki jumped up and came back with my handbag. "Oh, no, it stopped."

I took my handbag and the ringing started again.

"Better see who that is, Doc." Manny glared at my handbag, his micro-expressions a copy of Vinnie's suspicion.

I took the phone from its designated place and frowned. "It's Émile."

"Answer it and put it on speakerphone." Manny shifted to the edge of the sofa. "That criminal better have a good reason for phoning at this time of the night."

I swiped the screen. "It's late, Émile."

"That is true, Genevieve." His tone was friendly and relaxed. "Forgive me. I just wanted to make sure you are okay."

"Why are you asking, Roche?" Manny's tone wasn't friendly. Or relaxed.

"Colonel Millard? Ah, I'm on speakerphone again. Well, then. I was phoning because I've heard through the grapevine that there was an explosion at the opera house. Genevieve, I phoned because I was concerned about you."

"I'm well." I glanced at Phillip, thinking of his exceptional communication skills. "Thank you for asking."

Émile chuckled. "Is… um… Is everyone else well too?"

"You'll be disappointed to know we all survived, Roche." Manny's top lip pulled up. "I would feel even better if I can come and arrest you."

"Maybe another day, Colonel. I might have something else that will make you happy. I'm having my IT guy email you all the arrestable secrets I could dig up on the other three men who also tried to join us in the beginning."

"I hope you're sending me names as well. A list of crimes is not going to do me any good. I might come arrest you then for wasting my time."

"You're getting names, dates and crimes all wrapped up in a beautiful bowtie."

"Good." Manny slumped back on the sofa. "Good."

"You should take some lessons from Genevieve on polite phone conversations." Émile paused for a second. "Genevieve?"

"Yes?"

"It was an honour meeting you." His tone had lost its teasing quality. I wished I could see his face to measure his sincerity. His voice sounded honest. "I hope the next time we speak, it will be under much happier circumstances."

"What next time? Stay away from her, Roche." Manny sat up and again moved to the edge of the sofa.

I shook my head at him, tapped the speakerphone icon and brought the phone to my ear. "You were a great help during this investigation. I won't forget that."

"I know." He cleared his throat. "I'm really trying to do the best I can for my family. I hope you can see that."

"It is clear." I was taken aback by the uncertainty I heard in this alpha male's voice. "And I respect your attempt."

A loud exhale sounded over the phone. "Thank you, Genevieve. I will now let you get back to your friends. You've got good people there."

"I know." I looked at everyone's concerned faces staring at me. "I know."

I ended the call and looked up in surprise when Nikki was standing in front of me holding out her hand. "You're going to want to put your bag back, right? I'll do it."

I put my phone back in its place in my handbag and gave it to Nikki. She smiled at me and walked to the dining room table. I turned to Francine. "Why didn't Julien's remote control work?"

"Jammers, baby. Jammers." Francine winked at me, picked up her tablet, swiped the screen a few times and turned it for me to see. Onscreen was an electronic device that looked like some kind of receiver. "Pink's truck has one of the best jammers I've yet seen. It will jam up to twelve different frequencies. We chose the most common frequencies used for remote controls and smartphones and a few more for good luck. We didn't want to take a chance, so Pink didn't let the GIPN guys use their usual comms in case they set off the bomb. They did the whole evacuation with hand signals."

"There was a small possibility that Travere would use an electrical detonator, but Edward was convinced he would use the same as Brun had used," Manny said.

"Why?" I moved closer to Colin when Nikki sat down too close to me.

"Because Edward's team had investigated the university explosion and had traced the explosives to a theft in a mining storehouse in the west of France. The explosives had been locked away in a safe, so that had been easy to notice with the safe door standing wide open. The storehouse has loads of other stuff as well. Only when Edward pushed them did they do a stock take and found two remote controls missing."

I thought about this. "Then how did Julien know to set a timer to the explosives?"

"Yeah." Manny shook his head. "I must admit that I'm a bit surprised that little pussy had a backup plan. I didn't see that one coming."

Francine tapped on her tablet again. "While we were waiting for you to get back to us after the explosion, Pink and I did more research on Julien. We checked his credit cards for any recent activity and found that he'd been to an internet café late last night. People are so stupid. If you're going to research bomb-making stuff, you should wear a disguise and pay cash for your internet access.

"Anyhoo. Since we didn't want to waste time, Pink and I took a quick peek at the search histories of all the café's computers. And what did we find? A search for setting a timer device to a bomb. Idiot."

"Supermodel, you can't just go around hacking internet cafés like that. There wasn't any imminent threat."

"There was." Her voice was high and dramatic. "A threat of being killed by the suspense of not knowing how a tenor could have such a backup plan. It was a real threat."

Manny's lips thinned and he turned away from her. "Thanks for being quick on your feet, Doc."

"I don't understand."

"I'm bloody thanking you for paying attention and acting quickly."

"And being very gracious about it." Colin's tone was wry.

"Oh, shut it, Frey."

"I have a question." Phillip put his mug on the coffee table. "Why didn't Professor Gagneux or his judge father report Arnaud Brun? Surely they must have known he'd escaped from prison."

"Huh." Manny scratched his stubbled jaw. "I'm definitely going to be asking the professor that when the doctors allow us to visit tomorrow."

"Something makes me think you're going to make them allow you." Phillip smiled. "What about the judge?"

"He had a minor heart attack when he heard about the university explosion. He's in the hospital next to his son." Manny's lip twitched. "Easy arrests."

"Want to hear my theory?" Francine put her tablet on her lap and didn't wait for anyone to answer. "I'm thinking the professor and the judge are in a secret society planning to overthrow the European Union. They already had their new secret governments, spies and soldiers in place. They wante... uh... no, this is not working so well." She shrugged. "Maybe they were just feeling horrid for the life Brun had as a kid and were overcompensating."

That made sense. But I was not going to enable Francine by admitting to something that we hadn't confirmed yet.

"I bow at your feet, Oh Great Mistress of Nonsense."

Nikki laid her torso on her thighs, her head hanging down and her arms stretched out. "May I learn from your Highness?"

Francine's eyes widened in pleasure, then narrowed when her tablet buzzed. She swiped the screen, frowned, then looked at me with excitement. "Marco Gallo opened the email I sent to him. I got him. I got him!"

Nikki raised her head. "Is that another one of your theories?"

"Oh. Oh, sorry, Nix. I totally ignored my minion." Francine winked at Nikki, who sat up and pushed her fingers through her hair. "I will teach you my mad skills at coming up with great theories as soon as I follow up on this."

"Do you have Gallo's location?" I didn't care if Francine created a thousand more ridiculous theories. Not if she could send law enforcement officials to arrest Marcos Gallo.

Francine tapped her tablet screen for a few more seconds and sighed. "No. He turned his computer off and most likely removed the battery."

"Then what's the use of your email?" Manny asked.

"The first step would be to wait for him to turn his computer on again. Then I can download everything he has on his computer. Between that info and the location of where he connected to the internet, we can track him."

"Provided he connects to the internet."

"He will," I said. "On Wednesday."

"When he sends you another email." Francine rubbed her hands. "I'll be waiting for him."

"We need to get him, Francine." Colin's sombre statement caught my attention.

"What do you know, Frey?"

"I heard back from my sources. The diamonds in Léon Blanc's home safe trace back to a heist in Brazil three years ago. Seven people died during that heist."

"Bloody hell." Manny frowned. "Did we find out anything about the passports?"

"Yeah." Vinnie pushed a whole cookie in his mouth and talked past it. "I read some of the translation from Blanc's music books. I checked out the last few pages and he mentioned Gallo there. It seems like Gallo was blackmailing Blanc because Blanc was blackmailing the other dudes. That's how he got Blanc to get him those empty passports."

"Have all the books been decrypted?" I was very curious to see if there was any information that we didn't already know.

"Yup." Vinnie winked at Francine. "Franny's programme made quick work of it, but I didn't read anything else."

Francine's tablet pinged and she swiped the screen. "Huh. Daniel says they've found the bodies of two bodyguards in the woods you suggested, Genevieve. They'll continue the search tomorrow."

"Their families can now have the closure of a funeral." I was often right, but in this instance I took no pleasure in it. I wasn't naïve enough to think the other bodyguards who were reported missing were going to be found alive. Yet a small part in me hoped for that outcome.

Vinnie's fists pressed against his thighs. "Those men were doing their jobs. They didn't deserve to die. Not like that."

"You're right, big guy." Francine lowered her tablet. "But at least Brun won't hurt anyone again. Nor will Julien."

"And we still have to find Gallo." Manny cleared his throat. "But that's not going to happen tonight. Tomorrow we can go through the new intel we have. Right, supermodel?"

Francine's expression lightened. "I can't wait to see if Gallo has turned on his computer. And I want to get into those music book secrets. Ooh, imagine all the dirt there. I'm sure it will even help us catch Gallo."

Manny took her tablet and held it out of her reach. "Can you track him now? Right this very minute?"

"I don't know. Give back my tablet." She reached up, but Manny handed it to Vinnie. "Vin, gimme."

Manny grabbed her hands. "Supermodel. Look at me."

It took her three seconds before she looked at Manny. "What?"

"Can you track Gallo tonight?"

"If he connects to the internet, yes."

"What if he connects to the internet tomorrow?"

"I can track him then too."

"Then sit back, drink your hot chocolate and stop working on that despicable tablet. Tomorrow is another day. Leave it for then."

"Ooh." She pulled her hand from his and slowly dragged her manicured nail down his arm. "I like it when you get all manly and demanding."

"Oh, for the love of Pete." Manny pushed her hand away and sat back in the sofa. "You'd drive a saint to drink, woman."

The bantering continued. Vinnie made more hot chocolate and brought more cookies. I didn't join in the banter. I didn't know how. But I did observe the pleasure, happiness and contentment on each face as the night progressed. I was exhausted from the last few days' investigation and tonight's deception followed by the explosion. I was also curious to follow up on the music books, the diamonds and passports. Yet I had no desire to leave this positive atmosphere. My nightly ritual, my bed—I corrected my thoughts—*our* bed didn't give me the same deep sense of well-being as watching my friends who were like family enjoy being together.

Manny was right. Tomorrow was another day.

~ ~ ~ ~ ~

Be first to find out when Genevieve's next adventure will be published.
Sign up for the newsletter at http://estelleryan.com/contact.html

~~~~

Look at the paintings from this book
and read more about 3D-printed art, Verdi and Berthe Morisot at:

http://estelleryan.com/the-morisot-connection.html

Other books in the Genevieve Lenard Series:

Book 1: The Gauguin Connection

Book 2: The Dante Connection

Book 3: The Braque Connection

Book 4: The Flinck Connection

Book 5: The Courbet Connection

Book 6: The Pucelle Connection

Book 7: The Léger Connection

Book 8: The Morisot Connection

~ ~ ~ ~ ~

Please visit me on my Facebook Page to become part of the process as I'm writing Genevieve's next adventure.

and

Explore my website to find out more about me and Genevieve.

CPSIA information can be obtained at www.ICGtesting.com
Printed in the USA
LVOW11s1404180216

475692LV00003B/28/P